ALL THINGS PERFECT

Mary Bond has been writing since childhood. She also works as a skills trainer. She lives in Dublin with her husband and has two daughters and a son. *All Things Perfect* is her second novel. For more information please visit *www.mary-bond.com*.

Also by Mary Bond

Absolutely Love

MARY BOND

ALL THINGS PERFECT

TiVOLi

Tivoli
an imprint of Gill & Macmillan Ltd
Hume Avenue
Park West
Dublin 12
with associated companies throughout the world

www.gillmacmillan.ie

© Mary Bond 2006
ISBN-13: 978 0 7171 4082 4
ISBN-10: 0 7171 4082 2
Print origination by Carole Lynch
Printed and bound by Nørhaven Paperback A/S, Denmark

*The paper used in this book is made from the wood pulp
of managed forests. For every tree felled, at least one tree is
planted, thereby renewing natural resources.*

A catalogue record is available for this book
from the British Library.

1 3 5 4 2

To Derek, Michelle, Declan and Barbara
with thanks for all the love and support

Acknowledgments

Thanks to my family, circle of relatives, friends and work colleagues for endless enthusiasm and heaps of support. It means everything to me. Special acknowledgment to Olive, my mother, and Clare, my mother-in-law, for constant love and encouragement.

Much appreciation to Sheila Crowley for her invaluable help and commitment, and to all at AP Watt, especially Linda and Naomi.

A big thank you to Alison Walsh, for her kind encouragement and enthusiasm, and to the team at Tivoli, Gill & Macmillan, including Aoileann, Dearbhaile, Emma and Sinead. And to Kristin Jensen for her excellent copy editing.

And many, many thanks to all of you lovely readers who have written and emailed me at mary@mary-bond.com. It's really great to receive all the heartening messages and enthusiastic feedback.

A word of thanks also to the Irish Girls, fellow Irish writers, for their friendship and support.

Last but not least, special gratitude to Michelle, Declan and Barbara for bringing about the wonderful trip that helped to inspire *All Things Perfect*. And to Derek, for coming around the world with me and always being there.

And thank you, God.

Mary Bond

Prologue

'Come on, you can do it. Arms out, bend the knees, look up straight,' Mel grins.

Chloe hesitates. 'You make it look so easy.'

'It *is* easy. I've just had more practice, that's all.'

Chloe adjusts her goggles against the dazzle of the sun on blinding white snow and repositions her ski poles. God. She's really nervous, and she's hot inside her ski suit. It's easy for Mel to talk, she's gone skiing plenty of times, but Chloe is a complete and utter novice. She's already fallen off the ski lift – *twice* – and the whole thing had to be halted, which was most embarrassing, and right now she's beginning to think she has two left feet.

All around her on the snowy nursery slopes, eager skiers are silhouetted like stick insects, jerkily moving against swathes of glittering white expanse. But not her.

'Come on, one more try. I'm right beside you.' Mel is confident and reassuring.

Chloe takes a lungful of cold, crisp air. This is it. She has to get the hang of this skiing thing or else she's going to ruin her friend's holiday along with her own. She should really have got up early enough that morning to join the beginner's class, but the party last night with the guys from London went on for hours. She replays her friend's instructions once more in her head, then with a shaky smile, she gets into position and pushes...

And she's off. By some miracle she's moving across the dazzling slopes, feeling the rush of the wind on her face, her feet snug in their heavy boots, her skis rattling across the surface of the powdery snow. Mel is moving slightly ahead of her, her dark hair flying in the breeze, her mouth curved in a big, wide smile. Snowy slopes stretch as far as the eye can see, and far below them, tucked in under the lee of the mountain, are the jumbled rooftops of the skiing resort. Chloe feels laughter bubbling up inside her and some kind of happiness lifting her soul. She's skiing in the breathtaking panorama of the Italian Alps. She feels as though she's on top of the world. To look at her a few short years ago, who would ever have imagined that life would bring

Chloe Corrigan this far? And it's only the start of things to come. Of that she's determined.

Mel warms her hands around her glass of Baileys coffee. 'Why don't we take a trip on a skidoo tomorrow?' she suggests as they relax in the bar that evening. Her dark hair still feels a little damp from the shower, as she never has the patience to blow dry it thoroughly, but it doesn't matter. She and Chloe have managed to grab the coveted seats by the log fire and in no time her damp tendrils will soon dry out.

'A what?' asks Chloe.

'A skidoo – a kind of motor bike, you've seen them around, great fun altogether. I'll drive and you just have to hang on tight and soak up the scenery.'

'Thought you couldn't wait to show off on the scary mountainous slopes with those London guys,' Chloe grins at her.

'Hey, I'll do that later in the week when you've found your feet. C'mon, it'll be fun!'

It's more than fun, Mel thinks the following day as they whirl along a rough track cut into the steep white mountain at more than sixty kilometres an hour. It's some kind of catharsis for her. The exhilarating sense of speed, the feeling of freedom as they hurtle along, the blood singing in her veins as the vast landscape unrolls all help to paper over the empty space deep inside her.

There are no reminders of the last time she went skiing, just four years ago. There's only the sparkling, snow-covered mountain peaks that stretch on forever, a landscape that gleams whitely even in the small hours of the night and dazzles relentlessly by day. And, of course, the frantic après-ski, with the resort lit up like fairyland and laughter and music resounding out across the snowy terraces. And she and Chloe, feeling free and easy and having a ball.

'I dunno how I'll face work on Monday,' Chloe lightly moans on the last night of their holiday. The week has flown by. The guys from London have already gone home. The coach is collecting the Dublin gang at four in the morning and it looks like the party is going to last all the way to the airport and onto the plane. It's going to take her days to recover. For the first time in her life, Chloe glories in being able to say that she needs a second holiday in order to recover from the first one.

'I thought you'd be dying to get back to your desk in Premier Elect,' Mel teases.

'Come off it, I'm not that much of a workaholic.'

'You are so. I never thought I'd persuade you to take time out for this holiday.'

'Yeah, January is usually hectic, but I don't care how cluttered my desk is, it's been brilliant, and the best holiday I've had in ages. I loved our break in Benidorm last year, but it's great to have a change from the usual Spanish beach.'

4

'We could have an even better holiday, you know,' Mel suggests.

'Like what?'

'Ever fancied Australia? Maybe taking a year out?'

'A year? Are you serious?'

'I'm deadly serious. Two weeks in Spain or Greece is fine, but it's about time we really spread our wings and saw something of the world while we're still in our twenties. A year in Australia would be the trip of a lifetime.'

'It would take some planning.'

'Course it would. We couldn't do it overnight. We'd need some serious savings behind us. Think of the fun we'd have.' Mel leans forward and rests her elbows on the table. She's wearing a dark green jumper and it brings out the colour of her eyes, eyes that are shining with enthusiasm. 'We're only young once. I know you're keen to get ahead in your career, but this would be a marvellous learning experience for you and I'm sure your job would be waiting for you when you come home.'

'We'd have to think about it.'

'Sure. Think about spending all week long cooped up in the office and our usual Saturday night, fighting for space in the bars and nightclubs or waiting for a taxi in the rain at three in the morning. Or wet Sundays with your uniform draped over the radiators and the smell of damp in our flat. There has to be something more exciting out there.'

5

All the way to the airport, on a coach jammed with revellers determined to squeeze the maximum hilarity from the remaining holiday hours, and while Mel dozes fitfully beside her, Chloe thinks about it.

Chloe sees her pale reflection mirrored in the window as the coach travels through the dark, pre-dawn hours. It changes gears and whines along steep and twisty roads that clutch precariously to the side of ghostly white mountains. She watches the blue-grey dawn slowly lighten the frozen Italian landscape. Chloe never imagined herself enjoying the luxury of a skiing holiday and it's been just perfect. Now Mel's suggesting Australia, something else she never imagined. A year out, a learning experience. Sunshine and beaches, parties and fun. A world away from Dublin weekend nightlife and the daily office routine. Trust Mel, the restless free spirit who rarely stays in a job for longer than six months, to come up with the idea. Mel, the friend who helped her take the first steps away from her humble beginnings…

And maybe it will turn out to be just as perfect.

Part I

Chapter One

Late-night Friday nights were a very bad idea, Chloe decided as she flopped on the sofa and flicked through the latest copy of *Hello!*. They seemed a great start to the weekend, of course. Trouble was, you spent most of Saturday nursing a hangover, never mind fretting over the amount of funds that had disappeared in the space of a few short hours. Funds that were supposed to be nestling safely in her bank account for Australia.

Not to worry, she consoled herself as she toed off her sandals and propped her feet on the sofa. It didn't hurt to break out now and again. She listened to Dublin summer rain beating against the windowpane and wondered what life would be like on the other side of the world. A far cry, she fervently hoped, from a cramped flat in Harold's Cross and relentless grey skies.

She and Mel had spent most of last weekend poring over brochures and planning their itinerary. Sydney first, Mel suggested, then maybe up along the Gold Coast. Then Ayres Rock, of course. Chloe had stifled any qualms she felt at interrupting her fledgling career by gazing at long golden beaches and shimmering blue skies and reminding herself that it would be an education in itself. They planned to head off at the end of October. It would give them plenty of time to save and they would arrive just in time for the Australian summer.

She was debating whether it was safe to take another two Solpadeine to ease the throbbing in her fragile head when she heard a racket in the hallway outside her flat. The new tenant moving into the empty bed-sit upstairs, she guessed. Mindful of her aching head, she cuddled further into the sofa and tried to ignore the commotion. But she perked up at the sound of the muttered expletive that echoed in the hallway, because it was impossible to remain oblivious to the fact that the voice was masculine, and very attractively masculine at that.

Chloe got off the sofa and opened the door. And an ordinary Saturday afternoon turned into something completely different, for it seemed as though Adonis himself had marched straight out of the Aegean Sea and into the hallway outside her flat. The summer rain was so heavy that the tall, dark-haired hero was drenched and the cardboard box he was dragging into the hallway had practically turned to pulp. Chloe's wide grey eyes scanned all six foot one of him, from the raindrops beading his dark hair, to his bright blue eyes, to the saturated hip-hugging jeans, and she forgot all about her hangover.

'Hi there,' he grinned. 'Sorry for disturbing you.'

'Disturbing me?' Chloe laughed and shook her blonde head and said it had been a rather dull Saturday afternoon up to now.

'Adam Kavanagh.' He shook her hand. 'And I promise I'll behave like a perfect neighbour from now on.'

'Chloe Corrigan. So you're the new neighbour,' Chloe said as she looked up at him from her five foot three vantage point.

'Yeah.' He smiled a lopsided smile.

'You're very welcome,' Chloe smiled in return, and suddenly found herself inviting him in for a neighbourly drink. 'It'll give you a chance to dry off. You can finish unpacking your car when the rain eases.'

'You sure?' he asked. 'I'm not exactly...' He ran a hand through his wet hair, dislodging raindrops onto his blue denim shirt.

'Nonsense,' she insisted, opening the door a little wider.

'Okay, sounds good.' He stepped inside and glanced around at the cosy living room and tiny alcove of a kitchen. 'Nice spot you have here.'

11

'It'll do,' Chloe said with false nonchalance. What on earth had she done, she wondered frantically, to deserve the spectacle of this god standing in the middle of her cramped flat on a wet Saturday afternoon?

'I share with Mel, a friend of mine,' she explained. 'We moved in together when she came up from Galway. We have a shoebox of a bedroom each and the landlord has the nerve to call it a roomy two-bed flat!'

She followed the path of his eyes as he looked at the buttercup walls, the terracotta throw covering the sofa, the array of plants along the windowsill, the scented candles by the fireplace. In the draught from the open door, wind chimes tinkled melodiously above the window. Chloe whipped up her copy of *Hello!*, where Posh and Becks were strategically relaxing in their multi-million pound mansion, and dumped it on top of the pile of Australian brochures that tilted precariously against the wall near the fireplace. She shoved her feet into her sandals and closed the door.

'It was really dingy when we moved in,' Chloe said, trying to make casual conversation as she went to the fridge. She took out two chilled bottles of Bud and passed one over to him. 'I did the walls and painted over the ghastly wallpaper,' she said, suddenly anxious to keep talking. 'Mel put the lucky chimes over the window and she looks after the plants.'

'It's a lot brighter than the bed-sit I have upstairs,'

he grinned, making her heart turn upside down. 'Although I don't intend to stop too long,' Adam continued. 'This is only temporary for me.'

'Same here,' Chloe said. 'We're only passing through. In the meantime, I can always give you a hand if you want to do a spot of painting,' she suggested casually, crossing her fingers behind her back. 'I'm an expert in camouflaging even the biggest and gaudiest cabbage rose.'

'Sounds promising.' He took a slug of beer and his keen eyes appraised her.

It wasn't fair, she sighed, that a pair of blue eyes could melt all her insides with a single casual glance. She couldn't wait to tell Mel.

* * *

Mel ran into him at the gate. Literally. Head down against the rain, she wasn't looking where she was going and she head butted him in his chest.

'Wow, I didn't think I was that much of a babe magnet! You must be Mel, the girl from Galway.' He gave her a cheeky grin and she bristled.

'How do you know?' she challenged, disgusted with her blatant curiosity.

'Oh, I know everything.' He made it sound like he already knew her deepest, darkest secrets and it put her immediately on edge.

'Don't be ridiculous.' She tossed her head and brushed past him. He was full of himself, she decided, and far too self-assured. The kind of guy who usually got up her nose. She felt oddly cross as she stomped up the path and into the shelter of the hall.

'Did you say hello to Adam?' Chloe asked when Mel got in.

'That fella I bumped into outside? I guess you've already been talking to him. He seemed to know all about me.'

'No, he doesn't,' Chloe laughed. 'We just had a drink because he's moving in upstairs. Isn't he's gorgeous?'

'Speak for yourself.'

'Mel! Don't you think he's a fine thing?'

'Not a bit. He thinks he's great and I can't stand those types.'

'I think he's great as well…'

* * *

The first time they went to bed, it was even better than Chloe had expected. Afterwards she lay against Adam's shoulder and told him of her plans to go to Australia with Mel. So she wasn't interested in any kind of serious relationship, Chloe said silkily as she traced his angular jawbone and let her hand drift to his six-pack stomach.

And neither was he, Adam assured her as he curled an arm around her. He was busy setting up KVL Solutions, his new web application company, with his business partner, Rob Lyons. It would take time, energy and dedication, which he had in spades. Most weeknights he worked late into the evening. Soon he'd be earning megabucks, but for the moment he wanted no strings, no ties and certainly no commitment. The second time they went to bed they enjoyed it so much that they agreed it would be a shame not to repeat it from time to time over the next few months.

Mel breezed in the hall door one Friday evening just as they were heading up the stairs together.

'Gone for the evening, Chloe?' She raised an eyebrow.

Chloe smiled impishly. 'Yeah, Mel, don't worry, I'm not being abducted. We're just painting Adam's bed-sit.'

'But we can't agree on a colour scheme, so it's going to take longer than we thought. Much longer,' Adam said, dropping a kiss on the top of Chloe's head.

Chloe giggled.

'I suppose you might as well have some fun while you're saving for Australia,' Mel said, and Chloe's giggle subsided when she saw the cool glance that her friend threw Adam.

'That's the whole idea, Mel. We're having lots of fun,' Adam smiled as he caught Chloe by the hand and led her up the stairs.

* * *

'Don't you like Adam?' Chloe asked Mel the next day.

'Yeah, he's only gorgeous,' Mel shrugged.

'He doesn't think you like him.'

'Really.'

'He thinks you see him as a threat to our friendship.'

'You must be having great conversations altogether.'

'Don't worry, he's lovely and all that, but he doesn't mean anything to me. Honestly. I'm still on course for Australia.'

* * *

They painted his bed-sit together, a warm saffron shade. Chloe felt happy when Mel came down off her high horse and donated a plant. It was a spider plant, she explained, and they almost took care of themselves, so Adam should be able to manage it. Chloe bought scented candles and lit them on dusky summer evenings. She usually saw Adam at the weekends, sharing a bottle of wine in his small bed-sit and a few hours in his bed. Often they didn't even get as far as Adam's bed, and enjoyed it all the more.

Sometimes they went out for a few drinks on a Saturday night and met up with friends, including Adam's friend Henry, and Henry's latest girlfriend. Adam and Henry had grown up together in Athlone and had gone to college in Dublin. Henry worked in the bank. He had recently become the proud owner of a one-bedroom apartment nearby and it was impossible to keep track of the women in his life. Every time Chloe saw him, it seemed he had a different beauty clinging onto his arm. Chloe was pleased when Mel sometimes joined the gang, because she didn't want her to feel left out. Even though Mel and Adam sometimes bickered over silly things and tried to get the better of each other, it gave her friend the chance to see for herself that things between them were all very casual and relaxed.

Chloe rarely stayed the full night in Adam's bed-sit. No sense in getting too attached, she smiled, her grey eyes soft and earnest. The main thing was that they were enjoying themselves and they each understood the rules. And as the summer months slowly advanced, Chloe's Australian fund mounted up.

'I was never so rich,' she said to Adam one lazy Sunday afternoon in August as they lay together in bed.

'Hmm. Rich and sexy. What a dangerous combination,' he grinned.

'And I've applied for a career break,' she added.

'Do you want to go back to the building society?' he asked idly as he sifted his fingers through her blonde hair.

'Oh yes. Believe me, I've worked hard to get where I am,' she told him. 'I'm there two years now and

I've every intention of picking up my career again. It's very important to me. And Debbie Driscoll, my boss, said there's no problem, although they'll miss me. So things are falling nicely into place.'

As August slipped into September, Chloe and Mel applied for their visas. As soon as they arrived and everything was in order, they planned to confirm their flight details with a city centre travel agent.

Then, on a Wednesday afternoon in September, everything changed.

Chapter Two

Chloe bumped into Adam in Westmoreland Street. During her lunch hour, and in the middle of the passing crowds and the noisy traffic, they came face to face on the pavement.

'And where are you off to?' Adam smiled, his blue eyes crinkled against the glare of the early autumn sun.

'Back to the office to put in another wildly exciting afternoon,' Chloe said, feeling an unexpected bubble of excitement at bumping into Adam like this. 'You look all spruced up, quite the high-flying executive.' She eyed his razor-sharp suit and bulging leather briefcase.

'And so do you,' he said. 'I don't normally see you in your work uniform,' he grinned.

'Thank God for that.' She dismissed her bottle-green jacket and skirt. 'Anyway, what are you doing in this part of town?'

'I was supposed to be meeting a new client,' Adam explained, 'but I've just got a message on my mobile to say he can't make it. Some domestic crisis or other.'

Chloe laughed and ran a hand through her blonde hair. 'I can't believe the dynamic Adam Kavanagh has been stood up on account of a domestic crisis. I didn't think you acknowledged those kind of things.'

'This is a first,' Adam admitted. He took her arm and led her across to the inside of the pavement, out of the path of the busy crowds. 'But I'm not that much of a slave driver,' he continued. 'I know these things can happen.'

'So you're human after all,' Chloe laughed. 'And now what will you do with your afternoon, while the rest of us are slogging away?'

He shrugged. 'Well, I had diaried the whole afternoon for our meeting.'

'It's too nice an afternoon to be stuck in an office,' she said. 'And you weren't going to be there anyway. I dare you to take it off,' she challenged.

'Do you now.'

'Yeah, go back to your flat,' Chloe suggested. 'Change out of that suit of yours, get into your jeans and head out to the mountains. Or the sea.'

'Is that all you can come up with?' Adam grinned. 'I have a far better idea.'

Then he leaned over and whispered in her ear.

She wondered afterwards what would have happened if she had insisted on going back to the office. She wondered what would have happened if Adam's meeting had gone ahead as scheduled and she hadn't bumped into him at all. Or supposing it had been lashing rain and she had stayed in during lunch hour.

As it was, and almost before Chloe realised it, they were running across Westmoreland Street together, laughingly dodging the traffic. They were hurrying over to the Fleet Street car park, where Adam had left his car. As he negotiated the exit ramps, Chloe pulled out her mobile and phoned in an excuse to the office, forcing her voice to sound normal. Adam nosed out onto the quays, turned left into Parliament Street and took a right for Harold's Cross.

And instead of sitting dutifully at her desk, Chloe spent the afternoon making love to Adam and sipping Italian wine as September sunshine filtered through the drawn Holland blinds.

And then the unthinkable happened.

'Marry me,' Adam urged.

'Yeah, sure,' Chloe giggled.

Adam's bed-sit was warm and slightly stuffy. Chloe's face felt flushed. The duvet was rumpled, the pillows scattered, and the bottle of wine they had licked off each other's bodies was empty. Outside, she heard the early evening traffic that snarled through Harold's Cross gathering momentum. She looked to where the angle of the sun had shifted and now it pressed against the top of the cream Holland blinds, bathing the room in delicate light, turning her soft skin a creamy gold.

'No, I mean it. Will you marry me?'

'Sure thing, Adam.' Chloe licked her finger and drew it slowly down the inside of his forearm.

'And don't try to distract me.'

'Is this better?' she asked impishly, raising herself slightly off the pillows. She pointed her tongue and began to flicker it against his muscular flesh, tasting his skin, following the path her finger had made.

'Chloe!' Adam pulled his arm away. 'I'm serious. Will you listen to me?' The bed shifted under his weight as he moved on top of Chloe and pinioned her hips between his strong thighs. Then he caught her two hands in one of his and held them captive on the pillows above her head. 'You can't escape until I get an answer,' he warned.

'Who said anything about wanting to escape?' Her voice was husky.

Adam leaned over and kissed her hard.

Chloe caught her breath. He moved within her, sweetly, sharply, his eyes never leaving her face, and sent her tripping right over the edge. There was no doubt about it, she thought, ebbing into the afterglow, relaxing against his body. Adam Kavanagh, who resembled nothing short of a sex god on legs, was equally brilliant in bed.

Later, when his breathing had returned to normal, he said, 'You haven't answered my question, Chloe.'

She sighed. 'You're such a messer. You know I'm off to Australia with Mel and you're the original Mister No Strings.'

'I was.'

Chloe frowned. She sat up in bed and suddenly felt goose pimples all over her skin and she pulled the duvet around her creamy breasts. Adam reached out his hand and gently peeled the duvet away. Once again, he leaned over and kissed her. This time she felt his lips gently moving over hers, his tongue dipping into the warmth of her mouth, and Chloe was already sliding down amongst the pillows, her body tingling in anticipation of his touch, when he stopped abruptly, got out of bed and padded across to the window.

'Let's have some fresh air on the subject,' he said, lifting the blind.

'Someone will see you!' Chloe giggled. She admired the sight of his naked back. He was tall and well built, his wide shoulders tapering to a narrow waist, the long indent of his backbone running down to the compact curve of his bum.

What a way to spend a Wednesday afternoon.

'See me? They'd never be so lucky,' Adam said. He released the catch of the window and all at once the noise of the traffic increased and a draught of cool air stole across the bedroom, carrying with it the faint scent of diesel. Adam pulled down the blind again over the partly opened window and went back over to the bed.

Chloe squealed as he hauled the duvet off her and cool air hit her body. He lifted the duvet, gave it a vigorous shake and smoothed it back down. Then he plumped up Chloe's pillows and tucked them behind her head.

'That better?'

'Much better,' she smiled. Adam straightened his own pillows, then slid back into bed and held her close.

'As I was saying, it was all very well in the beginning, wasn't it? You with your bags practically packed, and me out for some fun.'

'You made it clear that you wanted no commitment.'

'Maybe I did at the start. But did you ever wish that things were different between us?'

Chloe frowned. 'What exactly do you mean?'

'Did you ever think of me in a different light, other than the good-looking fella from Athlone in the upstairs bed-sit? The good-looking fella who was fine for a laugh and a joke and really great in bed…'

'Great in bed? When did I ever say that?' Chloe teased.

Adam tweaked her nose. 'Seriously, Chloe, did you ever wake up in the middle of the night and reach out and wish I were there?' His arms curled around her and he held her even closer. As his voice went on, Chloe felt as though some kind of spell was being weaved around her.

'Did you ever find yourself thinking about me at odd times during the day? Or miss me in the evening if I wasn't around?' He looked at her steadily. 'Does it bother you that you'll soon be saying goodbye as you head off on your travels? Or am I just a handy number in your life, someone to while away the time as you wait for your visa to come through and your new life to begin?'

'That's quite a long speech, Adam,' Chloe said slowly.

Somewhere out in Harold's Cross an ambulance siren cut through the snarl of the traffic. A gang of schoolgirls passed by on the pavement outside, the noise of their careless laughter fading into the distance. The Holland blinds stirred against the window frame, and when Chloe straightened up and saw the expression in Adam's eyes, her throat suddenly constricted.

'Are you trying to tell me...' She struggled to find words.

'I'm not trying to tell you anything, Chloe. I'm asking you to marry me. Don't go to Australia. Stay here and marry me.'

'Wow.' Chloe didn't realise she had been holding her breath until she gasped for air. 'What happened to Mister No Strings?'

Adam smiled. 'He started off with the best of intentions, believe me, but one by one they fell by the wayside, thanks to a curvy little blonde who crept into his heart. I didn't plan on this happening, Chloe, but I've fallen in love with you.'

Chloe's whole life shifted out of focus. Everything she had known up til then fractured around the edges and became so utterly confused that she was almost afraid to look.

'I've taken you by surprise, haven't I?' Adam said. He reached out and ran his fingers through her hair.

'Yes, you certainly have,' she said weakly. Never in a million years had she expected this.

'I'm doing this all wrong,' he grinned. 'We should be out in a fancy restaurant. I should have a bunch of red roses with a little box placed carefully in the flowers. I'm not much good at proposals, I'm afraid. I haven't had much practice!'

'You really mean this, don't you?'

'Of course I do. I love you, Chloe. You've come to mean everything to me and I can't bear the thought of you going off to Australia. I'll miss you so much that it's distracting me during the day and losing me sleep at night.'

'And is that the reason you're asking me to marry you? So I won't go away?' She asked, feeling suddenly light headed.

'I want to marry you because I love you, the way we laugh and talk together and the way your grey eyes look at me when we make love. I even love the freckles on your nose and the way you stomp around when you're in bad humour. You're ambitious and a go-getter, and I want to be with you all the time and share your life and, above all, make you happy.'

He looked as though he meant every word he said. She felt his lips on her forehead and cheeks, then warm on her neck and in the hollow at the base of her throat. He bent his head and she felt his lips on her breasts, and then he looked at her, his blue eyes hopeful. 'Well? What do you have to say?'

Her heart lurched and Chloe felt as though the landscape of her life suddenly clicked into focus once more. And as she took a tentative peek, she realised that nothing looked the same.

'I'll have to consider this very carefully,' she smiled, and she felt as though even her voice belonged to a different person. 'I mean, my bags are practically packed, and here I am, all set for the adventure of a lifetime. Now you've thrown a right spanner in the works, Adam Kavanagh.'

'Good. We'll have a proper celebration soon,' Adam said.

'I haven't given you an answer yet,' Chloe pointed out.

'But I always get what I want,' he teased.

'Snap. You've met your match. I always get what *I* want.'

'Is there anything I can do to help you reach a decision?' he asked as he nuzzled even closer to her.

'I'm sure there are lots of things,' she said playfully.

Adam pulled off the duvet and Chloe's breath caught at the look in his eyes as they began to make love again. And even this was different. This time, as Adam drew her into a never-ending spiral, mouth and hands touching softly and tantalisingly, Chloe felt as though she was being brought somewhere new, somewhere way beyond normal reach, to a pinnacle she had never visited before, had never known existed.

It was late that night by the time Chloe returned to the flat. She tiptoed across the living room floor, thankful that there was no sign of light from under Mel's bedroom door. Chloe couldn't possibly have faced her.

Not just yet.

Chapter Three

'And keep the focus...hold, hold...now exhale in position and relax...inhale and slowly bring your arms up. Very good. Now moving to the other foot...'

Twenty-two women of varying shapes, sizes and ages changed position across the community centre hall. They breathed in and out in unison as they balanced on their mats, held the focus, held the stance, held their breath when instructed, then exhaled noisily on command.

Fashion slaves were sleek in skin-tight lycra mini tops and figure-hugging bottoms that displayed toned arms and pert bums. Others were muffled in comfortable tracksuits or oversized T-shirts. For the past hour they had all gone through their paces, from breathing exercises, to stretching routines, to yoga asanas and now the class was coming to an end. The session ended with the Relax position. Sarah, the calm, serene instructor, lit a lavender-scented candle and turned on music. Relaxing sounds and scents wafted around the hall as everyone got down on the floor.

Mel climbed into her comfy sleeping bag and lay prone. Although it had been a sunny September day, the evenings were drawing in and the scuffed linoleum floor was cool and draughty. Some of the class covered themselves with tracksuit tops or jackets as they lay on their assorted mats, and the fashion slaves in micro lycra braved the chill, but Mel was glad to be cocooned in the comfort of her cosy sleeping bag.

'Chin in towards your chest,' Sarah began. 'Relax your body onto the floor…close your eyes…gentle breathing now…'

Mel wiggled her toes. She had kicked off her sports shoes earlier. Closing her eyes, she began to relax. She started to feel as though she was drifting away, drifting on the tide, weightless, worriless, ageless. She pictured a beach somewhere, a tropical beach, the bowl of an azure sky, the expanse of shimmering turquoise waters, the long stretch of glittering sands and tropical trees in the foreground. She felt the warmth of the sun on her body, the touch of a gentle breeze on her face whispering in from the wide sweep of the ocean.

Heaven on earth.

After a while, Sarah's voice broke across her reverie, bringing the session to a close. It was difficult to return to reality, to come back to a hall that cried out for a lick of paint, to a chilly September evening in Dublin. And it was only Thursday, not yet Friday, so there was another day of boring work ahead of her before the weekend finally arrived.

Then she remembered and couldn't stop the wide grin from spreading across her face, or the rush of joy lifting her spirits. The visas had arrived. They were on their way to Australia. The tropical beach, the warmth of the sun, the sweep of blue-green oceans would soon become a reality.

Bliss. Pure and utter bliss.

It wasn't too difficult, then, to get slowly to her feet, a tall, lithe figure at the back of the hall. It wasn't too difficult to step back into her shoes, to reach down and tie her laces, to fix the waistband of her grey tracksuit bottoms and straighten her plain black T-shirt, to flick her fingers through her short dark hair, and come back to the humdrum routine of her life in Dublin.

The hall emptied quickly. Sarah doused the candle and switched off the music. The class pulled on jackets, lifted mats off the floor, said goodbyes all around and left in groups of twos and threes, trooping out the door, juggling bundled-up mats, car keys and bottles of water.

'You look happy,' Sarah remarked as Mel

reached the doorway and waved goodbye.

'So I should,' Mel smiled, emphasising her high cheekbones in her classic, heart-shaped face. 'I'm off to Australia soon, with my friend Chloe.'

'You lucky thing. My cousin Elaine's over there on a one-year visa. She's based in Sydney right now and she loves it. I must give you her address and e-mail. The Irish tend to hang out together a lot; she'll make sure you're invited to all the best parties!'

'Nice one. You can think of me doing my yoga on Bondi Beach at six in the morning as the sun is coming up.'

* * *

Mel strolled home in the chilly evening air. She pulled up the zip of her tracksuit top and carried her rolled-up sleeping bag under her arm. It was a fifteen-minute walk from the community centre to the flat in Harold's Cross and she enjoyed being out in the fresh evening air after the slightly stuffy confines of the hall.

It was her favourite kind of evening. The sun had long since set, but streaks of pink lingered in the western sky. She breathed in the clean scent of cut grass as it drifted across the still, calm air. She would be seeing plenty of sunshine in the coming months, she smiled to herself as she strolled along, feeling a nugget of joy and contentment spread out from her stomach.

The visas had arrived that morning after Chloe had left for work. Mel had put them away safely and was going to make a flourish of producing them as soon as Chloe got home. As it happened, Chloe hadn't arrived home that evening before Mel had left for her yoga class.

Chloe hadn't been around last night either, so she was bound to be home by now and Mel quickened her pace. They should go out and celebrate at the weekend. Forget about their budgets for once and go on the razz.

Her step was light as she walked around by the grounds of Mount Argus. She strolled past the small park where people were out walking their dogs in the calm September twilight, and she headed up to the pedestrian lights. Adam's friend, Henry McBride, was coming towards her, hands in his pockets, hurrying across the road to avoid the oncoming traffic, not seeing her in the gathering dusk until he had almost reached her side.

'Hi, Henry,' she said, pressing the button for the pedestrian lights.

'Well, if it isn't my all-time favourite,' he said, and even in the twilight she saw the twinkle in his eye.

'All-time favourite what?' she asked, not really expecting an answer. She knew Henry too well by now. 'Where are you off to?'

'I'm going home. I was trying to get my hands on Adam, but there's no answer.'

'Did you try our flat?'

Henry shrugged. 'I tried Adam's bed-sit and your flat. There's nobody in.'

The traffic halted, the pedestrian lights changed to green and the bleep sounded for Mel to cross the road. Someone honked a car horn, but Mel ignored it. 'Are you sure Chloe's not home?' she asked, stalling at the kerb, some of her excitement draining away.

'My dear Melissa,' Henry began.

'How many times do I have to tell you that my name is not Melissa?' she corrected sharply.

'But Mel has to be short for Melissa,' Henry said mildly.

'No, it doesn't,' she insisted.

'Then what else could it be short for?'

'Never mind,' she said. Once again, the green man lit up and the bleep signalled that it was safe for her to cross. She had one foot on the road when Henry called her back.

'Why don't you come for a drink with me?' he suggested. 'You're not in a mad rush anywhere, are you? What's the point in going back to an empty flat?'

A drink with Henry? Mel hesitated. He wasn't really her type, but it was only a quick drink. She'd been looking forward to showing Chloe the visas, but it seemed that that would have to wait a little longer. And she was dying to talk about her plans, to celebrate a little. As Henry waited in the gathering twilight, she stepped back onto the pavement to the accompaniment of another blast of a car horn.

'Oh, shut up,' she called to the driver. Then she turned to Henry. 'I might take you up on that drink. But what about Serena or Sylvia or whatever her name is at the moment?' She stood in front of him, almost as tall as him, and looked at him questioningly.

'It's Stephanie, actually,' he grinned. 'And let's not concern ourselves with her.'

By now Mel had fallen into step with Henry and she turned back the way she had come, down the road and around the corner to the local pub. 'She mightn't be too happy if you bring another woman out for a drink.'

'Ah well, that's her problem,' Henry said.

'Oh forget it.' Mel stopped in her tracks. 'Look, I'm not exactly dressed for the pub and I'm in need of a shower.'

'Come on. You look fine to me, only what the hell is that under your arm?'

'It's my sleeping bag.'

'And what on earth are you doing going around with a sleeping bag rolled up under your arm? No, on second thought, don't even answer that question. Might give a man ideas.'

'You'll have to guess.'

'Apart from being always prepared, like a good girl guide, I'd hazard a guess that Chloe has chucked you out.'

'Nothing so sensational. I've just come from my yoga class.'

'Yoga? What have sleeping bags got to do with yoga?'

'Don't tell me you've never tried a spot of yoga.'

'Are you allowed an alcoholic drink after that?'

'Yes, I am, and what's more, you're buying,' Mel retorted as they reached the pub.

Henry opened the door, releasing a rectangle of light and a blast of noise into the calm evening air. The pub was packed with Thursday evening regulars and they had to push their way over to two seats in the corner. Mel folded her sleeping bag and stuffed it under her seat. Henry pushed through the crowd at the bar and Mel watched as he placed the order and waited for his Guinness to settle.

Henry wasn't handsome in the conventional sense of the word, but he had a kind, intelligent face, and his eyes seemed to be always laughing at the world. She supposed that a lot of women would find him attractive. He was a little taller than she was and his auburn hair was cut so short it was almost spiky. She wondered what exactly made him tick. He sensed her watching and he turned and winked at her, returning with a pint of Guinness for himself and a bottle of Miller for Mel.

'Cheers,' she said, lifting the chilled bottle. 'Our visas for Oz arrived today.'

He clinked his pint glass against her bottle. 'That's great news. So you'll probably have a going-away booze-up.'

36

'Sure. You can bring your latest squeeze and give me and Chloe a good send-off.'

'And Chloe's happy to leave Adam?'

'Yeah, why shouldn't she be?' Mel tipped her bottle and took a gulp of Miller.

'Oh, nothing. They seem to be together quite a lot.'

'Only at weekends. And Adam doesn't mean anything to her. They've made no secret of the fact that they're only using each other for sex.'

'Convenient, if you think about it,' Henry said.

'I've far better things to be thinking about.'

'So have I. The weekend's almost here and I have to make some plans.'

'Like where you're going to bring Serena…no, Sylvia.'

'Stephanie.'

'Do you ever call them by the wrong name in the heat of the moment?' she asked.

'It's an occupational hazard,' he grinned.

'God, Henry, how many have you put through your hands? No, sorry I asked that.'

'If you mean what I think you mean, not quite as many as you'd guess,' he answered. 'And what about you?' he asked.

'Oh, you know me. No one's ever going to tie me down,' she smiled, her green eyes glinting.

'You haven't answered my question.'

'That's as good an answer as you'll get.'

'So you don't want to confide in Henry? Pity. I

thought we had something in common, you and me.'

'We're the last two people in Dublin to have something in common,' she scoffed. 'For starters, you've a whopping great ball and chain around your neck.'

'I wouldn't exactly call Stephanie a ball and chain.'

'I didn't mean Stephanie, I meant your mortgage.'

'That's an investment,' he objected. 'Having a mortgage makes far more economic sense than paying rent.'

'Now the banker in you is coming out. And that's another thing. You're stuck in a nine-to-five boring old job until you reach your pension so that you can pay your mortgage. I'd hate a job like that. I love temping. I can come and go as I please.'

Henry shook his head. 'So that's what you think of me, a boring old banker stuck in a dead-end job with a noose around his neck. What an exciting picture.'

'Do you ever feel stifled? Or smothered?' she challenged.

'Why, do you?'

His question was so swift it caught her off guard. 'I did once,' she admitted.

'Oh?' His eyes were suddenly sharp.

She smiled. 'Let's just say I made a bid for freedom and I haven't looked back.'

'Was it a man?'

'I don't want to talk about it.'

'Sorry, I've put my foot in it again.' He looked so earnest that Mel had to smile.

When they had finished their drinks, he insisted on walking her home.

'It's only down the road,' she said. 'Honestly, there's no need.'

'Yes, there is,' he insisted. 'I always see a lady home. I'm a secret gentleman at heart. You left that out of your description of me.'

She pulled on her tracksuit top.

'Better not forget your bed,' he said as he bent down and gathered up her sleeping bag. They went out into the evening air.

'Handy things, these portable beds. Did you ever try it in one of these?' he asked as they strolled down the road past gaudily lit takeaways and deserted shops that were shuttered for the night.

'No, I didn't,' Mel laughed. 'But I'd imagine it's a little awkward. Not much room to manoeuvre.'

'That's what a lot of people would think,' he said. 'But you should try it sometime, out under the Australian stars. You might be pleasantly surprised.'

* * *

Mel had been delayed, Chloe thought with relief as she sat on the living room sofa watching a repeat of *Holby City*. She was wrapped in her pink dressing gown, her feet propped up on the squashy beanbag in front of her, studiously painting her toenails a vibrant shade of strawberry shimmer. Her face was shiny under a layer of replenishing night cream. A myriad of scents drifted out from the bathroom, and the living room was filled with the pungent smell of nail varnish. Chloe felt like congratulating herself. She looked as though she had spent an innocent evening in, going through her usual beauty routines. She certainly didn't resemble someone who had scarcely slept a wink the night before or who had spent the whole day with her thoughts in chaos.

After a restless night, she had dragged herself into the city centre office of Premier Elect Building Society. When her phone rang at ten o'clock that morning, she knew instinctively that it was Adam. And when he asked her if she had come to a decision, she hesitated. She glanced around at the nearby desks, but thankfully, no one was paying any attention to her.

'Chloe, darling, last night I asked you to marry me,' he said as silence stretched between them. 'Is it that difficult a decision?'

Last night, Adam Kavanagh asked me to marry him, Chloe reminded herself.

'God, no,' she said breathlessly. 'It's just that I still can't believe it. I'm totally amazed. But I can't possibly talk right now. I'm sure you understand,' she finished hurriedly as the sight of Debbie Driscoll striding down the floor towards her desk unnerved her completely.

'Okay,' Adam had said. 'I have to work late tonight. I might pop in to see you afterwards?'

'Can we leave it for tonight? I...I might need an early night. After last night...'

'Are you sure you're not trying to avoid me?' Did his voice sound a little chilly or was she imagining it?

'Adam,' she murmured, terrified of being over-heard, 'the whole thing is so fantastic that I just need time to get my head around it.'

'Okay, I believe you.' Thankfully, his voice sounded warm. 'Enjoy your early night and I'll see you Friday evening.'

She had stayed on in town after work and had wandered aimlessly in and out of Grafton Street boutiques, eventually arriving home empty handed. The flat was quiet and she suddenly remembered that Mel was at her yoga class. Chloe heated up a Marks & Spencer pasta dish in the microwave, but abandoned it half eaten. She pulled off her uniform suit and headed for the minuscule bathroom. Just do normal things, she told herself as she stepped onto cool tiles. Keep busy. Keep occupied. Focus on something other than the mad scatter of your thoughts.

But as she stood under the warm spray of the shower and sponged her body with milk and honey shower cream, then slathered on her favourite aloe vera moisturiser, everything that had happened was whirling around and around in her head.

Just remembering the look on Adam's face when he asked her to marry him and the feeling inside her when they had made love afterwards made her knees go weak. She suddenly ached for him again. His insistence, as they strolled home late last night, that she was the one for him. Words she had never expected to hear from Adam Kavanagh.

Chloe wiped the steamy mirror and stared at her reflection. She wondered why she still looked exactly the same on the outside. Silky blonde hair framing her oval face, her petite figure curving in and out in the right places – thank you, God. But when she looked closer, she thought she saw something new, something different reflected in the depths of her wide grey eyes.

If she said yes, she would be planning a wedding instead of a trip to Australia. If she said yes, there would be people to tell. His parents. Her parents. And Mel.

Chloe's hands shook as she squeezed her face pack and she almost spattered her eyes. She cleaned the splashes away with a cotton wool pad and forced herself to calm down. She got into her dressing gown, sat on the sofa and turned on the telly. Forget about everyone else. She could be married to Adam, who she had automatically assumed was strictly out of bounds. Sexy, eligible Adam, the kind of man she had dreamed of marrying but always thought was far out of her reach. Suddenly he was well within her reach.

She only had to say yes.

Chapter Four

Mel breezed into the living room, bringing a whiff of cold air and the unmistakable odour of a pub. 'You look as though you've spent the whole evening pampering yourself,' she said.

'I do, don't I! You're late tonight,' Chloe said casually as she replaced the top on the bottle of nail varnish. It was a bonus that Mel was delayed. There would be less time to have to pretend, less time to keep up the act, less time to look as though everything was perfectly normal.

'Yeah. I met Henry McBride and we went for a drink.'

'You were out with Henry? I don't believe you.'

'I bumped into him on the way home from yoga. He was looking for Adam but he wasn't in, and you weren't home either, so we ended up going for a drink together. He's mad, he is. I don't know how his girlfriends put up with him. No wonder there's such a constant turnover.'

'He's okay, really. According to Adam, he usually dumps them and not the other way around. I wasn't home because I stayed on in town to have a look up Grafton Street.'

'Buy anything nice?'

'No, I didn't see anything.'

'Just as well you're not splurging your hard-earned cash. You'll be glad of your funds when you're in Australia.' There was a lift in her voice that should have forewarned Chloe, but she chose to ignore it in her attempt to steer the subject away from dangerous ground.

'Why don't you sit down and relax, Mel. I'll put on the kettle.' Chloe got up to escape to the kitchenette, but Mel stopped her.

'No, you sit down. Sit down and close your eyes. I have a surprise for you.'

'What's this all about?' Chloe asked. A vague apprehension flickered inside her.

'Don't worry, just do as I say and all will be revealed,' Mel said happily.

Chloe sat back on the couch and tried to close her eyes. She desperately ignored the alarm bell that was beginning to jangle, but even as Mel dropped something onto her lap, she knew.

The visas. They had arrived. Of all the times, of

all the nights. As she turned the envelope over in her hand, she knew that it would be impossible to hang onto her composure, to pretend.

Mel was chattering, nineteen to the dozen. 'We'll have to celebrate, Chloe, hang the budget. I was dying to tell you…Go on, open it…Couldn't wait to see you…I told Henry, of course, had to tell someone…How about a big celebration tomorrow night?' She finished with a loud whoop, 'Ozzie, here we come! I don't know how I managed to work today. God knows what mistakes I made with the orders!'

Chloe's envelope felt stiff and alien in her hands.

'Chloe, is something the matter?' Mel asked, stopping abruptly in her tracks.

Chloe felt as though she was in some kind of trance, that somewhere deep down inside she had switched off, that it wasn't really her sitting on the sofa in her pink dressing gown. She heard Mel talking again, her voice anxious.

'Is it your parents? Have you had bad news?' Mel leaned over and gave her a gentle shake. 'For God's sake, what's the matter? I'm beginning to get worried.'

'I don't know how I managed to work today either,' Chloe eventually said as she twisted the envelope around and around in her hands. 'It was impossible to concentrate.'

'Why? What's happened?' Mel sat down beside her and looked anxiously into her face.

'Last night…me and Adam…'

'Adam? Is he hurt? Did he have an accident?'

And then the words came out in a tumbled rush.

'He asked me to marry him.'

There was a stunned silence that seemed to go on forever. Then she heard the sound of Mel's laughter. 'He what?'

'I told you. He asked me to marry him.'

There was another silence, then Mel said in a hard-edged voice, 'Doesn't he realise that we'll be off away soon?'

Chloe remained silent. She looked steadily at her friend, and for a long time afterwards, she remembered the expressions that flitted across Mel's face as the realisation sank in. For a long time afterwards, she couldn't get even a whiff of nail varnish without remembering the look in Mel's green eyes.

'Chloe? You've not said yes, have you?'

'Not exactly. But I'm thinking about it.'

'But Chloe…' Mel spluttered. 'You're only twenty-six, you've your whole life ahead of you. The last thing you want is to be tied down. The last thing you need is a wedding hanging over you. Think of it! Travelling around Australia with Adam tracking your every move, waiting for you to come home to him. It'll ruin everything. We won't be able to really let rip, the two of us.'

Chloe's stomach was churning so much that she could scarcely breathe. 'You're missing the point,' she said. There was nothing else for it but to look her squarely in the eyes, and this time, before she spoke, Mel knew.

'Chloe – no!'

Chloe whispered, 'Adam doesn't want me to go to Australia. He wants me to stay here and marry him. But look, I haven't made any decision yet.'

'Yes, you have.'

'I told Adam I needed time to think.'

'Time to think?' Mel's green eyes glittered. 'I'm not stupid. I know by your face. You want to marry him instead of going away. After all our dreams and plans. Maybe you've known for ages and just didn't bother to tell me. Let Mel go ahead and arrange the visas. Let Mel scrimp and save. Pretend everything is all right.'

'You're getting it all wrong.'

'Am I? I wouldn't have heard any of this, only for the bloody visas arrived today. I bet you wouldn't even have opened your mouth. No wonder you hung on in town this evening. You were trying to avoid me.'

'I wasn't trying to avoid you. I've spent the day in bits. The last thing I want to do is hurt you. I never meant for this to happen, really, Mel. Neither of us did. It started out as a casual fling, that's all, but things have changed. Adam and I...well...'

'Don't tell me you suddenly can't live without him. And turn that bloody telly off. It's doing my head in.'

Chloe automatically picked up the remote and the frantic resuscitation scene in the emergency room

47

blacked out as she put the television on stand by.

'Mel, look at it from my point of view,' she began. 'Adam loves me and wants to marry me. This is a dream come true for me. I never expected anyone like Adam to want to marry me. I could have a wonderful life with him, we could be very happy together.'

'Happy? How do you know?'

In spite of everything, Chloe smiled abstractedly. 'I just know. Adam didn't mean for this to happen either, he had no intentions of getting serious about me, but as time went on, things changed. He loves me and he wants to marry me. If I didn't know you any better, I'd swear you were jealous.'

'Jealous? No way. You know what I think about commitment.'

'Yes, I suppose I can't blame you. I understand if you're angry and upset.' Chloe felt sudden tears welling up in her eyes.

'Chloe, can't you see that you have years ahead of you for marriage and all that, but you won't always be able to take time out and travel. It's a chance of a lifetime. It's *our* dream. It won't happen again.'

'It's a dream for me to marry Adam,' Chloe insisted. 'Something I never thought was possible. I'm mad about him, Mel, but I kind of blanked it out because I thought I hadn't got a hope. For me, marrying Adam is a chance of a lifetime, some-thing that won't happen again.'

'If Adam really loves you, he'll wait for you.'

'Maybe he would. But how can I take that risk? You see the way other women look at him. I couldn't compete against that, not if I'm thousands of miles away. He'd soon get fed up with e-mails and phone calls. He's only human, after all.'

'I don't know what to say.' Mel shook her head. 'What the bloody hell is so great about him anyway?'

Chloe tried to pull herself together. In the space of twenty-four hours her life had turned upside down. The Wednesday afternoon when she had bumped into Adam in Westmoreland Street seemed a lifetime ago. And Mel was angry. But instead of quaking in her dressing gown, Chloe was beginning to get angry in return. It wasn't the end of the world for Mel. She should be happy for her, happy that Adam wanted to marry her and that he loved her enough to make a proper commitment. He didn't just want them to live together, like so many other couples nowadays. He wanted to *marry* her.

'Everything,' Chloe said calmly. She began to smile. 'He's the best lover I've ever had and he wants to marry me. What more could anyone want? I almost feel sorry for you, Mel, because you just don't know what you're missing.'

* * *

She shouldn't have said that, Chloe agonised as she tossed and turned in bed. Mel was hurting enough

49

without rubbing salt into the wound. After Chloe's taunting boast, she'd disappeared into her bedroom and slammed the door.

All the same, Mel wasn't short of opportunities. Mel was tall with long shapely legs that she usually hid under her jeans, and she had a nice slim figure that Chloe had often envied. She never had to keep an eye on her weight. She had huge green eyes and eyelashes like Bambi's – sooty Connemara eyes, Chloe had once heard some lyrical boyfriend describe them as. She could have any man she wanted if she set her mind to it. There was something about her carefree, casual attitude that attracted them. But she hadn't always been so carefree and casual, Chloe remembered as she lay restless in bed. The Mel Saunders that Chloe had first met and befriended years ago in Irish college had been a different girl entirely.

* * *

At first Chloe was horrified when she won a scholarship to the Irish-speaking college outside Galway. At fifteen years of age, it was very uncool. But nonetheless, she went because she was determined to better herself, and her class teacher was so encouraging and supportive that she couldn't let her down.

She spent the first week in a welter of embarrassment. She hadn't got the right clothes, the right accent or anywhere near enough pocket money to keep up with everyone else. Nor could her parents afford to drive down at the weekends and bring her out to dinner in posh Galway hotels. She was so caught up in her all-pervasive misery that she didn't notice the tall, dark-haired girl with the prim and proper air until halfway through the second week. She was a native Irish speaker from the locality and was acting as an assistant. She was whisked home each evening by her father in a big swanky car. She looked as stiff and awkward as Chloe, and she was just as equally cold-shouldered by the noisy, popular gang. They found themselves left stranded together on the sidelines when teams were picked for a basketball match. Chloe was crawling with mortification when this girl caught her eye and smiled a conspiratorial smile, and they became instant friends.

They continued to keep in touch after Chloe returned home to Dublin with occasional phone calls, letters and, later on, e-mails. Chloe went straight into an office job when she left school, still dreaming of carving out a successful career that would elevate her beyond her working-class background. She was still living at home with her parents and brothers and stuck in a dead-end office job two years later, when out of the blue, a white-faced, tearful Mel turned up on her doorstep, dragging a suitcase. The bottom had dropped out of her world, she said. She had walked out of college and left

Galway for good. She was never going back. Could she bunk in with Chloe just for a while?

It took Chloe two days to mop up Mel's tears as she poured her heart out. It took Mel two weeks to find a job and somewhere to live and then she asked Chloe to flat-share with her. It was tiny, but it was in Harold's Cross and was the first step for Chloe away from her humble beginnings. And moving into the flat with Mel gave her further impetus to start realising her ambitions.

She enrolled for an evening college course. She would need a decent third-level qualification if she really wanted to get on, wouldn't she? Mel smiled indulgently and helped her complete the application form. The prim schoolgirl Chloe had met in Galway had vanished. It was as though she had shaken off her skin and adopted a new one, one that was happy to settle for a series of temporary jobs and tear out on the town at every opportunity. Now and then, she managed to drag Chloe away from her books for a much-needed break. And when Chloe had an attack of nerves the night before her first-year exams, Mel sat her down and told her calmly and confidently that she could do it. Which she did.

In time, Chloe persuaded Mel to join her in evening college and finish off her studies. Not necessarily for her career prospects, Chloe had wisely said, since Mel didn't have any such inclinations, but just for her own personal satisfaction.

They celebrated their final exam results in Santa Ponsa. They holidayed in Benidorm. They partied for a whole weekend when Chloe landed a great job in Premier Elect. Now, with Adam, Chloe had the chance to realise all her lifelong dreams. But instead of her friend being happy for her, Mel was angry and upset.

As she lay sleepless in bed for the second night in a row, Chloe was relieved that Adam hadn't put in an appearance earlier that evening. God only knows what Mel would have said to him. Chloe just couldn't have coped with any more scenes.

The next time she saw Adam, he would expect her answer. He wasn't the type of man to hang about. He was used to making big decisions every day, snap decisions that cost thousands of euro, decisions that involved pressing buttons or clicking a mouse where one wrong move could wipe huge databases.

Decisions that would frighten the life out of Chloe.

Yet why the hesitation? Did she doubt Adam's love? Did she feel she didn't deserve it? Was it the thought of meeting his parents? They couldn't possibly think she was good enough to marry their clever, intelligent son. And her parents already thought that in her ambition to make a success of her life, she was slowly but surely distancing herself. What the hell would they make of her plans to marry Adam?

* * *

The following morning, she tried to talk to Mel once more.

'At least let me explain how I feel, how much this means to me,' she began as Mel came out of the bathroom.

'You'll miss your bus if you don't get a move on,' Mel said curtly.

'I don't care if I'm late for once,' Chloe said. 'I don't want to fall out with you and I hate going into the office feeling like this.'

Mel shrugged as though it was none of her concern and Chloe felt worse than ever.

Chapter Five

'You knew, and you said absolutely nothing to me!' She almost choked on the words. 'You let me rant on like a feckin' eejit! You can go to hell, Henry McBride!'

'What on earth do you mean?'

Mel saw the welcoming smile change to one of puzzlement on Henry's face as he stood in the doorway of his apartment. He was in his stocking feet and his white shirt was billowing out from the waistband of his grey trousers. The buttons on his cuffs were undone and his tie was missing.

How dare he have the air of someone who was totally at ease, relaxing on a Friday evening after a busy week in the office? 'Don't play the innocent with me. You know exactly what I mean!' she fumed.

'I'm afraid I don't. And I'd much rather you came in. From the sound of it, I don't feel like having this conversation in the doorway.'

'And I'd much rather I didn't have anything to do with you, you slimy toad.'

'Slimy toad? That's original. I think you had better come in. And in spite of your bad temper, you're very welcome to my new and humble abode.'

He held back the door as she swept across the threshold in her faded denims and a navy fleece, straight into Henry's living room. In spite of her anger, she was pulled up sharply by the hotchpotch of new and old in Henry's living room. The floor was covered with expensive Coir matting. A Sky News reporter commented excitedly from a gleaming television set, and a modern Scandinavian coffee table, which held the remains of Henry's half-eaten meal, was drawn up in front of a faded floral settee. The windows were shaded with mint green curtains suspended precariously on a string, and a chrome uplighter in the alcove threw a luminous glow into the room. A Scandinavian bookcase inside the door was jammed with a medley of books and she caught the unmistakable scent of newness, of freshly painted woodwork and newly painted walls.

'I can't do everything at once,' Henry said. He pressed a button on the remote control and muted the television.

'There's no need to apologise to me, I don't care if your mortgage is proving a burden,' Mel taunted.

'The curtains are on order, but I'm hanging onto the settee until Christmas. I might get one of them things you throw over, to match the new curtains.'

'I'm very impressed. But you've no greenery, no plants. And as for your culinary skills…' She mocked his half-eaten pizza.

'Ah yes, there's a lot to be said for microwaves. It was one of the first things I invested in. Would you like to see the kitchen? It's only small, but really well fitted out.'

'Sorry, I'm not interested in the minute details of your thrilling mortgaged existence. Is Stephanie here?'

'No, she's not. You can check in the bedroom if you like, you're welcome to have a good look,' Henry offered.

'No chance, Mister McBride. I'm here to demand an apology for last night.'

'And I thought you were here for a social visit. What a shame. Would you like some pizza?' he offered.

He seemed to be not in the least perturbed by her angry air. What did it take to get through to him? Mel tried to compose herself, but it was almost impossible.

'I have another in the freezer,' Henry continued calmly. 'It only takes four minutes in the microwave. They're also great for socks, by the way, five minutes max, or alternatively there's the grill. Only that has the disadvantage of—'

'Cut it out, Henry.' God, was he for real?

'Can I offer you a drink? I have wine, believe it or not, a nice civilised Chilean pinot.'

'I'm not here to be sociable. I just want to know why you let me make such a fool of myself last night.'

'What's your problem, Mel?' he finally asked. 'I thought we had a very pleasant evening, a couple of drinks, a bit of chat, a nice stroll home in the fresh air. Now you're all agitated for some reason.'

'You let me rabbit on about Australia and the visas, and all the time you knew, and you didn't say a word.'

Henry looked bewildered. He stood in the middle of the living room, his hands in the pockets of his trousers, his eyes puzzled, and frowned at Mel. 'I really don't know what you're on about,' he said.

'You were the one who said it, Henry. Last night. I should have been paying more attention, only I was too excited, more fool me.'

'And what exactly did I say that has upset the normally calm and laid-back Mel?'

'You asked me if Chloe was happy to leave Adam. You were probably the first to know.'

'Mel, would you please start at the beginning? You're beginning to make me nervous, pacing around like that. You're upsetting the goldfish.'

'What goldfish?'

Henry quickly shook his head. 'Sorry, that was a joke. I'm thinking of getting a couple of goldfish, as I don't have any children or pets. Or plants, as you pointed out. But if I did have one, you would be upsetting it, the vibes, you know?'

'Jeez, you're mad!' It was hopeless. She shouldn't have bothered to come. Henry didn't give a damn.

'My granny wouldn't agree with you,' he said. 'She thinks I'm wonderful.'

'So does mine,' Mel quipped.

'Oh, so you have a granny.' Henry looked interested.

'I'm not here to discuss our respective grand-mothers.' Mel tried to control her breathing and she spoke slowly and distinctly. 'Adam must have told you. Is that why you were looking for him last night?'

'I haven't seen Adam since last weekend.'

'He's asked Chloe to marry him.'

'He's what?' The look of surprise on Henry's face was genuine. Mel's sharp anger immediately deflated, to be replaced by a hollow, empty ache in the pit of her stomach.

'Chloe told me last night, when I got home after "our very pleasant evening",' she said, echoing his earlier words.

'Marry her? But what about Australia?' Henry frowned and ran his hand through his spiky hair so that it stood up in uneven tufts.

Mel shrugged and there was a catch in her voice

as she answered. 'You tell me.'

'I think I will open that bottle of wine.' Suddenly, Henry was all business. Mel was ordered to sit down as he quickly cleared the coffee table of his cold, half-eaten pizza and disappeared out to the kitchen. But she couldn't sit still with her aimless thoughts, so she followed him out of the living room and into his small, bright kitchen.

'This is nice,' she said conversationally, looking around at the white wooden presses and clever use of the available space.

'Yeah, it's handy enough.' He reached into a wall press and took out two glasses. He opened the wine and filled the glasses and handed one to Mel. 'Now come inside and we'll talk,' he said.

All of a sudden, Mel wanted to forget all about Chloe and Adam and her sense of disappointment. She sat down on the faded floral settee and fingered the material. 'Where on earth did you get this? It's like a relic out of the arc.'

'Courtesy of one of my aunts,' Henry told her. 'Along with the curtains. She was doing a big clear out, or so she said. I think she was afraid I'd get myself into too much debt, so she was trying to give me a hand.'

'It's comfortable enough.' Mel sat back and took a sip of wine.

'It turns into a bed if anyone wants to stay over. Drink up, there's another bottle where that came from.'

'Aren't you going out tonight? It's Friday, after all,' Mel pointed out.

'I know you think I'm a rave partygoer and one of the leading lights of the Dublin clubbing scene, but no, I had planned on a quiet night in. Just let me switch off my mobile in case Stephanie disturbs us.'

'What will Stephanie think if she can't get an answer?'

'Don't worry about Stephanie,' Henry said calmly. 'Tell me about Chloe and Adam.'

'She told me she hasn't given him an answer yet,' Mel explained when she had brought Henry up to date. 'But she's going to say yes, I know she is. You should have seen the look on her face. She looked far more excited than she ever did when she talked about Australia. Apparently Adam is the man of her dreams.'

'So Adam must be good for something after all and not just weekend sex.'

'Who knows,' Mel shrugged. 'She's mad. I don't know how she can tie herself down to married life, at her age.'

'That's one of your big no-nos, along with a mortgage, I presume.' Henry's eyes smiled.

'That's ten times worse than a mortgage,' Mel insisted. 'I can't understand how people can make that kind of lifelong commitment. It's crazy. I mean, how could you possibly think that you want to spend the rest of your life with the one person?'

'Don't ask me.' Henry shook his head and refilled her glass.

'Chloe's mad. There's a whole world out there waiting to be explored.'

'I'm as surprised as you are, Mel,' Henry admitted. 'I thought Adam was far too busy with his company to start thinking about marriage.'

'Sorry for barging in like that and calling you horrible names,' Mel suddenly apologised.

'I'll remind you of them sometime. Call me anything you like, but of all animals, not a slimy toad, thanks very much.'

'I'll stick to plain old bastard,' Mel decided.

'Have you seen Chloe this evening?' Henry asked.

'No. She's obviously somewhere with Adam, filling him in on my reaction and swearing undying love.'

'Let me guess, you had words last night.'

'Course we had. How would you feel if your friend let you down at the last minute?'

'It would depend on why they let me down,' Henry answered slowly.

'Yeah, sure.'

'No, really, Mel. It would depend on the reason. Things aren't usually black and white.'

'So you think I'm being pig headed.'

'You were probably mad last night and not thinking straight.'

'Can you blame me? After all our careful planning, to turn around like that and…I just couldn't believe it.' Mel shook her head.

'I can imagine. But when you've calmed down, why don't you look at it from another point of view,' Henry suggested as he topped up her glass yet again. 'Supposing you were halfway to Australia and Chloe was homesick and really missing Adam, wouldn't that be worse?'

'I suppose it might,' she grudgingly admitted.

'Isn't it just as well that this is happening now, instead of when you're over in Australia and beginning to settle in? Supposing Chloe was over there, on the other side of the world, and very unhappy? You'd find that pretty suffocating, a weepy Chloe driving you mad.'

'You're probably right,' Mel conceded. She tried but couldn't prevent the faint grin from spreading across her face. 'But I'm still furious with Chloe,' she said.

'How long have you two been friends anyway?'

'We met in Irish college in Galway years ago and when I…when I came to Dublin we flat-shared and I ended up joining her in night school.'

'So you went to college?'

'Yeah. Thanks to Chloe I have a degree in Business Management. She had enough determination for both of us. I had already dropped out of university…and no, I'm not going to elaborate.'

'And I've no intentions of prying into your deep secrets. Looks like we've made short work of that wine,' Henry said, changing the subject. 'Why don't I open the other bottle?'

'Good idea,' Mel said. 'And what's that you were saying about a pizza? I don't want to put you to any trouble, only I'm feeling a bit hungry. This wine is going straight to my head. I tore over here as soon as I got home from work.' She gave him a sheepish grin as she tried to remember the last time she'd had something to eat.

Henry got up. 'Don't say another word. Just relax and have a look at my fabulous state-of-the-art telly while I get slaving in the kitchen.'

'Can I do anything to help?'

'Not at all. I can manage this single handedly. I told you, I'm an expert and frozen pizza is my speciality. See if there's anything on Channel 4.' He handed her the remote control and disappeared into the kitchen.

They watched Friday evening telly for a while and nibbled on slices of pineapple and mushroom pizza and a bowl of tossed salad that Henry, under cross examination, finally admitted came ready made. When they were halfway through the second bottle of wine and Henry went to top up her glass, Mel refused another refill.

'No thanks, I'm off now.'

'Back to the flat, to practise your yoga?'

'Back to the flat all right, but I'm not in the humour of yoga tonight. Although I could do with it. Any feeling of relaxation I had after last night's session soon vanished to the winds.'

'You can think of me stuck in the boring bank

when you're trekking through desert trails in the Australian outback.'

'That's if I go.'

'Of course you'll go.' Henry put down his glass and looked surprised.

'I told you, Chloe's probably not coming.'

'And you'd let something like that stand in your way? I'm surprised at you, Mel.'

'I hadn't really thought about going it alone.'

'Why the hell not?' Henry demanded. 'Don't be ridiculous. And don't be a stick in the mud like me. Go on off and see the world while you're young,' he urged. 'You've no ball and chain around your neck, no lifelong career to incarcerate you.'

'I just assumed that without Chloe…' Her voice trailed away.

'If anything, you'll have an even better time,' Henry insisted. 'The world is out there waiting for you, Mel. First stop, Australia.'

* * *

As luck would have it, she bumped into Adam when she was buying milk in the local shop on Saturday morning. He looked so bright and cheerful that she had the unmistakable urge to pour the carton of milk over his head.

'How's things, Mel? Have you been talking to Chloe?' he asked breezily.

'She told me she still hasn't decided yet, if that's

what you're wondering,' Mel drawled. 'So you didn't exactly sweep her off her feet, did you?'

He gave her a smile that was brimming with confidence. 'I took her by surprise, that's all. I think her decision is a foregone conclusion.'

'Must be nice to be so cocksure,' Mel shrugged as she walked out of the shop.

Chapter Six

Chloe selected three glossy magazines bursting with wedding tips and advice and joined the end of the checkout queue. She rummaged in her purse for some money and her engagement ring flashed, sending renewed excitement running through her. She had made the right decision. The rest of her life with Adam or a trip to Australia with Mel? How had she even hesitated?

'Let's get engaged immediately,' Adam had suggested when she agreed to marry him the previous Saturday afternoon, three days after he'd proposed. They had floated into town on a high and had chosen the ring together. Chloe had scarcely taken it off since. She still wasn't used to the look of the diamond solitaire on her finger and felt a warm thrill every time she glanced at it, which was quite often, as she had to remind herself it was really there, that all of this was actually happening.

She paid for her magazines and emerged into a bustling O'Connell Street. September sunshine filtered through the trees, dappled the pavement and licked the bright flower displays. She was glad of the slight breeze on her face after the warmth of the crowded store as she headed back to the office. She smiled to herself as she recalled the huge buzz of excitement when she had floated into work on Monday morning, flashing her ring.

'Forget about Australia,' she'd said to Debbie Driscoll, her supervisor, and to Emer and Tara and the rest of the girls in the Premier Elect office as she waved her left hand. 'I'm marrying Adam instead.'

It was impossible to put in a proper day's work at the moment. It was crazy, but scarily exciting, cancelling her trip to Australia, turning her back on all her plans and preparing to organise a wedding instead. Naturally, it would be the perfect wedding.

She would become Chloe Kavanagh. It sounded good. Some of the girls in the building society held on to their maiden names when they married, but she was happy to change hers. It was another step forward in moving away from the past.

No wonder Mel felt jealous. She would come around in time, Adam had said. It was funny how her whole life had taken on a far more significant meaning since the afternoon, barely a week ago, when she had bumped into Adam in Westmoreland Street. She felt like a happier, more confident person as she strolled along O'Connell Street. Even the sunshine seemed brighter and the sky a more brilliant blue and it was almost as though she floated on air.

* * *

'So you got what you wanted,' Mel said.

Adam paused at the bottom of the stairs. Bloody hell, the one evening he was home early from the office, he had to bump into Mel. There was something in the dismissive, slightly haughty way she looked at him that always managed to put him on edge. He wasn't used to be at the receiving end of disdainful glances from women. Right now he was tired and hungry, and he badly wanted a warm, refreshing shower and to make long, slow love to Chloe.

But there was no avoiding Mel. She was standing in the doorway of the flat, hands on her hips in confrontational mode, wearing denim jeans and a bright red top. Chloe had told him that Mel wasn't too impressed with her decision. Adam had hoped that she had calmed down a little by now. After all, she'd had a few days to get used to the idea. But from the look on her pale face, obviously not.

'Aren't you going to congratulate me?'

'Congratulate you? Why should I? If you really loved Chloe, you'd give her her year out and wait for her.'

Adam put down his briefcase. Mel was even more annoyed than he'd thought. Her green eyes glittered and he felt as though he was treading on dangerous territory as he forced himself to smile at her in a conciliatory fashion. He really didn't want to have a row with her. Hell, she was Chloe's friend, after all.

'Look, Mel, I'm sorry if the timing's a bit off—' he began.

'A bit off?' Mel interrupted. 'That's the understatement of the year. We've been organising our trip for months. You waited until we were just about to book our flight tickets. Convenient, to say the least. I'll be gone soon and Chloe will have no time to change her mind.'

'Hold on a minute. Chloe and I are in love. She's agreed to marry me of her own free will. I didn't force her into anything. Who says she wants to change her mind?'

'You're not giving her any opportunity, are you? Engaged already!'

'I guess I swept her off her feet after all!'

'I just hope for your sake that she's never sorry she turned her back on the chance to see something of the world.'

Adam smiled. 'Obviously, Chloe feels that marrying me is far more important than going away with you.'

70

'You really think you're something, Adam Kavanagh.'

'So I've been told.' He grinned disarmingly. He was on safer ground now. This he could handle. He picked up his briefcase. 'You never really liked me, did you?'

'You never really liked me either,' Mel said, stalling him. Her green eyes were light and full of candour and Adam felt as though she saw right through him. 'You put up with me because I'm Chloe's friend. But I bet you saw me as a bad influence on Chloe, someone who was leading her astray.'

'Funny, I thought you felt the same about me,' Adam countered. 'I always had the distinct impression that I was a nasty piece of work as far as you're concerned.'

'It must have been really bugging you that Chloe and I were going off together.' Mel's eyes narrowed.

'If you were any kind of decent friend, you'd be happy for Chloe,' Adam said.

'How can I be happy for her when I think she's making a big mistake? Marriage and all that is for the birds.'

'Come on, Mel, surely I have some good points? Do you not trust Chloe to follow her instincts?'

'Oh, she's following her instincts all right,' Mel blurted. 'The wrong kind of instincts.'

'Is that so? And what might they be?' Adam asked in a quiet voice.

'Never mind.' Mel backed down in the face of his fixed stare. 'I just hope that sometime in the future, Chloe doesn't regret that you tied her down.'

'You needn't worry about that,' Adam grinned wickedly. 'Chloe loves it when I tie her down.'

Mel looked at him scornfully. 'You really think you're a cut above everyone, don't you?'

'Actually, Mel, so do you,' he quipped as he marched up the stairs.

* * *

'Maybe not the jeans. They're too casual. What about these trousers and my white blouse? Or how about my lilac top with the black trousers?' Chloe asked.

It was the following Saturday morning. She stood in her lacy bra and pants by the side of her bed and reached across for her lilac top. Her half-packed weekend case sat in the middle of her bed, her wardrobe door wide open, and every available surface was awash with trousers, jeans, tops and blouses.

'Chloe, it doesn't matter. It's only a few hours. It's not a major expedition.'

'But I want to look my best. I would have bought something new, only you sprung this on me by surprise.'

'I'm good at doing surprises.'

'This is very important to me. I'm meeting your family for the very first time.'

'Just be yourself. They'll love you. As far as I'm concerned, you can wear your jeans. They look nice and sexy on you.' Adam caught her from behind, his arms around her waist, and he bent and nuzzled the back of her neck. Chloe straightened up and rested her body against the solid length of his. 'I can't look too sexy the first time I meet your parents,' she said as his hands began a familiar rove around her body.

'Why not?' Adam's voice was muffled as he kissed her shoulder and buried his face in her hair.

'I don't want your parents to get the wrong impression of me.'

'They'll just think I'm a very lucky man.'

'Adam! I can't have your parents thinking you're marrying me for all the wrong reasons.'

'And what reasons are they?' he demanded. Chloe tried to wriggle out of his grasp, but he held her firmly with one arm anchored across her waist as the other hand found ticklish spots she didn't even know existed.

'Adam, please,' she gasped, her laughter almost choking her.

'Please what?'

'Stop, please.'

'Are you sure you want me to stop?' he murmured against the side of her neck.

'Yes…no…'

73

Suddenly his hand stopped its crazy dance and began a slow exploration.

'What's that, Chloe? Will I stop now?'

Chloe groaned and felt her body melting. With his free hand, Adam shoved her half-packed case off the bed. It toppled to the floor, the contents scattering. He pulled Chloe down on the bed, on top of the pile of clothes. She heard the zip of his jeans as he tore them off, felt his fingers on her wispy pants and his body warm against hers. Before she had time to anticipate it, he was filling her up and sending her flying to that hot, sweet, special place. She heard herself cry out and heard Adam roar out loud. They lay panting in a tangle of arms and legs and Chloe's strewn clothes.

And Mel's bedroom door slammed shut.

'How come she's home this soon?' Chloe struggled to get up, shoving the sleeve of a blouse off her face. 'Shit! Shit! She must have heard us.'

'So what?' Adam pushed her back on the bed.

'I hate her hearing us.'

'Why? Mel's an adult. We're even engaged. So what if she hears a few groans? You can move in with me any time. Then we can make as much noise as we like.'

'It's very tempting, Adam, but I'd rather stay where I am for now, and try and patch things up with Mel,' Chloe said. 'We were great friends, and if I move out, I won't really have the opportunity for things to right themselves between us. And it's only a matter of time before she goes away anyway, three or four weeks, I think.'

'So she's definitely going off.'

'Yep. That's why she went into town this morning, to pay off her tickets... Aah, Adam!' she gasped as he began to caress her again.

'You'll just have to be very, very quiet,' Adam murmured with a devilish gleam in his eye. He caught her lips with his and his kiss went on forever, his tongue teasing the heat of her mouth. He began to kiss her all over and Chloe quivered silently beneath him. When she began to whimper softly, her grey eyes huge and beseeching, he covered her mouth with his hand. His blue eyes gleamed as Chloe suddenly bit one of his fingers. Then the bedsprings rattled as Adam climbed further onto the bed.

Chloe forgot about the bedsprings, forgot about Mel, forgot about everything as she moved beneath him. She felt gloriously loved, her happiness and joy spilling about her and around her.

* * *

In her bedroom, Mel firmly shut her ears. She focused on her favourite spot on the wall, on her poster of a dolphin leaping for joy on the surface of the wide blue ocean. Standing tall and straight, she began to take deep breaths, drawing the air in through her nose, feeling the air going right down past her rib cage, on down to her stomach, filling her up, holding for several seconds, then releasing it in a rush. After a while she began to feel relaxed.

She went over to her chest of drawers and began to sift through her clothes. She had one large rucksack bought for her travels, but she had a lot of stuff she couldn't possibly bring. She could ask Granny Alice in Galway to look after her things, couldn't she? She was going down soon to see her and to say goodbye. She heard muffled giggles coming from Chloe's bedroom, and in a determined effort to ignore them, she went over to her bag and took out the computer printouts with her flight details.

She felt a slight pang as she looked at her name on the top of the sheet, her proper name, according to her passport. It looked a bit forlorn by itself, with the absence of Chloe's accompanying name. It looked suddenly strange to her, a name she hadn't used in over four years.

So much for Henry's Melissa, she laughed ruefully.

Maybe she could give Henry her plants. They would look nice in his new apartment. He could put one near his goldfish tank, she smiled. Come to think of it, he probably wouldn't mind storing some stuff for her. He wasn't too bad when you got to know him. At least he had given her the encouragement to get going when she'd felt a bit downhearted. And right now, hearing the noise next door, she couldn't wait to be gone.

Chapter Seven

Chloe thought Adam had taken a wrong turn when the car swung in between two imposing gateposts and crunched up a curved gravel drive. Beautifully landscaped gardens and neat manicured lawns circled the front and sides of a sprawling bungalow. A full-sized conservatory extended to the right, cream shades partially drawn against the glare of the afternoon light. Chloe felt totally intimidated as she stepped out of the Peugeot on legs that had suddenly turned to water.

'God, Adam. I wasn't expecting this,' she said, trying to sound as casual as possible. Difficult, really, when her heart was pounding erratically.

'Ah, it's nothing special,' he said.

Nothing special? Was he for real?

'Chloe, stop worrying. You'll be fine. My parents will love you.'

Chloe was silent. She felt a wave of panic wash over her as they headed for the wide, pillared entrance porch. Adam had told her that his parents were in their late fifties, his father a chief executive in a midlands pharmaceutical firm who had a passion for golf and fishing and couldn't wait to retire, his mother a busy housewife who loved cooking and who kept herself occupied with a range of community interests. She knew Adam had come from a comfortable background, but she had no idea that his parents were quite so posh. Or rich. What on earth was she letting herself in for this weekend? What on earth was she letting herself in for, full stop?

But when his tall, handsome father answered the door immediately and his elegant blonde mother came out of the kitchen wearing a huge apron, a pair of slippers and a warm, welcoming smile, Chloe relaxed a little. And the first thing to strike her forcibly was that as far as Peter and Eileen Kavanagh were concerned, they thought the world of their blue-eyed boy and his happiness was paramount to them.

If they were a bit surprised at the speed of their engagement, or the fact that they'd first heard about Chloe the previous weekend, when Adam had phoned, they held their silence. They admired her engagement ring and Eileen Kavanagh even made a wish, turning it around on her own elegant finger.

'It's really beautiful,' she sighed, holding it to the light before returning it to Chloe.

It also became obvious to Chloe as they sipped gin and tonic aperitifs in the tastefully decorated lounge that as a child growing up, Adam had led a charmed life. He was the youngest in the family and born after a gap of nine years. Chloe was treated to a succession of family photograph albums and a display of his football trophies. When Chloe admired his graduation portrait, which showed a younger Adam proudly clutching his scroll, she was immediately informed that Adam had always been the brightest pupil in his class, sometimes a bit of a divil, and a terrific asset to the school GAA team. He had secured his place in university with ease, his mother said, and as Chloe probably knew, had graduated from there with first class honours.

'You never told me all this,' Chloe hissed at him at one stage.

'I'm far too modest,' he grinned.

'That's not what I meant. You've been spoiled rotten by your parents and you've had a really cushy number in life. You've always got everything you've wanted.'

'I told you that already.' He looked amused.

Dinner was served in the dining room that overlooked a decked patio to the rear of the house. Eileen made light of the five-course meal she had prepared – smoked salmon for starters, Wicklow lamb and seasonal vegetables for the main course, followed by fresh fruit pavlova, a cheese board and coffee and brandy.

'Nothing too fancy, I'm afraid. Just some plain home cooking,' she smiled. 'I hope the menu is okay with you?'

'Oh yes, of course, it's perfect,' Chloe answered. She tried to sound like she ate Wicklow lamb and smoked salmon starters on a regular basis.

'It's nice to get a chance to entertain,' Eileen said. 'There's just the four of us for dinner,' she explained as she invited Chloe to take a seat. 'My daughters and their husbands are joining us, but not until later. I didn't want you to feel we were all overwhelming you,' Eileen smiled, showing shapely cheekbones.

'Not at all,' Chloe said. Overwhelmed? That was surely the understatement of the year. She took a seat at the table laden with silverware and glasses. She looked at the array of silver cutlery at her place setting and fervently hoped she wouldn't make a fool of herself and use the wrong knife or fork. She could feel sweat prickling between her shoulder blades and she was almost afraid to answer when Peter asked her for her choice of wine.

'I have a medium Cabernet Sauvignon,' he suggested. 'Or you might prefer a full-bodied Shiraz?'

God. Was he going to fetch it from the cellar, she wondered absently, feeling suddenly giddy with nerves. They were bound to have a wine cellar in this mansion of a house. They appeared to have everything else.

'I think I'll stick to white,' she answered, forcing a confident smile.

'Any particular favourite?' he asked.

She was tempted to reply that her usual favourite was whatever cheapie was available in the supermarket special offer bin, but almost as if he sensed her reply, Adam broke in and suggested a Chardonnay.

'I have a nice fruity South African,' his dad suggested. 'Or would you prefer an unoaked Australian?'

Chloe was suddenly desperate for a drink, any drink.

Somehow she got through dinner all right and held her own in the conversation. Adam's parents were friendly and chatty. It was obvious they were delighted to see him. Eileen gently chided him for not calling down to see them often enough, but she understood he was extremely busy.

The only topic Chloe tried to avoid was her own family, and she sat on the edge of her seat as she glossed over them as briefly as possible. She was almost the opposite of Adam, the eldest child with two brothers born in close succession after a few years. They were still completing their education, she smiled. Her father was in the transport business, her mother worked part time as a retail merchandiser.

Okay, so she had embellished the truth, but so what?

She was just beginning to feel a little at ease over coffee and brandy when Adam's sisters swept in, complete with husbands in tow, and whatever frail composure she had gathered completely disintegrated.

Adam's sisters were in their late thirties, attractive and elegant, like their mother. There were friendly smiles all around as Chloe was introduced to Sandra, his elder sister, and her husband Sean Power, and Diane and her husband, Colm Barrett.

The distinct air of affluence about them unsettled Chloe. It went beyond the casual ease with which they wore their designer outfits and dripped gold jewellery from their wrists and necks. It was an aura of calm prosperity which hinted at lifestyles far beyond anything Chloe had ever experienced that put her on edge.

What had she expected, she asked herself crossly. She should have guessed from their privileged background that Adam's sisters would be moneyed and successful. Her chaotic thoughts flew ahead as she admired Sandra's pale lemon concoction that was surely straight from the Design Centre in Powerscourt Town House. Now that she was engaged to Adam, she would have to splash out on some decent outfits. And she wasn't talking Miss Selfridge or Top Shop.

'Champagne, everyone? Now that we're all here together, let's toast the happy couple,' Peter suggested. He popped the cork on a bottle of Bollinger and deftly filled the row of Waterford crystal flutes already lined up on a silver tray on the mahogany sideboard.

'You're a dark horse, Adam, all the same,' Sandra teased, her light blue eyes calculating. 'How long have you kept Chloe under wraps? The first I knew about all this was last weekend,' she said, gesturing in Chloe's direction with her champagne flute. 'I could hardly believe it when Mum phoned with the news.'

Chloe felt the champagne bubbles hitting off her nose as she took a quick gulp of the pale fizzy liquid.

'Well, Sandra, believe it or not, the first I knew of all this was also last weekend,' Adam laughed.

'Really? Chloe, I'm impressed. You must be even cleverer than Adam.' Sandra threw her a calculating glance. 'You've carried off something half the girls in Westmeath have been unable to do.'

Chloe almost choked. 'I think you've got it the wrong way around,' she ventured. 'It was actually Adam who took me by surprise.'

'Whatever way you managed to wangle it, there's a lot of broken hearts littered throughout Westmeath.'

'I think we should move into the lounge,' Eileen suggested, opening the connecting door and leading the way.

Chloe made sure to sit beside Adam on the burgundy sofa. After the warmth of his parents' welcome and their ready acceptance of her place in

Adam's life, she hadn't been expecting to run into a challenge from his witchy older sister. She imagined the giggle she could have with Mel about her, until she remembered that they were just about on speaking terms.

'So when's the big day?' his sister Diane asked, giving Chloe a friendly smile.

'Next year sometime, probably June,' Chloe told her, thinking that Diane seemed a lot more human than her sister.

'June?' Sandra frowned. 'Where on earth did you manage to book your reception at such short notice? Or have you crafty pair been engaged for longer than we know?'

'No, we haven't.' Chloe exchanged a glance with Adam. 'We've yet to make our wedding arrangements.'

Sandra laughed. 'You must be joking, surely. You do realise that most decent wedding venues are booked up a couple of years in advance. You'll never get anything for next June. How can you possibly—'

'I'm sure Adam and Chloe know exactly what they're doing,' Eileen intervened.

'There you are, Sandra,' Adam nodded at his sister. 'You don't have to worry about anything. We have it all under control, haven't we, Chloe?'

Chloe nodded thankfully. Adam to the rescue, with his unfailing confidence. It was one of the things that had attracted her to him in the first place and was obviously a legacy from his childhood, where everything had always turned up roses. Sandra changed the subject and began to talk about her job. Chloe learned that Sandra owned a boutique in Athlone. A thriving, hugely successful boutique, naturally.

'I'm run off my feet,' she boasted. 'I've just returned from Paris and I'm off to Milan next week. The stock is flying off the shelves. I was never so busy.'

'That's a good complaint,' Eileen remarked. 'Chloe's mother is in the retail business, isn't she, Chloe?'

Chloe swallowed. 'Well, she's more involved in the merchandising end of things.'

'At least she's gainfully employed,' Eileen laughed. 'I'm afraid I'm a lady of leisure.'

'Don't be ridiculous,' Sandra snorted. 'You almost work harder than any of us, between your this committee and your that committee. You never have a dull moment.'

Sandra's husband, Sean, was a publican with interests in the midland region, and according to Sandra, business was booming, as usual. The couple scarcely saw each other, they were so tied up with their respective businesses. They had one son, five-year-old Kian, who had just started school and was already showing signs of being way ahead of his class.

'He obviously takes after his favourite uncle,' Adam put in swiftly as Chloe tried to keep a straight face.

'I'm sometimes in Dublin on business,' Sandra turned to Chloe. 'Why don't we do lunch some day? We can talk wedding talk and I could advise you on dress styles, bridesmaids, going away outfits, that kind of thing.'

'That would be nice,' Chloe said politely, making a mental note to be tied up at an all-day meeting if Sandra Power ever phoned.

Adam's other sister, Diane, ran a local beauty parlour. Her skin was flawless, her hair a smooth blonde bob. She had two small daughters, Hannah and Megan.

'Two little handfuls,' she laughed, shaking her head. 'They're tucked up in bed right now, thankfully. Believe me, Chloe, I almost go to work to get a rest. I'd be lost without Colm's mother. She lives near us and comes in to mind the children when I'm at work. Colm's a building contractor, so it's all go!'

'I think it's vital to hang onto your job when you have a family,' Chloe heard herself say. 'Apart from the financial aspect, I couldn't imagine not working. I think I'd go mad without that satisfaction.'

Babies. Adam's babies. They hadn't even got around to discussing it, but at some stage they would have to think about starting a family. But not for a good while yet, she decided, and she would certainly be combining motherhood with her career.

It was almost eleven by the time they left. Chloe was glad to escape, to get away from Sandra's disconcerting glances, to flee from the strain of the last few hours and unutterably relieved that Adam had booked them into the privacy of a nearby hotel.

'Come down again soon. And you must stay with us the next time,' Eileen suggested as they said their goodbyes in the hallway. 'We've plenty of room, and now that you've met us, you know we won't bite.'

'Yes, of course, we'll do that,' Chloe said, then found herself being hugged warmly by Adam's mother.

'I'm sure these two lovebirds would rather have their own space,' Sandra suggested with a gleam in her eye. 'Isn't that why they've booked into the hotel?'

* * *

The following morning they went for a stroll on the shores of Lough Ree before driving back to Dublin. The sky was overcast, but here and there the sun struggled to get though the clouds and it glinted on the silvery waters of the lake. Out beyond the shore, several boats glided serenely along, sails at full mast. A family of ducks swam by the reeds billowing at the shore, cutting a V-shaped trail in the glassy water.

Chloe's attention was caught by two graceful swans who unfurled their wings and slowly rose up from the waters of the lake. They hesitated for a moment, suspended in the still morning air, then in balletic motion they wheeled around and set course for the other side of the lake. Like Adam and her, she mused, setting a course for a new life together.

'You're very quiet,' Adam said. 'My family too much for you?'

'No, I think it's all the excitement finally catching up on me. I thought your parents were lovely. Your mother's a dote and your dad a real gentleman.'

'I've been lucky,' Adam said. 'They never gave me anything but full support and encouragement.'

'You're right, you have been lucky. They made me feel very welcome. I'm not sure, though, if Sandra was too impressed.'

'Don't mind Sandra. She always acts the bossy older sister.'

'Bossy? That's mild. She seems to think you've left a pile of broken hearts behind you.'

'That's just Sandra for you.'

She took a deep breath of the crisp, clear air. Up to now, her engagement to Adam had seemed almost a fun thing, an excitement, an exhilarating change of plan. She had flourished her engagement ring with pride and a certain sense of accomplishment. She had felt as though she moved around in a cocoon of love.

Nothing mattered except their love for each other, she had said to herself as they lay together in the bed-sit in Harold's Cross. Who cared what their respective families thought? So what if Adam's family thought she wasn't clever enough for him?

But now that she had met Adam's family, things had shifted. No longer were they shadowy figures in the background to be disregarded at will. He had parents who loved him, who had given him every opportunity in life, who very proud of all his achievements. He had sisters to be reckoned with, family ties that couldn't be ignored, people who would now be part and parcel of their joint lives. People who would fully expect that Adam's charmed life would continue in much the same privileged vein as before, with a home and a wife straight out of *Hello!*, if his parents' home was anything to go by.

They would assume Chloe knew how to lay a table for a five-course dinner party. And even more hilarious, cook the meal. They would expect Chloe to know the difference between a Shiraz and a Merlot, and which type of glass was best for a Claret. And first and foremost, they would no doubt expect them to have the wedding of the year. It was everything Chloe had dreamed about as she was growing up.

Only it wasn't a pleasant dream any more. This was for real.

Chapter Eight

Chloe decided that it would be best to see her parents alone, then maybe they could meet Adam on neutral ground. On Wednesday evening, instead of going home from work, she got the bus out to the sprawling housing estate on the edge of the city where she was born and reared and had lived until she moved into the flat with Mel. The bus was jammed and took an age in the heavy rush hour traffic.

Thank God she didn't have to do this depressing journey every evening.

Chloe got off the bus and took a circuitous route past the broken glass spattering the pavement. In one sense, nothing had changed in twenty years. Some of the terraced houses boasted fussy new windows, ornate replacement doors and elaborate garden gates that would more than do justice to a small country estate. Nowadays, of course, there was more than one car parked outside every door, but the girls pushing baby buggies looked younger than ever and the lads drinking cider in the laneway were barely into their teens. The shop on the corner was secured with an assortment of barricades and shutters.

Thank God she had managed to escape.

Chloe's parents' house was one in an identical block of six compact terraced houses. The garden was the size of a mat and the replacement windows were modest. Her mother was surprised when Chloe put her key in the door and walked into the kitchen.

'Chloe! What brings you out here?' Irene Corrigan practically dropped the pot she had been lifting over to the gas stove. She was a small, spare woman with Chloe's grey eyes and an air of permanent activity.

'Surprise, surprise.'

'You can say that again. Thought we weren't going to see you until next Christmas, the way things are going.' She lit the flame, adjusted the pot on the stove and gave Chloe a welcoming hug.

'You know how it is, I've been busy.'

'Don't tell me. No one has time any more. Years ago we were all short of money, now it's time that's precious. Your dad's not home yet and there's no

91

sign of Brian or Rory. They're getting home later and later every evening, with the traffic.'

'The best thing I ever did was move into the flat. Some mornings I walk into work. How's Dad?'

'He's okay. A bit fed up driving that truck around morning, noon and night, but at least it's a job.'

My father's in the transport business, she had said to Adam's parents. It was the best way to describe a deliveryman, wasn't it? Her mother packed shelves in their local branch of Tesco, a retail merchandiser of sorts. And her brothers were completing apprenticeships, not the academic course of study that Adam's parents might have assumed. She tried not to feel too uneasy. After all, nowadays everyone had fancy job titles. For instance, there was no such thing as a typist any more. They were office administrators. So it was the same difference. Wasn't it?

'And how's Mel?' her mother asked.

'She's fine.'

'You should bring her out here again to visit us. I always thought there was something lonely about her. You're looking very well anyway.' Irene studied her daughter. 'It's still agreeing with you, city centre life.'

'It's not quite city centre, but near enough, I suppose.'

'It's the posh part of town, anyway, that's how I always describe it when the neighbours ask me where you've gone. Oh God, is that why you're here tonight? You've come to say your goodbyes?'

'What goodbyes, Mum?' Chloe had to reach forward and lower the gas under the pot of potatoes, as her mother was ignoring it completely.

'Australia! Are you and Mel heading off soon?'

'I think you should sit down, Mum. I want to talk to you.'

Irene immediately looked worried. 'What's wrong?'

'For God's sake, Mum, why should anything be wrong because I want to talk to you?' Chloe said impatiently.

'Are you in any kind of trouble?'

'Thanks a bunch,' Chloe said dryly. 'This isn't Rory or Brian speaking.'

'Sorry, Chloe.' Her mum looked abashed.

'There's a couple of things I want to tell you,' Chloe began as they sat at the kitchen table. 'First of all, I'm not going to Australia. I've changed my mind.'

'Oh, thank God! That's great news,' her mum said. 'Your dad and I hated the idea of you going that far away. Anything at all could have happened to you.'

'Anything can happen in dear old Dublin,' Chloe pointed out.

'Yes, but that's different. At least you're at home. Oh, I'm so pleased you're not going away, Chloe. Hold on til I put on the kettle.' Irene sprang to her feet.

Chloe waited until her mum had poured tea into bright yellow mugs to continue.

'So how come you're not going away?' her mum asked.

'I've met this fabulous man. Well, I've known him a good few months.'

'Chloe! You've a boyfriend! I'm glad. I used to worry about that sometimes. After all, you're gone twenty-six. Not that that means…' Her voice trailed off at the look in Chloe's eyes.

'Did you really think I couldn't get a fella?'

'God no, but it's nice to think you have a boyfriend. Most of the girls you went to school with have settled down by now. Did I tell you that Jean Cullen is expecting her second child? She's bought a grand house in the estate at the end of the road and her mother's over the moon.'

Some things never change, Chloe thought. Was that all her mother thought she was good for? Was that supposed to be the sum total of her ambition? Two babies by twenty-six and a house down the road?

'I didn't go to college and get where I am in my job to have two kids by twenty-six,' Chloe said stubbornly. 'Although I suppose that's good going compared to some of them around here. Fifteen or sixteen seems to be the average age of motherhood. And I haven't told you the rest of my news. That fabulous man I was telling you about, his name is Adam, and he's asked me to marry him.'

'Oh, Chloe!' Irene gasped and her hand flew up to cover her mouth.

'But before you jump to conclusions, number one, I'm not pregnant, and number two, I've no intentions of buying a house, grand or otherwise, in the estate down the road.'

When she saw the range of expressions that flitted across her mother's face, from astonishment, to joy, to anxiety as the full implications of her news sank in, Chloe wondered if she would be better off getting married to Adam on a desert island somewhere, anywhere, so long as it was far away from everyone.

* * *

Later that night, Adam dropped into the flat to say goodnight. Mel was already in bed and Chloe was sitting in the glow of the lamplight when Adam knocked softly on the door.

'My parents can't wait to meet you. My mum seems to think it's high time I settled down,' Chloe said.

'She's right,' Adam teased. 'And how about your dad? Is he expecting me to ask for his daughter's hand?'

'Of course. He's expecting a full declaration of your intentions.'

'And full disclosure of my financial affairs so that I can keep you in the manner to which you are accustomed,' he added.

'That wouldn't be too hard.' Chloe gave him a level look. 'You know my parents aren't in the same financial league as yours?'

'I don't see what it's got to do with you and me,' he said as he slowly began to undo the buttons on her blouse.

'It's just that our backgrounds don't have much in common. My parents thought it was great that I left school with an average Leaving Cert.'

'*I* think it's great that you left school with an average Leaving Cert,' Adam said, his hand reaching for the front clasp of her lacy bra.

'Sure, but that was the height of my parents' expectations,' Chloe said. 'They never encouraged me to go to college, the way yours did.'

'So what? Who needs college?' he said, drawing her close again.

'Easy for you to say, Adam,' she said. She lay back against his chest, listening to the steady beat of his heart through his shirt. His hands began to play with her breasts again, and she felt her nipples swell and harden. It would have been lovely just to melt under his touch, but now that they were getting married, it was important for Adam to understand exactly where she was coming from, wasn't it?

'I found myself in a dead-end job going nowhere fast,' she continued. 'My parents thought I was doing great, but I knew I could do a lot better. And when I moved out and went to college in the evenings, they nearly had a heart attack. They thought I was taking on far too much.'

'I don't know why you're anxious about it, Chloe. That's all in the past.' Adam bent down and began to nuzzle her breasts.

'You'll be meeting them next week.' Chloe's voice was suddenly breathless.

'Good.' Adam slanted a blue-eyed grin up at Chloe.

'I just want you to understand that their view of the world is so different to mine, and so different to that of your parents. My father was out of work for a good while when I was young. Times weren't easy.'

'Don't worry, Chloe, that's all behind you now.' He bent his head again and she sighed as once more she felt his tongue expertly flick at her nipples, sending delicious sensations throughout the rest of her body.

The words echoed in her mind later that night, long after Adam had left and she lay sleepless in bed. Times weren't easy, she had told him. It was all too easy, though, to string a few words together and sum up years of penny pinching, years of doing without things most teenage girls took for granted. In the years before the dawning of the Celtic Tiger, there had been barely enough money in the Corrigan household for essentials, never mind luxuries.

No words, however, could do justice to the feelings of being ashamed and embarrassed in front of her school pals, feelings that had haunted those interminable years until she was old enough to get a part-time job and have some money of her own. And even though her dad had eventually managed to get a permanent job and hung onto it for dear life for fear of a return to the bad old days, Chloe never forgot the many small humiliations, inflicted on her by the likes of Jean Cullen and her cronies, that had soured those early teenage years.

But as Adam had pointed out, it was all behind her now, wasn't it?

* * *

Adam met Chloe's parents and her two brothers the following Saturday night in the lounge of Bewley's Hotel. How the hell was she going to get through the next few hours, Chloe fretted as she looked at Des, her father, stiff and uncomfortable in his good charcoal suit. His funeral suit, he had cheerfully labelled it. How appropriate. His tie in particular seemed to be causing him annoyance and she fervently wished he'd leave it alone and stop fidgeting with it. Her mum, a chatty person who could be relied on to keep the conversation going, was unusually quiet as she sat on the edge of her seat in her plum-coloured twin set.

'Dunnes Stores sale,' she had mouthed to Chloe as she removed her best navy coat. Chloe had beamed approvingly. Anything to make her mum feel relaxed. It wasn't as though Adam was going to bite, after all.

Her two brothers, Brian and Rory, aged nineteen and twenty, looked as though they'd rather be out on the town having a few pints with the lads instead of sitting in the lounge of a Dublin hotel making polite conversation with their posh sister and her even posher boyfriend. At least they had scrubbed up well for the occasion, she noticed, grateful for small mercies.

She thought it was a mistake when Adam ordered champagne. Irene sipped hers carefully, almost suspiciously. Des tried to hold the delicate flute in a hand more accustomed to a pint glass. And although Chloe fixed them with a warning glare, Brian and Rory gulped theirs in double-quick time.

'A free drink is a free drink,' Rory hissed across to her when Adam was in conversation with Des.

'Isn't champagne supposed to get you drunk quicker?' Brian asked her. 'Something to do with the bubbles.'

Chloe threw her eyes up to heaven.

Then Adam ordered pints all around for the men, much to everyone's relief. Chloe decided she needed a brandy and Adam insisted that Irene join her.

'Try it with Baileys, Mrs Corrigan. If you sip it slowly, it's quite a pleasant drink. And we *are* celebrating.'

'Maybe I will,' she beamed. 'And please, call me Irene. None of that Mrs Corrigan nonsense.'

'And I'm Des,' Chloe's dad reminded Adam.

'Des and Irene, Brian and Rory, I envy all of you,' Adam announced.

Four pairs of eyes looked at him in puzzlement.

'You've had the pleasure of knowing Chloe far longer than I have. She's only been part of my life for a few short months, but she's made me extremely happy.'

Des and Irene beamed. Brian and Rory nudged each other. Chloe gulped her drink.

After that, they all got on like a house on fire.

'We're very proud of our Chloe,' Des told Adam. 'She's done very well for herself, you know. Worked very hard and been to college.'

'I love her very much,' Adam said. 'You needn't worry, I'll take care of her.'

'I'm sure you will, son. If our Chloe has chosen you, then that's good enough for us.'

'He's absolutely lovely,' Irene said later on in the ladies'.

'Yes, he is,' Chloe smiled at her mother's reflection in the mirror.

'Your dad and I just want you to be happy, Chloe.'

'I am, Mum. Very happy.'

'That's all we need to know.'

Chapter Nine

'I wouldn't if I were you.'

Chloe dropped the bath towel she had been examining. She wheeled around and came face to face with Sandra Power. God. The last person she wanted to see. Trust Sandra to spot her in the middle of a crowded Arnotts household department. How she had managed to single her out amongst the mounds of fluffy towels and the crush of shoppers was beyond Chloe's comprehension. Sandra must have some kind of killer instinct for homing in on her prey. Worse again, Chloe hadn't even got the safety net of saying she was on her lunch hour and had to rush back to the office, since it was a Saturday afternoon. Her brain raced through a selection of possible excuses, but nothing plausible came to mind.

'Hello, Sandra,' she said, resigning herself to the inevitable. 'How are things?'

'Fine, Chloe. Just up for the afternoon. And yourself?'

'Busy, of course. Things are hectic right now.'

'They'll get even busier, believe me,' Sandra smiled condescendingly. In light grey slacks and a white cotton jumper, she looked every inch as elegant as Chloe had remembered. Her gold earrings, her gleaming neck chain and her chunky bracelet were of the same unusual design. No doubt they had been specially commissioned for her. Her soft leather bag looked expensive enough to steal for its own value alone, never mind the contents. Her flawless complexion and perfectly symmetrical hairdo looked as though she had just stepped out of the beauty parlour.

And on that score at least, Chloe could look her in the eye. She had been in David Marshall's most of the morning, having her blonde hair conditioned and lightened. She had just spent the best part of an hour browsing around the cosmetic counters on the ground floor of Arnotts, sampling different make-up and perfume sprays as part of her action plan in updating her wardrobe and cosmetics now that she was engaged to be married.

'And how are the arrangements coming on?'

'We're getting there,' Chloe told her.

Sandra's blue eyes glared at a harassed shopper who had slightly jostled her in an attempt to reach the towel displays and she crooked an elegant finger and motioned for Chloe to step aside and join her away from the busy counter.

'Have you set a date for the wedding yet?' she asked.

'No, not yet, but we have several in mind.'

Talk about wishful thinking. Sandra had well and truly put the mockers on with her insistence that decent reception venues are booked up years in advance. The last two weeks had been an eye opener for Chloe as her stream of phone calls and enquiries met with negative responses. Marriage hadn't gone out of fashion after all. On the contrary, it seemed like the whole country intended to get married next year.

'Make sure we're the first to know, so we can schedule around it. We'll need plenty of notice.'

'Sure, Sandra.' Pity she couldn't arrange the wedding for when Sandra was away, preferably in a remote corner of the Far East.

'I don't suppose you've time for a coffee?' Sandra suggested as she checked her gold watch. 'I have half an hour to spare. It would be a great opportunity for us to get to know each other better.'

How come Sandra managed to make a cup of coffee sound like a royal command, Chloe thought irritably as once again she tried to come up with some kind of excuse and once more her thought processes failed her miserably.

'Well…I'm…'

'Far be it from me to interrupt your shopping,' Sandra said. 'Were you looking for towels? Maybe I can give you a hand.'

'Not at all, Sandra. I didn't really intend buying,' Chloe fibbed. No way was she going to buy for her bottom drawer under the merciless glare of Sandra's intimidating eye.

'Then coffee it is, if I'm not interrupting your shopping.'

They found seats in a corner of the busy coffee shop.

'I suppose Adam is working today,' Sandra said as she unfolded her napkin and placed it carefully on her lap.

'He's brought work home from the office so he can keep an eye on the football match.' Chloe cut a corner off her Danish pastry and popped it in her mouth. She hadn't really wanted it, but it gave her something to do besides concentrating on Sandra.

'He's very ambitious, that brother of mine. He always talked about setting up his own business from the time he was young. What's his partner's name again?'

'Rob Lyons.'

'Ah yes. Rob. And what's he like?'

'I've only met him a couple of times. He seems to be as determined as Adam to get things up and running and put the business on a secure footing.'

'It'll be an extremely busy year for Adam, all the same, between the challenges of getting his business off the ground, not to mention getting married. He seems to be putting rather a lot on his plate.' She gave Chloe a look of censure, as much to say that Chloe was to blame for her brother being subjected to such a frenzied schedule.

'As I said to you all already, it was Adam who took me by surprise and asked me to marry him,' Chloe said defensively.

'Goodness, Chloe, I never thought for a moment that you were the one who proposed,' Sandra trilled.

'When I first met Adam, he told me that he wasn't interested in any long-term relationship,' Chloe tossed. To hell with it. Sandra might as well know the truth in case she harboured any illusions that Chloe was dragging her little brother kicking and screaming to the altar. 'I had my own plans, you know. I was supposed to be going to Australia.'

'Australia?' Sandra's voice rose almost as much as her elegantly arched eyebrows.

'Yes. My bags were practically packed.'

'I didn't realise… And what exactly were you going to do in Australia, of all places?'

'Travel and work, of course,' Chloe shrugged.

'Like one of those backpackers, you mean.' Naturally, Sandra made it sound as though being a backpacker was the next best thing to being a vagrant. Chloe realised too late that whatever Sandra had thought at first of her suitability for her brother, or more to the point, her unsuitability, she had now surely plummeted in her estimation. Maybe she should have kept her mouth shut. No doubt the entire Kavanagh clan would be informed later that evening that Adam was throwing away his life for a might-have-been backpacker.

'Yeah, you know, a free and easy lifestyle,' Chloe said. 'Surfing on Bondi, picking strawberries in Queensland, camping under the stars.' Might as well give her something decent to gossip about. She would give them even more to gossip about when Adam and she eventually got married and set up home together. She felt more determined than ever that she would wipe Sandra's eye with her glittering wedding and fabulous home.

'So Adam saved you from all that.' Sandra looked as though he had rescued Chloe from a fate worse than death.

'Yes, he was a real knight in shining armour.' Chloe played along with her. 'I would have been going, oh, in about ten days' time.'

'That was a close shave. Mind you, we were all wondering why the hasty engagement,' Sandra smiled.

'Is that so? I'm not pregnant, if that's what you're worried about.'

'Oh no, Chloe. That didn't enter my head. And in any case, it would be the least of my worries. My brother does exactly what he wants to do,' she shrugged. 'He's responsible for his own life. Australia. I was wondering how you got him to propose.' Sandra looked shrewdly at Chloe.

'I didn't get him to do anything.'

'Yes, but that was quite a good hand you played, Chloe.'

'Do you think Adam asked me to marry him to stop me from going away? Is that what you mean?' Chloe suddenly simmered.

'I wouldn't have put it quite as bluntly as that.'

'So you don't think he really loves me?' She had had just about enough. The cheek of this stuck-up snob!

'No, Chloe, I didn't say that,' Sandra laughed hollowly. 'I would just be concerned that your travel plans might have meant a rushed decision. And I'd hate to see you hurt. Adam's had a very colourful past, as I'm sure you know.'

'He's not the only one with a past.' No doubt that's something else that would be burning up the phone lines in Westmeath, Chloe seethed.

'Maybe not, but I have to warn you that Adam has broken quite a few hearts.'

'Yes, you've already mentioned the broken hearts that are littering the Westmeath countryside.' Chloe's coffee had gone cold, but she sipped at the frothy liquid and watched Sandra's face over the rim of her cup, wondering if she was going to elaborate further. She was immediately sorry she had spoken. In one sense, Chloe didn't want to know. Adam and she had agreed not to take any baggage into their future life together. The last person she wanted any such information from was Sandra.

And Chloe didn't want to prolong this conversation any longer. She was tired of trying to keep one step ahead of Sandra and all her notions.

'That's another reason we were so surprised at the engagement,' Sandra began in a confidential voice. Right away, Chloe knew she wasn't going to like what was coming next. But even so, she wasn't in the least prepared for what Sandra had to say.

'He's told you about Jackie, I'm sure.'

'Oh yes,' Chloe lied. Jackie? Who the hell was Jackie?

'We were so sure she was the one. Girls were always chasing Adam, but Jackie seemed different. They grew up together, just friends at first, and then it turned to romance. Her father breeds, you know.'

'Breeds what?' Chloe asked automatically. Her mind was in overdrive as it seethed about Jackie and her relationship with Adam.

'Horses, of course.' Sandra looked at Chloe as though she had two heads. 'Anyway, getting back to Jackie. We were all expecting an Easter announcement. I believe her mother had already phoned the *Times* and enquired about the classifieds. You can imagine the upset it caused when it was all off!'

'Yes, absolutely,' Chloe agreed, nailing a knowledgeable expression to her face. She didn't want to hear about Jackie, especially when she sounded like the perfect match for Adam. Much more perfect than Chloe. A father who breeds, for God's sake.

What could be more appropriate? No, she didn't want to know, but in spite of herself, she was rooted to the spot, frozen in fascinated horror as Sandra, with cold-blooded efficiency, pulled the rug from under her dreams.

'I bumped into Jackie in Athlone on Good Friday,' Sandra continued. 'She was in floods and she didn't want to talk to me. We couldn't get anything out of Adam beyond the fact that he was finished with women.'

'I see.' Chloe didn't see. Not one bit.

'So there's Adam, sworn off women for life…'

When he met her, he had told her he was busy setting up his new web application company, just a few weeks after Easter. It would take time, energy and dedication and for the moment he wanted no ties or commitment.

The words echoed around in Chloe's head and she missed what Sandra said next. There was a horrible buzzing noise in her ears and it took every shred of willpower she possessed to continue the conversation in a normal tone of voice.

'These things happen all the time, Sandra,' she said as casually as possible.

'Yes, but that's what I need to know. He must have told you why they split up. Jackie's mother is a very good customer of mine and this is all extremely embarrassing. I regularly dress her for the Hunt Ball and the Christmas charity bashes. She had begun to discuss bridal wear with me and

I had planned to go to Paris to source some designer outfits. If I knew that Jackie had called the wedding off, then I could face her without feeling too uncomfortable. But if it was Adam who dumped Jackie… Can't you see the dilemma I'm in?'

'Not really,' Chloe snapped. 'It's Adam's business, after all, and I don't think he'd be too pleased if he knew we were discussing his former girlfriends behind his back. If you really need to know, then I suggest you ask him.' Which was exactly what she was going to do the minute she saw him, Chloe thought grimly. She looked at her watch, made a fake cry of horror, and told Sandra she just had to leave. 'I almost forgot. I have to collect my dry cleaning,' she said.

'We must get together properly,' Sandra suggested. 'We'll have a good natter about your wedding plans and I can give you loads of advice.'

'Sure, Sandra.' But not if I see you first, Chloe thought as she picked up her bag and made her way on shaky feet through the maze of tables and chairs.

* * *

'Why didn't you tell me?' She stormed into his bed-sit. She snapped off the portable television and silenced Gary Linekar in mid-commentary.

Adam looked up from his laptop and frowned. 'What's wrong?'

'Everything is wrong, Adam. Everything!'

'What on earth is the matter?' Adam pushed the laptop to one side.

Chloe's heart thumped. She had blindly found her way out of Arnotts with Sandra's words ringing in her ears. She had fought a path through Saturday afternoon shoppers on Henry Street as she rushed to the bus stop. All the way home on the bus she had gone over and over everything in her head. But now that she was face to face with Adam, she could scarcely get the words out.

Although maybe she didn't want to get the words out. Maybe it was best left unsaid, best left buried in the dim and distant past. And then God only knows when it might rear up and niggle her at unexpected times.

'I bumped into Sandra today,' she began, the words almost choking her. 'She had something very interesting to say.'

'Had she now?' Was there something in Adam's face, something that flickered in his blue eyes? Did he know exactly what she was going to say?

'Does the name Jackie ring a bell?' Chloe blazed. She could scarcely say the name. She couldn't believe how ill it made her feel.

'Ah. I see my big sister has been up to her usual mischief.'

'Mischief? Your sister has done nothing wrong, Adam.' Chloe shook with rage.

Adam frowned. 'Yes, she has, to judge by the state you're in.'

'Don't try to wangle out of this, and don't try to blame your sister for her innocent remarks. She thought I knew all about you and Jackie.'

'Innocent? Sandra? That's rich.' Adam grinned ruefully. 'That girl could win prizes for sheer bloody-mindedness.'

'I don't want to talk about Sandra, I want to talk about – about Jackie. And I want the truth.'

'Hold on a minute, Chloe. Let me get something straight here.' Adam stood up. She had almost forgotten how tall he was and her mouth suddenly felt dry. 'On the strength of a chat with my sister, you've got yourself all steamed up, and by the look on your face, you've already decided I'm guilty of something.'

'I haven't decided anything,' Chloe simmered.

'Yes, you have. You've burst in here demanding the truth, and you've told me I can't wangle out of it. What does that add up to?'

'And that's exactly what you're doing right now,' Chloe raged. 'You're trying to wiggle out of it.'

'I'm not trying to wiggle out of anything,' Adam said in a quiet voice. 'I'm trying to understand first of all how you managed to get yourself into such a fury.'

'It's very easy to understand,' Chloe spat. 'How was I supposed to feel when I heard you had been practically engaged just before you met me?'

'That's what Sandra told you?'

'I heard all about you and Jackie, from child-hood friendship to budding romance to the announcement ready for the *Times*. And if I recall properly, you were the one who told me you'd never proposed to anyone before.'

There was a silence, then Adam laughed ruefully.

'This isn't a laughing matter,' Chloe snapped.

'I agree. I'm actually disappointed in you, Chloe.' He shook his head.

'*You're* disappointed in *me*?' Chloe was practically speechless. Her grey eyes widened. 'What the hell do you mean by that?'

'I thought we'd already agreed that our past is behind us.'

'Come on, Adam, being almost engaged is different.'

'You took Sandra at her word and came tearing in here, ready to throw the book at me. That doesn't say much for your trust, does it?' He gave her a mocking glance.

Only then did Chloe realise that Adam was quietly furious. But why was he so angry? Was it because she had caught him out? Or was it because he was thinking of Jackie? Was he by any chance still in love with her?

'Trust?' she blazed. 'How can I trust you when you kept something like that from me?'

'You didn't even wait to talk to me,' Adam shrugged. 'You just got up on your high horse and went straight for the jugular.'

'Seems like I was right,' Chloe raged.

'There you go again. You're right and I'm

obviously the baddie. What does that say about us?' Adam waited for her answer, his arms folded, his blue eyes speculative.

All of a sudden, Chloe felt hot and cold. They were having a row, their first big row. She was right to be angry, right to feel he had kept something important from her, because this was quite, quite different from the few casual relationships she had assumed.

If only she hadn't bumped into Sandra, then this evening would have been like a normal Saturday. She would have bought the lilac towels she'd been examining and come home delighted with herself. She would have dropped up to Adam after five o'clock and gone straight to bed with him. Later on, they would have had a Chinese takeaway and gone out to the local pub for a couple of drinks.

Adam busied himself at the table and shoved the papers he had been working on into a pile by the side of his laptop.

'Go on then, tell me,' Chloe said, her voice shaky. The sooner Adam explained about Jackie, the sooner things would get back to normal. Right now, however, it didn't look as though bed was an option. Maybe they could rescue the Chinese take-away and the couple of drinks in the pub. All of a sudden she wanted to be sitting close beside him on a typical Saturday evening, sipping ice-cold beer and laughing and talking, discussing their wedding and honeymoon and where they might live happily ever after.

He turned to face her. 'So the little temper tantrum is finished now, is it?'

'I didn't have a tantrum.'

'Chloe, you were only short of doing a jig around the room. And now that you've calmed down, you want to know all the gory details.'

'The least I deserve is some kind of explanation.'

'I'm sorry, but I don't agree.'

'I beg your pardon?' Her voice was wobbly.

'You heard me. We already agreed to draw a line under our pasts. As far as I'm concerned, that still holds. In any case, it's obvious by your behaviour this evening that you've already thought the very worst of me. Explanations, as far as I'm concerned, are irrelevant.'

'That's not fair,' Chloe cried. 'I was totally shocked with Sandra's news. Naturally I was hurt that I didn't even know what she was talking about.'

'And instead of keeping your cool and deciding to discuss it with me, you get all hot and bothered and convinced that I'm not to be trusted. How do you think that makes me feel, Chloe?'

At that moment, Chloe didn't care how Adam felt. She only knew she was furious again – furious with Adam, who had neatly sidestepped everything, and furious with herself for expecting something different. All the way home on the bus, as she had gone over everything in her mind, she had pictured a final scene where Adam said how sorry he was for not telling her about Jackie, that she hadn't meant anything to him anyway, and that she, Chloe, was all that mattered.

By the look on Adam's face, that scene was a long way off.

'So I'm to be left in the dark as to what happened,' Chloe snapped. She was horrified to feel scorching tears at the back of her eyes.

'It's not up for discussion,' he said curtly.

'God almighty. You sound so cold and business-like. I never realised you could be such a ruthless bastard.'

'That's enough.'

'You'll go far,' Chloe sobbed as she wrenched off her engagement ring. 'With an attitude like that, God help anyone who gets in your way.'

Chapter Ten

'God, Chloe, what's wrong?' Mel gave her a startled glance as she emerged from her room on Sunday evening. 'Are you sick or something? Too much to drink last night?'

'Do I look hung over?'

'Well, sort of.' Mel's eyes hastily looked away as Chloe continued to glare at her.

What else had she expected, Chloe agonised. She knew that her eyes resembled red slits that were sunk in the back of her head and that her blonde hair was all mussed and untidy. Even her voice sounded raw and hoarse on account of a lump the size of a golf ball lodged in her throat. There was no hiding the fact that she had been crying. For about the last twenty-four hours.

Come to think of it, there was no point in hiding anything from Mel.

'You might as well know it's all off.'

'All off?' Mel looked puzzled.

'Yeah, me and Adam. Finished.' Chloe felt a physical pain as she said the words. There was no forgetting the expression on Adam's face as she had torn off her ring and hurled it back at him. She deliberately turned away from Mel, switched on the kettle and took a mug out of the press.

'God, I'm so sorry. I don't know what to say.'

'Don't attempt to say I told you so,' Chloe snapped defensively.

'Chloe, I wouldn't dream of it.'

'Sure.' Chloe took the milk out of the fridge and slammed the door shut, rattling everything inside.

'Look, I know we haven't exactly seen eye to eye the last couple of weeks, but you're still my friend. I don't like to see you so upset. Did you – or did…'

'I broke it off with Adam. I gave him back his ring and we're finished.'

Everyone was bound to find out sooner or later. Even Sandra. No doubt Sandra would be thrilled to hear Chloe had handed back her ring, following the revelation that Chloe had been planning on bumming around Australia until Adam intervened. She would probably think that Adam had had a lucky escape. And she wouldn't have the worry of coming face to face with Chloe's mother in her snobby boutique.

'Chloe! I'm really sorry.' Even through her red-rimmed eyes, Chloe could see the genuine empathy in her friend's face. She almost burst out crying again.

'I'll be okay,' she said gruffly.

Okay? Who was she kidding? In the whole of her life she had never felt so broken hearted, not even when she was enduring the worst of the taunts from Jean Cullen and her pals during those interminable schoolyard years.

Mel didn't look too convinced. 'And what about when I'm gone? Adam was supposed to be moving in here, wasn't he?'

'Don't even mention his name,' Chloe snapped.

'I'm going to Galway tomorrow, so I won't be around for the next few days...'

Chloe shrugged.

'I could postpone it for a day or two, if you want me to hang around.'

'Nah. You go ahead.'

'Are you sure? I know what it's like to have your world torn apart, Chloe. You were there for me when I landed on your doorstep, remember? I'd like to think I'm here for you if you need me.'

Chloe smiled weakly. 'Thanks, Mel, but it's okay, really.'

Adam had had his chance, Chloe fretted as she finally made some coffee. Wrapping her hands around the mug, she sat down on the sofa. Through the long lonely hours of Saturday evening and on into Sunday afternoon, she had fully expected his

119

knock on the door. And as the night wore on and the dawn crept through the window, she missed him so much that she began to feel ready to forgive him for being such an arrogant bastard, ready to accept whatever explanation he was willing to give.

It was all very simple, really. Just an honest explanation of what Jackie had meant to him. If he had broken it off with Jackie, all the better. However, if she had broken it off with Adam, then there was the chance that he had asked Chloe to marry him on the rebound. But there was an ominous silence from the bed-sit above. Chloe had checked and rechecked her mobile to make sure it was working. As the day slowly wore on and gave way to the evening and there was no sign of Adam, she felt sick and empty inside. She didn't want to know if he tried to contact her now. He had put her though so much torture in the last twenty-four hours that she didn't think she'd ever forgive him.

'You know I'm leaving tomorrow week?' Mel sat down beside her and threw an arm around her shoulders.

'I see you've been busy packing.' Chloe tried to smile a wobbly smile, but didn't quite succeed.

'Yeah, I got rid of loads of rubbish, and Henry's keeping a few things for me.'

'Henry?'

'I thought it was the handiest. You'll have more than enough on your plate the next few months—Sorry, Chloe, I forgot for a minute.'

Chloe mutely shook her head. 'Doesn't matter. It'll take time to get used to it. Never know, I might catch up with you in Oz.'

'Do you want me to see if I can book you in on the flights?'

'No, I can't think about anything like that right now. I still feel bad about the way I let you down. Are you sure you're okay about going off on your own?'

'Course I am. I'll be met in Sydney anyway. I just spoke to Sarah, my yoga teacher, yesterday. Her cousin Elaine is meeting me at the airport and she's putting me up for a while. Whatever happens, there's one thing I do know.'

'Yes?'

Mel gave her a hug. 'You'll get through this, I know you will. We go back a long way, don't we? You have the guts to make it, and you're a born survivor.'

She didn't want to be a survivor, Chloe fretted as she put down her mug and curled her legs underneath her. Not if this was what it meant, this awful, empty feeling, this sickening ache in the pit of her stomach. Somehow, though, all along, she should have expected this. She should have known that things were far too good to be true. She should have known that dreams don't really happen, just like that.

Not for the likes of Chloe Corrigan.

* * *

The two-thirty train from Dublin Heuston rattled into Ceannt Station in Galway on Monday evening a little behind schedule. Mel lifted her case down from the shelf above her head and joined the queue shuffling off the train.

Outside the station, she joined the queue for the bus that would take her out to Spiddal, where Granny Alice lived. As the bus trundled past familiar Galway landmarks, Mel was disgusted to find herself feeling nervous again.

Surely she should be over all this. Twenty-five years of age and four years gone from Galway, with only occasional visits to her gran, she couldn't believe that her stomach still contracted painfully when she neared the area of the city where she had once lived. She told herself to relax, it was okay, she wasn't going home this time, she wasn't returning to the scene of the crime. Anyway, her parents' house wasn't hers to go to, they were away in Cape Town indefinitely, and the house was leased to some learned professor who was lecturing in Galway University.

Spiddal was lit by mellow October sunshine when she stepped off the bus. The small village was a mecca for tourists and now, in mid-October, there were quite a few still around, making the most of the golden evening sunshine. Mel strolled down to the small sandy beach with its rocky out-crops. She drew in refreshing lungfuls of the crisp salty air. She felt the slight breeze tug at her hair and she watched the green waters of the Atlantic Ocean whisper and suck at the shore. On the near horizon, the blue-grey shapes of the north Clare coast seemed to float gracefully on top of the sea.

She felt instant peace.

She watched two children dressed in red outfits chase each other around and heard them laugh aloud. She had spent a lot of her childhood on this beach, playing with the sand, ducking in and out of the water. But had she ever been as carefree? Somehow, she couldn't recall.

Alice Saunders opened the door as Mel walked up the garden path.

'Hello, Alannah, come in, come in.' She threw her arms around her granddaughter and gave her a big hug. Her granny had only ever called her Alannah from the time she was small. Mel had once asked her what exactly it meant and why she insisted on calling her by that name.

'It means "beautiful child" in Irish.' Her granny's eyes had twinkled. 'It suits you much better than that mouthful your parents have given you.' Even now, into her twenties, her granny still used her pet name. And Mel loved her for it.

Alice Saunders was in her seventies. She was tall, like her granddaughter. Her once-dark hair was snow white, and it curled softly around her head. Her emerald eyes might have faded over the years, but there was no diminishing the inner spark that remained, and her skin was as soft as crumpled tissue paper.

123

She was a native Irish speaker and loved the language dearly. She had spoken Irish all her life, for the village in which she lived and the surrounding Connemara area was an Irish-speaking district. Her granddaughter was also a fluent Irish speaker, but the first time Mel had returned to visit, after fleeing to Dublin months earlier, she insisted she was beyond all that nonsense, as she cynically put it, and Alice hadn't the heart to argue.

'Are you hungry?' her gran asked as Mel automatically went down to her homely kitchen, with the cosy turf-burning stove and pine Welsh dresser, the flower-patterned curtains and matching tablecloth, the rush mats on the red flagstone floor.

'I'm starved,' Mel said, wrinkling her noise appreciatively. 'Let me guess, shepherd's pie?'

'I made it specially for you. Have to fatten you up before you go off to that heathen country. God knows what you'll be eating over there.'

'Gran! I'm very sensible about my food,' Mel protested gently.

'Don't I know you are, Alannah.' Alice ruffled Mel's dark hair. 'Thanks for coming down to see your old gran before you leave.'

'You know I wouldn't go off without saying goodbye,' Mel smiled.

'We won't think about that yet. Let's just enjoy our few days.'

Before her gran dished up savoury platefuls of shepherd's pie, Mel went down to her room at the back of the bungalow to freshen up and unpack. When she was growing up, Mel had often spent the night and occasionally the weekend with her gran while her parents were away. Even when she had moved to Dublin, her gran had told her that her room was there for her whenever she wanted to get away from the city; she was to come down whenever she felt like it.

She had even offered to have it done up, but Mel had been horrified. She loved it just the way it was, she insisted. She didn't want anything to change. She loved the pale blue wallpaper with its sprigs of flowers marching diagonally across the wall, the white wardrobe that held some of her clothes, her Spiddal clothes of warm fleece jacket, walking shoes and raincoat. She loved the heavier blue curtains that hung beneath the white wooden pelmet and the candlewick bedspread with a blue design in the centre. Her bed was soft and comfy, the kind of bed you could sink into, and the sheets and pillowcases always smelled of lavender.

Nothing had changed in the room since the days of Mel's childhood. And as far as she was concerned, nothing would change. Her gran, this room, the small house in Spiddal, represented the only piece of security she knew. It felt far more like home to Mel than the huge, echoing, four-bedroom house in Galway city where she had grown up.

* * *

125

Mel enjoyed the few days of peace and relaxation in the middle of her hectic preparations. She walked by the beach every day, sometimes in the autumn sunshine, sometimes in the soft drizzle of rain. Each night she slept like a log in the comfy lavender-scented bed and each day her gran cooked and baked, insisting that Mel have plenty to eat, feeding her homemade stews and soda bread, huge portions of cabbage and bacon and her favourite currant scones. In the evenings, they watched the news on RTÉ and her gran bemoaned the state of the world. They talked about anything and every-thing, anything at all, in fact, except Mel's parents.

It was late on Thursday evening, with Mel due to leave for Dublin the following morning, before her grandmother posed the inevitable question.

'Any chance you'll get to see your parents on your travels?' Alice finally asked.

'I won't be anywhere near them,' Mel spoke shortly. 'I'll be further around the world again.'

'They'll be home for Christmas,' her gran said.

'Where are they going to stay? The house is leased.'

'They might have to stay here.'

'Here? Couldn't they go to a hotel or something?'

'Maybe I'd like to have them,' Alice's tone softened.

'I'm glad I won't be around.'

'He's my son, Alannah,' her gran continued. 'And I love him almost as much as I love you. And I hate to see the rift between you. No, hold on a minute.' She put up her hand as Mel began to interrupt. 'I know it was your dad's fault and he was entirely to blame. But time has gone by and life is short, and your mother has forgiven him, so…?' She left the question hanging in mid-air.

'My mother is mad,' Mel said. She was on the point of saying more, that she would have kicked her father out for good, but she pulled herself up in time. What was the point in upsetting her gran any further? Her gran who had always loved her, who was always there for her, her gran who had been just as upset as she over her father's behaviour?

At the time, when Mel had thrown herself weeping inconsolably into her arms, Alice had been righteously indignant. But now, with the passage of time, she had obviously decided to follow her daughter-in-law's example and forgive and forget.

'Maybe Deirdre thinks she's doing the right thing,' Alice sighed.

'She just wants an easy life,' Mel shrugged. 'She's too weak to stand up to him.'

'Alannah, I know you probably think I'm a daft old soul who hasn't a clue, but I have been around on this planet a lot longer than you. And as far as human relations are concerned, nothing is ever black or white, remember that.'

Someone else had said that to her recently, Mel recalled. Henry McBride. She immediately bristled. It was so easy to talk, so easy to be wise if you were on the outside looking in. 'As far as I'm concerned, some things in life are crystal clear,' she stated.

Alice smiled. 'You remind me of myself when I was young, so sure I knew everything and that my view of the world was the right one. It'll do you good to get away, Alannah, broaden your horizons. It's an opportunity I would have loved at your age.'

'You were probably married at my age,' Mel said, relieved to be off the thorny subject of her parents.

'And with a couple of babies as well,' her gran said cheerfully.

'I suppose there was no such thing in those days as seeing the world before you settled down,' Mel said. 'Whereas nowadays, there's no such thing as settling down for life.'

'Not necessarily, Alannah,' her gran said gently. 'Human nature being what it is, people are still falling in love and getting married, and more importantly, staying married. But certainly, in my day, if you went to Australia it was for life, a one-way ticket. So make the most of it, make the most of every day, and whatever you do, make sure you come home at the end.'

'Of course I will. I'm only going for a year.'

Mel was up early the following morning. She was beginning to feel restless now, almost anxious to be gone, yet hating the thoughts of saying good-bye to her gran. She wandered into the front room and looked around at her gran's familiar posses-sions, the Donegal parian china and Galway Crystal in the glass-fronted cabinet, side by side with the inexpensive vases and ornaments a younger Mel had proudly bestowed on her.

She went over to the window and looked at the array of photos in frames along the curving windowsill. Mel aged four and starting school, already staring earnestly at the camera, Mel standing stiffly in her white Holy Communion dress, Mel looking serious and far too solemn in her secondary school uniform. A photo of her parents, Jim Saunders tall and handsome, Deirdre shy and pretty.

Mel had the tremendous urge to lift her arm and sweep the photo frames to the ground.

She was glad when the train finally rattled out of Ceannt Station later that morning and picked up speed, leaving Galway behind. Even the time it had taken to travel the jolting bus journey from Spiddal to Galway had eased the ache she felt at saying goodbye to her gran, had softened the picture in her mind of her gran standing by the hall door, smiling bravely and waving goodbye, telling her to make the most of everything, shoving some notes into her hand for an emergency, reminding her to bring a diary and keep an account of everything she saw, so that in time she could tell her old gran of the places she had been, the sights she had seen, when she came home again.

Mel leaned back against her seat as the train swayed through the countryside. She closed her eyes briefly and a single tear escaped and slid down the side of her nose. She wiped it away impatiently and firmly turned her mind to the next few days.

There was nothing to stop her now, nothing between her and the plane journey to London and then on to Singapore, en route to Sydney.

Chapter Eleven

The traffic flowing up the inside lane of Dame Street came to an abrupt halt behind Henry's battered old Renault as he pulled up at the bus stop. There was an instant volley of car horns that pierced even the Saturday evening bustle. He leaned across the car and opened the passenger door.

'Hey, Chloe! Do you want a lift?'

Chloe took one look at Henry's face and burst into tears.

'C'mon, jump in,' he urged. Chloe stood transfixed in the queue for the bus as tears poured unchecked down her cheeks.

'Chloe, get in quick, before I'm arrested.'

She moved forward, hesitantly at first, then a little more briskly as impatient drivers who had tried and failed to swing out into the busy centre lane blared their horns even more aggressively. She almost fell into the passenger seat, her shopping bags in a tangle at her feet. Henry threw the car into first gear and accelerated up Dame Street, making an apologetic signal to the driver behind.

Grey clouds that had threatened all afternoon finally broke and within minutes the first tentative raindrops had turned into a steady downpour. Henry switched on his windscreen wipers and turned on the lights.

'That was well timed,' he remarked lightly, ignoring the silent tears coursing down Chloe's face. 'Another few minutes and you would have been drowned.'

Come to think of it, he realised, Chloe was almost drowning as he spoke – drowning in her tears. She gave a little hiccup, then bent forward and rummaged in her bag for a tissue. She blew her nose and carefully patted the area around her wide grey eyes.

'Sorry about that,' she said, her voice muffled. 'You must think I'm an awful eejit. Thanks a million for the lift.'

'Not at all. Just as well I spotted you. You're heading back to Harold's Cross?'

'I am, yes. I suppose you've heard the news?' She turned a tear-stained face to him, and Henry's attention was momentarily distracted from the traffic.

Chloe looked wretched.

'Yes, I have. Want to talk about it?'

'Not really,' she gulped.

'I'm sure everything will work out in the end.'

'That's exactly what Mel said, but you're wrong, both of you. It's finished. For good.'

'I see.' He was silent as he slowed to a halt at the traffic lights on Christchurch Hill. The rain was heavy and pedestrians darted across the road, huddled under the scant protection of umbrellas. Large pools of rainwater were beginning to form at the edge of the pavements. After a few minutes the lights changed, he released the handbrake and turned into High Street.

'Is Mel home then, from Galway?' he asked.

'Yes, she came home yesterday evening. You know she's leaving on Monday afternoon.'

'Any regrets that you're not going with her?' Henry could have bitten his tongue. He had an awful habit of putting his foot in it, of saying the wrong thing at the wrong time, and this was surely one of those times. Bad enough reminding Chloe that her engagement was off without reminding her that her best friend was flying out to a new life on Monday. But to his surprise, Chloe laughed, a short, bitter laugh, but a laugh nonetheless.

'I suppose it serves me right if I had any regrets,' she said. 'I messed up Mel by letting her down at the last minute. At least we're friends again. But no, I don't wish I was going off with her on Monday. Not the way I'm feeling right now.'

With that, Chloe hung her head and began to cry again, sobbing as though her heart was broken.

'Look, why don't we go for a drink or something,' Henry suggested desperately as they neared his apartment. 'Or if you prefer, I've a bottle of something back home?'

He was mad, he told himself, absolutely crazy. He didn't even particularly like Chloe all that much, but he hated to see her cry like this. He hated to see anyone so upset, and he was well used to weepy females pouring out their troubles on his shoulder. He seemed to be a magnet for them. One more couldn't make all that much difference, could it? He would do it as a favour for Adam.

'Oh, could we? Go back to your apartment?' Chloe asked through her tears. 'That would be great, Henry, thanks. I hate the thought of going back to the flat.'

* * *

Mel stepped out of the shop on the corner and looked up the road to Henry's apartment. And then she saw the car.

For just as she came out of the shop into the gathering gloom of the evening, felt the rain on her face and began to open her umbrella, Henry drove by in his ancient Renault. With Chloe was sitting in the front seat.

Mel watched as the car turned the corner, drove up to Henry's apartment and stopped outside.

Henry jumped out of the driver's side and ran up to open the door of the apartment block. He hurried back to the car and opened the passenger door, and out stepped Chloe, hampered with several carrier bags. Henry took some of the bags off her, then threw a casual arm around Chloe's shoulder before ushering her quickly towards the door of the apartment block.

What the hell was that all about? She knew Stephanie had been blown out recently, and Henry, ever the fast worker, no doubt had someone lined up to take her place, but Chloe... His friend's ex-fiancée, for God's sake. Somehow she had thought better of him. And better of Chloe. She lifted her chin and turned away and walked back to the flat in the pouring rain and the dark, threatening sky.

* * *

Adam was drinking in a pub in Temple Bar. He had dropped in to catch the second half of a Man U Premiership match. The pub was jammed and the match fraught with tension. As soon as it was over he made his way towards the door, anxious to get home. Chloe had blanked him all week. He had left her alone until Tuesday evening, giving her plenty of time to cool down and come to her senses, time to realise that she was being ridiculously childish. But it hadn't worked. Every time he had tried to phone her since, she had terminated the call. He had knocked on the apartment door several times, full sure she was inside, but the door remained firmly shut. Maybe if he tried one more time, Chloe would talk to him.

Then he bumped into some old friends from college.

'Hey Adam, how's it going?'

'Donal! Don't tell me you've been sitting here all the time!'

'Yeah, I came in for the match. On your own?'

Adam nodded.

'I'm here with Paul,' Donal said. 'Remember Paul McNamara? He's up at the bar. Hey, Paul!'

In the middle of the crush at the bar, a sandy-haired man turned around. He recognised Adam and grinned.

'Get Adam a pint,' Donal yelled. Paul gave him a thumbs-up sign.

'I really should be going,' Adam began. He didn't particularly want another pint. The pub was wall-to-wall clamour and noise and he wanted to go back to the flat and try and see Chloe one more time.

'Don't rush off,' Donal insisted. He pulled a stool out from under the table. 'Sit down and have a chat. Haven't seen you in years.'

'What are you up to these days?' Adam sat down. Maybe just a quick pint then, for old time's sake.

'Pretty busy,' Donal said. 'I'm in my old man's firm, been there since I left college. Working my way up. He's hoping to take early retirement as soon as I can take over the reins. Yourself?'

'I'm in partnership with Rob Lyons, remember, he was in the year ahead of us. We started out on our own at the beginning of the year and business is booming.'

'Fair play. That's the only way to make money. Work for yourself. I reckon I'll have my first million under my belt in the next couple of years.'

'Same here,' Adam said.

Paul elbowed his way through the crowd, juggling three pints of Guinness in his hands.

'Jeez, Adam, long time no see. Here, get that into you.' He handed him a glass.

'Cheers, everyone.'

'Cheers.'

They began to talk about the match and the idiot referee, the goal that seemed to be off side but should have been allowed, the penalty that should have been awarded instead of a free kick, the crazy half-time substitutions. Adam took a long gulp of his pint and started to unwind. It was cosy sitting here with his old mates, watching the rain stream down the stained glass windows. It had been a tough week at the office without the added stress of Chloe's cold obstinacy. It was good to get away for a while from the tedium of incompatible programmes and the ridicule of an engagement ring flung back in his face. It was no harm, either, to network with Paul and Donal. You never knew

137

what business they could throw his way, and vice versa.

When he was almost finished with his pint, he ordered another round.

* * *

Mel dumped her wet umbrella in the front hall, opened the door to the flat and switched on the lights. She was being ridiculous. Imagine thinking that Henry and Chloe…

It was just that there had been something almost protective in the way he had thrown an arm around Chloe's shoulders and escorted her into the apartment block. But that was just Henry's normal behaviour, wasn't it? An old-fashioned gentleman in some respects, and in others, an out and out rogue.

She felt restless and somehow uneasy as she ate her evening meal, almost wishing the hours away until Monday, wishing she could be gone. She switched on the television and flicked through the channels, in the end settling for *The Simpsons*. Chloe was bound to come home soon. Then she could suggest a drink and maybe rope in Henry as well. After all, she didn't really want to head off to the other side of the world without some form of goodbye.

* * *

'You're very understanding, Henry,' Chloe hiccupped.

She was on her third glass of wine, and for the first time all week, some of the raw ache in her heart felt a little soothed. Henry's apartment was quiet and tranquil. She sat in the living room beside the new fish tank and watched as a sprinkling of tiny goldfish freckled the oxygenated water with its bed of coloured stones and gently waving fronds. She could sit back and relax on Henry's couch with the new navy throw and not have to worry about the sound of Adam's footsteps going up the stairs or his floorboards creaking overhead.

He hadn't even attempted to contact her until Tuesday night. Tuesday night, for God's sake. The bastard. No wonder she had refused to answer his phone calls and ignored his knocking on the door of the flat. He could scarcely expect her to fall into his arms having completely ignored her for almost three days. She sipped her wine and felt its mellow tang in her throat. She preferred white, but she didn't say no to the generous glass of rich red that Henry had silently handed her when she had finally managed to pull herself together. And she didn't say no when he told her to sit down and relax for a while.

'Me? Understanding? Not everyone would agree with you,' Henry laughed.

'I don't care what anyone else says. I think you're very patient and tolerant.'

'If you knew me better you might have something different to say.'

'It's not just that I've had a glass of wine. I think you're very understanding for a man. And I don't care what Mel thinks.'

'Why, what does Mel think?'

'Oh, just that…' She had better not say that Mel thought he was mad, Chloe had the sense to realise, in spite of feeling a tiny bit tipsy. 'She just said she doesn't how your girlfriends put up with you.'

'I'm sure Mel said a lot more than that,' Henry laughed.

Chloe shrugged. 'God knows what she said about me, when I told her I wasn't going to Australia.'

'Don't worry about Mel. She's able to take care of herself.'

'I hope so. I really let her down.'

'Please don't start crying again, Chloe. Mel will be fine, believe me.'

'Do you think she will?' Chloe groped for another tissue without success. All that remained in the pocket of her trousers was a sodden ball of mush. Henry went out to the kitchen and returned with a kitchen roll. Chloe gratefully tore off a couple of sheets and blew her nose before taking another gulp of her wine.

'She's not as hard as she makes out, you know,' she told him. 'Underneath it all, Mel's really very soft inside. She hurts easily. And I should know.'

'I see. And how come you know?'

Chloe took another gulp of her wine. 'It's just something that happened before she left Galway.

Something she told me in confidence.'

'Something that happened to Mel, you mean?'

'Sort of. Look, Henry, it's Mel's business. Just forget what I said. I've been rotten enough to her already, but she'd kill me altogether if she thought I'd broken a trust.'

'You haven't, really.'

'No, I haven't said anything at all to you, have I? And as far as you and the rest of the world are concerned, Mel is as hard as nails.'

'I don't think that's entirely accurate either, but don't worry, we haven't had this conversation. And I don't know about you, but I'm starved.'

'I'm a bit hungry myself. Can I cook you anything?' He might have something handy in the freezer, she thought. Anything to delay going home.

'Not at all.' He went to the window and pulled aside the new navy hangings. Outside, it was already dark and rain spattered against the glass and slithered down the pane. 'It's a filthy night out, so there's only one thing for it,' Henry said as he reached for his mobile. 'How would you like some fish and chips? The chippers up the road will deliver.'

'Although maybe I'd better go home.' Chloe struggled to get to her feet. She could feel the effects of the wine and she felt decidedly woozy.

'Are you joking?' Henry replaced the curtain and turned from the window. 'I'm not sending you out in that weather. Stay and have some food and then we'll see. How about a nice fresh cod and some chips? And I can even supply salt and vinegar.'

'That sounds lovely.'

She hadn't realised she was so hungry, Chloe thought, as half an hour later they were tucking into hot golden chips and battered fresh cod, all the things you weren't really supposed to eat. She had only picked at her food all week and she had even felt her jeans a bit looser on her that morning as she had dressed for town. So now, having relaxed a little, she ate everything on her plate, even munching on the crispy batter, definitely forbidden food, licking her fingers afterwards, telling Henry she had forgotten how nice an ordinary plate of fish and chips could be.

They had just finished their food when Henry's mobile rang and he went into the kitchen to talk to whoever had phoned. He was gone for about ten minutes and for a crazy moment Chloe thought it might be Adam. But Henry said nothing when he returned to the living room, minus his phone.

'Can I ask you something, Henry?' Chloe asked in a small voice, feeling suddenly emboldened. The question had been hovering on the edge of her mind all evening, but she had been afraid to ask, and now it suddenly slipped out.

'Sure.'

'Did you know about – about Jackie?'

'In all fairness, I don't think it's me you should be asking.'

'Adam wouldn't tell me, that's why we – we had an argument.' Sudden tears welled up in Chloe's eyes.

'Chloe, there's really only one question you can ask.'

'What's that?' she gulped.

'Who's wearing Adam's ring? You or Jackie?'

'But that's the problem. You see, I gave it back to him. So I don't have it any more.' She helped herself to more kitchen paper and wiped her streaming eyes. 'Sorry about this, after you being so kind and understanding. I've ruined your Saturday night.'

'And I thought I had finally managed to cheer you up.' He gave her a mocking grin.

'But you did,' she said tremulously. 'You've been great. The wine was lovely, I definitely owe you a bottle or two and the fish and chips saved my life. I'll go home now, and leave you in peace.' Just as she struggled to her feet, the heavens opened. Heavy rain pounded against the windows of the apartment and Chloe shivered.

'Sit down and have one more drink. You'll be destroyed if you go out in that weather. As soon as the worst is over, I'll walk you around to the flat.'

'You're a real brick, Henry, thanks.'

'Don't think I've ever been called a brick before,' Henry laughed as he filled up her glass one more time. He turned up the dial on the central heating and put on the film on BBC1. It was a romantic comedy, ideal for a wet Saturday night. Then he tidied up after the meal and began to do the washing up in his small white kitchen.

Chloe sipped her wine. It was heavy and luscious. She felt tired now, exhausted, really, after the strain of the week. She heard Henry moving about in the kitchen. He surely wouldn't mind if she put her feet up and rested on his couch for a while. It was very tempting to ease off her ankle boots and slip her feet up on the couch. She would definitely go home soon, back to the flat, and get out of Henry's way. He might have plans for tonight. But it was early yet for nightclubs in town, barely ten o'clock, so he still had time to rescue the night for himself.

And then the wine, the food, the warmth of the apartment and the cosy feel of the thick cotton throw under her cheek combined to do what nothing else had done all week. Her eyes grew heavier and heavier, and she just had to close them for a little while, just a little while. It was impossible to keep them open. And then Chloe fell into a deep, dreamless sleep.

* * *

Henry had always thought his couch would come in handy if anyone ever wanted to stay over, but he hadn't quite expected to see the sight of Chloe curled up and dead to the world when he walked back in from the kitchen. Her blonde hair had fallen over her face and she barely stirred when he put out a gentle hand and brushed it to one side.

Then he went out to his tiny hot press, fetched a spare blanket and covered her sleeping body.

He had turned off his mobile a short while earlier in case Stephanie phoned again. She had already been on, calling him a sad bastard amongst other things. He had reminded her that they had mutually agreed to split, but that wasn't enough for her, so he had ended the call and switched off the mobile. Then he dimmed the lamp, lowered the sound on the telly, and sat back to watch the rest of the film in the only other armchair.

He remembered then that Mel was supposed to have phoned to arrange for him to collect her stuff for storage. She would scarcely phone on a Saturday night at this hour. She was more than likely out on the town, celebrating her escape to freedom.

It would be time enough, wouldn't it, to contact her in the morning.

Chapter Twelve

Mel poured herself another Southern Comfort. She might as well have a party by herself. No one else seemed to be interested. Cheers, Mel. She waved her glass in the air and took a mouthful of the fiery liquid. Best of luck on your travels. She took another gulp. Don't forget to send us a post-card or two.

She picked up the sizeable banker's draft that had arrived in the post all the way from Cape Town. It would be easy enough to tear it in two. It would be easy enough to ignore it completely. After another deep slug, she went to the window. Outside, the rain teemed down, slanting against the window, pockmarking the puddles, gurgling down drainpipes. All evening she had waited, fully expecting Chloe to arrive home any minute, fully expecting that they would head to the pub for a farewell drink. Adam was out of the question, but maybe Henry would have joined them, with or without his latest girlfriend.

She felt suddenly lonely, on her last Saturday night in Dublin. Normally staying in alone didn't bother her, as she was usually happy with her own company. But tonight, she felt in a strange kind of limbo. She clutched her glass of Southern Comfort and told herself to focus on the present. Forget the weather outside and the dismal sight of the flat, stripped of most of her possessions. She had nothing whatsoever to worry about. Just hours to get through before she boarded the plane.

As time went by and there was no sign of Chloe coming home, she began to wonder if, mad as it seemed, Henry was indeed comforting her after Adam had broken her heart. Maybe Chloe was comforting Henry, after he had split with Stephanie.

There was only one way to find out. She couldn't reach Chloe on her mobile, as it was lying, switched off, on their kitchen table. What the hell, she might as well phone Henry. It was only ten o'clock and they had often met up around that time. She could ask him about collecting her stuff and see what he had to say. She reached for her mobile.

She wasn't too surprised when she punched in his number and the automatic service told her that the mobile she was calling was powered off. For wasn't that what Henry McBride did when he wanted no interruptions?

* * *

'Are you coming for something to eat, Adam?'

'Nah, you go ahead. I'm going home.'

'C'mon, a bit of Italian grub will soak up all that Guinness. Then you can start all over again, before we hit the nightclubs,' Donal suggested.

Adam winced.

'You're not going home. It's just after ten, and the night's only beginning,' Paul said as he threw an arm around Adam and the three of them half walked, half staggered between the crush of tables, stool legs and people and almost fell out of the pub into the wet Dublin night.

Blanketed in a fog of noise in a corner of the pub, and drinking steadily through the early evening hours and on into the night, Adam had lost all track of time. Donal and Paul looked as though they could go on forever, but Adam felt decidedly drunk, and even more so when he hit the air.

He had forgotten it was raining. The air was heavy and damp and if the huge pools of surface water on the pavements and the road were anything to go by, he had just missed the worst of a deluge. It was still falling steadily. He could feel raindrops trickling down the back of his neck and wetting his hair. The cobblestones were dangerously slick, and Adam watched his step as neon lights refracted on the dizzying, shifting surface.

They stopped outside an Italian restaurant, and a young couple came out arm in arm, laughing and talking, bringing with them a mixture of garlicky scents that wafted out into the street through the brightly lit doorway.

'C'mon, Adam, in we go. They'll squeeze us in somewhere,' Paul said as they stumbled through the doorway. However, Paul was being over-optimistic. The three of them were firmly but politely told that the restaurant was fully booked and they had no option but to trundle back out into the wet night.

'Try Parliament Street,' Donal suggested as they stalled at the corner. 'There are a few places up along there. We'll get in somewhere.'

'You go on, but I'm going home,' Adam said, holding up his hand as Donal and Paul protested. 'There's someone I want to see,' he went on. 'If she'll talk to me.'

'What do you mean, if she'll talk to you?'

'Ah, you know yourself, we had a bit of a row.' He began to back away. No point in mentioning the engagement ring that was hurled back. No point in mentioning Chloe's door remaining firmly shut in his face. And there was no point in mentioning the hurt and the anger that was surfacing again inside, now that the relaxing Saturday evening interval in the pub was over.

'I wouldn't waste my time. I'd get rid of her if I were you.'

'Yeah, Adam. Plenty of nice babes out there.'

'You're right there. See you around.' Adam moved away.

'Sure thing. Keep in touch.'

Adam turned up the collar of his jacket and began to head home. He had no change for a bus and taxis were gold dust on a Saturday night in Dublin, so he decided to walk. Might help sober him up, he decided as he trudged around by the Central Bank and began to head up George's Street in the falling rain.

When he was halfway home, he dropped into a fast food bar and demolished a large burger. As he sat on a stool munching his food through a fog of alcohol, he caught sight of his reflection in the glass window. His hair was slicked with rain, his jacket damp and dishevelled, and he was sitting hunched over the table, looking for all the world like a dejected down and out.

Saturday night in Dublin and he scarcely recognised himself.

* * *

Mel turned off Channel 4 and clumsily put down her glass. Swaying slightly, she dragged herself into the shower, holding onto the rail as warm water sluiced down her body. She felt a little better after

150

the shower and she towelled herself dry, putting on clean pants, a pair of blue fleece pyjamas with teddy bear motifs and a thick pair of ankle socks. She lurched back into the living room to turn off the gas fire before she went to bed. Then she looked at the half full bottle of Southern Comfort and decided to have one last drink.

After all, it was her private party. Although her hands were shaking a little, she finally managed to light the lavender-scented candles on the mantel-piece and switched on the stereo. All her favourite CDs were packed, so she rooted clumsily through Chloe's, selected Madonna and inserted it into the slot. She sat back on the sofa, feet curled under her, glass in hand, as the candlelight danced and flick-ered, the air was tinged with the scent of lavender and Madonna sang in the background.

It was only when the knock on the door was repeated that she realised there was someone out-side the flat. Chloe. She must have forgotten her key. Mel staggered to her feet as the knocking came again, a little sharper, a little louder.

'For God's sake, I'm coming,' she said under her breath.

She opened the door and looked out into the dim hallway. It wasn't Chloe, home at last.

It was Adam.

Chapter Thirteen

Chloe stirred on the couch. She made a little noise that was half a sigh, half a whimper, then turned over and settled back into a deep sleep again. Henry got up from his armchair. Chloe was out for the count. He went to the window, pulled aside the curtains and looked out. It was after midnight and the street was deserted. The rain had eased considerably but there was no need to wake up Chloe and bring her home. She might as well stay the night and go home in the morning. He unplugged the television but left the lamp on, dimming the light as low as possible. If Chloe awoke in the night, she wouldn't get too much of a fright.

Then he went into his bedroom, got into bed and fell into a deep sleep.

* * *

Their voices echoed around the shadowy hall.

'Where's Chloe?'

'She's out.'

'Out where?'

'I dunno.'

Adam felt a wave of frustration washing over him. When the door of the flat had opened at last, he had fully expected Chloe to be on the other side, ready to fall into his arms. He hadn't expected to see Mel, which was silly, really, considering she also lived there. He was furious to have encountered Mel like this. Mel, who normally irritated him beyond measure, had caught him unawares. He felt damp and bedraggled and definitely the worse for wear. She probably knew exactly where Chloe was but wasn't going to tell him, and she would undoubtedly relish every moment of his uneasiness.

'When will she be home?'

Mel shrugged. 'I haven't a clue.'

'How come you're not out with her?' Adam pressed.

Mel glared at him across the threshold. 'That's none of your business.'

He looked beyond her into the dimly lit living room, candles glinting on the mantelpiece, music in the background, the scent of something wafting out around him, something floral, the single glass on the coffee table half full of amber liquid.

'So you're on your own?'

'I'm having a party all by myself,' she spoke lightly, but he saw something flicker in the depths of her green eyes.

'Celebrating what?'

'Adam, where have you been for the past few weeks? I'm off on Monday. Getting the hell out of this country, thank God. And if you don't mind, I'm feeling chilly out here so I'm closing the door. Now are you coming in or what?'

The flat, with the glowing candles and warm gas fire, was a far more inviting prospect than a cold and lonely bed-sit, even if it did include an acerbic-tongued Mel. And there was always the chance that Chloe would come home at any minute.

'I'll come in for a while,' he said. He stepped across the threshold and Mel closed the door.

'Do you realise you're soaking?' she asked.

He shrugged. 'It's not too bad. I'll just throw off this jacket.'

'Here, give it to me. I'll put it on a chair in the kitchenette. I'll get you a towel for your hair. And I suppose you'll have a drink? Someone might as well join in my private celebration.'

'Yeah, why not.'

She poured him a Southern Comfort and handed him a glass, then finished the contents of her own glass in one long swallow and filled it up again. He towelled his hair so that it stood up in dark spikes all around his head and Mel began to laugh.

'What's so funny?'

'Nothing. Just that I've never seen you so messy looking. And right now, you look like a hedgehog.'

'And I've never seen you in your sexy pyjamas before.' The words were out before he realised, and had he been less drunk, he would have checked himself in time. He cursed himself when he saw the expression on Mel's face.

She stared at him for a long moment. 'You men,' she spat. 'You're all the same.'

'Sorry, Mel, I've—'

'You're not a bit sorry.'

'Look, it was a slip of the tongue, that's all.'

'Just have your drink and then you can leave,' she said.

Adam put down his glass. 'If that's your attitude, I'm not surprised you're sitting here on your own tonight. Where's Chloe?'

'Never mind where your darling Chloe is,' Mel snapped.

'You're just covering up for her, aren't you?'

'You've been drinking, haven't you?'

'At least I was out with friends and not hitting the bottle alone,' Adam taunted.

'Maybe I prefer to be alone rather than go out with friends,' Mel blazed.

'You've been let down, haven't you?' Adam challenged, as again something flickered in Mel's green eyes. 'You were expecting to go out, but you've been let down. By Chloe. And it must be another man. She would only let you down on account of another man, wouldn't she?'

'It's none of your business,' she snapped.

'You're loyal to the bitter end, I'll give you that much,' he smiled. 'I don't think I'd be quite as loyal and forgiving as you.'

Mel laughed bitterly. 'Forgiving? Me? You don't know me all that well, Adam.'

'How come you're sitting in the flat on your own, tonight of all nights? Surely there's a long line of admirers you have to say goodbye to? Or are you afraid they might manage to persuade you to stay?' He was definitely drunk. Otherwise he would never have asked the normally bristly Mel such a personal question.

Mel laughed harshly. 'Sorry to disappoint you Adam, but no one has asked me to marry him instead of going to Australia because I'm good in bed. But I'm sure that doesn't surprise you.'

'I didn't mean it like that.'

'No?' Her green eyes mocked.

'What about your family?' he asked, trying to change the subject. 'Surely they want to see you off with a bit of a fanfare?'

'Family?' Mel shook her head. 'I don't have much in the way of a family. Unless you think a generous bank draft solves all problems... Oh God, never mind.'

She abruptly turned away from him, and folding her arms in front of her, she stood facing the mantelpiece. One of the candle flames fluttered wildly for a few moments before it flickered and died. The sound of Madonna was low in the background. Mel stood rigid, as though she was trying to hold herself together. The thought crossed Adam's mind that there was something very vulnerable about the tall, slender shape of her in her blue fleece pyjamas.

'Mel? You okay?'

'Just go, will you?'

Her voice sounded odd, almost as though she was about to cry. Surely not. Not the sharp, caustic Mel. He was imagining things. But he felt a sudden tension in the room and it made him uneasy. Maybe he'd best leave. He turned and put his hand on the door and was just about to open it when he heard a muffled sob.

'Mel?' He couldn't pretend he hadn't heard. He just wished he weren't feeling so drunk. He turned back into the room and tentatively reached out to her and his hand touched her dark wavy hair. It felt springy and alive under his touch. 'Mel, what's the matter?'

She still didn't move, so he dropped his hand to her shoulder and he turned her to face him. 'I didn't mean that the way it sounded, about your boyfriends, or your family,' he began. Her green eyes were shimmering with unshed tears and it seemed absurd to see the tough, gutsy Mel suddenly so defenceless. 'God, look, I'm sorry if I said the wrong thing.'

'It's nothing,' she said, brushing the tears from her eyes and shaking her head. 'I'm drunk and I'm just being silly.'

'I could never imagine you being silly,' Adam said. 'Drunk perhaps, clever, yes, irritating, most definitely, but never silly.'

'Irritating? Me?'

'Sometimes.'

'Like when I'm telling you the truth?'

'Yes, I suppose.' What the hell was he getting himself into? Still, it was easier to go along with her than try to explain why she sometimes irritated the hell out of him.

'And anything else? Besides being clever. I know about that already.'

'Already? So someone else has you sussed?'

The flicker was back in her green eyes, a consciousness, a knowledge lurking in the depths of her eyes. He thought she was going to start crying again. But she straightened her shoulders and almost imperceptibly pulled herself together.

'No one has me sussed, Adam,' she tossed. He felt a bit relieved that she looked more like her usual self again. 'You said I irritated you,' she continued as she smiled mockingly, all trace of tears now disappeared. 'I wonder why.'

'You're a bit like me. You're stubbornly proud and in your own way, you're full of yourself.'

'So you admit it, now. You think you're better than everyone else.'

'And so do you, Mel,' he grinned. 'That's why we get on each other's nerves.'

'Get lost. I annoy you because I haven't joined the Adam Kavanagh fan club,' she taunted.

'Maybe it's the other way around,' he swiftly responded. 'Maybe you set out to needle me because I never showed any interest in you.'

'Sorry to disappoint you Adam, but I'd never lose sleep over that. Not if you were the last man alive. Your sort are all the same.'

'And what sort is that?'

Mel's green eyes glinted and she lifted her chin and challenged him. 'You're so used to getting exactly what you want, that you think you just have to click your little fingers and women will fall all over you. I'm sorry, but you don't impress me.'

The room suddenly fell silent as the CD came to an end.

Adam's silky voice broke the silence. 'I'd no idea you had such a poor opinion of me. What have I done to deserve it? Or maybe I should be asking what have I not done?'

'It's too late in the day to be thinking about that now.' Mel drained her glass. 'I'm throwing you out. I've had too much to drink and I feel wrecked.'

'That's right, get rid of me before I ask any more awkward questions.'

'Don't be ridiculous. Out you go. I'm tired.'

'Fair enough.' Adam put his glass down on the

coffee table. A little unsteady on her feet, Mel went across to the door to open it.

'Seems an awful shame,' Adam said, hesitating in the doorway. The hallway was cold and chilly and the damp smell of the earlier rain still lingered.

'What does?' Mel asked. She was propped against the frame of the door and her green eyes were full of the light sarcasm that never failed to put him on edge.

'Seems an awful shame that you're heading off around the world with such a low opinion of me.'

She smiled a slow, mocking smile. 'Poor Adam. You just can't accept the fact that not everyone wants to jump into bed with you.'

'Who said anything about bed?'

They stared at each other in silence.

'Is that what this is all about, Mel?' Adam's voice was soft, almost a murmur. 'Bed? Is that what I haven't done? No wonder I haven't impressed you. Well, we can't have you going off to Australia with a gap in your education, can we?' He let the words fall into the shadowed hall and watched for her reaction. In a corner of his mind he knew he was drunk and shouldn't be doing this, thinking this, saying these words, he shouldn't be feeling this unmistakable leap in his groin, but he was suddenly beyond reason.

Mel didn't move. He reached out and touched her springy hair, felt the curve of her pale cheek, saw the look in her eyes before he kissed her, the look of surprise as he bent down and touched her small, soft mouth with his. And after that, there was no going back. He was still kissing her as they moved back into the living room, back to the scented candles and warm gas fire, and he used the back of his foot to close the door firmly behind them.

He was still kissing her as his hand reached for the top of her fleece pyjamas and fumbled with the buttons, and slid inside to her cup her silky breast. He heard her gasp as he tore open the remaining buttons and pushed off her top and put his mouth to her high, firm breasts. He heard her sigh as he knelt in front of her and pulled down her pyjama bottoms and white panties, and felt her shudder and her fingers gripping in his hair as put his mouth to the hot moistness between her legs.

He thought he was going to explode as the throbbing in his groin intensified and became utterly unbearable. He stood up, opened his belt, flung off his jeans, and eased down his black boxer shorts. He pulled Mel across the couch, shoving a cushion under her hips and sank into sweet, blessed release.

Chapter Fourteen

'Mel? Don't tell me you're still in bed!'

'Just getting up now.'

'God, Mel, you're as pale as a ghost. What's up?' Chloe paused inside the door of Mel's bedroom.

'A couple of drinks too many last night.' Amongst other things, Mel thought silently as she reluctantly sat up in bed and faced the day.

'Where did you go? I'm only getting home now from yesterday's shopping trip,' Chloe began.

Mel was hoping she would go away, would leave her to wallow alone in her frozen misery and guilt, but instead Chloe sat on the edge of the bed and made herself comfortable. 'I bumped into Henry on the way home from town,' she chatted, 'and he brought me into his apartment for a drink and you'll never guess…'

You ended up having lustful sex, Mel thought grimly as she ran her fingers through her sleep-tossed hair.

'I put my feet up for a few minutes and fell asleep on his couch. And Henry didn't want to disturb me so he left me asleep for the night.'

'You slept on Henry's couch?'

'You see, I got a bit upset about Adam. Henry asked me back for a drink, so I had a few glasses of red wine. Then the rain was so bad that I hung on and had another drink. I could feel myself nodding off and the next thing it was eleven o'clock this morning. I couldn't believe it.'

'It didn't do you any harm, did it?' Mel said, thinking how perfectly innocent it all sounded and heartily wishing she could feel as innocent as Chloe obviously did at this moment in time.

'Anyway, Henry's waiting outside. I was going to walk home this morning, but he decided to drive me around and collect your stuff.'

'Tell him it's all ready and I'll be out in a minute.'

'Will do.' Chloe left as Mel got out of bed. Seconds later, she stormed back into Mel's bedroom. 'What the hell is Adam's jacket doing here?'

'He dropped in last night, looking for you. His jacket was soaking so he took it off for a few minutes. He must have forgotten all about it.'

'The swine! He probably left it there deliberately to see if I'd return it in person. Fat chance. I'm

163

dumping it out in the hall. Has he not got the message by now? It's over, finished. And I hope you told him I was out on the tear.'

* * *

Mel and Chloe went out to lunch to a pub just off Grafton Street. They ordered from the bar food menu and after their meal, they had a couple of drinks.

'The usual?' Chloe asked.

'Just a shandy for me,' Mel said.

'Are you okay?'

'I'm fine, why?'

'It's just, well, you're much quieter than usual. And you've only picked at your food. Are you having second thoughts? Or are you still annoyed that I'm not going with you? Especially the way things have worked out with me and Adam.'

Mel shook her head. 'God, no. I'm really sorry about that Chloe, but to be honest, I just want to get going.' All of a sudden, Monday afternoon couldn't come quickly enough. 'What are your plans?' she asked.

'I don't know, really. I suppose I'll hang on in the flat for another week or so, until I find somewhere else.'

'You're moving out?'

'You bet. A fresh start away from Adam is what I need. I don't know how I got through this week in work. I was even hauled into Debbie Driscoll's office on account of a stupid mistake I made.'

164

'Jeez.'

'You can say that again. The only good thing that came out of it was she told me that if I kept my mind on the job I'd go far.'

'That sounds good.'

'Yeah. She said that with the right dedication and commitment she could see me carving out a good career for myself. So maybe it's just as well I'm not going away. A year out would be a year lost and in time I want to be sitting where Debbie was sitting,' Chloe said. 'I want the bright, orderly office, the big leather chair and the vase of flowers on the desk.'

'Good for you, Chloe, you were never short of ambition,' Mel said, relieved to be off the topic of Adam. The knowledge of what she had done was settling like a heavy weight in the pit of her tummy. It was impossible to ease her sense of guilt, to stifle the rage she felt, to calm her frantic self-reproach. And it was impossible to come to terms with how stupidly she had behaved. Still, she had only a matter of hours left now, a few hours to hold herself together in front of Chloe, a few hours to hope that she wouldn't run into Adam.

* * *

Mel was up early the following morning in spite of her restless, guilt-ridden night. When the kettle boiled she made the tea, rescued Chloe's toast from

165

becoming incinerated in the ancient toaster and fished Chloe's umbrella out from under a pile of magazines. She went out to the hall door with her friend. The October morning was grey and damp and the air was thin and cool. She gave Chloe a hug, suddenly knowing exactly how Judas must have felt, and she saw a sudden sheen of tears in Chloe's eyes as she finally stepped back from the embrace and put up her umbrella against the light misty rain. Then Chloe hurried down the driveway and ran across the road towards the bus stop, barely in time to catch the bus, and Mel closed the door with a sigh of relief.

* * *

Henry phoned later that morning.

'Henry's limo at your service, madam. Would you like a lift to the airport?'

'No thanks. I hate farewells.'

'How about I drop you off outside Departures?'

'You must be really dying to get rid of me.'

'I hope it's not that obvious,' he laughed.

'Go on then, you can give me a lift. The set down stop for Departures is perfect.'

He called at five to three. Mel was oddly relieved that she wasn't on her own as she looked around the flat one final time. Henry kept up a light banter as he heaved her rucksack onto his shoulders and asked her why she was bringing the kitchen sink. He told her to make sure she had a good look at the grey clouds and drizzly rain as it was probably the last time she would see them for a while. He had her out the door and sitting in the front passenger seat of his ancient Renault before she realised it.

It was cold and breezy and the skies were grey when Mel stepped out of the car at the Departures terminal, shivering in her light blue jacket.

'Wait here till I get a trolley.'

'It's all right, I can manage.'

'Do as you're told and stay there a mo.'

He returned steering a trolley. He lifted her rucksack onto it and turned the handle towards Mel. 'There you are, makes life a bit easier for you.'

'Thanks, you're a pal.'

An airplane screamed directly overhead. It descended slowly from the leaden sky, almost skimming the top of the airport buildings in its downward curving plunge.

'Well go on, off you go,' he said. 'Send me a postcard from the Great Barrier Reef.'

'Sure thing,' she smiled. She gripped her trolley and felt the weight as she began to propel it forward. He put his hand on her arm and kissed her gently on the forehead. She saw his tawny eyes smiling, and the breeze lifting the spikes of his auburn hair.

'Godspeed,' he said, then got into his Renault. Mel wheeled her trolley along the pavement, waving at him as she walked along, then disappeared into the airport terminal.

* * *

'What's going on?' Adam asked.

It was the following Sunday morning. He had showered and dressed, putting on his blue Wranglers and a navy cotton jumper. He decided to walk to the shop on the corner for the Sunday papers and his favourite breakfast roll. He put on the kettle and, feeling decidedly peckish, picked up his jacket and hurried down the stairs.

Chloe was standing in the hall, surrounded by an assortment of cases and plastic bags.

'What does it look like?' she asked. She lifted her chin and stared defiantly at him. He saw the dark circles under her wide grey eyes, and the way a smattering of freckles stood out on her pale oval face. Above all, he sensed the unhappiness that was scarcely concealed by her defiant stance and he felt a rush of love for her and a sudden urge to take her and crush her in his arms.

His stomach contracted as he thought of his encounter with Mel. It had haunted him all week. He didn't normally make mistakes, but that one went right off the scale. Surely it was the worst thing he could ever have done to Chloe. And something to be pushed to the darkest corner of his mind. Forever. They must have been mad, Mel had fretted afterwards as she scrabbled for her under-wear. It had never happened, he had answered tersely as he slammed out of the flat. Funnily enough, he was almost beginning to believe that.

'It looks like you're on the move,' he said.

'How clever of you to work that one out.'

'And where are you off to?' He tried to keep his voice casual.

'I don't think that's any of your business, Adam.' Her voice was clipped.

'I see. Well, best of luck.'

He headed towards the front door, put his hand up to open it and suddenly wheeled around again, just in time to catch the raw, lost expression on her face before she masked it with a look of cool indifference. He wanted nothing more than to take that wounded look off her face and to see her smile. When Chloe smiled at him as though he was all her dreams rolled into one, it made him feel ten feet tall.

'It might be no harm if I had your address,' he began.

'Give me one good reason why,' she snapped.

He shrugged. 'In case any post comes, I can re-direct it. The landlord mightn't bother with it.'

'You hardly think I'm relying on him,' she said contemptuously.

There was a loud knock at the door and Chloe jumped.

'Taxi for Miss Corrigan. Is this all your stuff? Maybe you should have ordered a minibus,' the taxi driver joked, oblivious to the chilled atmosphere in the hall.

'Don't worry, we'll squeeze it all in. I'll give you a hand,' Adam offered magnanimously, noticing that Chloe seemed suddenly frozen to the spot. He took a plastic bag in each hand and headed down the driveway to the taxi waiting at the kerb. In no time at all, Chloe was tucked in the back seat, surrounded by her belongings.

'Now, miss, what part of Terenure exactly?' the taxi driver asked.

Chloe glared pointedly at Adam. 'Goodbye, Adam.'

Adam hesitated by the passenger door. 'Go on, Chloe, tell him where you're off to.'

'Yes, time's pushing on and I've another fare waiting,' the driver said irritably.

As she gave the taxi driver her address, she darted a furious glance at Adam. He slammed the door and waved her off, with a huge grin on his face.

Part II

Chapter Fifteen

When Mel left Dublin on a grey October day, she thought that nothing would ever excite her again, that nothing would send the blood running a little quicker through her veins.

She was very much mistaken.

Life began again for Mel on the October afternoon the Qantas jet began a curving descent into Sydney Airport, and from the skies above Sydney, she caught a glimpse of the city. It resembled a toy city from her sky-high vantage point, the Harbour Bridge a perfect symmetrical arc, the harbour itself a splash of calm blue silk and the white sails of the Opera House a dreamy shimmer on the southern foreshore.

Her breath caught in her throat and it seemed almost a crime that the Qantas jet had to continue a descent that brought her down to a wide concrete runway amidst a jungle of bright airport buildings that glinted harshly under the Australian sun.

'Hi and welcome, you must be Mel.' A tall, fair-haired girl, casually dressed in white shorts and a pink sleeveless top, broke free of the waiting crowds in the noisy arrivals hall.

'Yes, I am.' Mel looked at her quizzically.

'I'm Sarah's cousin, Elaine.'

'You were very quick to spot me!'

'It's easy to spot a fellow countryman out here, and with those emerald eyes you couldn't be anything but Irish!'

Mel grinned. 'So much for trying to look cosmopolitan.'

'Is this all your luggage?'

'Yep, one ten-ton weight of a backpack and a carry holdall.'

'Well c'mon, my banger is parked in the wrong place at the wrong time, so let's shift ourselves!'

Mel picked up her backpack, hoisted it onto a trolley and followed Elaine. The minute she exited the cool air-conditioned arrivals hall, she felt the warmth of the sun on her face. She had arrived. She was here now, on Australian soil. All of a sudden, she felt a giddy sense of freedom.

'How was your journey?' Elaine asked as she weaved through Sydney traffic. 'You stopped in Singapore, didn't you? Were your flights okay?'

'Yes, everything went fine.' Mel forced her mind

174

back to the conversation, her head full of the sights, sounds and smells of Sydney. She sat in the front seat of Elaine's old Vauxhall and let it all wash over her, jagged skyscrapers silhouetted against the sunny sky, heady thoughts of the Harbour Bridge and the Opera House waiting to be explored, the feeling of spring in the air, a warm spring at that and a far cry from murky, autumnal Dublin.

The glorious feeling of being a far cry from murky, autumnal Dublin.

'Singapore was hot and humid,' Mel said. 'I was wrecked when I landed, it was much warmer and damper than I had expected, but the time difference worked in my favour because I could legitimately hit the pillow pretty soon after I got to the hotel.'

'I came through Bangkok on the way out, but I might go back through Sing. I'd love to see it.'

'How long have you got left on your visa?'

'Just six months. You'll soon find that practically every week there's a leaving party or a welcoming party for someone or other. Hardly anyone stays beyond a year.' She threw Mel a quick glance. 'This week, we're having the welcoming party for you!'

'That's great,' Mel grinned.

'It'll give you a chance to get to know some of the gang. Did you manage to bring the Barry's?'

'Yes, I did. To tell you the truth, I thought Sarah was only pulling my leg when she said you were looking for Irish tea bags.'

'Oh no, Barry's tea is gold dust out here. You'll

175

make friends for life if you can supply them. There's nothing like an Irish cup of tea.'

'I can hardly imagine.'

'Wait till you see, Mel, when you're here a while your tongue will be hanging out for it,' Elaine said chattily. 'Every so often we get tea sent out. Our mums are sick of the price of the postage, though, so whenever we hear of someone coming out, we always put in a request. Cadbury's chocolate is something else we miss, and as for Tayto, I could murder a packet of Tayto.'

Mel laughed. When she heard the sound of her own carefree laughter, it almost surprised her. It had been a while since she had felt so relaxed and cheerful, a long time since she had enjoyed a truly light-hearted moment.

'Tayto crisps!' she giggled, feeling suddenly grateful to Elaine.

* * *

For the first few weeks, Mel did nothing but chill out. The two-bedroom apartment where Elaine lived, along with her friends Sally and Janet, was a cheerful free-for-all in the middle of a jumble of apartment blocks not too far from Bondi Beach, where rented accommodation was the norm and parties and barbies were a constant. There was a never-ending stream of newly arrived backpackers coming into the area, balanced by a constant flow of tearful departures and promises to stay in touch.

Mel soon got to know her way around the city by bus, rail and ferry. She felt a jolt of surprise at some of the English-sounding names – Hyde Park, Paddington Market and Oxford Street – and was intrigued at other Aussie-sounding names such as Wooloomooloo, Homebush and Parramatta.

She strolled around by the Opera House, and nothing she had seen on the telly prepared her for the feeling of being there in the flesh. As she stood on the famous steps looking upwards at the arrangement of sail-like crescents that folded gracefully into each other, she tried and failed to put her finger on the sensations washing over her. The closest she could come up with was a feeling of reverence.

She fell in love with Darling Harbour, and on a perfect November day, she donned a regulatory Bridge suit, clipped on a safety harness and spent three hours climbing the superstructure of the Harbour Bridge, following a guide up ladders, through catwalks and over arches. It was the most uplifting three hours of her life. The exhilarating view of the harbour, with its ripples of inlets and coves and myriad boats and ferries streaming through the waters, foamy trails in their wake, took her breath away. She felt as though she was on top of the world.

She checked out the nearby beaches, the golden crescents of sand, the shimmering blue-green ocean and the warm whispering breeze she had dreamed of during damp Dublin days. But she didn't practise her yoga on Bondi. She was surprised to discover that she preferred to travel further down the coast to the slightly quieter Coogee and Bronte beaches instead of hanging around the noisy, brash Bondi, with its louder-than-life beefy bronzed males, its equally bronzed flaunting females and blatant beachfront commercialism. Even the rolling surf, she thought, seemed made to order.

Her days slid easily by, and she was absorbed into the here and now, into a whole new easy way of life. Living for the moment, Mel never looked back and never looked beyond the following day. She lost track of time and was amazed to find that a month had elapsed without her realising it.

And then she had an e-mail from Chloe.

From: Chloe
To: Mel
Subject: Adam!

Hope you're enjoying the Oz experience!

You'll never guess – brilliant news – Adam and I have kissed and made up. It's a long story, and I've no time to fill you in right now, but I'm wearing his ring again. You can think of me up to my neck in exciting wedding plans while you're having the adventures of a lifetime in the outback. Gotta fly, heaps to do…

So happy I could burst.

Chloe xx

Mel's heart lurched as she stared at the screen. *So happy I could burst.* She hadn't expected this. She hadn't thought that Adam Kavanagh, God's gift to women, would have patched things up with Chloe. She hadn't thought that Chloe would take him back. And from the sound of the e-mail, Chloe obviously hadn't a clue what had happened.

God. Mel closed her eyes for a minute and tried to calm her breathing. She felt as though she was choking and she tried to get a grip on herself. After all, what had happened? Nothing, really. It had been over in minutes. It hadn't meant much to either her or Adam, which made things even worse, in a way. It wasn't every day that you betrayed your best friend with an exploit that meant little or nothing to you.

She shivered in spite of the heat of the day. She logged out of her e-mail and walked out of the internet shop. She told herself there was no point in panicking, not right now, not in this faraway world of endless blue skies. The Australian spring was warmer than an Irish summer, and November weather meant wearing white cotton shorts and a blue T-shirt and sipping chilled Australian beer out on the balcony. She might as well have been on a different planet.

'I might get a job for a couple of weeks, just something temporary,' she said to Sally and Janet as they sat sipping Tooheys New! on the small balcony outside the living room on a sunny Monday evening. A job would keep her occupied and give her less time to think.

'That's all you'll get,' Sally cautioned. 'You can only work for three months at a time on your visa.'

'That's fine. I just want to top up the bank balance a little. Does anyone ever manage to stay out here beyond their time limit?'

'I suppose it's not impossible. But it would be hard to get a job. You have to show your visa once you register with an agency,' Janet shrugged. 'The only black market kind of work you could get would pay very badly. And then the police often have spot checks on the buses coming into Bondi. It's not worth the hassle. You're only here a wet week,' Janet laughed. 'You don't know how you'll feel at the end of a year. You might be dying to go home.'

'I doubt it,' Mel smiled guardedly. 'Anyway, what are your plans?'

'We're due to leave in April, worse luck!' Sally said. 'We're finishing up in our jobs in February and travelling around a bit before we leave.'

'Where to?'

'Definitely Cairns, Darwin and Ayers Rock. You're more than welcome to join us.'

'I'll think about that,' Mel smiled.

'In the meantime, I think it's my turn to go to the fridge. Same again everyone?' Sally got up.

* * *

Mel's first job was in a gift shop off Pitt Street, a temporary position until Christmas. It kept her busy and by degrees, as the days drifted by, it helped her push Chloe's e-mail to the back of her mind. It was weird to be stacking shelves full of Santa Clauses, red festive candles and decorations in a cool air-conditioned shop, only to go out on her dinner hour to find the atmosphere simmering with heat. It was funnier to see Christmas cards illustrated with snow scenes, but it was even more of a novelty to have a barbie on Bondi Beach on Christmas Day, to duck and dive in and out of the lacy surf wearing a red bikini and a high-factor sunscreen, to munch on snags and chunks of barramundi and to feel the warmth of the Australian sun on her body.

The only awkward moment came when the girls phoned home on Stephen's Day.

'There's no point in trying to phone on Christmas Day,' Elaine had said. 'It's impossible to get through as the lines are usually jammed. So first thing Stephen's morning, we'll get cracking. It'll still be Christmas Day in Ireland.'

The sun was high in the sky when everyone stumbled out of bed, complete with hangover and bleary eyes. Except Mel.

'Aren't you going to phone your family?' Elaine asked Mel. 'If you're stuck for a phone card, I'll probably have a few minutes' credit left on mine.'

'No, it's okay, I've already been in touch,' Mel grinned. It wasn't really a fib. She hadn't actually said that she'd phoned, had she? And she had been in touch with her family, hadn't she? She ignored the voice in her head which said that a quick e-mail to her mother in Cape Town and a postcard of Sydney Harbour to her gran when she had arrived in Australia, followed by Christmas cards posted early in December, scarcely constituted being in touch. She would like to have phoned her gran, but she couldn't phone Galway. Either of her parents might answer the phone. And she didn't even want to think about them, let alone talk to them. She didn't want to know about Ireland, not here, not now, in this bright new sunshiny life where it didn't really exist.

The real celebrations were held on New Year's Eve. All day long and into the evening, crowds swelled along the foreshore of Sydney Harbour in the blistering heat and Mel was beginning to wonder what all the fuss was about. She was just glad she had donned a wide-brimmed cotton hat and brought a plentiful supply of sunscreen and bottled water. But it was worth the wait when they had a perfect view of the magnificent fireworks illuminating the sky over Harbour Bridge, welcoming in the new year and turning the warm Australian night into exotic daytime.

She signed on with a recruitment agency in the new year and within two weeks had a job in the back office of a firm of real estate consultants. It was mainly data input and boring as hell, but at least her colleagues were friendly and she was getting paid for being bored, and it wasn't going to last too long. She had decided to head off with Elaine and the girls and join them on their travels. They were travelling by bus and rail, as Elaine didn't trust her ancient Vauxhall to get them as far as Cairns, never mind Darwin or Ayers Rock.

'Anyway, I've no intention of driving those long distances, let alone in a non air-conditioned hulk,' Elaine said.

'The bus suits me,' Mel said. 'It's a good way of seeing the country first hand.'

'And we'll be staying mostly in hostels.'

'Nothing wrong with hostels as far as I'm concerned.'

'That's settled, then. Sally and Janet will be delighted you're coming with us. We'll have to have a party and maybe invite the gang next door around.'

The gang in the apartment next door was currently a group of three hurling maniacs from Kilkenny. Mel had often teased them as to how they survived so far from home without their precious game.

'Don't worry your pretty little head,' she was told. 'We'll be back home in plenty of time to see Kilkenny lift the All-Ireland trophy!'

The night of their farewell party, it seemed the whole block was crammed into their small apartment and that the nearby Bottle Shop had been depleted of its entire stock of beer and wine. Mel had never seen so much drink all together in one place. They would need a skip, she thought fleetingly as she opened another bottle of Sauvignon Blanc, two skips even to get rid of all the empty cans and bottles, never mind holding a garage sale to offload their excess belongings.

But it was only a fleeting thought because she forgot about skips and cans and garage sales as she poured one drink, then another, and another, and became very pleasantly drunk.

'Will you miss me?' She threw saucy green eyes at Brian, one of the Kilkenny hurling fans from the neighbouring apartment. They had somehow found themselves squashed into a corner together, in among the tangle of partygoers. The air was stifling even with all the windows open, and the party spilled out onto the tiny balcony. Someone had turned on the music and Robbie Williams was barely discernible against the babble of voices.

'Course I will. Life just won't be the same without you.' Brian threw his arm around her shoulders and squeezed her. He bent to give her a peck on the cheek but somehow it missed and he kissed her soft mouth instead. Mel automatically drew away, then changed her mind and kissed him back.

He was nice, his kiss was pleasant, his lips smooth and warm on hers, and it was a good feeling to have a pair of man's arms around her again. She hadn't been with a man since she had come out to

Australia. She hadn't been with a man since – well, that had never taken place, had it?

They sank to the floor, sitting close together in the corner amidst the noise and heat of the party. Eventually, looking at her flushed face and the dark tumble of her hair, Brian asked her if she wanted to go next door. She nodded, and they rose to their feet. Mel grabbed a bottle of wine and a couple of cans of beer and followed him out the door.

They made love on his narrow bed, and he laughed gently and teased the white bits of her body, where her bikini usually covered her fair Irish skin. Mel laughed in return and sat astride him, her green eyes glinting, her pale breasts gleaming as she moved back and forth. She felt like someone who had been parched for a long time, without even knowing it. She sighed as much with pleasure and relief as over and over she felt her body ripple and surge and flood with calming ease.

The following week, the girls packed up and left, handing the keys to the agent, carrying their backpacks along with their dreams as they headed for the bus station. Mel sat on the northward-bound bus and craned her neck for a final glimpse of the Harbour Bridge before it disappeared from view, lost behind the jagged city skyline.

Chapter Sixteen

As the girls toured Cairns and Darwin before travelling on to Ayers Rock, Mel lived for the moment, each day bringing something new to look at, something fresh to explore, whether it was an early morning hot air balloon ride over a misty dawn-soaked Cairns, or a journey to the lofty, cathedral-like surrounds of the tropical rainforest. The day they travelled out to the northern end of the Great Barrier Reef, Mel decided she wanted to stay there forever.

'Looks like rain,' Sally grumbled as they got ready for the trip. It was the second week of their stay in a hostel in Cairns. They had to board their coach at Trinity Wharf and it was bringing them up the coast to Port Douglas, where the catamaran was departing from.

'Cheer up,' Mel said brightly. 'Rain or no rain, this will be a trip to remember.'

'It's just a bit overcast, it'll clear up,' Janet said as she squashed a bikini and a towel into her shoulder bag.

'You're being optimistic,' Sally said.

'It shouldn't make any difference,' Mel shrugged impatiently. 'You'll be swimming underwater if you want to look at the reef, so you'll be getting wet anyway!'

Light rain began to fall as the coach journeyed northwards along the Captain Cook highway, and through the rain-misted windows Mel's eyes followed the wide sweep of the ocean to her right and the mountainous rainforest curving up and away to her left. In spite of the drizzle, it seemed every twist and turn of the road revealed a more splendid view and her heart lifted. She would never tire of the succession of different sights and sounds, the feeling of freedom, living from day to day.

Sitting in the middle of a catamaran speeding out to the Great Barrier Reef in a group of tourists drawn from all nationalities, Mel spotted a girl with a John Connolly paperback poking out of her holdall. Her heart flipped as her thoughts immediately flashed to Dublin and Ireland, and the e-mail Chloe had sent last week.

From: Chloe
To: Mel
Subject: Wedding date!!!

Big news! 2.00 pm, August 30th. Can't believe it's all happening. I'm mad busy with preparations. You've no idea how much there is to organise! Adam says I can have whatever I want. I want us to have the best, most perfect wedding. I'm giving you plenty of notice to book your return flight! Enjoy yourself, but not too much, I need you over here on August 30th!

Chloe xx

PS A horrible thought – hope you get this e-mail and that you're not stuck in some godforsaken outback that has no internet!

She had to ignore it in much the same way that she ignored the knot of tension it caused in her stomach. She had to put it to the back of her mind. At least for now. Chloe had unwittingly given her an excuse to hold off on her reply for the moment. She told herself that she was far away, both physically and mentally. And maybe, just maybe, anything could happen between now and the end of August. Adam might get cold feet. Chloe might change her mind, and the wedding could just as easily be called off.

Otherwise she didn't see how she could return to Dublin ever again. Right now, in the catamaran bouncing across the Coral Sea, she told herself she was enclosed in a protective bubble, far away from everything going on back home.

Gradually the rain cleared and the sun burned through the clouds, and by the time they reached the visitor site, which was a floating platform anchored in the sea just above the northern end of the reef, the skies were a brilliant blue and the sea an expanse of rippling aquamarine, stretching into far-off infinity. Here and there, shadows on the surface of the waters indicated where the reef was close underneath, and Mel felt as if she was in heaven.

They caught their first glimpse of the reef in a semi submersible. They went down into blue cavernous depths, into a world of thousands of colourful flickering fish and undulating, living coral reef. The whole environment of the coral reef was extremely fragile, their guide explained. Damaging the reef was prohibited, he explained, and even the floating platform was moored carefully so as to avoid any kind of harm to the reef. An incorrectly anchored boat could ruin many square miles of living reef, and if they decided to go snorkelling or scuba diving, they were prohibited from standing on the reef at any time. Mel watched, fascinated, as a glimmering school of tiny blue fish passed under the submersible and reappeared on the other side without altering their fluttering kaleidoscopic pattern by a centimetre.

Back on the floating platform, Mel and Elaine got ready to go snorkelling. Sally and Janet opted out.

'Sorry, but I just can't do it. I hate the thoughts of putting my face in the water,' Sally excused herself.

'And I don't fancy swimming with millions of fish all around,' Janet sheepishly admitted.

'Chickens!' Mel said tartly, watching a little girl of six slip confidently into the water with her dad. 'Surely the whole idea of coming out here is to snorkel?'

'You can look after our stuff,' Elaine suggested as Mel and she stripped down to T-shirts and bikinis and joined the queue for the snorkelling equipment.

Mel spit on the inside of her mask, rubbed it briefly and rinsed it in salt water. She fitted her mask around her eyes and adjusted her bright yellow snorkel. Then, putting on her fins and reminding herself to breathe only through her mouth, she sat on the edge of the submerged platform and let herself slip into the sunlit water.

Suddenly she was in a whole new world.

She felt weightless and free as she glided just under the dappled surface, suspended between the coral underneath and the sun-speckled surface and the swarms of darting fish. She moved lazily and slowly though the warm water, full of wonder at this magical, peaceful environment, which was new to her, yet thousands of years old.

'I'm never going home,' she said to Elaine as they held onto a guide rope and tread water while they caught their breath. 'I want to stay here forever.'

'So do I,' Elaine laughed.

'No, I mean it,' Mel insisted. 'I'm never going home.'

After a while they swam slowly back, clambered aboard the floating platform and queued for a buffet lunch. They joined Sally and Janet and sat on the top deck of the catamaran as they ate cold chicken and pasta and fish, enjoying the feel of the warm sunshine and the sight of the wide aquamarine ocean stretching away forever.

'Mel says she's never going home,' Elaine grinned as she picked up a chicken leg.

'Sooner or later you'll have to go,' Janet said. 'Our time is rapidly running out. What is it girls, another three weeks?'

'I don't know how I'm going to face it,' Sally sighed. She put down her plate and pushed it to one side. 'The more I think about going back to Dublin, the more depressed I feel.'

'We all feel depressed about going home,' Elaine pointed out. 'Rain and Dublin city gridlock doesn't appeal to any of us. However, we've no choice.'

'At least you're going home to normal lives,' Sally blurted. 'You're not going back to face parents at loggerheads and about to split up. I knew they were having problems, but I just heard last week that the split is definite. It's really awful.'

'That's bad news,' Janet sympathised. 'I moan about my parents, but at least they're happy. And together.'

'Cheer up, Sally,' Mel said unexpectedly. She opened her bottle of water and took a long swallow. 'It's much better for everyone that they split up instead of living a lie,' she continued. 'There's nothing worse than trying to pretend.'

'But they've been married twenty-eight years!'

'So? What's marriage anyway?' Mel shrugged. 'It's only a piece of paper. At the end of the day it means nothing.'

'I'd like to think that twenty-eight years counts for something.'

'Take it from me, Sally, there's not much point in agonising over it. You've your own life to lead.' Mel checked her watch. 'I think we've time for another spot of snorkelling before we leave. How about it, Elaine?'

She wanted to get back into the water again, back into the semi-shaded underwater world, and more than anything, back to that feeling of peace and tranquillity.

I want to stay here forever, she had said to Elaine. She thought of those words as she glided effortlessly along in the blue-green water, darting shoals of fish zigzagging out of her way, the coral reef a silent living landscape beneath her. And at that moment, she was suddenly filled with a sense of calm confidence, for right then, everything seemed possible.

* * *

When the girls eventually left Cairns, they travelled to Ayers Rock, the huge sandstone mass in the middle of Australia and one of the most famous tourist attractions, and this time it was Mel who held back.

'What do you mean, you're not going to climb?' Elaine asked.

'Just that. I'm not going on the climb.'

'C'mon, Mel, you can't give this a miss,' Janet insisted.

'Nope. I'll mind the bags and you three go ahead.'

'This is so not you, Mel,' Sally remarked. 'I thought you were always the have-a-go type.'

'Mostly I am,' Mel agreed. 'But not this time.'

Mel was relieved when they went ahead without her. They would have laughed, she felt sure, had she told them the real reason she didn't want to climb Ayers Rock.

She had watched the sunset turn it to molten red the previous evening. She'd had dinner under the Australian stars as the evening folded into a velvety night and the huge rock loomed its shadow across the desert floor. It had cast a spell on her and she wasn't going to break that spell. Elaine and her friends would never understand. No way could she admit that free and easy Mel thought there was almost something sacred about a huge flat-topped mound of rock that almost seemed to hover between the dry, scrubbed earth and the endless blue sky. No way could she confess that 'have a go'

Mel preferred to stand back and look this time.

And she didn't want to climb because it seemed like an insult to the native Australians, the Aborigines. She couldn't find it within her to trample all over what they regarded as ancient mystical territory. It was far better, surely, to wonder at it from a respectable distance, this huge, eerie, red sandstone mass that dominated the desert landscape for as far as the eye could see.

* * *

They journeyed northwards to Darwin and Mel finally replied to Chloe's e-mail. Her fingers were shaky on the keyboard as she told her she was delighted with her news and yes, she was travelling a lot and internet cafes were thin on the ground, and not to expect to hear from her that much. She knew she was evading the issue of returning home in time for the wedding, but it was just about all she could do right then.

The days blurred and ran into each other and all too soon it was time for Elaine and her friends to leave.

'We're stopping in Singapore for a couple of nights,' Elaine told her as they began to pack up.

'Best of luck,' Mel said.

'You won't be too long after us,' Sally pointed out.

'Me? I'm never going home.'

'Yeah, we all said that, but it doesn't happen that way,' Sally smirked.

'Watch this space,' Mel smirked in return.

She had decided to move back to Cairns as soon as the girls had left. The easy way of life in the town appealed to her. The backpackers arriving in their droves and the holiday makers constantly on the go helped to create a casual atmosphere. It was just the kind of place to live from day to day. And of course there was the proximity to the sea, the long stretches of tropical beach, and out beyond, the peace and tranquillity of the Great Barrier Reef.

What more could she want?

An extension to her visa, she decided as she said farewell to the girls on the morning they left for Darwin Airport. Otherwise, in a few short months she'd be the one packing up to leave.

'Oh, Mel, I do envy you,' Sally said unexpectedly as she gave her a goodbye hug. 'Everything is water off a duck's back with you. I wish I could be more like you, happy go lucky, able to take life on the chin.'

'Sure, life is great. Why shouldn't I be happy go lucky?'

'It's time we were off,' Elaine said. 'Everybody got everything? Passport, tickets, plastic?'

They were gone in a flurry of hugs and waves and bulging backpacks and for the first time since she arrived in Australia, Mel was alone. She looked out the window of the hostel at the sight of the traffic trundling through modern, suburban Darwin and tried to figure out the quickest way back to Cairns.

* * *

Mel stayed in a hostel in Cairns for two weeks until she found a bed-sit to rent. It was small and compact and had just the bare essentials, but it suited her. Better still, when she opened the window and craned her neck, she was able to catch a tiny, far-off glimpse of a fragment of blue that was the Coral Sea.

She got a job in a family-run restaurant in Cairns, serving tables full of tourists and transient backpackers who came in for the early evening specials. The music was lively and the tables were turned over fairly rapidly, so she was constantly busy, but the dress was casual, the atmosphere relaxed. Dan, the manager, had a bit of a sharp tongue, but she worked hard and kept out of his way. She earned good tips, which bumped up her small wages, and she got fed every evening, so she managed nicely without going near her bank account.

It was the winter in Cairns, but you'd never have guessed it, not with heat up to thirty degrees at midday and nights so balmy that you didn't need a jacket. Some early mornings she took a run along the Esplanade, up as far as Trinity Wharf, drinking in the sight of the Coral Sea stretching away to her left. And other early mornings she turned over in bed and touched skin to skin with whoever she had met the night before.

It was something she had never really done before, but life was different now; she was different. It was easy to single someone out from a group, to give him an encouraging grin, to see him hang back when his friends had left the restaurant, to watch him having a couple of drinks at the bar while she cleared tables and finished her shift. It was exciting to know that he would ask her if she would care to join him at the late night bar down the road, and it was gratifying to feel a rush of anticipation at the thoughts of getting into bed with him later that night.

And, most important of all, night after night, layer upon layer, it papered over hazy memories of another time in another life when she had touched skin to skin with Adam on a wet October night.

* * *

'Pardon the corny line, but do you do this often?' Mack asked her, eyeing her over a pitcher of beer in a harbour-front bar.

'Do what often?'

'Make it obvious you're interested.'

'I'm not that obvious, I hope.'

'Nah, you're fine.'

'Good, because I do it a lot,' Mel grinned.

He was a Canadian lumberjack having a year out. He was six foot two, blond and well built and she looked forward to having his arms around her, to feeling his big strong body on hers. He had come into the restaurant with his two backpacking friends earlier that evening and their eyes had locked and Mel had known immediately that they would spend the night together.

She was halfway into her three-month stint in the restaurant and enjoying every minute of the free and easy lifestyle. Before Mack there had been Colin, an electrician from Edinburgh with a persuasive Scottish accent, and before him, Rick.

'A lot?' Mack queried.

'I suppose that's an exaggeration. Now and again,' she admitted.

'So I'm not someone special. There goes my fragile male ego.' Mack made a funny face.

'Of course you're special. Don't you know that everyone's unique?' Mel flirted with her green eyes.

'Where did you say you're from?'

'Ireland.'

'That explains it. The Celtic mystery in your green eyes.'

Mel grinned. 'Don't worry, you've passed the test.'

'I didn't realise there was a test.'

'Of course there is. I don't let men into my bed all that easily. They have to be tall and strong and reasonably handsome. And understand the rules.'

'Rules?' His blue eyes held hers.

'Easy come, easy go.'

Mack stayed almost a week, making spine-tingling love to her with his big strong body until the early hours of every morning. On her day off, Mel went out to the Great Barrier Reef with him and his friends and they snorkelled together, drifting just under the surface of the warm blue waters, and as she glided along, cocooned in a calm floating world, Mel's inner sense of peace renewed and refreshed itself.

Mack moved on, Darwin bound. He said he would look her up if he ever came back to Cairns, and Mel smiled and waved goodbye but knew deep down inside that he wouldn't try to contact her again. And that was exactly the way she wanted it.

She was jolted out of her easy come, easy go existence by another e-mail from Chloe.

From: Chloe
To: Mel
Subject: Wedding Alert!!

God, Mel, where are you? Why haven't you e-mailed recently? I need you home to do bridesmaid. Your year is almost up. Surely you don't mind coming home a teeny weeny bit early? I'd like to have my best friend beside me on my special day! It wouldn't be the same without you! Please let me know as soon as possible. Time is running out and

I have zillions of last-minute preparations to make. Adam's sister is driving me mad. My own mother is having daily heart attacks. You've no idea of all the plans that have to be finalised, of how mad busy I am. I can't wait for you to see my dress, and even yours is gorgeous. I've chosen taffeta rose, it will be absolutely perfect on you. I've put a provisional deposit on a dress in your size, you'll look fabulous in it. Please, please tell me you'll be home in time.

Chloe xx

Chapter Seventeen

Why had she bothered to check her e-mail? There were times when it was far better to remain in blissful ignorance. This was surely one of them.

Feeling sick with tension, Mel logged off and went up to the cash desk in the internet café. As she handed over a five-dollar bill and stuffed the change in the pocket of her jeans, she couldn't help thinking that for all the modern-day advances in telecommunications, there was a helluva lot to be said for remaining incommunicado.

She didn't want to know about Chloe's wedding, let alone bridesmaid dresses. After all, how could she possibly wear taffeta rose and follow Chloe up the aisle and watch her exchange vows with Adam Kavanagh? It was out of the question. Up to now

she had tried to put the wedding and all its implications to the back of her mind, but it couldn't be
ignored any longer.

Mel opened the door of the internet café and
went out into the Cairns afternoon. It was warm
and moist with the hint of a drizzle. The blue sky
peeped through snatches of puffy clouds, and palm
trees rattled in the slight July breeze.

She could just ignore the e-mail, couldn't she?
Pretend she hadn't read it. Act as if she didn't know
anything about it. She started to cross the road,
heedless of the approaching motorbike, and almost
went under the front wheel. At the last second she
jerked back onto the pavement and crashed into a
bicycle parked by the palm tree, losing her balance
and falling ignominiously to the ground on top of
the bicycle.

'Hey there, you okay?' The motorcyclist jammed
on the brakes, pulled up in a screech of tyres and
whipped off his gleaming black helmet.

'Does it look like I'm okay?' she glared, strug-
gling furiously to rise to her feet. The end of her
jacket was caught in the frame of the bicycle and it
was difficult to free herself. The more she struggled,
the more her jacket became entangled. The motorcyclist leaned forward, tugged gently at her jacket
and righted the bicycle at the same time, extending
a hand to Mel, and she managed to get to her feet
and dust off her jeans.

'I dare say there's no bones broken,' he drawled

in an accent that Mel found hard to place. He had tight grey hair, a pair of interested blue eyes, and now that she could see it properly, a dangerous-looking motor bike.

'It's a Harley Davidson,' he said proudly.

'Very nice,' Mel shrugged.

'Very nice?' he echoed, with a gleam in his eyes. 'That's an insult. It's bloody beautiful!'

'Right then, it's bloody beautiful,' she grinned wryly. She guessed he was in his mid-fifties and he carried an air of been there, done that, worn the T-shirt.

'That's more like it,' he approved. 'And what part of Ireland are you from?'

'Who says I'm from Ireland?'

'Your soft Irish brogue, number one, and those green eyes couldn't come from anywhere but the Emerald Isle.'

Mel smiled. 'I'm from Dublin, well, Galway originally.'

'Out backpacking for a year?'

'Guess I am,' she replied.

'I think half the Irish population has come through here by now. I'm Sean, by the way, Sean Maguire, originally from Limerick.' He thrust out his hand and gave her a warm smile.

'Mel Saunders,' she smiled in return. 'You don't sound as though you're from Limerick.'

'Then I've been out here too long,' he said.

'What's too long?' Mel asked curiously.

'Fifteen years.'

'How did you manage to stay out here for fifteen years?'

'It's a long story,' Sean said. 'But much as I'd love to stay chatting to a nice Irish girl such as yourself, I'm afraid I'll have to defer it for the moment. I'm already late for an appointment. You sure you're okay?' he asked as he reached for his helmet.

'Yep, no bones broken.' Mel waggled her legs.

'I'll be around Cairns for the next couple of days if you fancied a drink, a coffee or whatever. Give me a chance to catch up on the Irish goings on. And a chance to apologise for sending you flying.'

Mel shook her head. 'It was my fault, I wasn't minding the traffic.'

'Is that a yes or a no for the coffee?'

She hesitated.

'Sorry, Mel, you're probably not used to strange men coming on to you in the street, never mind trying to knock you down,' Sean grinned, his tanned face breaking into hundreds of tiny creases.

'It's not that…'

'You don't want to be seen with someone old enough to be your father.'

'Nonsense,' she smiled.

She could have kicked herself when he didn't pursue it, when he bade a cheerful goodbye, put on his helmet, started his Harley and roared away. She crossed the road, watchfully now, and walked down to the road to the apartment block where her small bed-sit was tucked into a corner of the third floor.

There would have been nothing wrong with going for a coffee or a drink. And there would have been nothing wrong with finding out how Sean Maguire from Limerick had managed to stay in Australia for fifteen years. The main thing on her mind was getting to stay in Australia, wasn't it? But with her hesitation, she had well and truly blown her chance of getting any information from Sean.

The restaurant was busy that night. It was a seventies night and the music was loud. Mel found it difficult to concentrate. What would happen if she completely ignored Chloe's e-mail? Supposing she just kept away from internet cafés for the next few weeks? Pretend she had gone off to a semi-deserted Whitsunday island? After all, who'd know? She worked in a daze, accepting orders, lifting plates heaped with food, checking for drinks, but her mind was elsewhere. One couple were kept waiting so long for their starters that they complained to Dan. Mel rushed to apologise, rummaging in her order book for the docket she had forgotten to hand in, feeling totally stupid.

After that she tried to focus on the job, but thoughts of Chloe's wedding kept hammering away in the corner of her mind. A gang of back-packers arrived and took over a large table out on the sidewalk. They had obviously been drinking.

They were loud and boisterous and every sentence began with 'G'day mate', as they changed their minds time and time again about their orders, until Mel's patience was finally stretched to the limit.

'Right lads,' she asked crisply, pen poised at the ready. 'Is that your final order?'

'Yeah, that's our final answer,' someone laughed.

'Didn't think they had *Who Wants to Be a Millionaire* here in the outback,' one sandy-haired lad guffawed.

'This isn't the outback,' Mel answered crisply. 'And if you want to get fed, you'd better let me know what your order is.'

'We already gave you our final order, miss,' the sandy-haired lad said cheekily.

'Right so.' Mel turned on her heel and crossed to the hatch to the kitchens and left in the docket. She cleared off a table while she waited for their starters, knowing that at least she had come to one decision. Whether she was going home or not, doing bridesmaid for Chloe was out of the question.

What did she mean, whether she was going home or not? Surely she wasn't going to have a choice in the matter? Time was slipping through her fingers, wasn't it? Even if she didn't get back to Dublin until after the wedding, she would have to face Chloe sooner or later. She didn't have the luxury of hiding out in Australia indefinitely.

She felt something uncurl in the pit of her stomach and she accidentally knocked over a saltcellar.

It clattered onto the tiles, once more attracting Dan's attention. She hurriedly replaced it and refilled the dish of tomato sauce, gave the table a final wipe and neatly arranged the chairs.

She collected the starters for table twelve, the gang of noisy backpackers, and weaved through crowded tables to the sidewalk, where the night air was cool and scented in comparison to the hot, stuffy atmosphere in the restaurant.

'This isn't what I ordered!' The sandy-haired lad glared at his Buffalo wings.

'And I don't eat this crap!' Another lad picked up a lettuce leaf from his plate and flicked it across the table.

'Okay, I'll check it out,' Mel said, trying to hang onto her patience, convinced she was correct. They were just looking for trouble. She scanned her copy of the order, but there were so many changes and items crossed out that she had difficulty in following her notes. God knows what the kitchen staff had deciphered.

'What did you order instead?' she asked resignedly, lifting the offending plates, conscious of Dan's eyes boring into her back.

'What's wrong now?' He practically barred her way as she returned to the kitchen with the starters.

'They changed their minds,' she shrugged.

'Try and keep your mind on the job,' he snapped, 'and not on whoever you're going to take home tonight!'

Mel's face flamed. 'I beg your pardon,' she said haughtily. 'I work hard at my job, I hardly ever make mistakes and what I do in my spare time is none of your business.' She swept back to the kitchen and returned several moments later with fresh orders, fervently wishing it was time to go home. The sooner she got shut of these backpackers, the better.

She hurried across the sidewalk over to their table, had almost reached it and was just about to hand over their starters when she tripped over something on the ground, lost her balance and fell headlong. The plates slewed out across the table, losing their contents and tipping over drinks, which ran across the table in a series of tiny rivers and poured on the backpackers' laps and into their food, and for the second time that day, Mel landed in a heap on the ground.

The backpackers stood up and shook off bits of food and tried to mop up wet patches on their jeans with paper napkins. Mel scrambled to her feet and looked in horror at the mess. At first she thought someone had tripped her up on purpose. How else could she have lost her balance like that? At the same time as she saw Dan bearing down purposefully upon her, she spotted Sean Maguire out of the corner of her eye. He was sitting at the next table and sheepishly sliding his crash helmet underneath his chair.

'This is the last straw!' Dan snapped. 'I've a good mind to let you go.'

'Jeez, mister, it was an accident,' the sandy-haired backpacker spoke up. One leg of his jeans was saturated.

'You can't just fire me like this!' Mel protested.

'No, you can't just fire her. It was an accident.' Another backpacker, with a crescent of green pepper stuck to his T-shirt, came to her rescue.

'I'm afraid I'm entirely to blame,' Sean Maguire said, standing up. 'Mel tripped over my crash helmet. Please allow me to make good the damage.'

'Is this another one of your mates?' Dan sneered at Mel. 'No wonder you were distracted!'

'I don't believe this,' Mel fumed and her green eyes glinted. 'How dare you!'

'You can leave at the end of your shift.'

'I'll do no such thing,' Mel said heatedly. She whipped off her striped apron and flung it on the ground. 'I'm leaving now, because I quit.'

She was trembling as she turned on her heel and went to the cloakroom to collect her purse. She was so angry she could hardly see in front of her as, head held high, she strode back through the noisy, brightly lit restaurant and out onto the sidewalk, past a fuming Dan and a cheering gang of back-packers, out into the balmy Cairns night. Further down the road, Sean Maguire was waiting patiently.

* * *

'So what are you going to do?' Sean asked as he poured her another glass of wine.

'I'm not in a hurry to get another job,' Mel shrugged. They sat outside a restaurant near the seafront. Sean was eating lobster, but Mel wasn't hungry. She was beginning to calm down a little and was quite content to sit there, out in the evening air under a string of twinkling lamplights. She watched the lights flickering on the waving fronds of nearby palm trees as she sipped her wine. She felt the night breeze whispering in off the inky sea, tickling her neck, lifting her hair away from her face. 'I've enough money to keep me going for a while,' she said.

'Are you sure? I feel very bad about the whole thing. You've lost your job on account of me.'

'Don't be silly,' Mel smiled. 'Dan was on my back all night. He was waiting for a chance to let me go. Anyway, I would have had to leave soon with my visa restriction.'

'All the same, I wish there was something I could do.'

'You can tell me how you managed to stay here for fifteen years,' she suggested, sipping her wine and feeling it slither coolly down her throat.

'You want to hear the story of my life?'

'Only the interesting bits.' Mel gave him an honest grin.

'Okay, I'll give you the shortened version. I came out here for a year and fell in love. I married an Australian girl, Lauren, and eventually became a citizen, but unfortunately she died five years ago.

There were no kids. And I haven't been back to Ireland for years.'

'Sorry about your wife.'

'So was I.' He was lost in thought for a moment. 'Cancer,' he said briefly.

Mel wordlessly shook her head.

'Anyway,' he continued, 'work kept me going. I now have my own business in Port Douglas, minibus hire. Busy all year round, I'm glad to say. What about you? What's the story of your life?'

'I don't have any interesting bits,' she said. 'The most exciting thing I've done is come out here.'

'That's a start. Any particular reason why you don't want to go home?'

'Who says I don't want to go home?'

'You have that look on your face.'

'You're right. I'd give anything to be able to stay on here.'

'Anything?' Sean grinned.

'Within reason, of course.'

'I might be able to help you there,' he suggested tentatively, his eyes appraising her. 'Seen as how I've lost you your job, and that I'm a fellow countryman and all, I'd like to be able to do something.'

'It doesn't matter about the job, really. But how on earth could you help me?' Mel asked. Something inside her took root, a burgeoning expectation, a tiny germ of hope. She was ready to grasp at a straw. Anything at all would do, anything that would help her to remain on the other side of the world as Chloe walked down the aisle with Adam Kavanagh.

Chapter Eighteen

Chloe felt as though she was watching herself in some kind of slow-motion sequence as she floated out through the door of St Paul of the Cross, Mount Argus, out through the church porch, down the granite steps, into warm August sunshine and her new life with Adam.

She saw herself moving in the tableau of white silk and sunshine, her billowing veil, her wedding dress rustling, sunlight playing on her face and beaming on the gathering of friends and relatives who were shiny and sleek in elegant new clothes. Voices were raised in greetings and laughter, cars lined up shiny and sleek in the car park. There was a constant whirr of camera shutters and a flurry of excitement around her, the bride.

213

'Chloe! You look absolutely fantastic. Glad you took my advice about Kian! He's very smart.' Sandra Power kissed the air in the vicinity of Chloe's cheeks before sailing on by, as elegant as ever in a lilac creation straight off the Paris catwalk.

'Chloe, smile for the camera!'

'Chloe, you're beautiful. Where on earth did you get that fabulous dress?'

'Chloe, look this way!'

'Congratulations, Chloe. You and Adam make a lovely couple.'

'Welcome to the family, Chloe,' Adam's sister Diane said as she gave her a hug.

'Chloe, the photographer is looking for you.'

'Chloe, over here!'

'Happy?' Adam murmured as they posed for photographs in the landscaped grounds adjoining the church.

'Very,' she smiled, clutching her spray of roses.

'You look incredibly beautiful.' His blue eyes admired her and Chloe's heart turned over.

'I never thought I'd feel like this today.'

'Like what?'

'As though there's some kind of magic in the air.'

'Wait til tonight,' he murmured as he dropped a kiss on her nose.

'Now, now. You can hold that til afterwards,' the photographer called out. 'Let's get this show on the road. Where is the mother of the bride?'

They grouped and regrouped, and Chloe posed

so many times for so many photographs that she felt as though she was on a photo shoot for *Hello!*.

'You were right, Chloe, the grounds here are just perfect for photographs,' her mother admitted when they had a quiet moment together afterwards.

'Wait until you see the grounds of the hotel. But you can see why I didn't want to get married in your local church,' she said cheerfully, making light of the blazing row they'd had when Chloe announced her intention of getting married from the church near her flat.

'I just thought it would have been nice for all the neighbours to see you walking up the aisle,' Irene smiled wistfully, 'not to mention getting an eyeful of all this glamour and the flashy cars. I don't think I ever saw so much style all together in the one place before.'

Chloe smiled. 'You look very stylish yourself, Mum.'

'Yes, I do, don't I?' Irene twirled around in her royal blue ensemble. 'I suppose I should thank you for dragging me around almost every boutique in Ireland until you were satisfied! I probably would have settled for something more practical.'

'It was worth it, wasn't it?'

'Definitely. I don't feel out of place with all this smart sophistication.'

'And why should you? You're the mother of the bride, after all. If you want to make an impact, you don't settle for second best. Sandra pulled out all the stops for the Westmeath contingent,' Chloe

215

said. 'I lost count of the times she winged it over to London or Paris.'

'She's the sister who works in the boutique?'

'She's the sister who owns it, Mum.'

'Good job you reminded me. I hope I don't put my foot in it with Adam's family. They seem very nice.'

'Of course they are.'

'And I've warned Brian and Rory to behave.'

'So have I,' Chloe grinned.

'Your dad has practised his speech off by heart. It was very good of Henry to write it for him, wasn't it?'

'Henry didn't mind, and it saved Dad from having a nervous breakdown.'

'What about my nerves? I'm just glad we had the chance to meet Adam's parents beforehand, and break the ice.'

'Yes. Peter and Eileen are lovely, aren't they? I told you there was nothing to worry about.'

'Oh dear, your dad's buttonhole is almost falling off.' Irene's eyes followed her husband's progress as he moved through the guests gathered in the church grounds. 'I better catch up with him. Can't have him going around like that on the video,' she smiled as she hurried in his wake.

The day floated by and all the big important things and the small minute details Chloe had fretted about clicked together and fell into place and everything unrolled almost seamlessly, as perfect a wedding day as anyone could wish for. She forgot about the frenzied hours she had spent scrutinising hotel packages and wedding menus and available dates before being fortunate enough to secure a luxury hotel just an hour's drive outside Dublin. And it looked very impressive on the coloured themed invitations – 'and afterwards at a reception in Ballyglen Castle'.

She forgot all about her stressful search for the perfect wedding dress, the argument with Sandra over Kian's pageboy outfit, the argument with Adam over the wedding list, the frantic hunt for the exact colour of hair ribbon for her flower girls, Megan and Hannah, the countless times she had analysed the guest list, the mounting headaches as she fastidiously arranged the seating, and her mother's growing anxiety that finally drove Chloe to threaten to abandon the whole thing at the eleventh hour and get married on a beach in Barbados.

And she forgot about her huge disappointment when Mel had finally e-mailed and said that no, she couldn't do bridesmaid, she wouldn't be home, not this August, not even next August, she had extended her visa for another couple of years and was staying in a place called Port Douglas.

'I can't believe this!' she had wailed at Adam.

'How did she manage to do that?' Adam asked.

'I really don't care how she did it. I'm so disappointed she won't be here on my special day. It won't be the same without Mel,' Chloe fretted.

Then, looking at him curiously, she said, 'You look almost glad, Adam. Are you happy she's not coming home?'

'What difference is it to me?'

'I could have sworn I saw something like relief in your face, as though you don't want to see her. Do you still think Mel's a bad influence on me or something?'

'Chloe, she made no secret of the fact that she thought you were mad to marry me,' Adam said. 'Maybe it's just as well she's staying away.'

'Is that it? Don't tell me you're still holding that against her?'

'I don't want her coming home and upsetting you.'

'Look, we're getting married. I'm on top of the world. Nothing Mel could say or do could possibly upset me, except missing my wedding day,' Chloe said. 'We're best friends. I'm just terribly disappointed she can't be my bridesmaid. I'll ask my cousin Fiona, but it won't be the same as having Mel.'

But all the hectic preparations were forgotten about as the wedding day unfolded. Chloe didn't want the day to end. She wanted to hold on to this feeling of being in a magic circle, where everything was bright and shiny and new and full of golden promise. But even as the sun slipped westwards almost imperceptibly, the day slid slowly by and one minute Chloe was getting into a silver-grey Rolls Royce outside the church and holding a fizzing champagne flute in her hand and the next she was sitting in the luxury of the hotel dining room, amidst a sea of white napery and rose petals, the chink of cutlery and glasses, drifts of laughter and conversation and everything overlaid with the sweet scent of floral arrangements and Adam, who had just vowed to love her for the rest of her life…

The evening guests began to arrive, more friends and far-flung cousins and a gang from the building society, including Debbie Driscoll, Tara and Emer. Henry, all day long the impeccable best man, started to flirt outrageously with Fiona. Adam's little nieces began to droop with tiredness. Then Chloe was circling the floor in Adam's arms and the band was playing 'Wind Beneath My Wings' and Chloe didn't want that moment to end either, because right then, Adam was indeed her hero, and right then everything was perfect.

But come to an end it did, and the wedding day concluded in a flurry of hugs and kisses, fond farewells and happy ever afters before Chloe and Adam disappeared into the luxury of the hotel bridal suite and the sumptuous four poster bed. The following day, they jetted off to Majorca.

* * *

At first Chloe had been upset at the choice of Majorca for a honeymoon.

'Majorca? No one goes there on honeymoon, Adam!'

'Chloe, it's the best we can get at the moment. The travel agent said she'd hold it provisionally until ten o'clock tomorrow morning.'

'That's ridiculous. There has to be somewhere more upmarket than Majorca. That's fine for kids who want to get drunk and get laid. It's not where you go on honeymoon.'

'It's a four star luxury hotel in landscaped grounds with direct access to a secluded beach, and it's a million miles away from a noisy resort. It'll be ideal, Chloe.'

Chloe felt as though she was going to cry. After all the glittering wedding plans she had carefully put together, her brilliant honeymoon in Hawaii was disappearing down the tubes, thanks to a massive contract Adam had just negotiated for his fledgling company. He had worked really hard to get this contract. It was going to launch KVL into the big time. She was thrilled with Adam's success, of course she was, but what a pity that on account of the tight scheduling he'd had to agree to, he couldn't possibly take more than a bare week away from the office, so a tiring, long-haul trip to Hawaii was out of the question.

But Majorca? Whoever went on honeymoon to Majorca?

'Maybe if we wait until the last minute, something better will turn up,' Chloe suggested.

'Yes, we might be lucky to get a studio apartment in Hersonnissos or Ibiza. I know you're disappointed, and I promise I'll make it up to you.'

'No one will believe that we're off to Majorca for our honeymoon!'

'Is that what this is about? What other people will think?' Adam suddenly flared.

'No, of course not,' Chloe hastily assured him, feeling a sickening lurch in her stomach. The last thing she wanted was a row so close to the wedding or a return to those awful, heart-wrenching days when she and Adam had split up. 'It's just that I wanted us to have the best wedding and honeymoon we could possibly have,' she explained, forcing herself to calm down. 'I've been working very hard to make sure everything will be perfect for us.'

'I want us to have the best as well, and Majorca will be perfect, I promise.'

And it was. The island of rugged mountains, scented pine trees and long sandy beaches was bathed in sunshine. The hotel, set amongst picturesque grounds, was every bit as luxurious as Adam had described. Chloe's cases were full of delicate wispy lingerie and sheer satin nightgowns that Adam slowly peeled off, kissing her soft flesh inch by inch, making love to her in the purple afterglow of a warm sunny day as the whispering sea outside their hotel room turned to a crumpled grey silk sheet.

Whether they were lazing by the pool during the day, strolling on the beach in the evenings or making love as the sun slid beneath the horizon,

Chloe was on top of the world. She was married now, married to Adam. She was Chloe Kavanagh now. Nothing could take that away from her. Those awful days she had spent in turmoil after she had broken off their engagement were well and truly behind her. She was right to have made up with Adam, she thought as they strolled hand in hand on the golden beach.

Less than a week after she had moved out of the Harold's Cross flat, he had turned up at her new address, a cramped bed-sit in a noisy part of Terenure. Why can't you trust me, he had said. It had been three long miserable weeks since she had broken off the engagement and she was feeling so lonely and broken hearted that she had melted into his arms.

He never told her what exactly had happened between him and Jackie. He had known her all his life, he said in a dismissive tone of voice, and they had grown up together. But it was Chloe he loved, Chloe he wanted to marry. Curled up beside him in her narrow single bed, Chloe felt the touch of his skin against hers, felt her heart soothed with his words and she didn't really see the point in asking him why he couldn't have simply explained all this in the first place.

The following week, she moved back to Harold's Cross, back to the flat she had shared with Mel, only now she was sharing it with Adam.

'I thought this flat would have been snapped

up,' she said, looking around at the all too familiar walls.

'It was,' Adam smiled as he took her into his arms. 'I snapped it up. For us.'

Chloe put her engagement ring back on and began to plan the wedding of her dreams. Everything came together quite, quite perfectly. She was called into Debbie Driscoll's office on a cold wintry morning in February, and informed that she had been successful in her promotion application, effective immediately.

The house, then, was the icing on the cake. In early June, Chloe was browsing through a weekend property supplement when she spotted an advertisement for an exclusive new launch on the south side of Dublin.

A unique development in a sylvan setting, the advertising blurb for Abbey Manor promised. *Exciting and innovative, act today to avoid disappointment.* Everything about the house looked perfect. It *was* perfect. And even though she was grappling with guest numbers and wedding lists, she made a frantic telephone call to the selling agents, followed by a frantic phone call to Adam's office, and by the following afternoon, Adam was signing on the dotted line and a cheque for the booking deposit was changing hands.

* * *

She had everything in the world to look forward to, Chloe smiled to herself as the Aer Lingus jet thundered down the runway, lifted into blue skies over Palma Airport and turned in a wide arc on course for Dublin Airport.

'Happy?' Adam asked.

She caught his hand. 'Very. And you?'

'I know our honeymoon was short and sweet, but it was perfect. It had the two things that matter most.'

'What's that?'

'You and me.'

'Oh, Adam, I wonder how many of your knife-wielding competitors would guess what a romantic little heart you have under that steely surface.'

'None of them, I hope! It's back to business with a bang first thing on Monday morning. You won't see much of me for the next few weeks, I'm afraid.'

'I'll be busy myself.'

'You certainly will. Now that you're my wife, you'll have to start ironing my shirts.'

'Get lost!'

'Hold on a mo, that's part of the deal,' he grinned.

'I'll be busy getting our new house organised.'

'There's no point in thinking about that until after Christmas. It won't be ready for months.'

'It'll fly in, and if it's anything like organising a wedding, I'll be up to my tonsils. I'm glad it won't be ready for a while. I don't think I could have handled a wedding and a new house all at the same time. Not if I wanted to do everything properly.'

'I can't imagine you not organising anything properly,' Adam teased.

'Aren't you lucky you married me?'

'Didn't I tell you I always get what I want? Chloe, I…'

'Yes?'

'Just remember I love you and I want you to be happy. Always.'

There was no reason in the world why she shouldn't be happy, Chloe thought as the Boeing 737 droned on to Dublin and home.

Chapter Nineteen

Once again, Chloe found herself browsing the magazine shelves. This time it was the myriad of glossy house and home magazines that held her transfixed. Their house wouldn't be ready for occupation until early the following summer, so they had plenty of time to plan. Chloe's eyes raked the display of shiny magazines before she finally made her selection. Adam was looking after all the red tape in between his hectic working schedule. Chloe was going to make sure they had the house of their dreams.

She persuaded Adam to drive them out to the new estate on a blustery afternoon at the start of November. A few semi-detached houses at the entrance to the estate were already completed, all of them already bedecked with smart blinds and drapes.

'That'll be us, Adam,' she said, admiring the speed with which the newcomers had settled in. 'I can't wait. It'll be such fun!'

They parked the car and walked down to the end of the muck-encrusted road where wire mesh fencing barred their access to the rest of the building site. Lengths of steel scaffolding surrounded shells of houses in various stages of completion. The breeze tugged at Chloe's hair and slapped against sheets of tarpaulin and whistled through gaping apertures that were waiting for window frames and doors. Bright yellow earthmovers and cylindrical cement mixers were silent silhouettes against the heavy rain clouds. The light was draining rapidly from the grey November sky and Adam pulled up the collar of his wool overcoat against the chill of the breeze.

'There's not much to see,' he said. 'I think we should head back before it rains.'

'I just wanted to get a feel for the place,' she said. 'I think our house will be somewhere over there.' She gestured vaguely towards the far right-hand corner of the muddy field.

'If that's the case, it doesn't look like they've even dug out the foundations.'

'It's exciting, isn't it? To think that that's where we'll live, our very own home, and we'll be able to watch it going up bit by bit.'

'I wouldn't plan on traipsing out here too often in the winter,' Adam cautioned.

'I'm definitely coming out to have another look at the show house. I need to take some measurements. And I want to have another look at the kitchen presses before we decide.'

'Decide what?'

'I hardly think we want the standard show house style. They're a bit bland. I'm sure we can do a lot better.'

'I thought the kitchen looked okay, but I'll leave that up to you. You'll be the one spending the most time in it.'

She threw him a dirty look and began to laugh when she saw the teasing light in his eyes.

'C'mon, let's get back to the car,' Adam urged. 'I can feel drops of rain.'

Arm in arm, they ran up the road, avoiding the spatters of muck, past the newly occupied houses where glowing lamps were being switched on to dispel the dull grey afternoon. Chloe's hair was tossed and her hands felt cold and they barely made it back to the car before the tentative drizzle turned into big fat raindrops.

As soon as they got back to the flat, Adam closed the curtains against the wet November evening and turned on the gas fire. Chloe lit orchid-scented candles and poured two glasses of wine. She reached for a *Better Homes* magazine and was about to open it when Adam stilled her hand and reached for her instead and they spent the rainy evening making love, swiftly, slowly and passionately.

* * *

In the end, their house wasn't ready for occupation until the following July. Adam was caught up with a new business project, and although he organised the mortgage and scheduled the visits to the solicitors, all the other details were left up to Chloe.

She scoured house and home magazines, getting ideas, planning designs and co-ordinating colour schemes – primrose yellow for the kitchen, a warm apricot for the hall, a striking lavender and sage for the bathroom and en suite. She haunted the showrooms of the kitchen suppliers, the tilers and the wardrobe fitters. She went shopping for kitchen appliances. Adam gave her carte blanche and told her to buy whatever she wanted, so Chloe put a deposit on a range of gleaming Neff appliances.

'I thought it was stressful organising a wedding, but this is ten times worse,' Chloe said to Adam on a Saturday morning early in April as they lay in bed.

'What's wrong now?' he asked.

'On top of everything else, they've just gone and lost our order for the hand-painted kitchen tiles. And if they've lost that, they probably have the other tiles mixed up as well. God knows what they're putting into the en suite. I'll have to go back into the suppliers myself and sort it out and it means another half day off work. Debbie Driscoll will love me.'

'Cheer up, Chloe. So what if the extra sockets are in the wrong place or they forget that we changed the fireplace surround? And what about the kitchen? They might fit the show house standard instead of the fancy design you've set your heart on.'

'Sure, no problem,' Chloe scoffed at the teasing light in his eyes. 'I'm not signing for the house until everything is exactly as we want it,' she insisted as she slid out of bed.

'Where do you think you're going?' Adam's arm snaked around her bare midriff.

'I've loads to do. I want to make a list of things to check for, while it's still in my head.'

'Come back here this minute. I haven't finished with you yet.'

Chloe fell back upon the pillows and momentarily forgot about her checklist and the half-ready house. She felt the rush of desire inside her as Adam's blue eyes smiled a lazy Saturday morning smile and he pulled her into his arms.

* * *

'I don't like to see you worrying so much,' her mum said a couple of weeks later.

Chloe counted to ten and relaxed her grip on the phone.

'We're paying over the odds for all the additional extras, so of course I'm a bit anxious,' Chloe said patiently.

'Just be glad you'll have a roof over your head. Everything else will come afterwards. You can't expect to have everything perfect from the start,' her mum advised.

'Why not? Might as well get it right first time.'

'I dunno, Chloe,' Irene sighed. 'I think you're putting a lot of pressure on yourself. Your dad and I were over the moon when we moved in here, even though we had hand me down curtains and bare floors for a couple of years.'

'Hello, Mum, things are different nowadays.'

'That doesn't mean they're any better. Des and I were very happy, even though we had to struggle.'

'Of course things are better nowadays. You should be glad we don't have to struggle so much and that we'll have a fabulous home in an upmarket estate.'

'I *am* glad for you, Chloe. Just so long as you're not overstretching yourself.'

'We've had this kind of conversation before, when I started night college, for instance. Why can't you just be happy that I'm making such a great success of my life?'

* * *

Time after time, Chloe braved the muck of the building site in order to chivvy the foreman along and make sure the house would be ready on schedule and to her and Adam's satisfaction. The first day the foreman allowed her entry across the threshold, past the stone-riddled excavation that would be their front garden into the dusty hallway littered with builders' debris, into half-finished rooms where windows were shrouded in cement-spattered sheeting, Chloe could sense the shape of the house to come. She could imagine the elegant living room, with its smart Valencia fireplace, the bright and airy kitchen with the primrose yellow walls, blue hand-painted tiles, beech units and a natural slate floor, the sumptuous master bedroom complete with designer wardrobes and a king-sized pine bed.

They went for a farewell drink in the local pub with Henry and his latest girlfriend, who he introduced as Kim, an English model.

'You're not sad to leave Harold's Cross, then?' Henry asked. 'Very handy to town. You won't be able to walk to work any more, Chloe.'

'I'm not a bit sad, Henry. I'll easily cope with commuting. Onwards and upwards, as the saying goes.' Chloe raised her glass. 'Here's to Abbey Manor.'

She felt like pinching herself. Her new life with Adam was turning out to be everything she had dreamed of.

Chapter Twenty

'Adam, I have the travel agents on the other phone and I just wanted to make sure you're okay for the last week in August.'

'What's happening the last week in August?' Adam tore his eyes away from the flickering computer monitor.

'Adam!' Chloe squealed.

'Sorry, sorry.' Adam ran an impatient hand through his hair. 'It's our wedding anniversary, isn't it?'

'Yes, our very first, *and* our holidays.'

'What holidays?'

'Our holidays,' Chloe sounded impatient. 'Remember? Somewhere foreign, sunshine, nice hotel, etcetera? You said you'd be able to take a week off. And it would be nice to celebrate our first wedding anniversary in style. How do you fancy a week in Fuerteventura? A four star hotel on the beach?'

'Fuerta what? And I don't remember saying I could take time off.'

'Adam! We talked about it ages ago.'

'That was before we got the contract for Ryan Insurances. We've just moved into a new house, and I took some time off for that.'

'All the more reason for a holiday,' Chloe pointed out. 'We need a proper break away after all that stress. I don't want to lay eyes on another electrician or carpenter or see a scrap of builder's dust for the rest of my life. And we've had no real holiday since our honeymoon.'

Adam sighed. 'I'll have a word with Rob and take a look at the scheduling. I'll phone you later this morning.'

'It'll have to be before lunch, or the holiday will be gone,' Chloe insisted.

Adam put down the phone and stared into space. A week away from the office was the last thing he needed. KVL was busier and busier and he was working long hours each day as it was in order to stay on top of things. In one sense, though, Chloe was right. The last few months had been hectic for the two of them and they needed some kind of a break. And he loved Chloe and wanted to make her happy. He already had something special planned for their first wedding anniversary. If the ghost of a memory flickered at the back of his mind occasionally, he ignored it completely. All his life he was successful at everything he had turned his hand to. There was no reason in the world why his marriage shouldn't be equally as successful.

No reason whatsoever.

* * *

Chloe gave her credit card details over the phone to confirm the holiday booking and promised the travel agent that she'd call in that evening after work to fill in the necessary documents.

'Adam and I have to decided on Fuerteventura,' she said casually during lunchtime in the canteen.

'Oh?' Tara Conroy raised her eyes. 'I believe that's fairly quiet.'

'You're not looking for the same as us, Chloe,' Emer said.

'And what's that?' Chloe asked.

'Men, men and men!'

'Speak for yourself, Emer. I don't believe in spending my well-earned holidays in pursuit of men,' Tara said. 'If it happens, it happens,' she shrugged.

'Yeah, sure.' Emer looked at her in disbelief.

Chloe let the conversation wash over her. A couple of years ago she and Mel would have been looking for sex and excitement on a Spanish beach. Now she had all that and more, with Adam.

'You can take that grin off your face, Chloe,' Emer said. 'I envy you with that hunky husband of yours, heading off for a week in the sunshine. But there's no need to rub it in!'

'I didn't mean to upset you,' Chloe laughed. 'Can't help it if I look happy!'

'I'd be afraid I'd get bored with the same man,' Tara remarked cattily.

'If you were married to Adam, you wouldn't,' Chloe smirked, equally cattily.

There was no point in admitting that she didn't really see enough of Adam in order to get bored. He was working six days a week and he might have to put in some extra time in the run-up to the holidays. They were going to a party the following Saturday night, a housewarming plus meet the neighbours, in Kaz O'Reilly's house, and Chloe was fervently hoping that Adam would be home in plenty of time.

She had already met Kaz. She was a tall, blonde, friendly woman a little older than Chloe who lived four doors down. She had stopped to introduce herself when Chloe had been out polishing her mahogany hall door. Chloe had also met her next-door neighbour, Emma Boylan. Emma and Kaz had moved into Abbey Manor within several days of each other, and they both had small children.

She was looking forward to getting to know

them a little better, Chloe thought the following Saturday as she spent the afternoon arranging and rearranging the contents of her kitchen presses. Not that she wanted to live in anyone's pocket. God forbid she ended up like her mother, with neighbours dropping in whenever they felt like it, borrowing this and borrowing that, full of gossip and advice. That was unlikely to happen in Abbey Manor. Apart from briefly meeting Kaz and Emma, all Chloe had seen of her neighbours so far had been shiny BMWs, Mercs and zippy sports cars tearing out of drive-ins at unearthly hours in the morning and returning late in the evening.

Adam came home just after six. Chloe was soaking in a scented bath when she heard Adam's footsteps in the hall.

'Up here, Adam.'

'Aha. So this is what you're up to,' he grinned as he stuck his head around the bathroom door. As with the rest of the house, no expense had been spared. Chloe had ordered a superior bathroom suite, complete with large corner bath and Jacuzzi jets. The mosaic tiles on the wall were a perfect match for the floor tiles and mounds of fluffy sage and lavender towels were arranged on the heated rail.

'Care to join me?' She sat up briefly so that he caught a glimpse of her foamy breasts, then slid back down in the water.

'That's not fair,' he said, his blue eyes charged with something that made her insides contract.

'You've given me no choice.' In four seconds flat he had whipped off his clothes, and he was already aroused as he stepped into the bath beside her.

There was plenty of room. Adam's eyes were dark with desire as he took Chloe's slithery body into his arms. Afterwards, he wrapped her in a big lavender towel as he carried her through to the king-sized pine bed in their lilac and cream bedroom. He patted her gently all over until she was dry.

'What about my moisturiser?' she asked huskily.

'Can't forget about that,' he murmured as he took the bottle off her hands.

He began to apply aloe vera body lotion, his fingertips massaging in slow, circular movements across her shoulders, along her arms, across her breasts, and he was massaging the silken cream to her thighs when he stopped, unable to continue any further. Chloe sighed as his mouth followed the trail of his fingers. She was almost weak with renewed longing by the time he slid inside her and she caught her breath as she felt the answering spirals in her own body. They dozed off for a while, their bodies slick and entwined, until Chloe looked at the clock and eventually tore herself out of his arms and off the bed.

She opened the wardrobe door. 'I don't know what to wear tonight.'

'Your sexiest underwear,' Adam suggested, leaning forward and gently pinching her smooth bum. 'If I'm getting bored I'll just have to look at you.'

'Are you not looking forward to meeting the neighbours?'

'You're just dying to get a look inside Kaz O'Reilly's house,' he remarked shrewdly.

'So what?' she grinned. 'I'd like to see how it compares with ours. And I'd like to meet some of the neighbours.'

'Tell you what. Why don't you leave off your knickers? That'll really keep me on edge.'

'No way,' Chloe laughed.

'I won't be able to resist you.' He suddenly bounded off the bed and made a lunge for Chloe. She squealed in delight and ran from the room. She darted down the stairs, excitement thudding through her at the feeling of running naked through her own house and the thoughts of an equally naked Adam running after her. She veered towards the sitting room, thought the better of it, and ducked into the utility room.

'Scaredy cat!' Adam mocked as he caught up with her and cornered her in the small room.

'Anyone could see us,' she gasped, her heart thumping.

'Not in here they won't.' His eyes gleamed as he reached behind her and pulled down the blind. 'Ever tried it on a washing machine?'

* * *

They were the last to arrive at the party. Kaz gave her a keen quizzical glance as she held open the hall door, and Chloe felt sure that the last couple of lecherous hours she had spent with Adam were written all over her face.

About half a dozen couples were congregated in the big farmhouse-style kitchen, which Chloe quickly appraised. Nice enough, she thought, but not quite as up-to-the minute as her own. Apart, that was, from Kaz's flagstone floor, which was eye catching and stylish. She mingled with the crowd, exchanging introductions, and accepted a glass of Chardonnay and a smoked salmon cracker from Tom, Kaz's husband.

'Help yourself, and don't be shy,' he gestured expansively to a long table full of finger food and bottles of wine. Chloe scanned the variety of food and was relieved to note that there was nothing on offer that she couldn't have concocted herself, thanks to her range of well-thumbed cookery books.

'We should really have put on name tags, like first day at school,' Emma joked.

'Yes, it's impossible to remember everyone,' Chloe agreed.

'You've met my husband, Philip, haven't you?'

'I think so,' Chloe looked around.

'He's the one with the least amount of hair,' Emma joked. 'Now please introduce me to that gorgeous hunk you came in with. I'd say he's the one with the biggest amount of testosterone!'

They were younger than most of the other couples. From what Chloe gathered, listening to fragments of conversation, a move to the four-bed detached grandeur of Abbey Manor had been a move upmarket to their second home for the majority of the other couples. She watched Adam out of the corner of her eye as he made himself at ease, chatting and flirting, and she decided that as well as being the youngest couple, they were by far the sexiest. The combination of Adam's height, his hips neat in his figure-hugging jeans and his fine woollen sweater showing off a flat belly, in addition to his air of casual authority, made him stand out in the crowd. Chloe wore her size ten black leather trousers and a sleeveless, slinky top. She had refused to go knickerless, but had put on her black leather thong in front of Adam and told him he could anticipate the pleasure of peeling it off later that night.

She felt good as she chatted to Kaz and Emma, sipping wine and laughing over horror stories about builders and snag lists. Adam winked at her across the room and she winked back in return, and for the first time ever in her life, she felt as though she had finally arrived.

This was it. She was married to the sexiest man in the room, she was mingling with the affluent neighbours in Abbey Manor and, what's more, she was one of them. She, Chloe Kavanagh, belonged to this luxury lifestyle.

The previous Saturday she'd had Adam's family up to visit and it had been a marvellous success. It had been worth the months of frantic running and racing as she went all out to get their new home exactly as she wanted. It had been worth the hectic, last-minute preparations as she cleaned and cooked and pored over her Jamie Oliver cookbook, just to see the look on Sandra's face as she showed everyone around the house and finally led them into the dining room.

She hadn't needed a glass of wine to put her on a high.

Kaz threw open the double doors to the dining room, saying that she didn't want everyone huddled in the kitchen, and Chloe was glad of a further opportunity to throw her eye around and make a favourable comparison with her own home. She admired the beautiful portraits of Kaz's children, five-year-old Shauna and three-year-old Sam.

'They're in bed for the night,' Kaz explained. 'Don't want them tearing around, making a nuisance of themselves. Anyway, it's way past their bedtime and it's such a relief to get them up the stairs.'

'I know the feeling,' Emma said fervently. 'I'm always more relaxed when Alex and Matthew are asleep. They're two little devils,' she finished proudly.

'How old are they?' Chloe asked. She had spotted them playing out in the back garden at weekends and thought they looked cute in their colour co-ordinated dungarees.

'Three and four. Yes, I know,' Emma smiled contentedly. 'Just a year in the difference! Of course, Philip was as proud as punch, two sons in quick succession. He thinks the world of them, and behind it all, he was delighted with proof of his virility.'

'Men,' Kaz shook her head. 'I'll never forget the look on Tom's face in the labour ward when Shauna was put into his arms,' she continued conspiratorially. 'Then, of course, he was chuffed when we had Sam, a little lift to his ego.'

'And if you think Kaz's house is nice, you should see the children's bedrooms, Chloe,' Emma enthused. 'They're fantastic. I don't know where Kaz gets her ideas from!'

'You can have a look another time,' Kaz smiled. 'Let's change the subject for now. We mums could talk all night about our offspring, but we'd only bore you to tears, Chloe. We'll get together sometime Emma and swap labour ward horror stories.'

'Yes, I'd love that.' Emma looked pleased. 'If we can organise some time in our hectic lives!'

'Do you both work?' Chloe asked.

'Do we what?' Kaz laughed. 'We never have a minute. I'm out nursing three or four days a week and Emma practically runs her own business.'

'Not quite!' Emma protested.

'Don't mind her. She's a partner in a soft furnishing design company, and if you ask me, she runs the show.'

'And what do you do, Chloe?'

'I'm the customer service manager in Premier Elect.'

'Oh, very good,' Kaz approved. 'We can talk to you if we have trouble with our mortgages.'

* * *

'You seemed to be enjoying yourself,' Adam murmured later, much later, long after he had slowly peeled off Chloe's thong. They were sprawled on the sitting room sofa and Chloe felt weak in the aftermath of their lovemaking. They hadn't even got as far as the bedroom. When they had returned from the party, Adam had closed the hall door and pulled her into the sitting room, his blue eyes locked on hers as he eased her sleeveless top up over her breasts and slowly slid down the zip of her black leather trousers.

'You seemed to be enjoying yourself too.' Chloe nuzzled into his chest, half asleep.

'They're an okay bunch.'

'I'm glad that our house is every bit as smart, if not smarter, than Kaz's.'

'Of course it is, you ninny. It should be, after all the money we've spent.'

'Emma was telling me they went to Fuerteventura last year and it was lovely, so we should have a nice holiday.'

'Good. Philip was trying to get me to join his golf club.'

244

'You don't play golf, do you?'

'No, but I might give it a go. It's just as important to be able to network out on the golf course.'

'Of course. Another thing that could be important is starting a family.'

'Yeah, sometime in the future,' he agreed. 'And now I think we'd better move upstairs and get some sleep.'

* * *

They were strolling along the sand dunes on a warm evening in Fuerteventura when Chloe brought up the subject again.

'You do want children, don't you, Adam?' she said, idly watching a fluffy-haired little girl in a pink outfit toddle along between her parents. Her arms were upstretched as she held both their hands, and every so often they lifted her into the air between them and she let out the most adorable chuckles. The little girl's father smiled across at his wife and Chloe thought they made a lovely family.

'Yes, of course, eventually,' Adam said.

'Like next year, or the year after?'

'What's this, Chloe? Twenty questions?'

Chloe laughed. 'I'm just wondering how you'd feel about being a dad.'

Adam was silent for a few moments. 'I suppose it must be pretty wonderful, to think that you've helped to make another human being.' He frowned at her suspiciously. 'Are you trying to tell me something?'

Chloe shook her head. 'I'm just looking forward to the next few years, that's all.'

'Aren't you satisfied with the way things are at the moment?'

'Of course I am, I'm perfectly happy. I can't help wondering, though, what our babies would be like.'

'If they're our babies, they'd be brilliant, of course,' he grinned. 'Maybe if things go well, we could start thinking about it sometime next year?'

They strolled along in the deepening twilight. Chloe's thoughts flew ahead to the nursery that would be decorated, the gurgling baby in a beribboned Moses basket, the professional portrait adorning the sitting room wall and, last but not least, Adam's sense of pride. She pictured him holding a little baby in his arms and her heart contracted with emotion. All they needed to make their happiness complete was a baby of their own.

Next year, Adam had said. Maybe she should stop taking the Pill soon. After all, it often took up to a year to conceive when you came off the Pill, and she'd been on it for a helluva long time. And if she conceived, say, next summer, it would be another nine months, so it would be the following spring before they would have a baby. By then they would be two and half years married and she would be almost thirty years old – perfect timing.

And after all the preparations and the excitement of the wedding, and then moving into the new house, life had settled down again. It would be nice to have something new to plan for, something new to look forward to.

Towards the end of their holiday, they celebrated their first wedding anniversary, and Adam surprised her by handing her a set of keys as they finished a romantic evening meal.

'What's this?' she asked.

'Your anniversary present,' he smiled. 'It'll be waiting for you at Dublin Airport. I'll give you a clue. You won't have to borrow mine any more.'

'Adam, it's not…?'

'You have to guess.'

'It's a car, isn't it? Adam, you're a demon!' She threw her arms around his neck and told him she was the happiest woman in the world.

* * *

It was easy to stop taking the Pill. Chloe needed to have her prescription renewed a month after they returned from holiday. It was an easy enough matter not to bother going along to the doctor. After all, if she wanted to become pregnant the following year, she would need plenty of time to get back to normal, plenty of time to adjust, after years of taking it. And there were vitamins she would have to take in advance, to make sure her body was in tip-top shape. She looked upon the next few months as a time of preparation for her pregnancy.

And, as usual, everything would be quite perfectly planned.

Chapter Twenty-one

'Aren't you going to congratulate me?' Tara Conroy beamed.

Chloe looked up from her desk, automatically scanned Tara's left hand, and smiled quizzically at her. 'Sorry, Tara, you'll have to enlighten me.'

'I've just been promoted,' Tara glowed. 'Customer service manager, same as yourself, but I'm moving to a different branch, not sure yet which one.'

'Well done,' Chloe duly offered her congratulations. 'That's great news.'

'I'm not the only one with news, I believe,' Tara crooked an eyebrow.

'So you've heard.'

'Word travels fast in this place. When are you due?'

'Next July.'

'Then it wasn't a holiday baby,' Tara swiftly calculated. 'I thought you might have been carried away by the sun, the sea and the Sangria.'

'Carried away? As if!' Chloe laughed dismissively.

'And you don't mind an interruption to your career?'

'What interruption? I'll only be missing for a few months.'

'Yes, but your priorities are sure to change. That could have an effect on your career.'

'I'm not sure I follow you, Tara. Debbie Driscoll has two children and I'd say she manages quite well, wouldn't you?' Chloe's tone was clipped. Cheeky bitch. Give Tara a promotion and all of a sudden she's an expert on staff motivation.

'Yes, I didn't mean—' Tara began hastily.

'And Adam and I are really looking forward to having a baby,' Chloe said firmly, willing herself to believe every word she uttered.

* * *

When her period didn't arrive and her breasts began to feel heavier and more sensitive, she had thought it was her hormones reacting to the effects of coming off the Pill. Then, to compound her confusion, her mother had noticed it first.

'And have you any news for me?' Irene had asked as they sat at her kitchen table. Chloe had driven over for a visit one of the many evenings when Adam was working late. Even though she was nervous of parking her smart new car outside the door, it was better than watching her mother perch awkwardly on the edge of the luxury sofa in the sitting room at Abbey Manor or watching her thinly disguised anxiety as she spotted yet another new and expensive gadget in Chloe's gleaming kitchen.

'I've no news, but I have the holiday photos of Fuerteventura,' Chloe said, rummaging in her black leather bag.

'I'll never be able to keep up with you, Chloe,' Irene sighed as she looked at the glossy photos. 'You're really living the high life, you and Adam. A new home, a luxury holiday and your own car, all in the space of a couple of months. I don't know how you do it.'

'Now, Mum, don't start. We both have good jobs. Adam's business is flying at the moment,' Chloe said reproachfully.

'Did I say anything?' Irene looked aggrieved. 'I know you work hard for everything. Too hard, sometimes.'

'At least we give you plenty to boast about,' Chloe smiled.

'The neighbours are sick listening to me,' Irene admitted. 'Especially Maura Cullen. Are you sure you've no other news?' she asked, giving Chloe a funny look.

'Like what? Let's see, we're off to a party in Emma Boylan's house next weekend. She's my next-door neighbour and a good friend of Kaz, who lives a few doors down. I'm hoping to have something for the neighbours in my house before Christmas.'

'Your neighbours are important. I'm really glad to see you getting on with them.'

'I don't get on with them in the sense you mean, Mum, because we don't see all that much of them.'

'Don't tell me, you're all busy, busy, busy. Rushing out to work at the crack of dawn and coming home late in the evenings.' Her mum shook her head. 'Anyway, Chloe, if you want to keep your news to yourself for the moment, I understand. It's probably early days yet and it's as well to make sure everything is okay before you make the announcement.'

'What announcement? What exactly are you on about?'

'Chloe, it's obvious. You have that bloom about you. I'm really thrilled for you, but don't worry, I won't tell anyone. Your secret's safe with me, for the moment. Just don't ask me to hold my tongue for too long!'

'What secret?'

'The baby, of course!'

Chloe scarcely remembered driving home afterwards. Her mother was mad. She couldn't possibly be pregnant. There was no sense in trying to explain that it would be months before Chloe had

252

that kind of news. All the same, when another week passed and her period still hadn't arrived, and she began to feel nauseous at odd times during the day, she bought a pregnancy test. It was just to set her mind at rest, she assured herself, feeling a little silly as she went into her en suite and followed the instructions to the letter. She couldn't believe her eyes when the test was positive. She was still in a state of shock when she broke the news to Adam later that evening.

'What do you mean, pregnant?' He looked at Chloe in alarm. 'Are you sure?'

This wasn't the way it was supposed to be, her mind screamed. Not like this.

'Of course I'm sure.' She swallowed a sharp sense of disappointment. 'I'm expecting a baby, *our* baby. Aren't you happy about that?'

'How did it happen? We had barely discussed it. I do want to have children, but I thought we weren't having planning on having any for a long time yet…'

Me as well, Chloe felt like yelling. Never in her wildest dreams had she expected to fall pregnant almost instantly, and she felt cheated. Cheated of the months of anticipation as she watched her diet and popped her vitamins, and decided at leisure which gynaecologist to attend. Cheated of the months of making love in anticipation, of the excitement of watching and waiting and planning, the excitement of picking the perfect moment, creating the perfect scenario and breaking the news to Adam, an Adam thrilled with the idea of becoming a father…

Cheated of being the first to know. She found it hard to believe that she hadn't noticed the change in her own body, that she had been blissfully unaware. That someone else, albeit her mother, had spotted it first. Was that why she felt so tired and deflated, instead of being on top of the world?

'Oh, Adam, just think, a baby of our very own,' she began, dredging up every atom of enthusiasm she could muster and mentally crossing her fingers. 'Don't ask me how it happened. All I know is that it's much sooner than we expected. You must be very virile, you potent bastard,' she grinned at him, forcing herself to look relaxed and cheerful. 'This will really complete our happiness, won't it? We'll be the perfect little family.'

'I suppose if you look at it like that,' he smiled slowly. 'Me, a dad! It'll take a bit of time to get used to the idea. But so long as you're happy…'

'Of course I am. We have months and months to get used to it.'

When her expected date of mid-July was confirmed, Chloe realised that she had become pregnant almost straight away after stopping the Pill. She e-mailed Mel immediately. She wished that Mel was there with her so that she could tell her the news in person and watch her delighted reaction. She told her that although she'd missed the wedding, she had better be home in time to do godmother and she received a reply within a week.

From: Mel
To: Chloe
Re: Subject: Baby!

That's great news, Chloe, congrats. Hard to imagine you being pregnant, let alone being a mum! Look after yourself and have a great Christmas. It's summer over here and very warm.

Don't know when I'll be home, so don't count on me for anything.

Mel xx

Chloe felt deflated. It was far from the reaction she had expected. Her friend didn't sound all that interested in Chloe's momentous news. She was having a *baby*. Mel hadn't even bothered to include Adam in her congratulations. What did she mean, she didn't know when she'd be home? Just how long *was* Mel going to stay in Australia? Mel was notoriously bad about keeping in touch, but she'd rather not have got this particular e-mail, Chloe decided as she stabbed the keyboard and deleted the message.

Just before Christmas, she broke the news to family and friends. Her mother was overjoyed that the news was finally out in the open, her father quietly proud. Brian and Rory asked could they wet the baby's head, or did they have to wait until after it was born.

'You wait until it's born, you eejits,' Chloe said impatiently.

'Does it hurt?' Rory asked, fixing his glance somewhere in the region of Chloe's abdomen.

'I'm not even going to answer that question,' Chloe sniffed.

Henry was delighted with the news. When he called out to Abbey Manor to see them over Christmas, he brought a little golden teddy bear and said he was really looking forward to being an uncle of sorts.

Adam's parents were equally delighted. Peter and Eileen said that they couldn't wait to be grandparents again.

'You're fast workers, you pair.' Sandra looked at Chloe shrewdly as they lingered over after-dinner drinks during a Christmas get-together in Athlone.

'We didn't really see the point in waiting,' Chloe smiled, sipping her pineapple juice.

'No?' Sandra raised her eyebrows. 'I thought you would have liked more time to settle into your new house.'

'We're well settled in by now. We have everything just as we want it.'

'You're such a good organiser, Chloe, that you probably even know the sex of the baby so you can colour co-ordinate the nursery, right down to the light bulb.'

'How did you guess, Sandra?' Chloe smiled sweetly. 'The doctor told me it'll be either a boy or a girl.'

'Don't forget I carry a range of maternity clothes,' Sandra carried on. 'You can have a look at my catalogues if I don't have what you fancy in stock, and I can order it in. It's important to look your best, even when you're feeling like a gigantic piece of blubber.'

'I hope my sister's not trying to put you off, Chloe.' Diane breezed into the dining room in time to hear the last of Sandra's words.

'It's a bit late now if I was,' Sandra laughed shortly.

'How are you feeling, Chloe?' Diane asked. 'Have you still got morning sickness?'

'I'm fine,' Chloe fibbed. 'I really feel great.'

There was no point in mentioning that morning sickness was incorrectly labelled. It should be called morning, noon and night-time sickness. And there was no point in admitting that her boobs, delicately tender to begin with, were fast becoming a no go zone, with their acute sensitivity. So sensitive, in fact, that Adam could only admire at a distance. As for the exhaustion, it was totally unexpected and totally overwhelming.

But in front of Sandra, naturally, everything was great.

'Enjoy feeling great while it lasts,' Sandra snorted. 'You've months ahead of you yet.'

'Some people sail through pregnancy with no problems at all,' Diane said as she began to clear the table. 'The one sure thing, Chloe, is that by the time you have the baby, you'll have listened to reams of advice and heard plenty of gory details from the world and its mother. And by the way, don't buy a thing in the way of maternity clothes until you see what I have. I've tons of stuff I can loan you.'

Chloe tossed in bed that night beside a sleeping Adam. He was snoring contented little snores while she lay on her back and stared at the ceiling, one hand on her tummy. She wasn't ready for this. She wasn't ready for maternity clothes, for back-ache, for heartburn, for needing the loo so often, for getting fat and cumbersome. She wasn't ready to have a baby. But like it or not, she was going to have a baby in less than seven months' time.

The weeks slipped past and Chloe felt as though her body had been taken over. She turned up for her appointments in the antenatal clinic and joined women of all shapes and sizes going through the motions of blood tests and weigh-ins and blood pressure checks. She went for an ultrasound and was far too concerned with holding onto her bladder, terrified she would pee, to make much sense of what the doctor was saying.

But afterwards, when she looked at the fuzzy Polaroid picture of the tiny infant forming inside her, and when she awoke one bright February morning and felt better than she had in ages – no nausea and no wretched exhaustion – she began to think that maybe she could handle this after all.

She had planned the perfect wedding and the perfect house. Okay, the timing was a little too soon, but she would make sure she and Adam had the perfect baby. He would make a wonderful dad, of that she had no doubt. And she would be the perfect mum. And when she felt the first flutterings of life, just as the snowdrops blossomed in her patio planters, she was so excited she phoned Adam immediately. This was more like it. This was the way it was supposed to be.

By degrees, her tummy expanded until she had no choice but to start wearing looser clothes. True to her word, Diane turned up in Abbey Manor one Saturday afternoon with a suitcase full of maternity outfits.

'Take your pick. It's mostly tops and trousers. If you don't want anything, no worries,' Diane said cheerfully. 'There's no point in forking out for outfits you'll only wear for a few months. And believe me, you'll be only too glad to see the back of them.'

'Thanks, Diane. I'm beginning to balloon a little already. God knows what I'll be like by the end!'

'You'll be fine. You'll get your figure back no problem. Where's that brother of mine? Working as usual?'

'Not today, believe it or not. He's out playing golf, or dare I say, learning to play. Now that it's coming into the spring, he's hoping to take it up and go out now and again.'

'Don't let him neglect you. You'll need all the help you can get in the first few weeks after the baby is born.'

'Where's Megan and Hannah?' she asked. She would have liked to see Diane's little girls and to have seen them in her house, to get an idea of what it would be like to have children running around.

'They're gone to the kiddies cinema special with Colm. Then he's going to bring them to McDonalds. I escaped off for the day and I'm going into town to do some shopping, lucky me!'

As soon as Diane had left, Chloe tried on some outfits, twisting backwards and forwards in front of the bedroom mirrors, feeling proud of her tiny bump. It wouldn't do to get too big. No way would she turn into a gigantic piece of blubber, as Sandra had phrased it. She had, of course, a growing collection of baby and pregnancy magazines, which were full of glossy pictures of cherub-like babies and adoring mums, and packed with advice on diet and exercise, which she religiously followed. Her baby would have the best possible start in life, and that included a mum at the peak of her energy and fitness.

On Saturday afternoons she went into town and checked out prams and cots and buggies and fingered delicate baby clothes, awed by tiny little vests, filigree matinee coats and miniature bootees. She hired a painter and decorator and had one of the spare bedrooms decorated as a nursery, done in primary colours with a Winnie the Pooh mural painted across one wall. Kaz and Emma were very impressed.

Her maternity outfits were smart and stylish, courtesy of Diane and thanks to a couple of shopping trips where she couldn't resist a pair of maternity dungarees and an expertly cut charcoal suit. She went to antenatal classes with Adam; he practised rubbing her back and she practised her breathing. She learned how to lie with a pillow between her legs to accommodate her growing bump. And together they learned how to make love in a variety of different positions.

She felt sexy and desirable in an earth mother sort of way, her skin glowed and her hair was full and glossy. Summer was on the way, the weather was getting warmer, the days longer and longer. They were almost a year in their new house and soon they would have a baby to add to their happiness.

'No, I'm not taking a career break,' she said a hundred times in answer to queries as she began to clear her desk in Premier Elect in preparation for the months of maternity leave. 'I'll be back in action in no time.'

'No, I'm not too posh to push,' she said to Kaz and Emma as she discussed the merits of natural childbirth over a C-section.

'Yes, we can make love up to the very end,' she assured Adam. 'Once I'm comfortable, it won't harm the baby.'

She read up on what to bring to the labour ward and began to shop, picking up soft white vests, babygros and fluffy white towels for the baby. She bought a range of smart cotton nightdresses and pyjamas for the hospital. She pictured herself sitting up in bed, chatting to visitors while the baby slept peacefully beside her.

'Yes, Mum, everything's under control,' she reassured her mum as her due date drew nearer. Her bag was packed, with all the essential items on the hospital list and more besides, the nursery was ready and waiting for its tiny new occupant and Adam was on stand-by in the office, prepared to drop everything as soon as she went into labour.

Of course everything was under control.

Chapter Twenty-two

From: Adam
To: Mel
Subject: Baby

Mia Kavanagh has arrived safe and sound. Eight pounds, two ounces, dark haired and blue eyed. Mother and baby are well. Chloe asked me to e-mail you asap.

Adam

The words danced in front of Mel and she felt as though she had been thumped in the rib cage. When Chloe had e-mailed to say she was expecting a baby all those months ago, Mel had felt slightly shocked. She had done her best to ignore it, in

263

much the same way she had tried to ignore everything else to do with Chloe and Adam. But now
they had a baby daughter. Things were completely
different.

Up to now their marriage hadn't seemed real to
her. Even though Chloe e-mailed occasionally and
Mel had heard all about the wedding of the year
and the house of their dreams – Abbey what's its
name – and Chloe's pregnancy, she still pictured
the two of them in the flat in Harold's Cross. It had
been easier that way. She still imagined them in a
casual relationship, a relationship that could finish
at any moment, where Chloe just used Adam for sex
and Adam was happy to oblige. But a baby on the
scene, a flesh and blood baby girl called Mia
Kavanagh, eight pounds two ounces and dark haired
like her daddy, altered the picture completely.

She logged out of her e-mail account and checked
again for any other messages on the business account,
but things were quiet for the moment. Good time to
take a quick break, she decided as she went out to the
small canteen off the main office and began to make
her lunch. She cut a crusty roll lengthways and filled
it with tomato and ham. She poured fruit juice into
a glass, sat down at the table and began to eat.

'Penny for 'em,' Sean said and Mel jumped,
almost spilling her juice. He was sitting at the table
in the far corner, wearing his usual Levis and
cotton shirt, drinking a mug of tea, the newspaper
spread out in front of him.

'I didn't see you, Sean.'

'That's obvious,' he grinned. 'You're lost in thought.'

'I've just heard news from Ireland,' Mel said without thinking.

'Ireland? Do you still keep in touch?' Sean looked surprised.

'Now and then,' Mel admitted.

'Well? Good news or bad?'

'My – my friend has had a baby. A baby girl.'

'Good news, so. Would that make you want to be at home? Maybe make you feel a little homesick?'

'Homesick? What's that?' Mel shook her head. 'It would make me want to stay away, if anything.'

'You don't fancy being called on for babysitting duties, I suppose.'

'Babysitting? I never thought of that. Having a baby puts paid to your social life. I suppose it changes everything, really.'

'I wouldn't know,' Sean said. 'Lauren and I weren't that lucky. It didn't happen for us. Maybe it was just as well, the way things turned out.' He folded his paper, took his mug over to the sink and rinsed it, leaving it upside down on the drainer. 'I'll be gone most of the afternoon,' he said. 'I've a party of eight to collect from the airport. I think Joe's due back at half four…'

'Joe's due back at five and he has to do a pick-up down at the marina,' Mel informed him briskly, only too happy to change the subject. 'And Dave's to do a run to collect a group from the Skyrail.'

'And Mark? Where's he off to?'

'Don't worry about Mark, he's busy as well. Everything's sorted, Sean, off you go,' Mel grinned. 'I have all the schedules organised.'

'Where would I be without my able assistant?' he joked as he picked up the keys to his minibus and went out into the warm July afternoon.

Where indeed would *she* be without the likes of Sean Maguire, Mel wondered as she watched him jump into the driver's seat of the minibus, reverse out of the small parking lot and head towards the Captain Cook Highway en route to the airport in Cairns.

It was too nice an afternoon to be stuck in the office. Outside on Main Street, blue skies filtered through the dappled shade of the trees. Sunshine squinted in through windows and slanted across her desk. The overhead fan whirred, creating ripples in the warm air, and Mel was tempted to shut up shop and go for a jog on the golden four-mile beach that stretched the length of Port Douglas.

She wanted to go for a run to chase the thoughts out of her head, to feel the sand between her toes and the sea breeze tossing her hair. Running along the strand, with the turquoise sea on one side and the green shelter belt of palm trees on the other, with the span of the blue sky overhead, she could empty her mind, switch off her thoughts and just be there in the moment.

But she couldn't leave the office. Sean's minibus business was booming, drivers were coming and going all afternoon, so someone had to keep an eye on the schedules and answer the phone. And she owed it to him to hold the fort after all he had done for her. Throughout the afternoon she was busy making bookings and confirming schedules and reassuring customers. She was so busy that she managed to put all thoughts of Chloe, Adam and the baby to the back of her mind.

When six o'clock came, she switched over to the answering machine, locked up the office and headed upstairs to the second floor to her tiny, self-contained attic studio. She reached across to switch on the lights, but changed her mind and instead looked out the dormer window, out into the gathering twilight, past the line of palm trees where in the far-off distance the mountainous rainforest was a vast, inky backdrop.

Somewhere on the other side of the world it was a sunny morning in July. Chloe was no doubt queening it in a hospital bed surrounded by visitors, with her new baby daughter asleep in her arms. A self-important Adam was almost certainly accepting congratulations and well wishes. Mel closed her eyes briefly, as though to blot out the picture.

She heard the rumble of Sean's minibus as it rounded the corner into the parking lot and he manoeuvred it in readiness for the morning. She heard the cluck of the closing door and Sean's footsteps as he came around the front of the building, and in the twilight she saw the top of his grey head appearing far below her window as he let himself into the building. She heard him taking the stairs two at a time to his flat on the first floor. She pulled the blinds, blotted out the night and switched on the amber-shaded lamps.

She was just about to plug in the kettle when she heard Sean bounding up the remainder of the stairs to her bed-sit and he knocked on the door.

'Are you on your own?' he asked.

'Yep. All alone and not a lover boy in sight.'

'Any plans for tonight?'

'I'm going out to find myself a lover boy, of course.'

'Oh. Forget it, so.'

'I'm only messing, Sean. I'm not going anywhere. I'm too whacked after such a hard day at the office.'

'That's too bad. You should have a word with your boss,' he grinned.

'He never listens to me anyway. He's an awful slave driver.'

'He sounds like a right old bastard. You don't happen to fancy a drink, do you?' he asked. 'I just thought you might like to wet the baby's head, you know, your friend's baby.'

'What brought this on?' Mel looked at him quizzically.

Sean shrugged his shoulders. 'Nothing in particular. One of my regulars handed me a bottle of

Scotch whisky today and I just thought…'

'Sean, to be perfectly honest with you, I don't particularly want to wet the baby's head,' Mel blurted. 'But I could certainly do with a drink.'

'That's a good enough reason, I suppose,' Sean grinned.

'No strings?'

'Mel, I know you well enough by now,' Sean sighed. 'Of course no strings. I wouldn't dare suggest anything otherwise.'

Mel grinned ruefully. 'Okay, you're on. It's a long time since I tasted a drop of Scotch.'

'Well, allow me to refresh your memory.'

'Lead the way.'

Mel switched off the lamps and followed Sean down to his flat on the first floor.

Chapter Twenty-three

She had been astonished at first, that evening long ago in Cairns when Sean had suggested that he might be able to help her stay in Australia.

'Come and live with me,' Sean had offered.

'Live with you? No. That's not on.'

'I don't mean live with me in the true sense of the word,' he had hastily amended. 'I live in a flat over my minibus business in Port Douglas, but there's a small studio apartment on the second floor. Well, it's really a converted attic. It would make a grand little bolthole, and you could have it at a very nominal rent.'

A bolthole? An attic studio? Sounded perfect. Pity she couldn't take up his offer.

'My visa expires in a couple of months,' Mel

unhappily admitted. 'Even if I took a chance and stayed on illegally, I wouldn't be able to find a decent job, and I couldn't support myself.'

'Who said anything about staying on illegally?' Sean suddenly asked.

'I don't understand,' Mel frowned. 'There's nothing I can do to stay, short of marrying an Australian. And no, Sean, apologies all the same but I'm not that desperate,' she said, anticipating his next suggestion.

'Ah well, neither am I,' he smiled, letting the pause lengthen between them. 'Fact is,' he continued, 'I'm never going to marry again, not after Lauren. I'll never fall in love again. She was the only one for me. I was forty years old when I met her and fell in love. Something like that comes only once in a lifetime. I don't want to sound corny and I don't normally talk about it, but I'm telling you this for a reason.'

'Yes?' she prompted.

'You see, Mel, I'm never going to get involved with anyone again. So without any motive whatsoever on my part, there's nothing to stop you and me from making out that we're partners, beyond a little bit of red tape. That way, you get to extend your visa by another couple of years and I have someone renting the studio.'

'Hang on a minute.' Mel drained her glass of wine in one gulp and Sean obligingly poured her another. 'Are you suggesting that we pretend to the authorities that we're living together?'

'We would be living in the same building. Separate apartments, of course. Everything would be above board. You'd have your life and I'd have mine. I wouldn't intrude on you and vice versa. We'd have to kinda come up with proof that we're in a relationship, shared utility bills, for instance. Maybe a bank statement, but we could sort that out.'

'There's one thing I don't understand.'

'And what's that?'

'Why do this for me? I scarcely know you. I could be anybody at all. And in a way, you'd be tying yourself down to me. It would look like that from the outside. And supposing you *did* meet someone else? Supposing you wanted her to come and live with you? That would upset the apple cart.'

'Hold on, one thing at a time. I told you, I'm not interested in having a relationship with another woman. Full stop. Anyway, who'd have me now? I'm way the wrong side of fifty and I've a face like an old leather shoe.'

'Don't be ridiculous,' she grinned suddenly.

'Life is short,' he said. 'It's far too short, Mel. And I have this urge to give a helping hand to a fellow Irishman. Or woman, as the case may be. It might help to lessen some of the awful sins I've committed down through the years,' he grinned. 'Or dissolve some of the blots in my copy book.'

'Very noble indeed,' Mel smiled, her heart racing a little. Was there any possibility that Sean's plan might work? Maybe there was light at the end of the tunnel after all. Maybe she could go on as she was, living from day to day, heedless of what had happened in the past, careless of what might happen in the future.

'And another thing,' Sean continued. 'You remind me of the daughter we might have had. You're like Lauren, spunky and quick tempered. Besides, I've lost you your job. And I nearly killed you today.'

'Yes, you did,' Mel agreed.

'So why don't you think about it?'

'Maybe I will.'

'Atta girl. If you want to stay in dear old Ozzie, make sure you give it your best shot.' Sean gave Mel his business card and told her to contact him as soon as she came to a decision.

'I'm just thirty miles up the coast in Port Douglas,' he said. 'It was a sleepy fishing village when I moved there first with Lauren. Now it's a major tourist attraction, but it hasn't lost any of its charm. There are strict guidelines as to what can and can't be built.'

'Yes, I was up there a couple of times already, on the way out to the Barrier Reef.'

'You'd be able to pick up a job no sweat, so long as you're not too picky. Can't say I'd recommend you as a waitress, however.' He tried but failed to keep a straight face.

'Thank a bunch,' Mel answered wryly.

'Don't wait too long if you want to take me up on my offer. The sooner we get things moving, the

273

better. We'd have some red tape to sort out. Come up and have a chat with me any time, if you like. You could have a look at the studio and check out the living arrangements.'

In the end, it was a straightforward choice between getting on a plane back to Ireland or moving into the small apartment on the top floor of Sean's premises and signing a few forms. In the end, it was no choice at all.

On the day of Chloe and Adam's wedding, Mel packed up everything in Cairns and got the bus to Port Douglas. Look forward, she told herself as the bus twisted and turned along the breathtaking coastal road, taking her yet again to another new experience.

By the end of October, she had secured a four-year extension to her visa and was working in a bar in Port Douglas, filling schooners and middys of beer five nights a week. She had painted her compact attic studio a relaxing shade of sea-haze green, scoured Port Douglas for some dolphin prints for the wall and picked up some hand-thrown pottery candle holders and two amber-shaded lamps. She felt that nothing could touch her now.

She got used to the tropical summer storms, the thunderous rain that darkened the sky and poured with furious energy. She did her yoga stretches on the long, curving beach in Port Douglas, idled by the picturesque marina looking at the boats and the catamarans heading out to the Great Barrier Reef, and sometimes she joined them, feeling re-energised and renewed as she floated in the calm, silky water.

She e-mailed her mother and told her of her plans to stay. After a while she tired of working in the bar, so she took time out and joined a safari into the rainforest, finding herself silenced by the soaring canopy of leafy vegetation and the sight of pure, sparkling streams. When she returned, she got a job in a souvenir shop until she was fed up selling T-shirts and mouse mats and baseball caps.

She met people from all countries and all walks of life, and now and again brought someone back to her attic studio to spend a night or two, and just as easily said goodbye. When Sean's business expanded even further, she went to work for him.

'You badly need some organisation around here,' she said, shaking her head at the mountain of paperwork he had allowed to pile up. 'I don't know how you expect to run a successful business when you can't even decipher your own schedules. And you shouldn't be spending all your spare time stuck in the office. What's the point in working so hard that you can't enjoy any free time?'

'Maybe it suits me not to have much free time.'

'Don't be such a workaholic. You said it yourself, life is short.'

'Okay, you're the boss,' he said, handing her the keys.

'I'm only a glorified dogsbody,' she said when he insisted on reviewing her salary after a couple of months. 'I don't want any more responsibility, so don't pay me any more.'

'Who says I was going to pay you any more?' he answered back. 'I'm just making sure I'm getting value for money!'

'In that case, I insist on an impartial assessment,' Mel rejoined.

Although she saw him on and off during the day and she lived one floor above him, Sean kept his word and kept his distance. Sometimes he disappeared for a couple of days at a time, slinging a bag over his shoulder and zooming off on his Harley. By and large they led separate lives and they rarely socialised together. And as the months went on, and one year slipped into the next, Mel thanked her lucky stars that Sean Maguire had almost knocked her down on a street in Cairns and had unintentionally lost her her job.

She was taken by surprise the evening he knocked at the door of her studio and invited her to join him for a Scotch. As a rule he didn't invite her for a drink like this, but she gladly followed him down to his flat. She didn't particularly want to be alone. Not this evening. Not when thoughts of Chloe's baby girl were spinning around and around in her head.

* * *

Sean's apartment was relaxing and comfortable, with clean whitewashed walls, huge abstract colourful prints and an assortment of souvenirs and memorabilia he had accumulated on his travels. Scattered on the sideboard, on the small table holding a lamp and arranged on the shelf in the kitchen were various photos of him and Lauren.

'Catch a whiff of that,' Sean said, passing her a glass of amber liquid. 'Ten-year-old malt, the real thing.'

'Mmm, nice all right. But I'm afraid I'm going to ruin it with a dash of Sprite,' Mel said, going over to the sideboard and helping herself to the mineral bottle.

'That's criminal,' Sean objected.

'It'll be even more criminal if I get as drunk as a skunk, which is what happened the last time I drank neat spirits.'

'Sounds interesting.'

'That's all you're going to hear, so don't get too excited.'

'I'm just trying to picture you drunk as a skunk.'

For an instant, the scene flared in her head like the flash of a camera bulb. Adam was pulling down her pants. Her fingers were coiled in his damp hair as his tongue began an intimate search. She saw her startled eyes reflected in his as she lay across the couch in the flat in Harold's Cross. She remembered her sudden, physical need as Adam thrust deep inside her.

Mel felt dizzy and her drink slopped over the rim of her glass.

'Mel? You okay?'

She took a deep breath and steadied herself. She sat down on Sean's cane sofa and counted to five, then she took a gulp of the warming mellow drink.

'Yes, I'm fine.'

'You went as white as a sheet. You had me worried for a minute.'

She forced a laugh. 'And I've barely taken a sip.'

'Was it something I said?'

'No, not at all.' Her green eyes glinted.

'Anything to do with the last time you were drunk as a skunk?'

'If I was that drunk, how would I remember?' she challenged.

He threw her a curious glance. 'Can't have my valuable employee getting dizzy from a whiff of Scotch. Sometimes it helps to talk, you know.'

'There's nothing to talk about.' She looked at him clear eyed.

'No? You know what they say, a problem shared is a problem halved.'

'I've no problems,' she said lightly.

'Of course not,' he agreed, just as lightly. 'How could a grand Irish girl like yourself have any problems? Isn't the world your oyster?'

'Exactly.'

'Once upon a time, I thought the world was my oyster.' Sean's leather chair creaked as he settled himself down and nursed his glass.

'And?'

'I had Lauren, we had a happy life, and the future looked good. In a matter of months, that was all gone. And I felt terribly angry. Angry with myself for falling in love with her in the first place, and angry with her for leaving me. Can you believe that? I was angry with the best woman in the world because she got cancer and died.'

'I suppose that's a natural reaction,' Mel said.

He shook his head. 'I was one hell of a messed-up guy. And I bottled everything up until one day I finally exploded, and it wasn't pretty. Anger is a terrible thing. By the time you realise you're only hurting yourself, it's sometimes too late. The damage can't be undone.'

'Sometimes it's right to be angry.'

'Yeah, if it makes you get off your butt and do something. But if it goes on too long, it's like a poison.'

Silence fell between them. Mel stared out the window. Sean hadn't bothered to pull the blinds, but there was nothing to see but the darkness of the night, broken by the glare of the street lamp and the occasional headlights of a passing car.

'I'm sorry about Lauren,' she said after a while. 'It must have been awful.'

'She was the love of my life,' he said simply. 'I don't know how I managed to keep going, but somehow I did. Hell, you keep waking up every morning and you have to get on with it. And you have to find a way to make the anger go away before it turns on you.'

279

'And how did you make it go away?' Mel asked.

'It was damned hard. That and the guilt. At the time, I couldn't see any way out,' he sighed. 'But here I am, five years later, still trundling along. One day at a time. I've made a sort of peace with myself. If things get too much, I go off for a couple of days. You know, it's her anniversary today. That's why I asked you to join me for a drink. I just didn't feel like sitting here on my own.'

Mel was more conscious than ever of the blonde woman in the silver-framed photograph smiling across at them from the sideboard.

'You shouldn't be on your own,' she said quietly.

'I'll never fall in love again.'

'You can't say that.'

'After what I shared with Lauren? No way.'

'But no love lasts forever. It just isn't possible.'

'Obviously, Mel, you've never really been in love,' Sean smiled at her. 'Another drink?' he gestured with his glass and got up from his chair.

'Thanks, and again I'm going to destroy it with some Sprite,' Mel said.

'Your loss.' He said as he reached for the bottle of Scotch.

'I'm afraid I'm cynical when it comes to matters of love,' Mel said as she sat back with her glass. 'I don't believe you can meet someone and know that you'll love them for the rest of your life. Someone always gets hurt.'

'Of course people get hurt. I did things I still regret, and Lauren was far from perfect. We had our ups and downs, but we loved each other, warts an' all. And that's what loving is all about.'

Mel slowly shook her head. 'I don't know how anyone can make the decision to tie themselves down to one person. It's crazy.'

'It's a little crazy all right,' Sean tried to explain. 'You meet someone who means the world to you, who gives a new dimension to every part of your life. Of course it's a risk. But you feel you just can't live without them. It's something deep down in your soul that you can't deny. Sorry,' he shrugged. 'I'm sounding all soppy here and Lauren would be the first to laugh.'

'Lauren would be the first to tell you to get out and start living again, as in really living,' Mel insisted. 'You said I reminded you of her – well, take it from me, she'd be very annoyed with you for staying stuck in the past. Maybe you'll never fall in love again the way you loved her, but that doesn't mean you can't have close friendships.'

This time Sean's face broke into hundreds of tiny wrinkles as he smiled. 'Maybe that's what I need, a daughter like you bossing me around.'

'Any time you want some free advice or a kick up the ass, just give me a shout.'

'Sure thing.'

* * *

281

After that, they got together for a couple of drinks now and again. Mel still maintained that there was no such thing as true love and Sean insisted otherwise. Mel told him that he had better get a life and Sean said he already had the life he wanted, whereupon Mel told him he was looking backwards instead of forwards.

She laughed when she heard that the Australian authorities decided to relax the visa rules to allow a two-year stay under certain conditions. But it would have been too late for her and not even long enough, and she was quite happy with her Port Douglas bolthole, particularly now that Chloe and Adam had started a family. Ireland was most definitely out of bounds.

She sent Chloe a card for the baby and, feeling ridiculously nervous, she bought a little pink fleece with two Koala bears embroidered on the front, parcelled it up and posted it off. She heard about the preparations for the christening of the decade, then almost as though fate had decided that Mel deserved some peace of mind, there was blessed silence from Ireland for a while.

Chapter Twenty-four

The shrill cry pierced the night.

Chloe awoke immediately. Not again. It was the third time that night that Mia had disturbed her and she just hadn't the energy to get out of bed. Maybe Mia would go back to sleep. Maybe her crying would stop in a minute. After all, Chloe thought as she peered at the clock, she had been up with her just two hours earlier, feeding her and changing her wet nappy.

'Chloe!' Adam grunted as the crying increased in tempo.

'Yes, I know,' she muttered hastily. Adam had an important meeting at half past eight in the morning and he couldn't be disturbed. Good job she wasn't back in work yet, Chloe thought as she dragged herself from the warmth of the bed and went into the nursery.

She lifted up the warm little body of her daughter and her heart flooded with love. Mia's crying instantly stopped. Chloe wiped away the minuscule tears on her soft, silky eyelashes and held her close. She had thought she loved Adam with all her heart, but it was nothing compared to the fierce, raw emotion that filled her heart when she cuddled her little daughter in her arms. She was the most beautiful baby in the whole world and when she smiled at her with her little rosebud mouth, Chloe wanted to sit holding her forever.

'Chloe!' She heard Adam's voice again, but she was too tired to answer, too tired to move. She felt as though she was still asleep, caught up in some dreamlike trance, so she snuggled further into the bed.

'Chloe! I can't find my blue shirt. I left it out for the wash last week.' She heard his voice as if from a far-off distance, and this time she felt Adam's hand on her shoulder. 'Oh, forget it!'

She struggled to open her eyes, but it was impossible. Surely she had closed them only five minutes earlier when she had settled Mia down again? Why was Adam disturbing her in the middle of the night? She was dimly aware of him stomping around the bedroom, and then there was blissful silence. She eventually dragged herself out of bed at ten o'clock in the morning. Adam was long gone, her blonde hair was sticking out all over her head in true scarecrow fashion, and Mia was crying again.

When Kaz unexpectedly knocked at midday, Chloe froze. Which was worse, she hurriedly agonised, Kaz detecting that her kitchen resembled the aftermath of a bomb strike, getting caught in a pair of tracksuit bottoms with her hair all messy, or the fact that Mia was still in her nightclothes and waiting for her bath? The most important thing that registered amidst her confusion was the fact that Kaz mustn't be allowed in. The next most important thing that registered was the fact that come hell or high water, she would never be caught short like this again.

The doorbell rang a second time and Chloe forced a cheerful grin on her face and ran her fingers through her hair as she went up the hallway to answer it.

'Hi Kaz. Sorry I can't ask you in,' she beamed. 'I'm just about to give Mia her morning bath. She makes such a splash that I put on these old tracksuit bottoms,' Chloe gave an apologetic laugh.

'No worries,' Kaz smiled. 'I hope I didn't disturb you. I'm off work today and I was wondering if you needed anything in the shops, to save you the journey.' She was wearing a new pair of stonewash denims and a crimson sweater and she looked so jaunty and smart that Chloe suddenly felt ancient by comparison. Even more enviable, Kaz was going shopping. All by herself. Something Chloe had taken for granted a few short weeks ago, it now seemed like utter utopia.

'No, I'm fine, thanks,' Chloe answered, giving herself a mental shake.

'Then I'll let you get back to Mia.' Kaz stalled for a moment. 'Everything okay?'

'Of course. Why shouldn't it be?'

'Oh, nothing.' Kaz backed down the driveway. 'See you, then.'

'See you.' Chloe pushed the door shut with relief.

She was testing the water in the pink baby bath with her elbow, just as the baby magazines recommended, when the phone rang.

'Hi Chloe.'

'Hi Mum. I can't really talk, I'm just about to give Mia her bath.'

'Again? That baby of yours must be the most spotless baby in Dublin. I'm not trying to interfere, but you don't have to bath her every single day. You're putting a lot of work on yourself.'

'Babies need a daily bath with all those nappy changes and puke.'

'It won't make much difference to Mia if she gets a quick top and tail on that fancy changing mat you have, every now and again, instead of a bath. You're far too scrupulous, Chloe. She can't be all that dirty and it would save you some time.'

'I don't need to save time. I'm well able to manage.' And remind me not to ask you to babysit,

286

Chloe thought to herself. No cursory top and tail would do her Mia.

'When you go back to work, you won't have time to bath her every day,' Irene pointed out.

'Of course I will. I'll just have to do it when I come home in the evenings,' Chloe said.

Irene sighed. 'You're a glutton for punishment. Have you made any decisions about who's going to mind Mia?'

'I thought I already told you. It was arranged ages ago. The local crèche has her name on the list and they'll have a vacancy at the end of October.'

'I don't remember you telling me. That's something else that's all different nowadays,' Irene sighed. 'Crèches with waiting lists. Grannies aren't wanted any more.'

'Most grannies are out at work, like yourself,' Chloe pointed out. 'I'm sure the last thing you want is to be stuck in the house minding a baby.'

'Not if it were my grandchild, but I don't remember you even asking me if I was interested. The thing is, Chloe, I hate the thoughts of Mia being brought up by strangers.'

'She'll be very well looked after, Mum. I checked everything out and discussed it with Adam and I'm more than happy with my choice.'

'Don't forget, I'm around if you ever need me for anything. It's no problem for me to take time off work if you're ever stuck or need a hand. That's what mothers are for and I'd be only too delighted.'

287

'I'm sure we'll be fine, but thanks all the same.'

Her mother hadn't seriously thought that she wanted her to mind the baby, had she? It was out of the question. The modern crèche in the nearby shopping centre, with its up-to-the-minute equipment and specially trained staff, was surely a far better option.

She was halfway through bathing Mia, pouring the warm water down over the back of her dark, downy head and away from her eyes, as advised in the baby magazines, when she had a vague recollection of Adam looking for his blue shirt early that morning. She had intended putting it in the washing machine yesterday. But Mia had been sick in her cot, so naturally all her sheets and clothes had to be stripped and immediately washed. Maybe if she did the shirt straight away and threw it in the dryer, he'd be none the wiser. With a bit of luck he might think he had overlooked it in his hurry to get out to work that morning.

She lifted Mia out of the bath and cuddled her in her soft bath towel, tickling her gently on the stomach, loving the feel of her baby-soft skin and her contented chuckles. The last thing she wanted was Adam thinking he took second place to Mia. One of the most important pieces of advice she had read was that new fathers must always be included, not pushed to one side by the baby. And neither did she want Adam to think that she couldn't cope. Mia was over two months old now. Those frantic early days, when she had been almost afraid to bath her tiny newborn little body, afraid to change her nappy, when her fingers had felt so awkward and clumsy with tiny buttons and sleeves and velvety arms and legs, were surely behind her.

* * *

Chloe returned to work at the end of October, and on her first day back, Debbie Driscoll called her into her office.

'And how are you, Chloe? How's the baby?' Debbie asked. She was wearing a beautifully cut light grey suit that Chloe couldn't help but admire. Size ten, Chloe guessed, conscious of her own bulging tummy straining at the waistband of her skirt. Six weeks, she had read, before she could expect to get back into her jeans. The way things were going with her, however, it would be more like twenty-six weeks.

'She's fine,' Chloe answered blithely. 'She's three and a half months now.'

'So she's well into an established routine and over that messy newborn stage. Nice time to come back to work,' Debbie approved.

'Yes, I have her placed in the local crèche. It's very convenient.'

Chloe told herself to keep her mind on the job instead of remembering the sharp pain she'd had in her heart when she handed a gurgling, pink-cheeked

Mia over to the girl in the crèche. She wondered how soon she could phone the crèche to see if Mia was all right. Then she pulled herself up sharply and smiled fixedly at Debbie.

'It's very important that you're happy with your childminding arrangements. It would be impossible to focus properly on your job otherwise,' Debbie said, sounding businesslike. 'I know it'll take a couple of days for you to ease back into things, Chloe, but I wanted you to be aware of a few procedures that have changed in your absence. I also have some news for you.'

'Yes?'

'I'm moving into a position in Head Office shortly, which means my job will become vacant,' Debbie began.

For a wild, heart-stopping moment, Chloe had a vision of Debbie offering her the vacant role. Then she realised that things like that didn't happen in real life and she struggled to catch up with what Debbie was saying.

'They'll be holding interviews for my position in about a month's time, and I suggest you apply. You haven't really acquired enough experience yet, but it will be good practice for you and show the powers that be that you're serious about your career. You are still interested in further promotion?'

'Absolutely,' Chloe enthused. 'I'm not one of those working mothers who are afraid to seek promotion in case it brings more responsibilities,' she gabbled, anxious to let Debbie know that nothing had changed in her determination to get on, that she was still the same competent Chloe. 'I know people might think my priorities have changed, but having a baby won't interfere with my career. As far as I'm concerned, nothing has changed,' she said, her grey eyes looking determinedly at Debbie.

Debbie frowned slightly. 'Yes, well, don't expect to be on top of things immediately. It will take you a few days to get back into the office routine.'

'I feel as though I've hardly been away.'

'Good,' Debbie smiled. 'Have a go at the interview anyway. I'll be moving into the corporate area, Chloe. It's a promotion, of course. I'm glad to say that I'll still be involved with the customer service end of things, but on a higher level, so you'll still be reporting ultimately to me.'

'Congratulations,' Chloe said warmly.

Afterwards, back at her desk, she tried to read over some of the internal memos that Debbie had given her, but it was difficult to concentrate. She phoned the crèche and felt silly for having any misgivings when she was confidently assured that of course Mia was fine. It seemed a long time since she had kissed her goodbye and an even longer time until she could hold her in her arms later that evening.

She would get used to this, she told herself. It was just a bit strange in the beginning. She went over her conversation with Debbie. Debbie thought she should apply for her job. In other words, she was good enough to be promoted. And she had impressed on Debbie the fact that motherhood wouldn't interfere with her career.

Chloe felt proud of herself all of a sudden. It was good to be sitting at her desk once more, to feel in control, to feel that she was doing a worthwhile job, to know that Mia was being well looked after in the extensively equipped crèche with the fully trained staff. It didn't really matter that she'd had to get up at six o'clock that morning to make sure everything was properly organised, Mia had her first feed and Chloe got her bag ready for the crèche. Then she had her own shower and did her hair and make-up. Adam had poured her a cup of coffee, kissed them both goodbye and wished her the best of luck. He had left the house at a quarter to seven, as he had to get out to Dún Laoghaire for an important breakfast meeting.

There was no reason in the world why she couldn't hold down a career and manage a baby, Chloe thought as she fell into bed that night. After all, look at Debbie. Debbie was well and truly on her way up the ladder. Debbie had succeeded in coping with sleepless nights, and she had no trouble handling the demands of running a home, two children and a successful career.

Chloe was asleep before her head hit the pillow. She didn't hear Adam coming out of the shower, was oblivious to him getting into bed beside her, and even more oblivious of the hand that curled around her breasts before he quietly turned over in bed and began to snore.

* * *

'And tell me, Chloe,' the chairman of the interview panel said. 'There are fifteen applicants and only one position. What makes you think you have the potential to fulfil the job requirements?'

Chloe's mind went blank as she looked at the three faces on the other side of the table. She felt hot and cold all over as she struggled to compose her thoughts.

'Let me rephrase that,' the chairman said with an indulgent smile, but the look on his face said it all. The interview was fast becoming a total disaster.

'Have you anything to bring to the job, Chloe, over and above the experience and qualifications of those other candidates? In other words, why should we pick you?' He finished with another indulgent smile.

What a shitty question. You didn't want to appear boastful and bragging, but neither could you afford to undersell yourself. It was very hard to strike the right balance and very hard to come up with something clever to say when you had been up all night with a sick baby, when you felt so tired that you couldn't even think straight.

'Since I'm not acquainted with the experience

and qualifications of the other candidates, I can only speak for myself,' Chloe began, feeling the sweat prickling between her shoulder blades.

'Yes, go on,' the chairman encouraged.

'I would bring many qualities to the job,' she continued. 'Over the years I've developed excellent customer service skills, leadership skills—'

'Leadership,' the female interviewer with the navy power suit pounced. 'Could you give the panel some specific examples of where you have displayed your leadership skills in the course of your career, Chloe?'

* * *

'Don't worry about it. It's not the end of the world,' Adam consoled her.

'I know it's not the end of the world,' she blazed, 'but I feel such a fool. I was hopeless.'

'I'm sure you weren't that bad,' he soothed.

'Yes, I was. It'll be a long time before I'm considered for promotion again.'

'I suppose it didn't help that you had little or no sleep last night. I could have looked after Mia. There was no need for you to get up,' Adam pointed out.

'There was every need when she was sick all over her cot. I couldn't leave you to deal with all that mess.'

Adam shrugged. 'I did offer. And you should really have asked your mother to mind her today instead of bringing her to the crèche, just in case.'

'Thanks, but no. Can you imagine the fuss my mother would have made? Anyway, the crèche has my mobile number in case of emergencies.'

'What's the big deal about promotion, anyway?' Adam asked. 'Don't you have enough on your plate as it is, without looking for more responsibility? You expect too much of yourself.'

'I'm well able to cope,' Chloe said sharply.

* * *

Chloe bumped into Emma in the supermarket on Saturday morning. Adam had gone off to play golf. Business mixed with pleasure, he had said as he kissed Chloe on the cheek before going out the door.

'She's an absolute dote,' Emma admired Mia, who was strapped into the baby seat of the shopping trolley. 'Look at her cute little jacket and her friendly smile! You must bring her to Alex's birthday party.'

'Yes, sure,' Chloe smiled, delighted with Mia's first invitation.

'It's next Saturday, and you can come as well,' Emma said cheerfully. 'I'll need back-up support. That's if you don't mind lots of messy ice cream and jelly. Whatever you do, don't wear anything too decent.'

'Thanks Emma, we'll be there.'

'How are things since you went back to work?'

'Fine. It's great to be back in action again,' Chloe said airily.

'You're looking terrific. I wish I could look half as good as you in the supermarket on a Saturday morning!'

The birthday party was a great success. Emma had invited neighbours and relations. The house was decked with colourful balloons, and even though it was a crisp, chilly day in early December, there was a bouncing castle set up in the back garden. Everyone thought Mia was gorgeous.

'Her party frock is really fabulous,' Emma's mother admired the plum velvet dress with the embroidered collar.

'And you're looking terrific,' Kaz said. 'New hairdo?'

'Yes,' Chloe smiled and bounced Mia on her lap. She had picked up Mia's dress during a mad downtown dash at lunch hour on Thursday. Her hair had been another frantic lunch hour dash, and a hurried sandwich on the go, this time on Friday. Thanks to strict closing times at the crèche, late night shopping and leisurely visits to the beauty parlour were a thing of the past. Everything had to be squeezed in during her lunch hour. Still, it was worth it, wasn't it? She knew she was looking her best and Mia really looked cute.

'Chloe always manages to look terrific,' Emma said, handing around a bowl of crisps. 'I don't know how she does it.'

'I have to look well on account of my job,' Chloe said. 'I'm facing the public day in, day out.'

'I thought it was on account of your lovely husband.'

Chloe laughed and refused the bowl of crisps. There was no point in dwelling on the fact that Adam had gone off to work that morning in a huff when she had got up earlier than usual to do the cleaning and vacuuming.

'Forget about the house for once,' Adam had said as she slipped out of bed.

'I can't,' she had said irritably. 'I'm bringing Mia to the party this afternoon and if I don't get my jobs done this morning, the house will look messy all week.'

'So?' His arm reached out to grab her, but she evaded it.

'Maybe you don't care, but I don't want it looking like a tip.'

She regretted her outburst the minute she saw the look on his face. What the hell had she been thinking of? More than anything she wanted to go back to the days of wild, uninhibited lovemaking, to feel his blue eyes admiring her body. It seemed such a long time ago that she had even noticed the colour of his eyes. They rarely had time for each other nowadays. She shouldn't have pushed him away. So she slid back into bed, telling Adam she was sorry, but he had thrust the duvet aside and got up.

'I might as well head into the office,' he had said, marching into the en suite.

'Here's your husband now,' Emma said as the doorbell rang. Chloe's heart missed a beat. She watched his six-foot frame stride into Emma's kitchen, noticing afresh how much marriage and fatherhood, along with the success of his business, had matured Adam. His aura of careless authority was even more defined. Along with his dark hair casually slicked into shape and his compelling blue eyes, he looked like all her dreams rolled into one. How could she have been so stupid as to have had such a silly row with him that morning?

'Hey, Mister Kavanagh, Philip's in the living room if you want to have a drink with him,' Emma said.

'I'll join him in a minute,' Adam said. Chloe felt weak with sudden relief as he greeted everyone in the room and included her in his warm smile. He had obviously forgotten about the row.

'How's my little princess? Enjoying your first party?' Adam picked up Mia in his arms and tickled her on the stomach. They both looked gorgeous, her lovely baby girl and her daddy in his indigo jeans, and Chloe's heart flipped over. She stood up and joined them, fixing Mia's tiny plum-coloured hair ribbon, and her heart was full when she thought of the perfect family tableau they made. Somehow, it made everything worthwhile. Christmas was just around the corner, and next year she would be thirty, a milestone she wasn't particularly looking forward to, but more importantly, Mia would be a year old and life would get a little easier.

For she was back at work a few weeks now and the six o'clock start in the morning was fast resembling some kind of sleepwalking scenario. Some mornings her limbs just wouldn't move quickly enough, and red taillights all the way into the city centre seemed to be the main focus of her bleary eyes. Sometimes she felt an almost physical pang of loss when she handed Mia over at the crèche, smiling and still warm from sleep. Other times she just felt blank with exhaustion.

But so long as she behaved like the perfect working mother, and looked like one on the outside, did it really matter?

Chapter Twenty-five

The Christmas party was in full swing. Wine and beer flowed fast and furious and a medley of Christmas songs blared from the music centre in a corner of the pub. Mel put down her glass and grabbed Ruth and together they danced round and round in a mad twist of arms and legs and crooked paper hats until Ruth finally gasped and begged for mercy.

'Where the hell do you get your energy from, Mel?' she demanded breathlessly.

Mel laughed and tossed back her dark hair.

Claire appeared beside them, complete with a Santa Claus hat tilted precariously on her head and a full bottle of chilled Sauvignon Blanc in her hand.

'Here, girls, you're looking dangerously empty. Hold out your glasses.'

'Don't bother with Mel,' Ruth giggled. 'She's not one of us. She doesn't deserve to get hammered.'

'Hang on a minute,' Mel said with feigned grievance. 'Who asked who to this party anyway?'

'I'll offer you another drink,' Claire said. 'Don't mind Ruth. She's always like this.'

'Like what?'

'Kind of contrary.'

'Thanks a bunch.' Ruth was miffed.

Mel took a long sip of wine and let their banter flow over her head. She was used to the two girls from Cork by now. They were passing through Port Douglas and had struck up a friendship with Mel, treating her as though she was their older and wiser sister. They all seemed so young, Mel thought. So young and carefree. Well, so was she, Mel reminded herself sharply. Wasn't she?

She tipped back her glass and reached for the bottle of wine that Claire was still holding, pouring herself another drink. She went out through the back door of the pub onto the warm, bright patio, where the sun was warm on her skin. It was too hot to wear anything but a pair of cotton shorts and a plain pink T-shirt, even though it was a Christmas party and Christmas songs were floating across the beer garden.

She couldn't remember how many glasses of wine she had drunk when she first heard the words of the song. Something to do with Galway Bay. She listened closely for a few moments and there was no mistaking it, for even the lads lounging on the patio were raucously joining in the chorus. They were singing about Galway Bay and bells ringing out on Christmas Day.

Mel froze. She felt hairs rise on the back of her neck, and in spite of the heat and the party mayhem going on around her, something cold ran through her bones. Port Douglas disappeared and all she could visualise was the shingle beach at Spiddal, the grey seas of the Atlantic and the low curve of the north Clare coast floating on the horizon. She could hear the haunting cry of the gulls and smell the salt-scented air. She could see it all quite sharply. She could even picture exactly how it would look on a clear, fresh Christmas morning.

The song went on and the verse came around again and again and it was being sung even louder and more uproariously. She couldn't rid her mind of the vision or get the words out of her head, even when some of the partygoers started to dance, jigging around and around, and she shivered and felt as though the sun had gone in.

'You okay, Mel?' Ruth was looking at her anxiously. 'I didn't mean that about the wine. I was only joking.'

'What?' Mel stared at Ruth as though she were a stranger.

'Mel, what's wrong?' Ruth asked, looking a little alarmed. 'Are you feeling okay?'

'Of course I am, I'm fine,' Mel said sharply. 'What's the name of that song?'

'The song?' Ruth stared at her as though she had two heads.

'Yes, the song that they played just now.'

Ruth's face cleared. 'You mean "Fairytale of New York"? Is it one of your favourites?'

'No, I think I hate it.'

'Oh. Why don't you have some more wine and we'll all get hammered together. Claire, pass over that bottle. Now.'

* * *

It was nothing. There was nothing for her to worry about, Mel reassured herself when she eventually surfaced the next day. She'd had too many glasses of Australian white. It was just a fragment of memory that didn't really mean anything. She wasn't going soft in the head.

She strolled down to the Marina Mirage in the shimmering December heat and reminded herself that she was halfway around the world, well away from everything and everybody. She had already sent Christmas cards and had e-mailed Chloe, who had replied with a brief one liner to say all was well in Abbey Manor. She had phoned her gran and Alice had said that her parents wouldn't be home this Christmas. More than likely they would be home for good in the summer. But that news didn't bother her. Nothing bothered her, for she was a million miles away from everyone, after all.

303

January drifted into February and then March, and Mel had forgotten all about the Christmas party when the main doorbell shrilled one Saturday morning. She skipped down the stairs and called out to Sean as she went past his landing.

'I'll get it, Sean, stay where you are.'

And she opened the door and came face to face with Henry McBride.

Chapter Twenty-six

He looked different, though at first she couldn't figure out exactly what it was. Then she realised that he had let his spiky auburn hair grow a little and his face was fuzzed with three-day-old stubble. And she wasn't used to seeing Henry McBride in a pair of Nike trainers, never mind Bermuda shorts, and she certainly hadn't been expecting him to turn up on her doorstep in Port Douglas on a warm Saturday morning.

'Henry!' she gasped.

'Thought I'd surprise you.'

'Surprise? I'm shell shocked! I don't believe this!'

'Can I come in?'

'Of course, of course.' Mel opened the door wide and Henry stepped into the narrow hallway just as Sean came down the stairs.

'Sean, this is Henry. Henry, this is Sean,' Mel gabbled the introductions. 'What on earth are you doing here? Sean, Henry is an old friend of mine from Ireland. I just can't believe he's dropped in like this!'

'Just thought I'd visit,' Henry grinned. 'Hello, Sean, pleased to meet you. As Mel said, I'm an old friend.'

'Good to see you, Henry.' Sean extended his hand. 'Any friend of Mel's is a friend of mine.'

'We can't just all stand here,' Mel babbled. 'Come on upstairs, Henry, and I'll try and calm down. God, this is mad!'

'I'm sorry I have to leave straight away, but I have to do a run to Cairns. I'll catch you later.' Sean jingled keys in his pocket and made for the door. 'I'm sure you've plenty of news for each other,' he grinned.

'Don't forget, Sean. You have to be back in time to drop a group over to the Skyrail,' Mel called out hastily as she began to bound up the stairs. 'Henry! C'mon. How the hell did you get here?'

He followed her up to her second-floor studio, and she stood in the middle of the floor and just looked at him, her green eyes bright with amazement.

'Pinch me, for I must be dreaming,' she said.

'You're not dreaming,' Henry laughed.

'Sit down, sit down,' she urged, almost dancing as she crossed the room and pulled out a chair. He sat down and looked at her, a bemused expression on his face.

'You're a hard woman to find, Mel Saunders,' he said.

'How did you find me? How did you get here? And why the hell didn't you e-mail me? God, Henry, tell me everything. Will you have a cup of coffee? Or something stronger?'

'It's a bit early for something stronger. Coffee's just fine.'

'Well?' she questioned as she plugged in the kettle and took two mugs out of the press.

'I decided to take your advice, Mel.'

'My advice?' Her hands shook as she spooned coffee into the mugs.

'Yeah, remember, do something wild, shake off the shackles.'

'Did I say that?'

'You were always saying things like that.'

'Yeah, I probably was,' she grinned.

'So I left Ireland straight after Christmas, to go travelling.'

'I don't believe it! What about your apartment? Your great investment?'

'I'm renting it out for while.'

'Don't tell me you've left the secure pensionable job.'

'I've taken a career break.'

She sat down at the table and shook her head. 'Never in a million years did I think you'd break free.'

'It was easier than I thought,' Henry grinned.

'And how did you find me?'

'I had an idea you were still in Port Douglas. I wanted to surprise you, so I didn't e-mail. I've spent the last two days here, asking around. I knew if I kept asking for a tall Irish girl with dark wavy hair and green eyes that I'd come across you sooner or later. I was just hoping you hadn't gone blonde or shaved your head or gone off with some eco warriors to save the rainforest.'

'Thanks very much.'

'And I was just about to add on your fondness for doing yoga with a sleeping bag, only last night someone in the pub down the road told me to check out this address, so here I am!'

'Lucky me that you didn't have to give away too many of my secret vices! I used to work in that pub,' Mel smiled. After the initial shock of seeing Henry on her doorstep, she was beginning to calm down. Henry had no hidden agenda. He had merely looked her up on his way around the world.

'You're a great one for keeping in touch. You should be ashamed of yourself, Mel,' he teased. 'A couple of cards in as many years?'

'You know how it is,' she shrugged. 'You move on, you get caught up in different things. When you leave Dublin behind, you tend to wipe the slate clean, and sometimes you don't want any reminders.'

'Is that really what happened?'

'Sort of,' Mel said guardedly. Henry hadn't

changed. He was still as perceptive as ever. 'I still can't understand why you didn't e-mail and let me know you were coming. It would have saved a lot of bother.'

'I didn't want to make a big fuss,' Henry shrugged. 'And you might have told me to stay away.'

Mel gave him a steady look. 'And you could have chickened out at the last minute if you happened to change your mind.' She ignored his protesting shake of the head. 'Don't worry, I'm delighted to see you. And you have given me a surprise, a lovely surprise. So tell me, where have you been so far, and what are your plans?'

'So far I've been around Thailand, and I came through Darwin and Ayers Rock. I'm here for a couple of weeks, then it's down to Sydney and over to New Zealand before I head home in April.'

'Fair play to you. I'm impressed.'

'And what have you been doing with yourself for the past three and a half years?'

'Have you got all day?' Mel grinned. 'I don't know about you, but I need more coffee.' She went over to fill the kettle again and shook her head as she looked back at him across the room. Henry McBride in her apartment in Port Douglas. Never in a million years…

'I have to go down to the office for a while,' Mel explained as she poured fresh coffee. 'I'll be as quick as I can. I've some paperwork to do and I have to make a couple of phone calls, then I'm free

309

for the rest of today and we'll catch up on everything. How long did you say you're staying?'

'I've nearly two weeks here.'

'Brilliant. I'll have a word with Sean and get
some time off. Oh, Henry, we'll have a great couple
of weeks!'

* * *

'And the million dollar question, Mel – do you
think you'll ever come home?'

Mel made a funny face and put down her fork.
'Dunno, really. Thanks to Sean, my visa will last
another couple of years. Just look around you,
Henry. Who'd want to go back to Dublin when
you have surroundings like this?'

They were having lunch on the boardwalk of the
Marina Mirage and Mel felt that even the air
seemed charged with a kind of energy and adventure. The breeze was warm on her face as she
watched three youths climb into a speedboat, pull
on lifejackets and roar out of the shelter of the
harbour, cutting a foamy white trail on the surface
of the water. In the near distance, the Mossman
rainforest was a dark green enigma encircling the
harbour, giving definition to the clear blue skies
and reflecting in the silky waters of the harbour.
Boats of all shapes and sizes bobbed and eddied
along by the jetties. Later on, the great silver catamarans would return from the vast blue ocean,

unroll their gangways and disgorge travellers who had spent the day out at the Great Barrier Reef.

'It's lovely, yes, but so are parts of Ireland. Don't you feel homesick from time to time?' Henry asked.

'Nope,' Mel shrugged.

'D'you not even miss your granny in Galway?'

'I phone Gran now and again. She's fine, she always sends her love and tells me to make sure I'm keeping a diary.'

'What about your parents?'

'What about them?' Mel said sharply.

'I presume you have parents alive and well?'

'Don't most people my age?' Mel answered flippantly.

'As a matter of fact, I don't.'

'God, I'm sorry, I forgot. They died, didn't they, when you were young?'

'They were killed in a car accident when I was four,' Henry said calmly. 'My granny brought me up, and my aunt Kate. I was the apple of their eye – still am – and they spoil me rotten,' he grinned, his eyes warm in reflection.

'So that explains it.'

'Explains what?'

'Why you're always so happy and relaxed.' Mel wiped her fingers on her napkin and poured another glass of iced water.

'You surprise me, Mel. Usually when I explain that my parents are dead, most people are full of sympathy.'

'Yes, I'm sure they are. But you were very young. And parents aren't always good for your health.'

'No?'

'Sometimes they can really mess you around.'

'You're not by any stretch of the imagination talking about yourself?'

'How did we get onto this subject anyway?' Mel said briskly. 'Hey, you're on holidays, let's lighten up.'

She felt relieved when Henry followed her cue. 'Sure,' he said. 'What's next on the agenda?'

Mel scrunched her napkin and dropped it on her plate. 'We could take a walk up Wharf Street, along by Anzac Park and around by the point. You'll have a terrific view of the beach from there. Then tonight, I'm going to treat you to dinner.'

'Dinner at your place?' Henry looked hopeful.

'Yeah. The one thing all backpackers have in common is that they love the thought of a home-cooked dinner, and I make a mean spag bol.'

'Do you often feed the poor unfortunates then?' Henry asked with a knowing glint in his eye.

'Now and again,' she tossed.

* * *

She shopped in Coles while Henry went back to his hostel to shower and change. She bought water-melon and pineapple, minced steak, tomatoes, puree, onions, button mushrooms and garlic and basil, crusty rolls, mineral water and a bottle of Australian red.

312

Back in her studio apartment, she lit candlesticks in her hand-thrown pottery candle holders, put on a CD of Mary J. Blige – nice and low, not too loud – and left the curtains open to the calm evening, where high, fragmented clouds patterned the violet sky. She hummed to herself as she browned the meat, tossed in onions and mushrooms and poured boiling water over the spaghetti. She dressed in a pair of pale canvas jeans and a soft white blouse and waited for Henry to arrive.

He arrived promptly at eight, freshly showered, his hair slicked back and not a trace remaining of his three-day-old fuzz.

'We'll have a great party tonight,' Mel said as she opened the door to him, and he handed her a bottle of Pinot Noir.

'We don't have to drink it all at once,' Henry said as he followed her up the stairs to the second floor. 'Nice smell,' he said appreciatively as he stepped into her apartment.

'Will you do the honours with the wine, please?' She handed him an opener. 'Funny to think you have to come all the way out to Australia for me to cook you a meal.'

'Tells you how desperate I was!'

'Didn't I tell you I was a brilliant cook?'

'So, Mel,' Henry asked when they were halfway through their dinner. 'What's really keeping you out here?'

Mel was winding her spaghetti around her fork.

313

She stopped momentarily and frowned at Henry. 'I've already explained that Sean Maguire made me an offer I couldn't refuse.'

'C'mon Mel, there's surely more to it than that. Unless…you and him…?' Henry raised a quizzical eyebrow.

'Don't be daft. Sean's old enough to be my father.'

'So? What difference should that make? I'm sure he fancies you rotten.'

'No way,' Mel spoke a little sharply. 'Sean's wife died five years ago and he's still in love with her memory, still stuck in the past. So it's all above board. Anyway, you should know me better than that. I'm not into relationships, full stop.'

'I'm just checking. You're an old friend, after all. I wouldn't like to think you're stranded out here. You're not short of money for a plane fare, are you?'

Mel laughed. 'Jeez, Henry, you're scarcely offering me a bank loan, are you?'

'No, it's just something that crossed our minds.'

'Whose minds?'

'Well, when I was talking to Chloe—'

'So you were discussing me, you and Chloe?' Mel asked tightly.

'Of course we were. You were supposed to be linking me as we followed Chloe and Adam back down the aisle on the happiest day of their lives. Remember? Bridesmaid? I was the best man.'

'That must have been exciting.'

'Chloe almost had a nervous breakdown when there was no sign of you coming home, and she had to ask her cousin to do bridesmaid.'

She watched as he tore off a piece of bread and popped it into his mouth. 'I didn't think it was that big of a deal.'

'You do realise that you got away with murder, don't you?' Henry grinned.

'Yeah, I missed the wedding of the year, then the house move, and now the baby.'

'And the christening,' he said, 'Don't forget the christening.'

'And does Chloe seriously think I can't afford a plane fare?'

'She can't understand why you're staying away for so long.'

'She's just annoyed she can't show off her dream house and perfect wedding photos and darling accessory baby,' Mel said sharply.

Henry was in the act of raising his glass to his lips when he put it back on the table.

'Is there something I'm missing here?' he frowned. 'You're scarcely still annoyed with Chloe for marrying Adam instead of coming out here?'

'Nonsense.' Mel's voice was brittle. 'You were right on one point, Henry. I'm enjoying it all the more without her. I can suit myself and I haven't got to worry about anybody else. Anyway, that's all water under the bridge.'

'It didn't sound like that to me.'

'Well it is. So c'mon, drink up.' She lifted the bottle of wine. 'We've plans to make for tomorrow.' She poured Henry a generous glass and refilled her own.

Water under the bridge?

As if.

Chapter Twenty-seven

Sean insisted that she took a few days off work to show Henry around.

'Don't worry about the office, we'll manage,' he insisted. 'And what's Henry doing staying in the motel up the road? I told you before, I've no problem with any of your friends staying over.'

'Henry's different.'

'Why should Henry be different?'

Mel laughed. 'He's not that kind of a friend, Sean. He's more like a brother to me, which would be awkward in a one-room studio.'

'He must need his head examined,' Sean scoffed. 'Unless he's, dare I ask…'

'Are you joking? Back home, he practically has a girl for every night of the week. And it's usually a blonde bimbo with six-inch killer heels and a decent pair of boobs!'

'More fool him. No chance of a bit of romance, then?'

'None whatsoever. Neither of us believes in all that happy ever after crap.'

'Pity.'

'That's why we manage to stay friends,' Mel insisted.

They went out to the Reef, and as the catamaran bounced through clear blue seas under the bright blue sky, Mel asked Henry if he still had his aquarium, because pretty soon, she said, he would feel as though he was actually in one, only this was a million times better. She showed him how to adjust his face mask and how to breathe through his snorkel. She slipped into the warm ocean waters with him and they moved together just under the sunlit surface, kicking lazily with their fins.

'This is amazing,' he gasped as they tread water for a while out by the guide ropes.

'How does it make you feel?' she asked.

'It's like a whole new dimension. I can't explain really.'

'Neither can I,' said Mel. 'I come out here every so often just to get back to myself. It makes me feel, I dunno, kind of calm and peaceful.'

'And humble and full of awe,' he continued.

'You realise you're just a tiny speck in the hugeness, the vast magnitude of this tremendous creation,' Mel voiced her thoughts.

His tawny eyes locked with hers. 'Exactly what I was thinking,' he said. 'For once, we have agreement of sorts. There's a poem about that...let me see...'

'Poetry, Henry? I wouldn't have thought you're the poetry type.' She tried but failed to inject her usual bantering tone into her voice and found it hard to tear her eyes away from his. He was looking at her as though he could see right inside her.

'It's food for the soul, isn't it?' He regarded her steadily. 'Some of my favourite poems make me feel calm and peaceful.'

She was almost tempted to ask him what his favourite poems were, but she quickly dismissed that thought. Then she frowned and shook her head as though to dislodge the droplets of water from her hair, but it was really to break the connection. She adjusted the strap of her black bikini and asked him if he was ready to go again.

They fitted their masks and snorkels once again and swam slowly back to the diving platform. Every so often Henry touched her arm and pointed to something that caught his interest – an unusual plant with fronds dancing to the movement of the water, a school of tiny fluttering fish, a baby turtle scuttling across his line of vision. And she smiled back at him in the dappled water, glad that the unsettling moment had passed.

* * *

'When are we going white-water rafting?' Henry asked later on the week. They had just spent the day in the rainforest and now they were relaxing over a meal in one of the many restaurants that dotted Port Douglas. Henry was digging into a prime rib steak almost the size of his plate. Mel was picking at a chicken salad and they both had ordered cold beer.

Mel's eyebrows shot up. 'Is this Henry McBride speaking? The respectable banker?'

'I'm not as dull and boring as you think I am, Mel,' Henry said mildly.

'I never said you were dull and boring.'

'Maybe not in so many words, but you made it very plain to me what you thought of boring, respectable people who stay in the same job for zillions of years and have a mortgage tied around their neck.'

'And what brought this on all of a sudden?' Mel put down her fork.

Henry shrugged. 'I'd like to think I've changed a bit, changed my image.'

'I thought you were happy the way you were. Why should you want to change?'

'I suppose deep down inside I was beginning to feel irritated that I'm such a play-safe person.'

'Play-safe? Pull the other one, Henry. Someone with as many girlfriends as you could scarcely be called play-safe!'

He smiled across the table at her. 'That's the

whole point. Loads of different girlfriends, no commitment, no ties – isn't that a form of play-safe?'

'How?'

'No ties, no involvement equals no feelings, no hurt. Point proven?'

'You're making it sound like a mathematical equation.'

'You know what I mean, Mel, and you're just as bad as I am, in a way.'

'C'mon, Henry, I'm lagging way behind you when it comes to counting scores!'

'I'm not talking about numbers, I'm talking about attitudes.'

'You think I'm dull and boring in my attitudes?' Her green eyes flashed.

'You're the last person in the world I'd find boring,' Henry said. 'But you're afraid to take a risk when it comes to commitment.'

'I thought you agreed with me that marriage and all that crap was for the birds?'

'Forget it, Mel.' He shrugged and took a slug of his beer. 'Who am I to talk about taking risks? I'm the one with the safe job and the mortgaged existence. Just so long as you don't think I'm a perfectly dull old sod.'

'Why should you worry about my opinion? I'm just an old friend, and when you leave next week, God knows when I'll see you again.'

There was a moment of silence. Mel toyed with a slice of green pepper before she eventually picked it up and absently chewed on it.

'You're right,' Henry said. 'But seeing as I am an old friend, just tell me one thing,' he asked.

'Yes?'

'Why do you need to go out to the Reef to feel calm and peaceful? I'm kind of puzzled. Surely you have exactly the life you want? You work when you feel like it, you have sex when you feel like it, no mortgage, no kids, no real problems, no real ties. Isn't that why you jumped through hoops to stay out here?'

'Jeez, Henry, you're an awful swine,' Mel said.

'I just thought if there was anything on your mind…'

'There isn't,' Mel snapped.

'Don't take offence. I just thought that living the way you are, you probably don't have many friends out here, and if there was anything you wanted to talk about, well, I'll still be around for a few days.' Their eyes met across the table. Henry's were calm and reflective, and once again, Mel found it almost impossible to tear hers away.

All of a sudden, and to her horror, she felt like telling him about her innermost fears and hurt, why she fled Galway and still barely spoke to her parents, why she couldn't possibly return to Dublin, and she sensed that Henry wouldn't flinch or turn away, that he wouldn't think any worse of her for turning her back on her mother, wouldn't think she was a horrible monster for having sex with her best friend's husband. Putting it like that,

322

however, it really sounded awful. She looked at him across the table and said the first thing that came into her head.

'Do you know, Henry, your hair is getting long. If it gets much longer, I'd nearly class you as a hippy. How's that for a change of image?'

* * *

They went white-water rafting two days later. Mel was surprised by how much she enjoyed it. She liked it as much for the thrill of the plunge and the sheer rush of adrenaline as the expression on Henry's face, and the fact that he was there, sharing the excitement, sharing the moment with her.

They went running on the Four Mile beach and Mel, who was used to jogging alone, was quite happy to have Henry jogging alongside her. They ran along the wide shelter belt of palm trees and Mel pointed out the succession of luxury hotels which backed onto the beach, secluded privately behind the trees. They ran back along through the surf, along the edge of the shimmering turquoise sea that stretched infinitely away under the blue bowl of the sky. Mel felt as though she could run on and on forever.

Henry aimed a kick of spray and it dotted her pink canvas shorts, and she aimed a kick in return, splashing his navy Bermudas. They ended up having a water fight of sorts, both spattered in foamy spray, both laughing and catching their breath as Henry gave in and declared her the winner.

On his last night in Port Douglas, they sat drinking schooners of beer on the boardwalk of the Marina Mirage.

'It's quite pleasant here,' Henry said, looking across at the yachts and boats bobbing on their moorings. The harbour waters had turned to pinkish grey, reflecting the twilight luminescence in the sky. 'By the way, whatever happened to your old sleeping bag?'

'I left that behind. I never managed to do it yet, under the stars,' she joked.

'You don't know what you're missing,' he told her.

'I'm sure I'll find out sooner or later. You're going to love Sydney,' she continued. 'Sydney Harbour has to be one of the loveliest spots in the world.'

'I haven't really thought about it,' Henry admitted. 'I left Ireland with an open mind, no real thoughts on what to expect, and so far everything has been great. I thought Ayres Rock was fantastic. Much more immense than I expected.'

'Tell me this,' Mel asked. 'Did you climb it?'

'No. Did you?'

'Me neither. Why didn't you?'

'You tell me first, then I'll tell you.'

Mel shrugged. 'This will probably sound silly, but I felt there was almost something sacred or mystical about it and I didn't want to trample all over it.'

He looked at her for a long moment. 'This will probably sound silly, but that's exactly why I didn't climb it. I didn't want to spoil the mystery.'

'So that's something else we agree on,' Mel said. Too late, she tried to sound flippant, to make light of the moment, to break the intangible connection, because all of a sudden he was looking at her again as though he could see right into her very soul. Her soul? What soul? She caught her breath sharply. She scarcely had any semblance of a soul left.

'Wait til you get to Sydney,' she babbled, eventually tearing her eyes away from his. 'Make sure you do the Bridge climb and see the Opera House. I thought Sydney was brilliant. I'm really looking forward to going back some time.'

'In that case, why don't you come with me?' he asked suddenly.

'Nah, I'll leave you to it. I'm happy where I am right now.'

'You don't fancy coming along and showing me the sights?'

Mel thought for a moment. She looked at him in the violet twilight and suddenly realised that nothing appealed to her more than showing Henry the sights of Sydney. Which was surely all the more reason, wasn't it, for staying put.

'I guess I'll pass on this one, Henry,' she said lightly. 'Let me get you another drink and I'll fill you in on everything you need to know.'

'So, have you any messages for Chloe?' he asked when she returned with two more beers.

'I hope she's happy, that's all,' Mel said glibly.

Henry frowned. 'I get the feeling there's something…you're not still a bit sore with her, are you?'

'Don't be daft. I scarcely think of her,' Mel fibbed.

'Are you not curious as to how she's getting on now that she has a baby?'

'I'm sure she's busy, making sure the baby has matching dribblers and soothers.'

'I'll tell her you're asking for her. She seems to be very happy, anyway. It's all worked out for her and Adam.'

'That's great.'

'You don't sound convinced.'

'It won't last.'

'And what makes you such an authority on Chloe and Adam?'

'I'm talking about marriage in general,' Mel hurriedly replied.

'Are you an expert on that?'

'Henry, I had first-hand experience of what seemed to be a perfect marriage. But it turned out to be nothing more than a sham.'

'Your parents?' he questioned swiftly.

'Who else?' she said bitterly, taking a long, cool gulp of her beer.

'But how could it be perfect?' Henry said reasonably. 'No marriage is.' He looked so composed and relaxed, so sure of himself, that Mel suddenly itched to slap his face. Henry hadn't a clue. Something inside her bubbled up and over and she began to talk, the words spilling out in a tumbled rush. Anything, she thought, to take that complacent look off his face.

'The thing is, they pretended it was. On the outside, we had the perfect life. My parents were the perfect couple and we were better than everyone else was. I was an only child and I had to be Little Miss Perfect, brilliant in school, class prefect, top marks all the time. I thought it was so important to do everything right and uphold the proud family tradition. You've no idea how hard I worked in school and how my classmates kept their distance from me. Even in university I worked hard and got good results because I was determined to do my parents proud and keep up the high standard.'

'That's fair enough,' Henry said mildly. 'Nothing wrong with trying to do your parents proud.'

'Oh yeah?' Mel challenged. 'And what do you do when you come home unexpectedly in the middle of the afternoon and catch your father having sex with his secretary? In the perfect marital bed?'

Chapter Twenty-eight

For a long moment, Henry was silent. Mel was beginning to wonder if he had heard her, if she had actually voiced the words out loud, when he spoke.

'You've never forgiven him.' He was still quite calm and relaxed, she realised. He didn't look as though she had just given him shocking news. And he certainly didn't look as though she had made even the slightest dent in his composure.

What the hell made him tick anyway?

'That's beside the point,' Mel began heatedly. 'He was living a lie. My mother was living a lie. And I was busting my guts to be the perfect daughter and get top marks in college. No boyfriends, no social life. They made a right fool of me. So it goes beyond all that forgiveness crap.'

'And that's why you're hiding out here in Australia.'

'Don't be ridiculous. I'm not hiding,' Mel scoffed.

'No?'

'It happened ages ago, Henry.'

'Like when?'

'I had just started third year. So I dropped out of college, left Galway and went to Dublin.'

'In other words, you ran away.'

'You hardly think I was going to stay under their roof. Although my mother was in bits when I found out. World War Three had nothing on it.'

'Did she know about – about your father's affair?'

'Yes, she did,' Mel sighed. 'She was ignoring it, hoping it would go away. We had just been on our annual skiing holiday. We used to go every year from the time I was about ten and play perfect happy families. But this time I kind of sensed some undercurrents between them. Then when I...when I found out, it brought everything out in the open. I suppose I upped and ran just when she needed me to give her some moral support.'

'So what happened? They split up?'

'My mother stayed with him, believe it or not. She told me it was just a once off, a temporary madness, and she wasn't going to throw away twenty-five years of marriage just for that. If I had remained on in Galway, I could have helped her to make a fresh start.'

'You can't beat yourself up over that, Mel. Your mother's an adult, capable of making her own decisions.'

Mel shook her head. 'I can't believe she wanted to stay with him, after he betrayed her like that. Things might have been different if I hadn't run off.'

'C'mon, let's go for a walk.' Henry drained the last of his beer. Mel threw her cardi over her shoulders, picked up her bag and scraped back her chair. They strolled along the boardwalk, away from the piped music, the groups of tourists sitting outside the brightly lit restaurants and away from the bursts of conversations and laughter. When they reached the perimeter, they leaned on the wooden railings and looked out across the harbour at the boats and yachts caught in twinkling lights that spilled out into the calm, inky blackness. Mel felt the sea breeze, cool and refreshing on her face, and took a few deep breaths and tried to clear her thoughts.

'My parents went abroad soon afterwards,' Mel told Henry. 'My father was offered a great job in the sister company of the electronics firm where he's one of the directors. My mother went with him. She saw it as a chance to make a fresh start. Right now they're in Cape Town. So it's all done and dusted. Past history.'

'Past history?' Henry questioned, turning to look at her in the twilight.

'Yeah.' Mel avoided his eyes. His direct gaze was unnerving her. 'As I said, it happened ages ago. I don't really know why I bothered dragging it up, an old family skeleton,' she half laughed, half shrugged.

'Do me a favour and just forget I ever mentioned it. I must be boring you silly talking about my wayward family, when we really should be making plans for your last day.'

'Hold on a minute, Mel.' Henry threw a casual arm around her shoulders.

Mel froze.

'Don't get all up in a heap,' he cautioned. 'Just hear me out.'

She was practically as tall as Henry and his face was almost on a level with hers as she turned to him.

'I'm not one for picking over the bones of old family skeletons,' he said, 'but I get the feeling that this one is far from done and dusted.'

'What do you mean?'

'You've never really faced up to it, have you? You ran away.'

'It was the only thing I could do,' Mel protested.

'Yeah, sometimes in the heat of the moment you need to get away, get some space for a while. Then you need to sort it out in your head. Sounds to me, Mel, like you've never sorted it out, like you've never forgiven your father.'

'So?'

'I'm sure you were hurting badly at the time; it must have been a shock. But you can't hold his actions against him forever. You need to let go and move on.'

'You don't know what it was like, Henry, always living up to his high expectations, always trying to be the perfect daughter, trying to be the best.'

'There's nothing wrong with trying to be the best.'

'He made out he was better than everyone else, and then I find him screwing his secretary. What kind of betrayal was that?'

'Can't you see, Mel, that it doesn't reflect on you? You worked hard, did well in school, got into college, but that's not something to be angry about or something to regret. Okay, so your father was cheating on your mother, that's hard to take, I agree. But that's a separate issue. They're adults and you can't solve their problems.'

'No, but it affected me. I couldn't continue on in college.'

'Yes, of course it affected you, but you could have chosen to rise above it all. You're your own person, responsible to yourself. You could have stayed on in university, moved into a flat or something. I bet you dropped out of college to spite your father, to hurt him for upsetting you. In those kinds of scenarios, you only end up hurting yourself,' he finished softly.

Mel moved back abruptly, out of the reach of Henry's arm.

'What did you study, philosophy or something? How come you think you know all the answers?'

'I don't know all the answers,' Henry said, 'but I think you're still angry with your father, and in that sense you're tied to the past, Mel, just as much as

Sean Maguire is. You can't control your parents' actions any more than they can control you. And you can't go around thinking all marriages are doomed on the basis of your parents' experience.'

'And what makes you the great expert on life and love?' Mel sneered. 'I suppose you think infidelity is okay?'

'No, I don't think it's okay. But depending on the circumstances, some marriages can overcome it, just as they can overcome other types of problems.'

'Don't be ridiculous, Henry. We're talking about being unfaithful here.'

'So? Look around you. Nobody's perfect, Mel. Otherwise the world would be dead boring. You have to live and let live.'

'Live and let live,' she echoed. 'And it's okay to be disloyal.'

'Come on, Mel, that's not what I said. Grow up. You're beginning to sound like a tiresome sixteen year old and not an adult in charge of her life.'

'This is a brilliant conversation.'

'I'm not getting anywhere with you, am I?'

'And where exactly did you expect to get?' she snapped. 'You don't understand, Henry. You bloody well don't know the half of it.' Her voice wobbled and she turned away from him and gripped the smooth wood of the handrail and stared out across the shadowy harbour.

Her own words echoed in her ears. A once off. A temporary madness. Infidelity. Oh, God. Just as well Henry didn't know the half of it. The sooner he was gone, the better. If he stayed around Port Douglas much longer, God only knows what else she'd come out with, what other can of worms would be opened. She had said more than enough already. 'Maybe it's just as well that you're heading off tomorrow,' she continued, and now there was a cold edge to her voice. 'I don't think I could take any more of Henry McBride's school of positive thinking.'

'I'm only trying to help,' Henry said amicably.

She still hadn't pricked his calm composure, hadn't unsettled him in any way.

'For the last time, I don't need any help,' Mel fumed. 'I'm quite happy the way I am. So please get off my back.'

'Okay so, I think get the message. Loud and clear.'

She felt a moment of regret, a moment of remorse when she heard the tone of his voice. But it was better this way.

She was relieved that the following day was his last day. They went for a final stroll along the beach in the warm sunshine.

'Fancy coming out to the airport?' he asked. 'Sean's taking me in his minibus.'

'No thanks, Henry, I don't think so. Airport farewells and all that just aren't my scene.' Her green eyes were perfectly clear.

'I guessed as much,' he hesitated, his eyes searching hers. She thought he was going to say something, and she could feel herself stiffen in anticipation, but he must have noticed her reaction, for he laughed and ruefully shook his head, tipped her playfully on the shoulder and said he'd race her to the steps at the end of the beach.

After a quick, breathless run on the golden sand, they said goodbye. Henry was going back to the hostel to finish his packing. Mel told him she was going to stay on the beach for a while. Henry pulled her close and hugged her briefly and she felt the solidity of his chest against her and his arms around her. Somehow her nose got in the way when he went to kiss her, and they ended up bumping faces and cheeks, Mel's face soft and curved against the hard planes of his.

'See you around sometime.' He gave her a lop-sided grin.

'Yeah, sometime,' she smiled in return. She kicked at the sand, sending up a golden, grainy cloud, then turned and began to stroll down the beach as he stuffed his hands into the pockets of his jeans and walked away.

Chapter Twenty-nine

Sean found her sitting in the darkness of her room.

She heard him returning from his final run, heard the slam of the minibus door, and soon after, his tread on the stairs. And even when she heard him coming up to her second-floor landing, she didn't move from her seat by the window, so when he knocked lightly and put his head around the door, he let in a flood of light from the passageway and she blinked.

'What the hell are you doing, sitting in the dark?' Sean barked.

'Jeez, Sean, you don't need to roar at me like that,' Mel said.

'You gave me a fright, that's all. What's up?'

'There's nothing up. And I wasn't sitting in the dark. There's still some light in the sky and the moon has just come up.' It was a pale moon surrounded by cobwebby clouds, not very bright just yet, just barely a glimmer.

'It looks pretty dark to me,' Sean said. 'I have a pressie for you, so you'd better switch on a lamp or something.'

'A pressie for me?' Mel leaned across and turned on a lamp, illuminating a corner of the room, and Sean closed the door behind him

'Henry asked me to give you this.' He handed her a small packet. Wordlessly, Mel took it from him and left it on the shelf beside the lamp.

'Did he get off okay?'

'Yep, most likely he's halfway to Sydney by now.'

Sean looked at Mel, concern evident in his eyes. 'I hope you're not sitting here alone in the dark because you're missing him.'

Mel shook her head. 'I told you, he's not that kind of a friend.'

'Yeah, so you said.'

'Anyway, I'm glad he's gone,' she said tonelessly.

Sean's eyebrows shot up. 'Really?'

'Yeah, he was doing my head in, butting in where he wasn't wanted, thinking he had the answer to everything.'

'Ah, I see,' Sean said thoughtfully. 'In other words, he was being a real friend.'

'What do you mean?' Mel frowned.

'He must care enough about you to risk getting his head chopped off.'

Mel's green eyes darted an angry glance at him. 'I don't think I even want an explanation for that remark.'

'All I meant was he's the kind of friend who cares enough to try getting through that invisible barbed wire fence you have around you. Takes some guts to do that.'

'You don't know what the hell you're talking about.'

'No, I don't know the ins and outs of your life, Mel,' Sean agreed. 'But I can spot a barbed wire fence from about a mile.'

'Just go away, Sean.'

'No chance.' To Mel's acute discomfort he pulled across a chair and straddled it, resting his elbows against the back of the chair and facing her directly.

'I told you, leave me alone,' she said.

'If you think I'm leaving you here to wallow in self-pity, you've another thing coming.'

'Self-pity?' Mel snorted. 'I'm not feeling sorry for myself.'

'Don't forget, I recognise the signs. I was all too familiar with them myself.'

'So you're another expert on life and love,' Mel sneered.

'I should hope so. I had ten long years of living and loving.'

'And where exactly did that get you?' she asked heatedly. 'What good did it do you in the end?

Lauren's gone and you're clinging to the memory of a ghost.'

'That's more like it. Now you're sounding a bit more like my spunky Mel,' Sean smiled.

'I mean it, Sean,' she persisted. 'What's the point in thinking you're in love, of being in love, when after a few years it ends in tears and hurt?'

'It doesn't end after a few years. Real love never ends.'

'I never heard of anything so slushy,' Mel said vehemently. 'You'll be telling me in a minute that you go to mass every Sunday.'

Sean grinned, his face covered in creases, his blue eyes glinting. 'Where do you think I head off to at ten o'clock of a morning? Seriously though, Mel, the years I had with Lauren were the happiest of my life, and no matter how awful I felt after she died, no matter how terrible it was, I've no regrets. I'd do it all over again.'

'Even if it meant you spent the rest of your life looking backwards?'

'How come we got talking about me anyway?' Sean asked.

'You're a great one to talk about barbed wire fences,' Mel pointed out. 'You've one about six feet high moulded around yourself.'

'I told you, I know exactly what they look like. I also know what they do to you. All the more reason why I don't want to see you following me down the same old backwards track.'

339

'You must have been talking to Henry,' Mel shot.

'Hand on my heart, Mel, I wasn't talking to Henry about anything more important than the weather and the flying time to Sydney.' He paused for a moment and look at her curiously. 'But from the sound of it, you were obviously discussing me.'

Mel looked flustered.

'Is that what Henry said?' Sean persisted. 'That you're following the same old track as me?'

'No, not quite,' Mel said.

'What, then?'

There was silence in the room, except for the sound of the breeze rustling the trees outside on the street. Somewhere down the road a car door slammed and an alarm was activated. Finally, Mel spoke.

'Henry has this idea that I'm stuck in the past, just as much as you are,' she quietly said.

'And are you?'

'How could I be? Didn't I have the guts to up sticks and come halfway across the world?'

'Some people would call that running away.'

'Don't you start, Sean.'

'Well, whatever about me, that's one thing,' Sean sighed. 'I'm an old dried-up fogey. But you're young. You've your whole life ahead of you, full of living and loving. The whole world is out there for you, to grab what you want.'

'Yeah, sure.'

'Wake up, Mel! You do have a choice. You can stay here and quietly fester in the backwater of

340

things, or you can go on out there and come to grips with the life you really want.'

'Maybe I'm happy here. Maybe this is what I want,' Mel said.

'Could be,' Sean agreed. 'And perhaps Henry's wrong. Perhaps, even, you're not sitting here right now with a funny little ache in your heart.' He looked at her for a long moment and she was the first to look away.

'You have a choice as well,' she eventually pointed out. 'You said you and Lauren really loved each other, didn't you?'

Sean nodded wordlessly.

'Then surely the last thing she'd want is to see you living all alone for the rest of your life. Maybe you'll never love anyone the way you loved her, but you can't decide to lock yourself away forever.'

'Come off it, Mel,' he said resignedly. 'That's easier said than done. Look at me. I'm no oil painting. What have I got to offer? And who in their right mind would want me?'

She saw it in his eyes then, the lonely place his life had become. She saw the prospect of years of emptiness ahead. Afterwards she couldn't recall who moved first. She remembered asking Sean to hold her close, to give her a hug, to ease the funny little ache in her heart. She remembered reaching to touch his weather-beaten face and feeling his skin with her fingers and turning to kiss his cheek, and then his mouth. She remembered the way he

341

smiled in the amber lamplight, the way he softly sighed as she removed her jeans and T-shirt and reached to unbuckle his belt.

And it was different from anything she had ever known before. This was no lustful, urgent coupling, no heated empty embrace. It was something far beyond – a quiet sharing of hands and bodies, a calm soothing which smoothed the ruffled edges of her mind. A once-off healing she knew would never be repeated. Afterwards she lay peacefully in her bed as Sean pulled his jeans back on, kissed her gently on the forehead, tucked the bedclothes around her and went quietly down the stairs.

The following morning she opened the present from Henry. It was a little fluffy dolphin, grey with a white underbelly and a black shiny pellet for a nose. She shoved it away in a corner of a press.

As March and April slid past, Mel felt as though it was taking all her energy to live for the moment, that it was far more of an effort to glide smoothly through the days and focus on the here and now. She found she couldn't walk on the beach any more without thinking of Henry and his annoying remarks. She couldn't sit by the Marina Mirage and watch the catamarans heading out to the Reef without hearing his voice in her head, telling her to grow up. To hell with him. Thank God she had told him to get off her back. He wouldn't look her up again in a hurry. One evening, in a fit of pique, she e-mailed him and asked him to dispose of her belongings in whatever way he saw fit.

She toyed with the idea of going back to Sydney. She could blend into the casual anonymity of Bondi, with its seething hordes of backpackers from all over the world, and pick up the threads of her transient lifestyle once more. She tentatively mentioned it to Sean. He said he was going to sack her anyway and turf her out of her accommodation, anything to force her to move on and go forward with her life. She told him she had intended to leave anyway. He didn't want her in his hair, not when he was getting friendly with Joan, the new waitress in the seafood restaurant down the road.

'You should be okay with your visa for another while,' he said.

'Don't worry, Sean, I'll sort something out,' she grinned cheerfully.

'Is Henry in Sydney, by any chance?'

'God, no. Not now. Why?'

'I just thought you might be catching up with him, that's all.'

Mel laughed. 'And suffer another load of his interfering advice? No thanks! I'm going back to Sydney to blend in with the crowds, and to do exactly as I please. Henry McBride can get lost in a jungle somewhere, as far as I'm concerned.'

Yet she stalled when it came to booking her flight. She awoke, disturbed by her dreams, in the middle of the night and lay sleepless in bed with thoughts skittering around her in her head,

343

thoughts she was afraid to give voice to. She even checked out flights to Sydney on the internet, but hesitated when it came to booking one. During one of her sleepless nights, as she looked up into the dark Australian sky and watched the pin prick glitter of stars strewn across the southern depths, she finally surrendered and gave space to her innermost thoughts. Deep down inside, she wanted to go home. Back to Dublin, back to Ireland. She was tired of flitting from place to place, from job to job, from lover to lover. Most of all, though, she was tired of running away. It was a relief to finally face it, to voice it to Sean, to have it out in the open.

'Look, Mel, you have to grab what you want from life,' he advised. 'Don't be afraid. And don't waste time the way I did. Joan and I...I guess you could say we're very good friends. And it's all thanks to you. I owe you one.'

'I'm glad you're happy, Sean,' she said, her green eyes suddenly misty as he gave her a quick hug, and she felt a catch in her throat.

Before she changed her mind again, she booked her long-haul flight, Cairns International to Singapore Changi to London Heathrow, then finally Dublin. She wrote to her gran and sent a brief e-mail to her parents. And just in the nick of time, she remembered to send Chloe a birthday card. She would be thirty soon, surely a milestone.

She began to clear her things and pack her rucksack one last time, ruthlessly now in view of the long journey. But she found space for the grey fluffy dolphin with the white underbelly and the black pellet nose.

She wondered if she was making the biggest mistake of her life.

Part III

Chapter Thirty

On the bright June morning of her thirtieth birthday, Chloe just wanted to turn back time. And it wasn't because she regretted leaving her twenties. Suddenly, today, that milestone was totally irrelevant.

She entered the hotel where the Premier Elect workshop was being held, and for once in her life she ignored her gathering colleagues and the buzz of conversation in the conference room. She squiggled an illegible signature on the attendance sheet, stared blankly for several seconds before eventually spotting her nametag and slunk anonymously over to her designated seat. She stared vacantly at the flipcharts and projection screen placed at the top of the room.

She wondered how the hell she was going to get through the day.

'Good morning, Chloe! Seems like I'm sitting next to you.' A cheerful voice dragged her back to reality, and Tara Conroy pulled out the adjacent chair.

Chloe immediately wished she had stayed at home.

Promotion had made a new woman out of Tara. Her sleek dark hair was styled to obedient precision, and her perfectly proportioned figure managed to make even her dark green uniform look alluring. Naturally, she oozed vitality, energy and happiness. And naturally she was somehow sitting next to Chloe, on a day when she felt her whole world was falling asunder.

'Hi Tara,' Chloe replied politely, shifting her chair slightly to make more room for Tara at the table.

'Haven't seen you in ages,' Tara grinned, opening her black leather briefcase and taking out her mobile phone and a bottle of Lucozade. 'Our big day out. Beats being stuck in the office, I suppose. It doesn't seem a year since our last regional workshop.' She looked quizzically at Chloe. 'I don't seem to remember you here last year?'

'No, I was on maternity leave.'

'Oh, that's right. How's the baby?'

'Mia's eleven months now.'

'Knowing you, Chloe, I'm sure you're a natural.'

'Of course,' Chloe said airily.

'I really admire women like you who can handle motherhood on top of a career,' the cheerful twenty-something gushed. 'It must be quite a challenge to multitask successfully. Business is so demanding nowadays, isn't it? And motherhood deserves quality time. I intend to concentrate on my career first and get really well established. Then maybe later on…' She gave Chloe a confident smile.

Chloe's face felt frozen.

'There's quite a turn-out this morning,' Tara continued. 'Debbie is our facilitator today, so we're in for an interesting day.'

'Good morning everybody,' Debbie said, raising her voice against the murmur of conversation in the conference room. 'Our workshop today will discuss customer advisory operations and brief you on the innovations we hope to introduce over the coming twelve months,' Debbie announced. 'We'll start the morning with our introductions…'

Debbie Driscoll. Of all days to be surrounded by dazzling go-getters. Chloe wanted to cry.

'Chloe?' Debbie's voice registered in a corner of her brain. Chloe suddenly realised that the workshop attendees had been introducing themselves and now it was her turn.

'Good morning everyone, my name is Chloe Kavanagh, and I'm…'

God. Her mind had gone completely blank. She smothered a hysterical giggle and threw an apologetic glance around the room.

'And?' Another wide, encouraging smile from Debbie.

'And?' Chloe frowned.

'Would you like to share with the group what you hope to get out of today?'

Oh, God. Did they really want to know what she hoped to get out of the day? There was only one thing she longed for and she knew that unless a miracle took place, it wasn't going to happen. The whole room was waiting patiently for her response, so she dragged her scattered thoughts together and tried to formulate an acceptable reply.

'I'd like to see what's in store for the next twelve months,' she replied dutifully, lying through her teeth. She knew exactly what was in store for the next twelve months.

Total chaos.

'Excellent,' Debbie beamed and focused her dazzling smile on Tara.

'I'm so glad to be here,' Tara trilled, introducing herself clearly and articulately. 'I aim to continue to deliver best practice and ongoing excellence in the area of customer advice and I look forward to the exchange of ideas that are an integral part of the workshop.'

Once upon a time, she would have made a smart little speech like that, Chloe fretted. She helped herself to a bottle of still water from the selection on the table and tried to pull herself together as she sipped the cool water and watched Debbie in action. Standing by the laptop and projector, in her Karen Millen pale grey suit, Debbie looked as though nothing would faze her. She was cool, calm and collected. She handled awkward questions with ease and clarity, in perfect control of her job and in perfect control of her life.

Just like me, I don't think, Chloe agonised.

'Is everything all right, Chloe?' Debbie asked her during morning break as they helped themselves to tea and coffee.

'Yes, of course,' Chloe hastily replied. 'Why? Is there a problem?'

'No, no problem. I just thought you didn't seem your usual self.'

Chloe smiled brightly. 'Really? Everything's fine.'

'Good. That's what I like to hear.'

Somehow Chloe got through the day. She watched the workshop video and tried to contribute to the discussion afterwards, feeling as though she was wading through mud. And at long last the workshop came to a conclusion. She gathered her handouts and shoved them into her briefcase, said goodbye to Tara, Debbie and her fellow colleagues, and headed into the ladies room off the hotel foyer before she began the journey home. Out in the ladies, she leaned her forehead against the cool tiles of the cubicle wall and almost cried. As if things weren't bad enough already, now her life was really in a mess.

* * *

Superquinn was jammed. Adam managed to avoid collision as he steered his trolley up and down noisy aisles crowded with Thursday evening shoppers. Mia sat in the baby seat, fat dimpled fingers grasping the trolley handles, pink-clad legs pumping up and down.

He had collected Mia from the crèche as Chloe was attending a workshop in the city centre and would scarcely be home in time. It meant he had to rush out of the office early, but he had already factored that into his bulging diary on account of Chloe's thirtieth birthday. He had popped into Superquinn on impulse, suddenly realising that although he had a surprise planned for Chloe, he couldn't very well arrive home empty handed on the evening of her birthday.

Adam's tie had long since been abandoned and the collar of his crisp white shirt was undone. He was oblivious to the drooling glances darted in his direction. He made a beeline for the wine section, and ignoring the barrels of special offers, he aimed straight for the selection of champagne. Raking his keen blue eyes along the rows, he selected an excellent Bollinger and carefully placed it in the supermarket trolley.

'We'll give Mummy a nice treat, won't we Mia?' He tickled his daughter's soft, peachy cheek. Mia gurgled and focused her big blue eyes on her beloved daddy and pumped her fat little legs even faster.

He headed over to the confectionery section and picked out the largest box of gift-wrapped Lir chocolates he could find. Chloe had insisted that her birthday was to be kept low key. She thought they were going out for a meal on the Saturday night, just the two of them. As far as she was concerned, a table was already booked in Shanahan's on the Green. But Adam had gone one better. He had arranged for Chloe's mum to take Mia at the weekend and he was whisking Chloe off on Saturday morning for an overnight stay in the Slieve Russell Hotel in Cavan. This was a birthday surprise to make up for all the times he was absent from home.

Better still, he wasn't even going to bring his golf clubs.

He threw a couple of yoghurts for Mia and a carton of orange juice into the near-empty trolley. A wire basket would have been adequate for his few articles, but he had rapidly calculated that it would have taken twice as long to get Mia's buggy out of the boot, disentangle it and settle her in it. And it would have been more awkward to juggle buggy and basket around the crowded aisles. As it was, it had been difficult enough to unfasten Mia from her car seat harness and coax her to sit properly in the trolley.

Thank God he didn't have to do this too often. Computer down time was far easier to handle than a runaway trolley and a recalcitrant daughter. Just as well Chloe usually looked after the shopping.

Mia blew bubbles and smacked her mouth in glee as they waited at the checkout. Adam took a clean tissue from his pocket and gently wiped her little rosebud lips and small dimpled fingers.

'Forgotten your anniversary?' the checkout girl flirted as she scanned the Bollinger and box of Lir.

'It's her birthday, and of course I haven't forgotten,' he grinned as he handed her his platinum card.

'She's a lucky girl.' The checkout girl fluttered her eyelashes.

'I'll make sure to tell her,' Adam smiled again.

He came through the checkout, pushing his trolley in front, and paused at the Baker's Kitchen. There was a variety of cakes on offer, from a range of individual pastries, cream slices and chocolate éclairs, to birthday cakes and an assortment of cream sponges and Black Forest gateaux.

'What do you think, Mia? What kind of a cake will we get for mummy?'

* * *

Chloe unlocked the door of the cubicle and bumped straight into Tara, who was expertly redoing her already perfect make-up in front of the mirror.

Brilliant. Just brilliant.

'Hi Tara, not gone home yet?' Chloe forced herself to sound light and friendly when all she wanted to do was bawl her eyes out.

'I stayed back to discuss some customer targets with Debbie,' Tara explained. 'I'm looking forward

356

to initiating some new strategies, but it will have to wait until Monday. I'm on leave tomorrow as I'm off to Barcelona for a weekend break.'

'Oh, lovely.' Chloe's mouth trembled slightly as she forced a smile.

'I like to chill out at the weekends, but it's great to get away now and again.'

'Yes, it is.'

'And I'm not going directly home anyway.'

'Are you going out?'

'First of all, I'm having a good look around my favourite boutiques,' Tara said.

'Shopping?' Chloe frowned.

'It's Thursday, Chloe, late night shopping.'

'Oh, yes, of course.'

'Don't tell me you forgot!' Tara squealed. 'Oh, Chloe! You're gone all domesticated now. Anyway, after my retail therapy, I'm being treated to a romantic candlelit dinner,' she continued as she smiled into the mirror.

'You're all organised,' Chloe said as Tara whipped off her uniform blouse and produced a cream lace top wrapped in tissue paper from the depths of her briefcase. Tara smoothed on her top and sprayed herself and the surrounding air quite liberally with Estée Lauder Pleasures. She put back on her jacket and grinned.

'I have to be organised. My social life is hectic. I'm almost glad of the evenings when I enjoy nothing more than a long soak in the bath.'

'Enjoy yourself tonight,' Chloe said.

'I intend to. My credit card is ready for action, and before you ask, yes, he's gorgeous,' Tara winked as she picked up her briefcase. She sauntered jauntily out of the ladies, taking a cloud of perfume with her and leaving Chloe enveloped in a big black fog of envy. Long soaks in the bath, candlelit dinners, time to browse the shops or relax with a glossy mag were luxuries that now existed on another planet.

She drove home in her metallic blue Volkswagen Beetle. As she passed through the outskirts of Harold's Cross and prepared to slow down at pedestrian lights, she almost caught a glimpse of the old flat. But the lights turned green, the traffic surged ahead and the redbrick row of terraced houses was just a blur.

She was gripped by a surge of nostalgia. The good old days. Only at the time, she hadn't really realised how good they really were, had she?

Forty minutes later, she finally reached home.

Post had arrived during the day and she gathered it up from the hall and walked down to the kitchen. There was a faint scent of lemon, and only the low hum of the integrated fridge-freezer and the click of Chloe's high heels on the natural slate floor broke the silence. She threw open the window that looked out over the landscaped rear garden. The glazed ceramic pots she had planted up earlier that summer, in a fit of optimism one bright Saturday afternoon, were almost mocking her now with their cheerful tumble of colour.

Chloe took a deep breath and let it out slowly. Then she sorted through the post. She put the bills to one side for Adam's attention and began to open her birthday cards. As she read the congratulatory messages, the love and best wishes from family and friends, she felt tears gathering in her eyes.

I'm sure you're a natural, Tara's words echoed. *I admire women like you who can balance motherhood and a career.*

What a laugh. She was such a natural that she had everyone fooled, herself included, into thinking that she could cope expertly with motherhood and a career. And she was such a natural that she had spent the best part of the day trying to ignore her pukey tummy, terrified she would get sick over Tara's leather briefcase, afraid she would have to bolt ignominiously to the loo, and all the way home, nervous of ruining the upholstered interior of her Volkswagen Beetle.

Because to put the icing on the cake, she had awoken that morning to the stark realisation that she was pregnant once more.

She had spent the past ten days watching and waiting in vain for her period to arrive. She had clutched at a slender thread of hope. She was on the Pill. You don't get pregnant on the Pill. And lots of women had late periods, hadn't they? But underneath it all, she had known. And when she had awoken that morning, there was no mistaking the queasy tummy, the tender boobs and the pervading sense of panic.

Happy birthday, Chloe!

She couldn't tell Adam. Not yet. Telling someone else made it all the more real, and she didn't want it to be real. With a bit of luck she might have another couple of months before she began to show. Her mind swiftly calculated, and all of a sudden she remembered.

Quite clearly she remembered the how, the why and the when. Her mind flashed back to a wet Saturday evening last April, when she had sat drinking Californian Chardonnay in Kaz's country pine kitchen.

* * *

'Have another drink, Chloe, go on.' Kaz had passed over the bottle.

'No, I'm fine, I must be getting back. I'm gone ages and I only dropped in to have a look at the plans for your conservatory.'

'Nonsense,' Kaz said firmly. 'Mia's in bed asleep, you said so yourself, and Adam is bound to be glued to the match. He won't even notice you're missing. You're always running and racing and we hardly ever get the chance to have a chat.'

Outside Kaz's kitchen window, the April rain drizzled non-stop.

'Maybe just one more then.'

'Good girl, that's more like it.' Kaz generously filled her glass again. 'Now Emma, let's get back to our earlier conversation. What exactly were you saying about Brad Pitt's bum?'

'It just does it for me – you know what I mean,' Emma giggled.

And then they looked at Chloe expectantly.

'Come on, Chloe, you're next. What are your secret fantasies?' Kaz prodded with a gleam in her eye.

Chloe's mouth went dry and she took a large gulp of white wine. Problem was, she had nothing interesting to confess. But on the outside, her life was as blissful as could be, so she pinned a big smile on her face, ignored the ache in her heart and racked her brains for something seductive. And quite unintentionally, Emma came to her rescue.

'Who the hell needs fantasies with a husband like Adam Kavanagh?' Emma grinned provocatively. 'He's a walking, ready-made fantasy in himself.'

Chloe smiled and fingered her silky blonde hair and tried to look as though she and Adam enjoyed mind-blowing sex every night.

By the time she got home, Chloe was hammered. Adam laughed as he half carried her, half dragged her up the stairs. She remembered saying something to him about Brad Pitt's body but that Adam was everything she ever wanted. She remembered undressing swiftly and reaching for him and telling him she wanted to prove that they still had a terrific sex life.

But she had completely forgotten to take her Pill. She had taken two the following day, but thanks to an overdose of chilled white wine, she had been as sick as a dog. She thought she would have gotten away with it, as it was only the start of her cycle.

No such luck.

* * *

Chloe stared out at the landscaped back garden and felt her world caving in. She could put up with the puffy ankles and expanding waistline, the elephantine tent dresses and the scorching heartburn. What she couldn't possibly do, however, was cope with everything else.

Where had things started to go wrong, she fretted. What had happened to the bright and blissful Chloe who had glided radiantly up the aisle three short years ago? What had happened to the cheerful, confident Chloe and all her dreams? She stood in a daze and automatically opened the rest of her birthday cards. She opened a rude card from Kaz and Emma and came to the final envelope, the one with the Australian stamp. It was, as she had guessed, from Mel. For a long moment, the words danced in front of her eyes.

Happy birthday, Chloe! Hope it's not too much of a shock to the system! Thirty and all that! Anyway, guess what, I'll be home soon. The wanderer returns and will arrive back in Dublin before the end of the month, see u soon. Luv, Mel.

Just what the doctor ordered, Chloe thought sadly. Just when her dream life was falling apart, careless, carefree Mel, the original free spirit, was coming home.

Chapter Thirty-one

Pandemonium reigned when Adam arrived home. Mia had fallen asleep in the car and her cheeks were flushed, her soft hair slightly damp. Adam lifted her out, gingerly unfastening her from her seat, but as he walked into the kitchen, Mia awoke and began to cry.

'Give her to me.' Chloe held out her arms.

'I was hoping we'd manage to have our meal in peace,' Adam said, depositing a crying Mia in her arms and dropping a kiss on Chloe's nose. 'And how's my birthday girl? How did it go today?'

'Fine,' Chloe answered shortly as she balanced Mia on her hip and automatically hugged her. Fine, she felt like saying, if you don't mind feeling nauseous half the day and realising that your life, which is already stretched taut like an elastic band, is about to snap.

Adam headed back out to his car. He returned with Mia's bag and her buggy, dumping them in the kitchen, and he disappeared again. Chloe settled Mia in her baby chair, a beaker of orange juice in her hands.

'What's all this?' Chloe asked as Adam returned to the kitchen, his arms laden.

'Patience, patience,' he said. He put a Chinese takeaway bag on the countertop, and with the air of a conjurer opening his box of tricks, he opened more bags and produced the bottle of Bollinger, the box of Lir chocolates and the largest and gooiest Black Forest gateau that Chloe had ever seen. Her stomach did a complete somersault.

'Happy birthday, darling,' he said, drawing her into his arms for a kiss.

He insisted that Mia went to bed and that they set the dining room table for a proper celebratory birthday meal. It was a special birthday, after all, and he had something special to say. Nothing else could possibly go wrong, Chloe sighed as she picked at roast duck and helped herself to a small sliver of Black Forest. Then Adam told her he was whisking her off for the weekend as a birthday treat.

'You're what?' She almost choked on crumbs of gateau.

'I'm bringing you off to the Slieve Russell,' he smiled. 'My treat. I know it's only for one night, but if we leave early on the Saturday morning, we can make the most of the two days.'

'I told you I wanted no big fuss,' she said desperately.

Oh, God, especially now. A weekend away, with Adam's undivided attention, was the last thing she needed. She had banked on Adam being as preoccupied as usual over the weekend, giving her time to mentally adjust to the bombshell.

'It's a special birthday,' he insisted. 'You hardly think I was going to let that pass with just a meal out on a Saturday night? We can do that anytime.'

Chloe shrugged. 'I suppose it wouldn't be impressive enough for your clients, would it? At least now you'll have something decent to talk about.'

'Chloe!' Adam suddenly flared. 'I've gone to all sorts of lengths to free up the weekend so that we can head off first thing on Saturday, and this is the thanks I get? I'm doing it to impress my clients?'

Chloe's heart thumped. They were having a row. They were supposed to be enjoying a quiet meal in on the night of her birthday, and they were having a row. A row over a surprise luxury weekend away.

'Sorry, it's just that I wasn't expecting this,' she swallowed.

'That's the whole idea. I thought you'd be happy. You often say we don't see enough of each other.'

'You caught me by surprise. It's Thursday evening. I've loads of things to organise before we

366

can head off for the weekend. We can't just go off at the drop of a hat.'

'Of course we can. All you have to do is throw a few things in a bag for Mia and pack a few things for yourself.'

'It's not as simple as that, Adam. I've stuff to organise for next week as well. That's more hassle. When will I get that done? Clothes don't iron themselves, you know.'

She was appalled at the words tumbling out of her mouth. Where was the calm, collected Chloe that she loved to show the world? What had happened to Adam's capable wife?

She was beginning to fall apart, that's what.

'Sometimes there's just no pleasing you, Chloe, is there? Anyway, the Slieve Russell is booked, your mum's all set and we're going.'

'What do you mean, my mum's all set?'

'She's minding Mia, of course. She's delighted with the chance to have Mia to herself. You hardly think we're bringing her?'

'I don't want my mother minding Mia.'

'Why not? She's babysat before.'

'That was completely different. It was only for a few hours at night and Mia was asleep in her own cot.'

'What the hell is up with you, Chloe?' Adam fumed. 'I'm trying to organise a treat for your birthday and everything I do is wrong.'

From upstairs, they heard the thin wail of Mia's cry.

'I thought she was asleep,' Adam snapped.

'I'll go,' Chloe said resignedly.

'No, stay where you are. The kind of humour you're in, you'll only upset her more.' Adam stalked out of the dining room.

Bloody marvellous. On top of everything else, a stupid row over a weekend away that lots of women would give their eye teeth for. She was definitely losing it. Chloe poured more champagne into her John Rocha crystal flute and added a dash of white lemonade. This was turning out to be a bloody great birthday. She shouldn't even be drinking, although diluted champagne wouldn't do much harm, would it? And anyway, she had been drinking last weekend and countless weekends before. She had knocked back plenty of vodkas before she realised she was pregnant again.

Chloe got up from the dining room table and walked through to the living room. She sat down on the cream leather sofa and glared at the shaft of sunshine that slanted in through the front room window. The yellow rays licked the edge of the Venetian fireplace, slid past the surround sound centre and pooled in the corner by the green umbrella plant in the blue Habitat pot. She lifted her glass and extended her arm and looked at her French manicured fingernails holding the glass and watched prisms of light dance off the surface of the crystal.

She had it all, hadn't she? Everything she had ever wanted. She was sitting in her luxury Abbey

Manor home, a crystal flute of champagne in hand. Life was perfect, with her successful husband, her cute little daughter, her own career in the building society and a wardrobe full of designer labels. Adam had upgraded their two cars at the beginning of the year and outside in the cobble-locked driveway sat his plush BMW and her stylish Beetle. And he was about to whisk her away to a luxury hotel for a romantic weekend to celebrate her birthday.

It was a far cry from the days of cheap chain store joggers.

She should be feeling on top of the world.

* * *

Adam hushed his little daughter and settled her in her cot. He switched on a colourful mobile over her head and waited as Mia's eyes began to close, her eyelashes a dark curving fan on her pink chubby cheeks. He wondered what the hell had got into Chloe.

He had fully expected her to be delighted with his plans. He had expected her to appreciate the way he had thoughtfully freed up the weekend, booked the Slieve Russell and made the babysitting arrangements. And if he was perfectly honest with himself, he had expected to bask munificently in her gratitude.

He wasn't used to getting it wrong.

And if anyone should be on edge this evening, it should surely be him. An icy thread had slithered around his stomach when Chloe had announced that Mel was finally coming home. Now, with the benefit of a couple of stiff drinks, he felt a little calmer. There was no way Chloe could possibly have known what had happened one rainy night in October, he reassured himself. It was years ago, he reasoned, and there was no way she was going to find out, he decided as he tucked pink teddy bear blankets around his sleeping daughter.

He had far too much to lose.

* * *

Mia beamed and gurgled when they dropped her off at Chloe's parents' house early Saturday morning. The sun was climbing in the sky and it was going to be a beautiful June day. Already neighbours and children were out and about and Chloe was disgusted with the blatantly curious glances thrown in their direction.

It was a sight not usually glimpsed in the drab housing estate – a tall man getting out of the driver's seat of the shiny BMW, sexy looking in Levis jeans, a short-sleeved white cotton shirt and a pair of Ralph Lauren sunglasses, the smiling baby he scooped out of the car seat, pink cheeked and pretty in a yellow frilly dress and white broderie anglaise bonnet, the amount of expensive baby paraphernalia unloaded from the boot.

'She doesn't see enough of us,' Irene said. 'No

wonder she's so happy to be here.' She bounced a gurgling Mia in her arms as Adam went back and forth from the boot of his BMW to the small terraced house, unloading buggy, travel cot, baby walker, changing pad, a large box of nappies, supplies of bottles and formula and a bag of clothes.

'She's only staying for one night. What's with all this stuff?' Irene asked.

Don't start Mum, not now, Chloe said under her breath. 'I'll go through her things with you,' she answered, striving for patience. 'And I've made out a list of instructions about her food and clothes.'

Irene laughed. 'Instructions? Don't be daft, Chloe. Didn't I rear three of my own? If I run short of anything I can knock into any of the neighbours, there's always grandchildren around.'

Brilliant, just brilliant. Holding her temper in check, Chloe said, 'Mia's very fussy about her food.'

'You mean you're fussy. Far too fussy for your own good, I've told you. Just go off and relax. We'll be fine, won't we Mia? Your granddad and I are really looking forward to the weekend. We might go to the playground in the park if the weather holds.'

'The playground?'

'Don't tell me you haven't brought her to the playground yet?'

'Of course not. She's far too young,' Chloe said crisply.

'Right then. We'll stick to feeding the ducks, Mia, your mum's orders.'

'And don't let her too near—'

'I won't let her too near the ducks in case she catches anything. Honestly, Chloe, I give up. It's a wonder you trust me to mind her at all.'

You can thank Adam for that, Chloe thought viciously as she got into the car and yanked at her seat belt. She took a few deep breaths and tried to calm down. Kaz and Emma had sighed enviously when she had told them of her weekend plans. Forget about the house, they had said. Just go. Lap it all up.

The luxury, of course, Kaz laughed.

And Adam as well, Emma winked.

She would have to pull herself together. She watched Adam give Mia a goodbye kiss before jumping into the driver's seat. For the next couple of days, she would have to look as though she was enjoying herself, even though she just felt like crawling under a rock and hiding there for the foreseeable future.

* * *

The Slieve Russell was an oasis of tranquil luxury. A shimmering water fountain sparkled iridescently in the June sunshine and banks of flowers splashed riotous colour in the surrounding gardens as the BMW swept in through the wide, gated entrance.

Chloe just had to take it easy and unwind, Adam said. He had requested a deluxe room with a Jacuzzi bath and reserved a table in the opulent dining room for later that evening. They were going to make full use of the leisure centre and he had booked Chloe in for a facial and manicure. And it hadn't been too much hassle in the end, he said as they went up the elegant sweeping stairway to their room. Mia was happy to stay with her gran, and Chloe was to switch off her mobile. If there were any problems, Irene was to contact him, not Chloe, so there was nothing to stop her from relaxing completely.

She barely made it into the en suite bathroom in time, and she flushed the loo repeatedly to muffle the sounds of her retching.

They went for a stroll in the rolling parkland along a walkway that skirted the perimeter of the golf course. Sunshine filtered through the trees and the undulating landscape stretched for miles, green upon green, melting into the hazy distance.

'Are you sorry you didn't bring your clubs?' Chloe asked as they watched groups of golfers dotted about the perfectly appointed greens and pushing golf trolleys across the luscious parkland.

'I can always hire a set.' He threw her a questioning glance. 'Only joking, Chloe, this weekend is reserved for you.'

'Go and play, if you like, I'm not stopping you,' she said. Maybe if she had a few hours to herself, away from everyone, she could get her head together, she could try and made sense of what was happening to her life.

'Nonsense. I brought you here to relax. I can play golf anytime. Well, not in these surroundings, I have to admit.' He looked out across the championship course. Then he turned to her and threw his arm around her. 'C'mon. I can hardly remember the last time we had some precious time to ourselves.'

'Not since Mia was born, I suppose,' she said as she fell into step with him.

'Yeah. It's been a busy year all round,' Adam said. 'You're doing a great job, Chloe, holding us all together, and you're looking terrific, as usual.' He squeezed her waist. 'I'm so happy with you and Mia, the two women in my life. Look, let me show you…' He halted in his stride, fished in the pocket of his Levis, brought out his wallet and opened it. Inside one of the leather compartments was a miniature photo of herself and Mia.

'See? I know I may not be around as much as you'd like, but I'm working hard to give you everything you want and make you happy. And you're never far from me.' He took out the photo and silently passed it to her.

It was a photo taken at Christmas, before Mia was five months old. Chloe was smiling into the camera and Mia was in her arms, with a look of such utter trust on her little button face that Chloe's heart clenched.

Maybe now was a good time to tell him the news? Tell Adam he was going to be a dad once more? She handed him back the photo, her hands trembling a little, and Adam tucked it back safely into his wallet.

Maybe now…

'You know, Chloe, I was more than a little shocked when you told me about Mia,' Adam said suddenly. 'Don't get me wrong,' he hastily added as he threw his arm around her. 'I just wasn't expecting us to have a baby so soon, and I was worried about how we'd manage. Especially with the pressures of consolidating KVL.'

'We've managed fine, haven't we?' She nailed a smile to her suddenly pale face and waited for her heartbeat to return to normal.

'Thanks to you, we have. I don't know how you keep going.'

Chloe remained silent.

'I never realised that having a baby could be such a responsibility,' Adam continued. 'To have one little person so totally dependent on you…' He shook his head. 'But she's beautiful and adorable. Almost as adorable as you. Maybe in a few years' time, when KVL is more established and you can work part time, we can think about a little brother or sister. Hmm?'

Her throat felt as though it was clogged and she couldn't find the words to tell him her news. She couldn't even think of how to begin as they continued their stroll around the panoramic walkway in the warm June sunshine. She would have to forget about being pregnant for the moment.

Adam wouldn't notice for a while. And if he asked any awkward questions, she could pretend she was giving up drink for her new keep fit plan, because with sitting down all day in the office her tummy was getting a bit flabby.

* * *

'I think we should have a welcoming home party for Mel,' Chloe said later that evening as they ate in the hotel restaurant.

Adam dropped his knife on the floor. He signalled to a nearby waiter, who immediately replaced it. Calm down, he told himself. There was no need to jump at the sound of her name.

'I'm not sure that's such a good idea,' he said slowly. He topped up his glass of Merlot and gestured to Chloe, who refused a refill. 'I don't think Mel's the welcoming home party type. She'd hate that kind of a fuss.'

'According to Henry, life in Australia is one long party.'

'When were you talking to him about Mel?' Adam asked, sounding as casual as possible.

Chloe shrugged. 'Some time after he was home. April, I suppose.'

'And did Henry think she was happy over there?'

'She must have been, otherwise she'd hardly have stayed all this time,' Chloe pointed out. 'Henry seemed to think she'd live there forever.'

'Then I wonder why she's coming home now.' Adam toyed with his steak.

'She must have had a change of mind. According to Henry, she's still the same old Mel. Anyway, why are you so concerned? I didn't think you and Mel were great buddies.'

'No, that's true, we weren't,' Adam said. 'We never really saw eye to eye.'

Except once. And that hadn't exactly been a meeting of minds, had it? He pushed the thought out of his head and tried to concentrate on what Chloe was saying.

'Which is why I want to have this party,' Chloe insisted.

'I don't follow you, Chloe. Surely the fact that Mel and I don't really get on is all the more reason to keep her away?'

'Look, Adam,' Chloe began impatiently. 'Mel was a bit cheesed off with me because I married you instead of going away with her.' Chloe leaned forward across the table. 'We managed to make up before she went away, but I want her to see what a success we've made with our lives. Let her see us in action in Abbey Manor, throwing a party for our friends and neighbours. Let her see how happy we are.'

'Do you not think you could be tempting fate?'

'Tempting fate? What do you mean?'

'She'll take one look at Abbey Manor and that'll be enough to know that our marriage is a success.

Why rub her nose in it, or run the risk of getting her back up?' Adam put down his knife. He had scarcely tasted his steak. He reached for the bottle of Merlot and refilled his glass yet again.

Chloe smiled at him. 'I don't know why you're so worried about her reaction.'

'I'm thinking of you. She didn't bother coming home to do bridesmaid, and she's hardly kept in touch over the last four years. I really don't see the point in throwing a huge party for her.'

'She was my friend, Adam, my best friend.'

'Maybe she was, once. But things change, friendships change.'

'Mel and I will always be friends,' Chloe said.

Adam looked across the table at Chloe. He loved his wife. He loved it when she looked at him with her wide grey eyes, as though he was her favourite hero. He loved the way she dressed, the way she looked after her curvy figure, her outraged reaction when he teased her over her minuscule belly, the way she looked after Mia and him and their beautiful home and kept their lives running as though on well-oiled wheels.

Maybe they didn't make love as often as he'd like, maybe they didn't have the same time for each other – after all, their lives were very busy – but apart from his successful, demanding business, in Chloe, Mia and Abbey Manor, he had everything he ever wanted. And no one was going to take that away. Certainly not the likes of Mel

Saunders, returning from Australia for God knows whatever reason.

* * *

They swept out of the hotel grounds the following morning shortly before noon. Chloe looked out at the undulating countryside as they took the road to Dublin. It was a pleasant day for the drive, with a bright, expectant haze over the morning that promised sunshine to come.

She was glad she had thought of the idea of throwing a party for Mel. It had been a spur of the moment decision, and even as she had suggested it to Adam, she had mentally envisaged all the necessary preparations involved and almost backed down. But it was definitely the best thing to do, to put on her best face in front of her careless, free-spirited friend, no matter how much planning it took. She would show Mel that she had made the right decision in marrying Adam. She would invite their immediate neighbours, Adam's business associates and Henry. She would throw open the double doors downstairs and the house would look fantastic.

And planning the party would help to cushion the shock of her pregnancy and give her a different focus for the next couple of weeks. She was glad she hadn't yet broken the news to Adam. It would have spoiled the peaceful oasis of the weekend.

And it would be best if she could first come to terms with the pregnancy before convincing Adam that Mia needed a little brother or sister.

She told herself to relax in the passenger seat as Adam switched on a David Gray CD and the BMW cruised down the N3 towards Dublin. She told herself there was no reason to feel as though she was suspended in some kind of quiet calm before the storm.

Chapter Thirty-two

The welcoming home party was in full swing by the time Mel arrived.

She hadn't intended to be late. Even though she had often read about it on the *Irish Times* website, she hadn't expected Dublin city traffic to be quite so heavy. Neither had she expected the taxi to be twenty minutes late.

She hadn't wanted a party. She would have preferred to meet Chloe on neutral territory and go for a quiet meal. Thoughts of seeing Chloe and Adam and perhaps Henry, all together in the one place, had kept her on edge all day. But Chloe had insisted and told her it was all arranged.

So she felt slightly nervous as the taxi eventually swept in through the pillared entrance to Abbey

Manor estate and she felt even more jittery when it pulled up outside a very imposing redbrick detached house. In the dusky July evening, wrought iron lanterns illuminated the landscaped front garden and light glowed from the picture window to the front of the house. Chloe hadn't yet drawn the blinds, and against the glimmer of table lamps, Mel could see people moving about in the sitting room.

As she stepped up the cobble-locked driveway past two flashy cars, she glimpsed other details – double doors opened through to the back of the house, more people, a vase of tall, bell-shaped lilies, candlelight glinting on a marble surround fireplace, thick draperies tied back with gold coloured swags, a cream leather sofa with flame-shaded scatter cushions.

For a moment she wanted to turn and flee away from this opulence, away from this other world of screaming luxury, away from Chloe, Adam and Henry, back to the single room close to town, ninety euro a week including electricity. She would have run there and then, only someone had spotted her.

The mahogany door was thrown open and the noise of the party spilled out into the front garden. She heard Chloe's excited voice, and next thing Chloe was flying through the hall door, down the driveway and throwing her arms around her as though she would never let her go.

* * *

'I can't believe you're home at last,' Chloe said. 'It's wonderful to see you again.'

'It's great to see you too. You're looking marvellous. You *are* happy, aren't you?'

'Couldn't be better!' Chloe said brightly. 'And you look the exact same as the day you left, not a day older. Except for your nice golden tan, of course. And your voice! I think you've a bit of an Australian twang. Sounds unusual mixed with the Dublin tones on top of Galway!'

They were out in Chloe's fancy kitchen. Mel had been swiftly introduced all around, to what appeared to be a gathering mainly of Chloe's posh neighbours and Adam's business partner and acquaintances. Chloe had brought her on a whirl-wind tour of the house. Mel had been left with the impression of complete and utter affluence, from the luxury interior right through to the professionally landscaped back garden, complete with decking, patio plants and more well-heeled partygoers.

'I never expected…all this. You're certainly living in the lap of luxury,' Mel said. 'And as for little Mia, what can I say, Chloe, she's only adorable. You have a fantastic little daughter!'

Chloe lifted Mia up and balanced her possessively on her hip. A section of her dark hair was scooped up and caught with a miniature lilac ribbon that matched her frilly cotton dress.

'She'll be a year old soon, won't you Mia? Of course, it's way past her bedtime. I never keep her

383

up when I entertain,' Chloe prattled on as she jiggled Mia in her arms. 'But it's okay just this once, to meet her Auntie Mel.'

'I should hope so,' Mel smiled and tickled her cheek and Mia wriggled to get down.

'She's starting to walk now, but it's nerve wracking looking at her wobbling along. I'm terrified she'll slip on the tiles and hurt herself. I don't know what I'd do if anything happened to her.'

'The joys of parenthood,' Adam said as he came in from the shadowy back garden.

He had initially greeted Mel with cool detachment. If anything, he seemed even more suave and confident than she remembered. He looked the picture of relaxed contentment in his Levis and thin woollen sweater as he mingled with his guests in the dusky July evening. Now, in the recessed lighting of the kitchen, as he shut the patio door against the draught of cool air, Mel noticed the first signs of grey at his temples and the fresh lines fanning out from his blue eyes. If anything, they added an edge of maturity to his image.

'Here, I'll take her.' He held out his arms for his little daughter and Mel caught the glint of the wedding band on his finger and the loving look he exchanged with Chloe. Mia snuggled against her daddy's shoulder, burying her little head into the crook of his neck.

'Quite the proud father,' Mel said, keeping her tone as neutral as possible.

'Adam adores Mia,' Chloe enthused. She smiled at her husband. 'Mel was just saying she didn't expect to see us living in quite such luxury.'

'No?' Adam raised his eyebrows. 'We've worked very hard for what we have, both Chloe and I.'

'I'm sure you have,' Mel said evenly. 'It's a big change from the flat in Harold's Cross.'

'Harold's Cross seems like ancient history. We've come a long way since then,' Adam said just as evenly. 'But we do appreciate everything we have. And we're quite the happy little family, aren't we, Chloe?' Adam smiled at his wife and then he looked directly at Mel over the dark head of his little daughter.

'Absolutely,' Chloe agreed.

'I'll put Mia to bed, love. Everyone's okay for drinks at the moment, so you can catch up on all the news with Mel,' Adam said before going out of the kitchen.

'Your hair is nice,' Mel said, turning to Chloe. 'It seems to be blonder than I remember.'

'Do you think so? I thought it was nearly time to have the roots done again. I seem to be getting them done more and more often, but don't ask me why. God, Mel, it's funny to be having this conversation with you. The last thing I want to talk about is highlights or lowlights. Tell me all about Australia.'

'All? It was very free and easy. I travelled around, worked when I felt like it, mostly lived in one-room bed-sits, had a ball in general, great weather, of course.'

'And men? I'm sure there were plenty of men.'

'Oh yeah, loads,' Mel said casually.

'And what brought you back after all this time?' Chloe asked quizzically. 'You missed my wedding. I would have loved it if you had been my brides-maid. But don't worry, I forgive you,' she added hastily. 'I was beginning to think you'd never come home. Even Henry said that you seemed very settled.'

'Did he now? What else did he have to say?'

'He had a brilliant time, the best thing he'd ever done. He loved Sydney and thought New Zealand was the last word.'

'I thought he'd like Sydney all right,' Mel paused.

'I was really delighted when he said he'd look you up. I felt it was some kind of contact with you apart from occasional e-mails.'

'Yeah, I sure got a surprise. He's home now, I suppose?'

'Been home since April. He should be here tonight, don't know where he's got to. You know Henry, he could turn up at any time.'

* * *

Chloe felt like congratulating herself as she opened the kitchen presses and began to take out napkins and cutlery. It was time to serve the food and

386

everything was going according to plan. The house looked fabulous. There were bursts of laughter from the patio outside where Adam's business partner and acquaintances were still gathered. Neighbours were happily drifting about in the sitting room and dining room. There was plenty to drink. She had been wise to arrange for caterers to supply a salad buffet. It had given her more time to put extra finishing touches to the house.

And most importantly of all, Mel was impressed.

She didn't quite know what to make of Mel. It was wonderful to see her friend again. In one sense it was as though the last few years had never been. If anything, Mel seemed more carefree than ever. In amongst the sophisticated glamour of the residents of Abbey Manor and Adam's well-heeled acquaintances, she had turned up for her welcoming home party in a pair of beige combats and a plain green T-shirt. Much and all as she was delighted to have her friend back home, she looked a little out of place, Chloe decided. And as for her casual hairstyle, her messy dark hair was completely different to the smooth, elegantly coiffed gleam of every other woman.

Why, then, did she think that Mel had some kind of attraction about her, something she couldn't quite put her finger on? It defied all logic.

'Chloe, what are you up to?' Kaz's voice broke into her thoughts.

'I'm just getting the food organised.'

'Why don't you let Emma and me do that? Everyone can help themselves. You just relax and talk to Mel. She's lovely, isn't she?'

'Do you think so?'

'Yes, so refreshing, and I'd die for those green eyes of hers.'

Refreshing was one way of putting it, Chloe thought, her eyes on Mel as she sauntered over to join them.

'Mel, I've told Chloe that Emma and I will organise the food,' Kaz said firmly. 'And for once she's to do as I say. It's all ready, so it's just a question of putting it out.'

'You won't know where everything is, the plates, serving spoons…' Chloe hesitated.

'I'm sure I can find my way around a kitchen,' Kaz said dryly.

'There are certain things I had planned on using and you won't know…'

'We can always ask Adam if we're stuck,' Emma suggested with a glint in her eye.

'We'll make it a joint effort,' Chloe gave in as she took out some plates and directed Kaz and Emma to the integrated fridge. 'Mel, why don't you pour yourself some more wine and mingle. You're the guest of honour. On second thought, here comes Henry. You can chat to him.'

* * *

388

She didn't know what she had been expecting. It had been months since they had parted on the beach in Port Douglas, but to Mel it seemed like a lifetime ago. It had been even longer since Henry had dropped her out to the airport that grey October day when she had first left Dublin. Yet Henry looked the exact same as he had then, the same spiky auburn hair, the same untroubled expression in his eyes, and the same type of blonde bimbo clinging like a limpet onto his arm.

Why should she have been expecting anything else, Mel asked herself irritably as she moved forward to say hello.

'This is Samantha,' Henry introduced her. 'And of course she's from Westmeath, the best county in Ireland! Samantha, this is Mel, remember, I told you all about her.'

'Oh yes, the girl who went off to Australia,' Samantha giggled. 'And this is your homecoming party?'

Samantha looked about nineteen years old. She was wearing a leather miniskirt that barely covered her bum and a sleeveless wrap top out of which a pair of creamy breasts overflowed. Mel immediately felt like a tall skinny lamppost in her combat jeans and T-shirt the colour of her eyes.

'Yes, Chloe insisted on throwing a bash for me,' Mel said easily. 'To get me back into circulation, so to speak.'

Henry's tawny eyes gleamed. 'I wouldn't have

thought the residents of Abbey Manor would have been high on your circulation list.'

'Why not?' she challenged him.

'Unless you've changed, Mel, I thought you'd run a mile from the mortgaged-to-the-eyeballs, married-to-the-job types around here.'

'Henry, I'm going to get a glass of wine,' Samantha interrupted in a breathy, little-girl voice. 'Can I get you anything?'

'White for me, thanks,' he said. He watched with an indulgent expression on his face as Samantha tottered off on ten-inch killer heels, then turned to Mel and asked her what had finally brought her home. 'You've scarcely decided to settle down, seeing that Chloe and Adam are making a go of it,' he said, raising an eyebrow.

'Mockery doesn't suit you,' Mel scoffed.

She was distracted for a few moments as Samantha made a mini drama of tottering back to Henry complete with two very full glasses of wine clutched grimly in her hands. If she held them any closer to her chest, Mel thought, or teetered any further on her high heels, the contents would surely spill over onto her generous breasts. For the next few seconds she tried to rid her mind of the unsettling picture of Henry licking the wine off Samantha's cleavage.

Why exactly had she come home? She watched Henry make a fuss of Samantha as she handed him his glass and wondered why she had flown back halfway around the world.

Glad as she was to see Chloe, she hadn't come home to mingle with the posh snobs in Abbey Manor. And neither had she come home on account of something she had felt during a Christmas party. That would be tantamount to admitting that she was soft in the head. And it certainly wasn't anything that Henry had said to her on a beach in Port Douglas. As she watched him laughing with Samantha, he seemed a million miles away from the Henry she had encountered in Australia.

So why was she standing in Chloe's dream kitchen, surrounded by people she didn't really care for, as Adam strutted his best party host persona and Chloe fluttered around in her gilded cage, and together they flaunted a united front to the world? And Henry, good old Henry, flirted as usual with his latest conquest? Some things hadn't changed in the time she'd been away.

And other things had altered out of all recognition.

She felt a wave of dizziness wash over her, so she took a couple of deep breaths to steady herself and pinned a bright smile to her face as Samantha tipped her apologetically on the shoulder.

'Adam's finally agreed to bring me upstairs to take a quick look at Mia,' Samantha said breathlessly. 'She was asleep the last time I was here and I didn't see her. But Adam promised me a sneaky look if I don't disturb her. I'll see you later, Mel.'

So Henry had already brought Samantha out to Abbey Manor. No matter. There was no reason in the world for that piece of information to even register with Mel. Samantha disappeared in Adam's wake, her hips wiggling with every careful footstep, and once more Henry turned to Mel.

'Come on, Mel, let's have it, there must be some reason why you decided to come home at last.'

Mel shrugged. 'If you must know, Henry, my visa expired,' she fibbed. 'I had to come home before I was booted out of the country. Otherwise I'd still be there.'

'I thought that had been sorted for you? Didn't that Sean fella work something for you?'

'Yes, but that was only temporary,' Mel told him.

'And is that the only reason you came home?' He looked at her closely and Mel was suddenly reminded of the moments of connection she had felt with Henry on the other side of the world. And that was where they belonged, wasn't it?

'Of course. What other reason could there possibly be?' she challenged him, meeting the gaze of his eyes for as long as she could.

Henry was the first to look away. 'Chloe told me you have a roof over your head already.'

'Yes, I have a bed-sit off the South Circular.'

'That was quick. I was afraid you might have been stuck for somewhere to stay, and unfortunately my emergency couch is out of the question right now.'

'I've kinda guessed as much,' Mel said swiftly. 'So you're still in the apartment?'

'Still there, still feeding the fish, still paying the mortgage, but at least it's more than doubled in value since I bought it.'

'Good for you.'

'I had to replace the car, though.'

'Aw.'

'One day she just gave up the ghost and clapped out on the Naas Road.'

'And what are you driving now?' Mel asked.

'I have an opulent Renault Laguna. Sometimes it's handy, working in a bank.'

'I suppose it has certain advantages,' Mel said dryly.

'And I still have your worldly possessions.' He gave her a questioning glance, his eyes once again searching hers. 'What the hell was that e-mail all about? Anyway, Mel, I didn't have the heart to dump any of your things, just in case you did ever come home.'

'I suppose I sent that e-mail in the heat of the moment,' Mel admitted with a wry smile. 'I'll get my stuff out of your way sometime soon.'

'Anytime, just give me a bell. I can even do home deliveries.'

They were interrupted again by Samantha as she click clacked back into the kitchen. This time she was all excited about Mia.

'Oh, Henry, she's gorgeous,' Samantha squealed. 'I just took a peep. You should see her, fast asleep, tucked up in her cot with her thumb in her mouth.

And her bedroom is just out of this world. All her fluffy little toys and…and…'

Suddenly Samantha's bottom lip trembled. Mel watched in astonishment as she tried to control it to no avail. Her whole face seemed to collapse as she started to cry, tears spilling down her cheeks, and she turned blindly to Henry and went into his arms and sobbed on his shoulder as though her heart was about to break.

Henry shook his head slightly as Adam frowned at him.

'I was half afraid of this,' he said. 'We'll slip out quietly. It's best if I bring her home.'

'You sure?' Adam asked.

'Positive.' Henry inched towards the kitchen door, a weeping Samantha clinging valiantly to him.

'What's wrong?' Chloe sensed the commotion. She had been putting the finishing touches to the buffet table, but quickly dropped the napkins to one side and followed Henry as he went out into the hall.

'Henry! Samantha! What's up? You can't leave yet. The food's ready. Are you not going to stay for something to eat?'

'Leave them, Chloe,' Adam urged.

'But what's the matter? What's wrong?'

'Forget it, darling,' Adam ordered as he put his arm around her shoulders. 'Don't upset yourself. It's nothing to do with us. Let's look after our guests. Did you say the food was ready?'

'Yes, well, okay, if you're sure,' Chloe agreed. She threw Mel a puzzled glance as arm in arm, Henry and Samantha went out into the lantern-lit front garden on the cool July night, and the hall door clicked shut. 'God knows what that was all about,' she shrugged. 'C'mon, you're the guest of honour and the night's still young!'

* * *

The night was endless. Mel picked at the delicious buffet that Chloe had laid on. She drank far too much wine. She felt an almost physical pain in her face as she talked to all and sundry about Australia, the sunshine, the barbecues, the beaches. She watched Chloe and Adam, laughing together at a private joke in the way only lovers do. She watched his hand lingering possessively on her hip as they chatted to one of their neighbours.

And all the time she wondered why the hell she had come home.

Chapter Thirty-three

'I wonder what was going on between Henry and Samantha,' Chloe said sleepily.

'Hmm?' Adam pulled back the edge of the lilac cotton duvet and slid into bed.

'That fuss with Henry and Samantha. What was going on?'

'I dunno.'

'You must have some idea, you're his friend, after all.'

'Henry and I don't talk that much.'

'I wonder if she's pregnant. It looked serious enough to me.'

'Ask him the next time you see him.'

'I can't just ask Henry if he got his girlfriend pregnant.' Chloe roused herself a little. She turned around to face Adam and adjusted the thin satin strap of her filmy nightdress.

'Ask Samantha,' Adam suggested dismissively. 'Women tell each other everything, don't they?'

'I'll see. The party went well, didn't it?'

'Terrific, Chloe.'

'What did you think of Mel?'

Adam yawned. 'Not much, to be honest.'

'It was great to see her, but I was expecting something different. And I thought she would have made more of an effort to dress up, or do her hair or something.'

'I didn't really notice.'

'Adam, a pair of combats, for God's sake, and a T-shirt. And she should really smarten up her hair, try and straighten it out or whatever. I thought she looked out of place compared to everyone else's slinky glamour.'

'What did you expect from someone who's spent four years tramping around Australia?'

'Yeah, you've just put your finger on it. I hadn't thought of it like that.' Chloe was silent for a minute and then she continued. 'I'll have to have a word with her. She is my friend, after all, and a little bit of advice wouldn't go astray. And I think I proved my point by having the party.' Chloe smiled sleepily in the lamplight. 'Mel was impressed with everything – our house, our friends, our lifestyle. It's perfectly obvious that I made the right decision in marrying you.'

'I don't know why you're so concerned about what Mel thinks. She can hardly expect to swan back into your life as though she's never been away.'

'Adam! We're friends.'

'Maybe you were, once. But four years is a long time and she scarcely kept in touch. We've moved on with our lives, but she obviously hasn't. If I were you, I wouldn't waste too much time on her,' Adam said crisply as he reached out and clicked off the bedside lamp.

* * *

Chloe dragged herself out of bed early the next morning. She had to get the kitchen back into shape after the party. Kaz and Emma had offered to come in and help, but she insisted that she could manage. Most of the heavy cleaning had been done the night before, so it was just a question of putting everything away in the right place.

She was showered and dressed and downstairs before Mia awoke and it was a novelty to look forward to a cup of coffee in peace. Out in the back garden, the sky was patchy grey and it was drizzling rain. A slight breeze riffled across the damp grass and she watched a lone sparrow pecking at the wet surface of the patio decking.

She shouldn't really be drinking coffee. Her tummy was still a little queasy in the mornings, but she badly needed a kick start, something to get through the endless round of tidying, feeding Mia, bathing her, dressing her, sorting the laundry, getting as much done as she could before she jumped on the treadmill at six o'clock the following morning. She looked at the pile of serving dishes waiting to be put away and she knew that the treadmill now extended to include the weekends.

It was worth it, though, wasn't it? Anytime she felt that things were getting on top of her, she only had to remember last night, and the terrific success of her party.

She still hadn't told Adam she was pregnant again. She was just having some breathing space, wasn't she? Some time to adjust. She had more than enough to cope with without facing another pregnancy, so it was easier to pretend it wasn't really happening.

The next thing on her list was Mia's first birthday. Chloe was planning a great party for her, including a bouncy castle and face painting. Kaz and Emma would be there with their children, Adam's sisters with his nieces and nephew and the two sets of grandparents. She would have to get her highlights done in advance. She had the most adorable dress picked out for Mia. She might get caterers to do the food again. It would take some of the work off her and give her plenty of time to make sure the house and garden were in tip-top shape.

She spooned coffee into a yellow mug and her thoughts turned to Mel. Why had she been so concerned about her friend coming home? Why had she thought that Mel's sassy, free-spirited out-look on life would be any kind of a threat to her? There was no need, after all, to worry about some-one who looked as though she had spent four years backpacking around Australia. If anything, she thought as she hugged her coffee cup in her hands, she could almost feel sorry for Mel.

* * *

'Hi Henry.'

'Hello?' His voice on the phone was impersonal.

'It's Mel.'

'Mel! Sorry, I didn't recognise you straight away. I'll have to get used to the sound of you again!'

'I'm just ringing about my worldly goods. I'll get them out of your way as soon as I can.'

'There's no rush, take your time.'

'I'm already home over three weeks, I think I have taken my time.'

'Three weeks? Time flies! If you like, I could drop your things over to you. You're off the South Circular and it's only down the road.'

'I can't put you to any trouble, Henry.'

'Don't sound so formal, it's no trouble.'

'I'd rather collect the stuff myself. I could drop over on Saturday afternoon?'

'Saturday afternoon is fine. See you then.'

* * *

On Friday afternoon, Mel handed over some of the savings she had brought home from Australia and became the proud owner of a red Ford Fiesta. It was four years old, one lady owner, and in great nick, the mechanic in the garage assured her. It would give her no bother, he said. She just had to get used to Dublin city traffic, Mel thought as she turned the key in the ignition, checked the mirrors and waited for what seemed like an age to join the stream of cars on the main road.

At two o'clock on Saturday she drove to Harold's Cross and parked outside Henry's apartment. Samantha opened the door. Her baby blonde hair was mussed. She was wearing a soft pink dressing gown that gaped open at her cleavage, and she had furry slippers with teddy bear motifs on her feet. She looked as though she hadn't slept all night.

'Sorry I disturbed you, Samantha,' Mel frowned. 'Is Henry around?'

'Come in, don't mind me. Henry was here up to five minutes ago. He's just gone to get a couple of bottles of wine. We were running a bit low,' she giggled, drawing the edges of her dressing gown together, 'and he thought you might like a welcome home drink. He shouldn't be too long.'

'No worries. Anyway, I can't have a drink, I'm driving. Did he leave out my things?'

Samantha giggled again. 'Yes, I think he did. There's stuff out in the kitchen that definitely doesn't belong there.'

The sooner she got out of there, the better, Mel decided firmly as she walked into Henry's living room.

It was much the same as she remembered, but the couch had been replaced with a modern-looking sofa that matched the curtains, and the walls were painted a warm peach. And he still had his small aquarium. There were a couple of new lamps dotted about and an interesting picture of the sun rising over the sea on the wall above the fireplace. Mel would have loved to stand and linger over it, only Samantha was right beside her, hovering at her elbow.

And Samantha's frilly underwear was draped all over the radiator.

'It's a nice apartment, isn't it?' Samantha said.

'Yes, very comfortable.'

'Although there's no comparison with Chloe's house…' Samantha left the rest of the sentence hanging in mid-air.

'Thank God for that,' Mel muttered under her breath, but Samantha caught the words.

'Do you feel like that too?' she chimed. 'I was nearly afraid to sit down in Chloe's house, never mind go to the loo.'

'I know what you mean,' Mel admitted.

'I'm glad you feel like that too and it's not just me,' Samantha babbled. 'Henry said you were okay. I was nervous about meeting Chloe and Adam, but he said there was no need to be nervous about meeting you, that you were cool.'

Did he now, Mel fumed. Cool? She didn't feel a

bit cool right now. She felt distinctly hot, with some kind of indefinable rage gathering in her chest.

'I'll just get my things,' she said to Samantha, forcing herself to sound calm.

'Are you sure you won't wait for Henry? He'll be sorry he missed you.'

'I'm busy this afternoon,' Mel said.

'Would you even have time for a cup of tea? It'd be really nice to have a chat with one of Henry's friends.'

Was she for real, Mel thought savagely. She spotted the corner of her black sack poking out of the kitchen door and went to pick it up. 'I'm afraid I'm in a rush, Samantha, maybe another time.'

'You'll have to call again. I'd love to hear all about Australia. Henry doesn't talk about it much.'

'No?'

'Although I can't complain about him. He really saved my life. He's great, he is,' Samantha gushed. 'I feel terribly lucky that—'

'Sorry Samantha, I really have to go.' Mel hoisted her sack and made a beeline for the door. It took two trips in and out to the car to collect the remainder of her things, and then, with a final wave at Samantha and completely ignoring her request to at least leave her mobile number, Mel put the car in gear and with a squeal of tyres did a three point turn and headed back down the road to the sanctuary of her bed-sit.

* * *

Mia's birthday party was a great success. Once again, Chloe was rushed off her feet with last-minute preparations. She had arranged for a professional photographer to come early in the afternoon, and he took portraits of Mia, sitting and standing, then a family group of herself, Adam and Mia. She had already picked out the exact spot on the wall where the portraits would be hung and she felt very proud of herself as she discussed the correct positioning with him after the photography session, especially as the Westmeath contingent had arrived early and had to listen to every word.

Try as hard as she might, Sandra couldn't find any fault with the bouncy castle or the face painter. Before she left, Diane paid her the great compliment of booking them for Hannah's birthday. Even though she fell into bed totally shattered, Chloe knew she had pulled it off admirably.

* * *

'To what do I owe this honour?' Mel glared as she answered the door of her bed-sit to Adam. Why hadn't she expected this, she simmered as she tried to close the door, but Adam put his foot in the gap and prevented her from closing it.

Adam smiled. 'That's a nice welcome for your best friend's husband.'

'How did you find me?'

'Simple. Chloe has already updated your details

in our address book.'

'I've nothing to say to you, Adam. We're not exactly great buddies, are we, you and I?'

'No, I guess we're too alike, aren't we? We both think we're a cut above, remember? Although I'm not feeling particularly proud of myself this minute. I just want to clear the air…sort out one or two little matters.'

'Like what?' Mel challenged.

'You know why I'm here,' Adam said coldly. 'And, if necessary, I'm quite happy to discuss it out here in the corridor.'

'I suppose you had better come in.' Mel grudgingly stood aside as he strode into her bed-sit. 'It's not exactly Abbey Manor,' she smirked.

'No, it's not, is it?' He gave her a thin smile in return.

Mel picked up the paperback she had been reading and put it away. 'You're scarcely here for a repeat performance, are you?'

'I want to remind you of our agreement.'

'Yes?' She wasn't going to make it easy for him. Let him sweat a little. Although he didn't look the least bit uncomfortable. His suit was razor sharp, his shirt and tie immaculate, even though he had put in a full day at the office.

'I want to remind you that Chloe's your friend,' he said, his voice clipped. 'She appears to have every intention of loyally picking up the threads of your friendship again.'

'And you, no doubt, were hoping I'd disappear off the face of the earth and never come home.'

'Chloe's happy, contrary to your expectations.'

'Really? That's not the impression I got.'

'What do you mean?'

'She might seem to be happy on the surface. But I get the feeling that underneath, Chloe's a bundle of nerves.'

'That's ridiculous. Chloe has everything she could want in life.'

'Maybe she thinks she has, but that doesn't necessarily mean she's happy.'

'I don't know where you're getting this idea from, Mel. I guess you're envious of the success we've made of things and I want to make one point perfectly clear to you.'

'Yes?' Her voice was sharp, her green eyes challenging.

'I love Chloe,' he said. 'I don't want to see her upset in any way. And we have a daughter. We're a family now. If you're any kind of a friend to Chloe, you'll respect that.'

'Emotional blackmail?' Mel said scornfully. 'I never thought you'd stoop to that, Adam Kavanagh. I seem to recall you were as much to blame as I.'

'I was totally pissed. So were you.' His blue eyes flickered over her.

'You're afraid, aren't you, Adam? Afraid that I'll upset your cosy little nest.'

'I'd prefer to think that you're more concerned with your friend's best interests.'

'I'd prefer you to leave now, if you've said your piece.'

He hesitated in the doorway. 'Look, Mel, I really regret what happened…'

'And why the hell do you think I stayed away for so long?' she fumed.

Her hands were shaking as she locked the door after him. She picked up her book and tried to read, but it was impossible. It was impossible to focus on the words when everything Adam had said, and the memory of that far-off night, were churning around in her mind.

Chapter Thirty-four

'Mel?'

'Hi Chloe, how are things?' Mel answered her mobile immediately.

'Great! I was wondering, would you fancy a night out? It would be nice to have a girly night. We didn't get the chance to have a proper talk at the party.'

'A girly night?'

'Yes, just the two of us. When are you free? Or would next Friday suit? I could get Adam to collect Mia from the crèche that night. He'll be working late every other night.'

'Next Friday is fine.'

'I could meet you in town around half five? Say, the Westbury? Do you remember where it is?'

'I do remember where it is, Chloe. I'll see you at half five.'

* * *

Mel was late. Chloe was sitting on a sofa by the window in the upstairs lounge of the Westbury and had nearly finished her gin and tonic by the time Mel eventually appeared. She felt a pinprick of annoyance. By rights she, Chloe, should have been late. After all, she was the one who had been up to her tonsils all day, dealing with clients and investments and all sorts of challenges.

She had deliberately chosen drinks in town after work. She would be coming directly from the office, the picture of the successful executive, complete with uniform and briefcase, having put in a demanding day at work. No harm in letting Mel see this side of her in action, and that in addition to her brilliant marriage and beautiful home, she also had a flourishing career.

And it would reinforce things for Chloe, help her get a proper sense of herself instead of this awful nagging feeling that her life was spiralling out of control.

'Hi Mel, sit down. What will you have?' Chloe signalled to the barman.

Mel took off her navy parka jacket. She was wearing drawstring trousers and a rugby shirt and her hair looked the exact same as it had on the night of the party. 'I think I'll have a pint of beer,' she replied. 'Whatever's on tap, Miller, Heineken,' she shrugged. She sat down in the opposite corner of the sofa and relaxed completely.

'Are you sure you won't have anything else? How about a G and T?'

Mel made a face. 'No thanks. Don't know how you can drink that.'

'It's an acquired taste,' Chloe told her.

'I've no intentions of acquiring it,' Mel grinned easily.

Chloe decided to let that go. There would be plenty of time to talk to Mel about smartening up her image. She ordered a pint of Miller for Mel and another gin and tonic for herself.

'And what are you doing with yourself these days?' Chloe asked conversationally.

'First of all, I'm trying to find my way around Dublin again,' Mel laughed ruefully.

'Yes, I heard you've bought a car.'

'That's right.' Mel frowned. 'How did you know?'

'Henry and Samantha were over for drinks last Saturday evening,' Chloe said. 'Samantha told us you were driving yourself around.'

'I see.'

'I thought Samantha would have been too embarrassed to set foot in our house again, after the party,' Chloe gossiped. 'But she wanted to apologise. We had a very pleasant evening. It was warm enough to sit out on the deck, and Samantha

410

was fine this time, but I never managed to find out why she was so upset.'

'Upset? That's putting it mildly.'

'I presume she's pregnant. But she seems very happy with Henry.'

'Pregnant?'

'That's the only thing I can think of. Henry or no Henry, at eighteen years of age it must be a bit of a shock. It probably only hit her when she laid eyes on Mia and saw a real live baby.'

Their drinks arrived and Mel took a long gulp of her pint. 'She's only eighteen?'

'So she told me. She appeared with Henry about two months ago. And you know what he's like, I took no real notice until all of a sudden I realised she was living with him. Must have been a case of instant attraction.'

'So she's being living with him for two months?'

'I suppose it's about that,' Chloe shrugged. 'Anyway, let's talk about us. We've so much to catch up on I don't know where to start.'

'A lot has happened since I left,' Mel said.

'And all of it good, of course,' Chloe said cheerfully. 'Adam and I got married, Mia was born, and now we're living in Abbey Manor in the house of our dreams,' Chloe grinned as she ticked off the items one by one on her fingers. 'And don't forget our two busy careers. I was promoted soon after I got married. As Adam said to you on the night of the party, it's a far cry from Harold's Cross.'

'And yet when I left Dublin you had broken off the engagement,' Mel pointed out. 'You were never going to talk to Adam again. I'd barely set foot in Australia when you e-mailed to say it was all back on and you were planning the wedding of the decade.'

Chloe decided to ignore Mel's smart comment about her wedding. 'Yes, we made up,' she smiled. 'It was just a silly misunderstanding. Adam explained everything.'

'Did he?'

'Of course.' Chloe quashed an annoying little flicker of doubt. Adam hadn't really gone into any details about Jackie and him, had he? She had just been so glad to see him on her doorstep that she had melted into his arms. Anyway, it was all in the past now. She hadn't even thought about Jackie in years.

'And are you happy, Chloe?' Mel's green eyes looked at her steadily.

'Of course, why shouldn't I be?' Chloe frowned. 'Adam and I are more in love than ever.'

'Does it not get a bit much at times, trying to keep up appearances?'

'Mel, whatever gave you that idea?'

'It must be tough going, trying to keep your home immaculate as well as looking after Mia and Adam and a career.'

'Nonsense,' Chloe protested airily. 'I'm well able to manage. Adam is brilliant.'

'Really? I got the impression that he works late most of the week and spends his weekends on the golf course.'

'Of course he's busy. KVL is flying. I don't think even Adam expected it to be quite so successful. And as for playing golf, it's only occasionally and that's where he networks, of course. But he's fully supportive of everything I do. So everything has worked out for the best.'

Mel drained her pint glass. 'Another drink?'

'Yes, okay.'

She shouldn't be drinking, Chloe fretted. She certainly hadn't meant to have three gin and tonics. It was bad for the baby. But it wasn't really a baby yet, was it? And this conversation wasn't going exactly as she had intended. Why should she feel she had to defend her lifestyle in front of Mel? Mel had nothing, really – a second-hand Ford Fiesta and a rented room, nothing at all to show for the last few years.

When the drinks arrived, Chloe decided to sip hers very slowly.

'Let's talk about you, Mel,' she began. 'What are your plans now that you're home? Ireland has changed in the time you've been away, but I can give you all the advice you need to get back on your feet again. That's one of the reasons I thought we might have this chat.'

'Really?'

'I'm well placed to give you whatever tips you need to get back into proper circulation. You've bought a car. That's a start. I presume you'll be looking for a job?'

'Yes, of course.'

'The thing is, Mel, I hope the length of time you spent backpacking around isn't going to be a disadvantage.'

'I wasn't backpacking around the whole time, you know, but thanks for the vote of confidence.'

'Let's be realistic,' Chloe said. 'Working as a waitress or lounge girl down under doesn't exactly equip you with skills suitable for the current Irish marketplace.'

'So what do you suggest?'

Mel's tone was a little cold, but Chloe quickly decided that Mel would see the sense behind what she was saying sooner or later. 'I'm just concerned that you've been four years out of the job market,' she continued. 'You might have to start on the bottom rung until you've gained some experience.'

'Thanks, Chloe, I'll bear that in mind,' Mel said sharply. 'I do have a degree, remember? Maybe I've finally decided to make use of it. Believe it or not, I have a couple of interviews lined up.'

'Have you? That's great,' Chloe said. 'So it's just a question of looking the part.'

'Looking the part?' Mel's green eyes narrowed.

'Well, your hair, for example,' Chloe began. 'Now don't get me wrong, it's nice, Mel, it was probably handy for Australia, but I've a terrific hairdresser who could really transform it for you. It's not exactly the latest style, is it?'

'No, but I've never paid much attention to the latest style.'

'I know. But if you want to be where I am in a few years' time, it's worthwhile paying attention to fashion and style and making the best of yourself. I mean, even the most famous celebrities reinvent themselves all the time.'

'You think I need to reinvent myself?'

'If you want to get a decent job and get on in life, you can't really look like someone who's hung out in Australia for four years,' Chloe said.

'I suppose I don't measure up to your exacting standards,' Mel said with undisguised sarcasm. 'Sorry to disappoint you, but I've no intentions of turning into an Abbey Manor clone.'

'Don't take it personally. You don't realise how much Dublin has changed. The job market has shrunk and it's very competitive. I'm only thinking of you,' Chloe insisted.

'Really.'

She wasn't getting anywhere, Chloe realised. Mel had a closed-up look on her face, as though she wasn't the least bit interested in what she had to say. She would be in for a lot of disappointment if she didn't get her act together. 'And Adam agrees with me,' she said suddenly, grasping at a straw.

'What the hell has Adam got to do with it?' Mel suddenly sat up.

'Well, besides it being a question of a decent career, if you want to find love and get a man…' Chloe began, glad that Mel was at last paying attention.

'Let me get this straight,' Mel said coldly. 'You think no one will love me as I am? And Adam God Almighty Kavanagh agrees with you that I need to be reinvented?'

'Please don't get all annoyed,' Chloe said. She should have guessed that Mel would overreact. Maybe she was going about this the wrong way. 'Look,' she began again, trying to adopt her most reasonable tone of voice. 'You've obviously come home because you realise your biological clock is ticking away and soon enough you'll want to settle down. I'm just trying to help.'

'Is that what you think? I want to settle down?'

'You'll be thirty soon, Mel. You must have become fed up with the free and easy life in Australia. You must want something more substantial from life.' Chloe hesitated at the funny look in Mel's eyes.

'Well go on with the expert analysis,' she said.

'What I'm trying to say is that you'd need to be a bit more image conscious if you want to find someone like Adam.'

'Adam?' Mel snapped. 'No thanks, Chloe!'

'Look, I'm only trying to help.' She had definitely got it wrong, Chloe fretted, and she hadn't expected a row with Mel. All she wanted was to give her some girly advice. After all, that's what friends were for, wasn't it? 'Tell yourself you deserve the best,' she said, trying to smooth things a little. 'Aim high. Surely you want a partner who's clever and ambitious and committed?' Mel couldn't argue with that, could she?

'And you think Adam's all those things?' Mel said, an annoying little smirk on her face.

'Of course he is,' Chloe smiled.

Mel began to laugh. 'Really? Don't be ridiculous,' she scoffed.

'I'm not being ridiculous. Adam's clever, he's very highly qualified. You only have to look at KVL to see how ambitious he is. And he's totally committed to me and Mia.'

'Come off it.'

'I mean it, Mel, our lives couldn't be better.' How on earth had she got into a situation where she was defending her lifestyle, Chloe simmered. She didn't have to justify herself to Mel, of all people.

Mel shook her head. 'You're putting a huge strain on yourself, trying to measure up to your high-class lifestyle, expecting everything, including Adam, to be perfect.'

'I think you sound more than a little bit envious.' Chloe tried to smile, to take the sting out of her words.

Mel laughed and her green eyes were full of mockery as she answered Chloe. 'If it took forever to reinvent myself, which I've no intention of doing, I'd never want to be where you are right now. And I certainly would not want to be married to Adam Kavanagh.'

Chloe frowned. 'You're still the same old Mel, aren't you? Henry was right.'

'What the hell was Henry saying about me?' Mel demanded.

'Nothing much, just that you hadn't changed a bit. And you're obviously still annoyed that I married Adam. I can't believe it. You're still jealous of me and Adam. You probably still think that all commitment stinks. It doesn't, Mel. Some people have the guts to make a go of things. Like Adam and me.'

'Yeah, sure.'

'You know, Mel, Adam told me to expect this.' Chloe gave a small smile.

'He what?'

'He didn't really want me to have a party for you. And he didn't want you coming out to Abbey Manor in case you got too envious of our lifestyle.'

'Is that what he said?' Mel asked incredulously.

'He was afraid that if you saw how well things have turned out for us, that it might get your back up. And obviously it has.' Chloe sounded resigned.

'I don't quite think that's exactly what he was afraid of, Chloe, when he didn't want me near the house,' Mel said. She took a mouthful of beer and watched Chloe intently over the rim of her glass. 'He didn't, perhaps, say anything about keeping me away because we don't really get on?' she asked. 'Or did he by any chance try to convince you there was no point in trying to breathe life into an old friendship?'

'Yes, but…'

'Ask him the real reason, Chloe. Ask Adam why he doesn't want me around. Go on, I dare you. And while you're at it, ask him did he always find me so dull.'

Mel had a peculiar look on her face. She finished the rest of her drink in one go and thumped the empty glass on the table. She stood up abruptly and picked up her jacket and bag. Then she pulled on her jacket and strode off in the direction of the staircase.

Chloe had the strangest feeling that her life was slipping into some sort of free fall.

Chapter Thirty-five

Afterwards, Mel had hazy recollections of sweeping down the staircase of the Westbury Hotel, almost crashing into the glass entrance doors in her haste to leave. She recalled the damp feel of the July evening, a crowd of giggling girls scurrying into Bruxelles, their high heels clacking, the flower sellers on the corner tidying up after the day, bruised flower petals on the red cobblestone footpath, and the scent of flowers drifting in the air.

She turned right and strode up St Stephen's Green, where she saw herself reflected in the windows of the shopping centre, a tall striding figure in a navy parka jacket. She went up Harcourt Street, circling strolling groups of people out for the night. She turned right at the top of the road and strode home to her bed-sit. It wasn't too far, a mile or so, and she needed to walk. To walk fast and try and clear her head.

And as she walked along, she waited – for a feeling of remorse, a feeling of guilt, for her conscience to get the better of her. But it never came. Instead she felt oddly numb. All the way along the South Circular Road, past terraces of redbrick houses and even as she turned into the avenue where her bed-sit was located in the third house on the right, she felt numb.

It was only when she caught sight of Henry McBride waiting patiently at the front door of the house that she burst into tears.

Henry McBride. The last person she wanted to see.

* * *

When Chloe arrived home, Adam was in the sitting room watching Sky Sports on the plasma telly. He had a glass of red wine on the coffee table in front of him and the *Irish Times* at his feet. The blinds were half drawn against the gloomy evening and a Tiffany lamp glowed in the corner.

'You're early,' he said.

'Yeah. How's Mia?'

'She's fine. Why, don't you trust me to mind her?' He raised an amused eyebrow.

'Of course I do. That's not why I'm home early. I'll be back in a mo.'

She went up to the bedroom, put down her brief-case and examined herself in the mirror. She looked the same as ever. There was nothing different about her face, her hair or the expression in her eyes. She could leave things as they were at this moment, with light July rain tipping against the bedroom window, Adam relaxing with a glass of red wine as he watched Sky Sports in the sitting room, Mia in bed asleep, herself with her wide grey eyes and sleek blonde hair, in love with her husband. In love with her life.

Things could stay like this. In another couple of weeks, she could tell Adam about the baby. He might be taken aback at first, but then he would adjust. After all, it wouldn't make a major differ-ence to his life. She was the one who would have to cope with the extra demands, somehow or other. She was the one who would have to juggle the house, her career, her marriage, Mia, the baby. Everything. She stared at her reflection in the mirror.

And for what? So that to all intents and purposes, everything would appear to be functioning beauti-fully in their perfect little world? Not a ripple denting the surface of their comfortable lifestyle?

Was she kidding herself?

What exactly had Mel meant? The mocking grin on her face had alarmed Chloe. Telling Adam about the baby seemed easy now. Telling Adam about the baby was nothing compared to the feel-ing of uneasiness lurking in the pit of her stomach.

But she could ignore the feeling, ignore the nausea, the sense of dizziness, the sensation of everything falling apart. Couldn't she? She could ignore her instincts and let them carry on as they were, Adam and Chloe, blissfully happy ever after.

Or she could ask him straight out what exactly Mel had meant by her words.

* * *

'What the hell are you doing here?' Mel asked. Tears poured down her cheeks and she rummaged feverishly and in vain in her jacket pocket for a hanky, so she dashed away the tears with the back of her hand.

'That's a nice reception, I must say,' Henry said mildly. He looked as unperturbed as ever. But then, Henry was always unruffled, wasn't he? 'I thought you might have asked how long I've been waiting here for you to come home,' he said. 'Or more to the point, asked exactly why I was waiting.'

She stayed silent, swallowed hard, and made a valiant effort to control the tears running down her cheeks.

'Don't you think we should go inside?' he asked gently.

Henry in her bed-sit was a no-no. Henry, with his perceptive eyes, taking up space in the small enclosure of her room, was something she couldn't possibly deal with right now. He was blocking her path to the front door, however, and she sighed quietly and wondered how the hell she was going to get rid of him.

'Mel, I think we should get in out of the rain, don't you?' he added as he touched her gently on the arm.

Up to then, she hadn't even noticed it was raining. The July evening was dark and grey, and drizzle eddied and danced about in the gentle breeze. She felt it on her face in between the rivulets of her tears and tasted it on her lips. When she looked at Henry she saw the misty droplets clinging to his auburn hair and drifting across the shoulders of his grey fleece.

'It's not very convenient right now,' she said in a stiff voice, backing away slightly.

'I'm a very good listener,' he smiled benignly.

'Henry, believe me, you wouldn't want to listen to what I have to say.'

'Try me.'

Her green eyes were bright with tears. 'I'm trying to forget about it, aren't I?' she said a little heatedly. 'I don't want to talk about it.'

'No unsolicited advice. I promise.'

'No, Henry.'

'Is it your parents?' he ventured.

Mel laughed ruefully. 'If it were only that simple. I'm afraid I've more than one skeleton screaming to get out of the cupboard. You don't want to know, and let's leave it at that.'

'Okay, you don't want to talk. Now that we've got that out of the way, aren't you going to invite me in?'

'No. I'm not very good company right now.'

'That doesn't matter.' His eyes caught hers, but she looked away.

'Can't you take a hint?' she said desperately. 'I don't want company, and certainly not yours.'

'If you don't want company, fine. But there's something I want to clear up with you, a misunderstanding. That's why I'm here.'

'Henry, you're the second person this week who's come prowling around in an attempt to clear things up,' Mel flared. 'I don't want things cleared up. I don't want to know. Okay? Now please, if you don't mind, I want to go inside. Alone.'

'All right,' he shrugged and stood aside as she swept past him into the relative shelter of the porch, put her key in the lock with a shaky hand, eventually opened the door and turned to close it behind her.

'So you're not the least bit interested in anything I have to say? Or why I was waiting patiently for you to arrive home?' he asked as he backed down the path in the July rain. There was a gap of six inches between the closing door and the frame. It never wavered by even a millimetre as Mel called out to him through the gap.

'You're right, Henry, I'm not the least bit interested.'

* * *

Chloe might have said nothing. She might have let life carry on, everything perfectly calm on the surface, continuing to gloss over the effort she had to put in to keep the show on the road. As she left her bedroom and went downstairs, she hadn't quite decided what to do. But when she went out to the kitchen to get a glass of chilled mineral water, she noticed her address book opened at the page holding Mel's details.

'What's my address book doing out on the kitchen worktop?' she blurted out when she returned to the sitting room. She sat down, not beside Adam on the luxury leather sofa, but on the recliner chair at right angles to him.

Adam frowned and continued to look at the football match.

'I didn't leave it out, Adam, so…'

'Chloe, stop fussing,' Adam was abrupt. 'I'll put it back in the drawer the next time I'm out in the kitchen.'

'I've already put it away. I was just wondering why it was out and opened at Mel's address.' She tried to sound natural, to cover the note of resentment.

Adam gave her a questioning glance. 'Mel's address?' There was a pause. 'Henry was looking for it.'

'Henry? What did he want it for?'

'How should I know? I didn't ask him.' Adam was irritable. 'He rang this evening and we were

426

chatting. Something came up about Samantha. You'll never guess, by the way—'

'I'm not interested in the finer details of Samantha's life,' Chloe snapped.

'Then Henry asked for Mel's address. As soon as I gave it to him he rang off. I didn't have a chance to tell him that she was out with you tonight.'

'And how did you know I had Mel's address?' Chloe's voice was tight.

Adam shrugged. 'I saw it already.'

'When were you looking for her address?'

Adam took his eyes off the telly long enough to glance sharply at Chloe. 'What's this? An interrogation? I came across it I when I was looking up something else, okay?'

'Really?' She willed herself to believe him. She willed herself to believe that he was looking at her like that because she was interrupting his all-important match, and not for any other reason.

'Yes, Chloe. I don't know what all the fuss is about anyway. Why is everyone getting excited about the whereabouts of a shabby little bed-sit?'

'I'm not getting excited. You are. And how do you know it's a shabby little bed-sit?'

'Because most rented accommodation is tatty.'

'Not necessarily,' Chloe argued. 'Some of the apartments in Henry's block are rented and they're quite state of the art. Maybe Mel's is equally modern.'

She was playing for time, putting off the inevitable. She hadn't yet come out and asked him any direct questions, like had he been to see Mel, and if so, why. Already her stomach felt as though it had turned to stone.

'Chloe, what is this?' Adam demanded. 'I don't know what you're getting at.'

'To be perfectly honest, Adam, neither do I. Is there anything to get at? So far I'm just trying to figure out a few things.'

'A few things like…?'

'Like is there any particular reason why you didn't want me to have a homecoming party for Mel? Is there any particular reason why you would prefer she kept away from this house? Away, in particular, from you?' She tried to keep the tremble out of her voice. She was holding her glass of mineral water so hard that she was sure it was about to crack.

'I can't believe you're getting into a state about this. Why don't you just calm down?'

'Why did she laugh at me when I told her that I think you're a terrific husband? I told her you were clever, ambitious and – let me see – committed, and she laughed at me.' Chloe's voice began to crack.

'Chloe, I don't know why you're making yourself so upset.'

'You're not answering me. You're avoiding the issue, just as you did when I asked you about Jackie.'

'Jackie?' Adam's eyebrows rose in disbelief. 'Christ, Chloe! What the hell brought this on? Are you sure you're feeling all right?' He stared at her so incredulously that she had to look away.

'I'm perfectly fine. I'm just trying to understand something, trying to understand why my friend and my husband don't get along, why my friend thinks there's a major reason you don't want her here in this house. And why you're evading the issue.'

'You'll waken Mia if you don't lower your voice,' Adam said briskly. 'It's obvious that Mel's jealous. I flagged this before now, didn't I? I told you she'd be envious of your life, your home, maybe even Mia.'

'Mel doesn't give a toss about our home,' Chloe said wearily.

'Chloe, forget about her,' Adam said with determination. 'She can't be much of a friend after all. She should be happy for you, glad that your life is turning out so well, instead of upsetting you with her silly notions.'

'I suppose you're right,' Chloe said slowly.

'You'd be mad to let her get under your skin,' Adam continued with renewed determination. 'Look around you, for God's sake. We love each other, we have Mia. It's only natural that Mel feels envious when you compare Abbey Manor to the shabby little room she's living in.'

There was a heavy silence. Chloe didn't realise she had been holding her breath until she suddenly felt suffocated. Her voice was strangled somewhere in the region of her throat as she faced him.

'And when, Adam, did you happen to see the shabby little room she's living in?'

This time, he was the first to look away.

'Adam! Why did you go to see Mel? You did go to see her, didn't you? What the hell are you covering up?'

'Look,' he began placatingly. 'Why upset the apple cart? We're fine as we are. Why look for trouble?'

'What do you mean, trouble? What's going on?'

'Okay, I did go to see her,' Adam admitted. 'Now that she's back in Dublin again, I don't want a situation arising where she might cause conflict between us, so I let her know that we were very happy, and I asked her to respect that, as your friend. Does that satisfy you?'

'No, I don't understand. You've scarcely spoken to her since she came home from Australia. How could you have known what she's thinking? She could have been delighted with the way things have worked out for us.'

'And do you think she's delighted?'

'I don't know what to think any more!' Chloe got to her feet and stood in front of the television set, blocking Adam's view. 'You're great at twisting things to suit you, Adam. Just tell me if there's any other reason you don't want Mel around.'

'I really can't believe this. I've had a hard day at the office, trying to salvage a project before it went belly up. The last thing I expected was the third degree when I came home. If this is what I get for babysitting Mia and letting you out for a drink, then forget it.'

'There you go again, avoiding the question.'

Adam sighed. He rubbed the bridge of his nose, the way he sometimes did when he was tired. Chloe wished it was just an ordinary evening, when she would suggest an early night and they would curl up in bed together.

'Chloe, I love you,' Adam said. 'You and Mia, both. I don't understand why you're going on with this ridiculous nonsense.'

'Neither do I. That's the whole point.'

'Now you're talking in riddles.'

'It's simple, Adam. Something is going on between you and Mel. And I'd like to know what it is.'

'I've had enough of this.' Adam stood up abruptly. 'What *I* don't understand, Chloe, is the whole point of this conversation.' He strode towards the door.

'Where are you off to?' Chloe asked, disgusted with the quaver in her voice.

'I'm going out,' he snapped, plucking his car keys off the hall table and disappearing out the door.

It seemed a long time before Chloe actually moved. She felt as though she was standing in front of the plasma television forever, looking at the glass of wine abandoned on the coffee table, the crumpled newspaper on the floor and the empty space on the sofa where Adam had sat. In reality it was probably only a few minutes before she crossed to the window and pulled the blinds down completely.

He had taken his car. Adam had gone out in a temper, with a glass or two of wine on him, and had

431

taken his car. Bloody great. He could be headed anywhere, she supposed – the pub down the road, the golf club, with its congenial bar facilities, or maybe Henry's apartment. In all their married life, he had never walked out of the house like that. Why had she started this? Why hadn't she left well enough alone? Surely she had learned her lesson after Jackie? Adam hated his love and commitment being questioned.

She went upstairs and checked on Mia. Her little daughter was fast asleep, lying on her stomach with her little bum in the air, the blankets kicked aside. Chloe's heart clenched as she fixed the soft pink blankets around her sleeping child before quietly leaving the room. Adam loved her and Mia. He had stormed out of the house because she had doubted his love.

She wandered into her bedroom and was momentarily startled when she caught sight of herself in the bedroom mirrors because she had forgotten that she was still in her green uniform suit. For her meeting with Mel, she had swapped her Premier Elect shirt for a soft linen top in natural ivory. She had thought she looked the picture of the snappy executive, out relaxing for a drink after work. She certainly hadn't looked like someone whose life was falling apart.

Adam could have gone over to Mel's. He could be arguing with Mel for putting silly ideas in Chloe's head even now. She took off her clothes and went into the shower. Maybe by the time she was finished, Adam would be home again.

But he wasn't. Chloe put on a wash and did some ironing and there was still no sign of Adam. She cleaned the bathroom and the en suite and there was still no sign of him. Then she reached for the phone and dialled Henry's number.

She could scarcely tell him she was looking for Adam, she realised all too late as she heard the ringing tone. Henry would think it was unusual for her to be looking for Adam at…she automatically checked her slim gold watch, but she already knew it was past eleven o'clock. But just before she had the presence of mind to put the phone down, Henry answered.

'Oh hi, Henry, Chloe here. You – you were looking for Mel's address?' she gabbled.

'Hi Chloe, yes thanks, Adam gave it to me.'

'He forgot to mention that she was out. With me. In case you called over and missed her, she should be home by now.'

'Don't worry, I've already seen her.'

'Was she at home? On her own?'

'Yes she was, well, earlier on, anyway. Why?'

'Oh, nothing.'

'Chloe…'

'Yes?'

'Did you think that Samantha was pregnant?'

'Isn't she?' Chloe replied, feeling as though she was on autopilot. 'She's very young, but at least she has you by her side. I suppose congratulations are in order?'

'God.'

Chloe was more mixed up than ever when Henry abruptly hung up.

Chapter Thirty-six

Adam eventually arrived home at two in the morning. Chloe was lying rigidly in bed and her heart began a suffocating thump when she heard his key scraping in the lock. She pretended to be asleep when he came up the stairs, but her heart sank all over again when Adam went into the spare bedroom and closed the door firmly behind him.

Rain fell heavily at around four o'clock in the morning. Chloe heard it drumming on the window, heard the swish of car tyres on the wet road outside. After that, she must have fallen into a fitful sleep because Mia woke her up at eight o'clock. For several panic-stricken seconds, she looked at the clock in horror. Then it dawned on her that it was a Saturday morning.

She went through the motions of feeding and changing Mia and downed two cups of strong coffee. She had a full load of washing churning away in the machine in the utility room and was emptying the dishwasher by the time Adam surfaced.

He came into the kitchen, pale faced and distant, and looked as though he'd had as little sleep as she.

'I'm going into the office,' he announced.

'What about dinner?' she asked automatically.

'Dinner?' He looked at her as though she'd suggested a trip to the moon.

'Yes, as in what time would suit you for dinner?'

She was mad. She was stark raving mad. Why wasn't she confronting him over the fact that he had stayed out til all hours last night? Why wasn't she letting him know she was furious because he had bolted out of the house instead of staying put and quietly explaining everything to her satisfaction? Instead she was being ridiculously polite as she asked him about dinner.

Pretending everything was perfect.

Adam stood in the doorway and shrugged. 'I've no idea what time I'll be home,' he said casually. 'I just hope you'll have come to your senses by this evening.' He turned and strode up the hall.

She was tempted to leave it at that. Maybe she was in the wrong. Maybe she had misinterpreted Mel completely. Let Adam go to the office, and maybe by the time he returned that evening it would all have blown over. They could open a bottle of wine and relax, and later, go to bed together. She wouldn't have to lie awake half the night wondering where he was. And everything would be back to normal. The perfect marriage of Chloe and Adam would be back on the rails again.

Or would it?

Adam began to open the hall door with the air of someone who was only too relieved to escape. All of a sudden, Chloe snapped.

'Hold on a minute, Adam.' She stormed up the hall, a yellow tea towel fluttering in her hand. 'You think you can swan off for the day and by the time you come home everything will be rosy in the garden again. Sorry, but it won't be.'

Adam shut the door and turned to face her. 'Don't tell me you're still hung up on a few silly remarks?'

'There's something going on that I don't understand and I'm sick of pretending that everything is fine, but I'll be damned if I'm going to continue,' Chloe said, her words carelessly spilling out.

Adam frowned. 'Pretending, Chloe? What are you talking about?'

'For starters, Adam, you haven't a clue how hard it is for me to keep things running smoothly around here. You're hardly ever around,' she continued heedlessly.

'What's this, Chloe? Insurrection time?'

'I just want you to appreciate how hard I have to work. You really don't know, do you? You don't know the effort I have to put in to juggle the house, the job, Mia—'

'Hang on a minute. What's this got to do with last night?'

'I'm trying to explain where I'm coming from.' Chloe was agitated. 'I'm just trying to point out how much of a struggle it is for me to keep going.'

'And you think I don't work equally hard?'

'Yes, I know you do. It's just that I find it very hard at times to manage, and I often let on that everything is all right.'

'Let on?' Somewhere she registered that Adam looked genuinely puzzled. 'What brought all this on, Chloe? If you're finding the going too tough, why didn't you say so before now? I thought you were happy.'

'I *am* happy,' Chloe insisted as she twisted the yellow tea towel around and around. 'I don't mind all the effort, the hard work. It's worth it, isn't it, so long as we have a good marriage? But there's no point in me killing myself if something is wrong, is there? I mean, it's one thing to pretend that I'm not too tired, or to pretend that it's no problem keeping the house spick and span, never mind the extra effort to make sure Mia and I are always well turned out. But it's another thing entirely to pretend, for example, that we have the perfect marriage.'

'What kind of pretending are you talking about? Where in God's name did all this come from?'

'I had plenty of time to think last night.'

'And you've decided to blow a hole in our marriage, is that it?'

'No, Adam.' Chloe hesitated before continuing, 'I think the damage has already been caused, and if that's the case, I don't see the point in carrying on like this, pretending everything is okay.'

'What damage?' He looked at her guardedly.

Chloe shrugged. She felt drained now, her immediate anger dissolved, replaced by a kind of tired resignation. 'Is there anything I should know about?' she asked. 'Anything that has you and Mel at loggerheads with each other, anything that made her stay in Australia for the last few years?'

Somehow she couldn't bring herself to ask the million dollar question, like what exactly did Mel mean when she said that Adam hadn't always found her dull? A remark that had kept her tossing and turning long into the night.

'You weren't the only one who had time to think last night, Chloe. So did I,' Adam sighed. He leaned back against the door and folded his arms. 'Now that she's home, I'm not putting up with Mel Saunders trying to drive a wedge between us. And I don't want any secrets between us, Chloe.'

He looked suddenly tired and defeated, and for the first time since she had known him, Adam looked uncomfortable. Almost uncertain. Chloe suddenly wished that she had left things alone, that she had let Adam go through the hall door, that she had left things as they were last night.

'Look, Chloe,' he began, his blue eyes looking contrite. 'I went to see Mel because I didn't want her causing any trouble. I didn't want her upsetting you.'

'What kind of trouble? What would upset me?'

'Something did happen…Mel and I…well…we were both pissed. It meant nothing, Chloe, you must believe me.'

'No, Adam! God, no!' She felt the cry of distress slicing through her body and was vaguely aware of the yellow tea towel fluttering soundlessly to the polished wooden floor.

'Look, Chloe, you and Mia are the most important people in the world to me and I'm not having a cloud hanging over us as long as Mel is around.'

'Is this some kind of nightmare?'

'Please don't look at me like that, darling. I'm really sorry. It was a huge mistake.'

'You can't mean…you and Mel…no!' Chloe choked. With a cry of rage she began to pound his chest with her fists. 'When, Adam, when?'

'Just before she went to Australia.'

'Just before Australia? And all this time…I don't believe this!'

'It was nothing,' Adam insisted. He took her hands in his and looked at her earnestly. 'We had broken up, remember? And I was drowning my sorrows. I knocked on the door of your flat, late one Saturday night, and it was the sorriest thing I ever did. Mel was there, alone. She had been drinking.'

'Get out, you bastard! Get out!' Chloe picked up the tea towel and ineffectually began to hit him with it.

'Have you heard me at all?' Adam pleaded. 'I'm really sorry, I don't even know how it happened. But I was absolutely twisted and it was over in minutes. It meant nothing whatsoever.'

'Of course it meant something, you prick! You betrayed me! Our marriage is built on lies and deceit!'

'Please, Chloe, listen to me. Our engagement was off at the time, that's how I was so drunk—'

'So you're blaming me? Typical of you, Adam. Always the golden boy! You never make a mistake, never put a foot wrong. Someone else is always to blame!' Chloe was shouting now and her voice was hoarse. Out in the kitchen, Mia began to cry.

'Get out!' Chloe cried. 'Get out of my sight!'

'I'm not going anywhere until we sort this out.'

'I'll sort it out pretty damn quickly, Adam. I want you out of my sight. Now!'

'Listen to me, Chloe, I thought I was doing the right thing by telling you what happened.' Adam held out his hands entreatingly. 'Now that Mel's back home, I'm not letting her come between us any more, so it's best that we clear the air and you know the truth.'

'Get out!'

'Look, Chloe, it happened years ago, long before we were married. You know I love you. Something

441

that happened on the spur of the moment a long time ago has nothing to do with us now, today.'

'You'll be telling me next that it should make no difference to our marriage, you bastard!'

'It shouldn't. We're the same as we were yesterday and the day before, and the day before that again.'

'That's a load of crap!'

'What happened between Mel and I was crap. Why should we let it matter to you and me? I was really drunk.'

'So that makes it all okay? Get out of my sight. I can't bear to look at you.' She was screaming at him now and it finally registered with him. Adam gave her a long remorseful look before going out the hall door and shutting it quietly behind him. Chloe began to thump the hall door, heedless of who might hear. Over and over she thumped at the door until her fists were sore.

She was quietly hysterical as she got through the day. She threw herself into the usual Saturday round of shopping, cleaning and laundry. She held Mia on her lap and looked at silly cartoons on the television because she needed the close, physical comfort of her daughter's body. She couldn't cry. She couldn't eat a thing. She couldn't even think straight. Everything Adam had said was strangled together in a painful lump somewhere inside her. She couldn't even begin to unravel what had happened, let alone make sense of it. The only thing she knew was that she couldn't bear to look at Adam and she didn't want to talk to Mel, ever again.

No wonder Mel had smirked at her when she had boasted about Adam and his commitment. No wonder she had stayed away in Australia. And she couldn't possibly have been bridesmaid to Chloe. She wouldn't have been able to keep a straight face as she stood beside Chloe while she and Adam exchanged vows.

Everything began to make dreadful, horrible sense.

By the time Adam returned home that evening, her mind was made up.

'I don't want you near me,' she said when he came into the kitchen. Mia was already in bed and Chloe was rinsing out her feeding dish and bottle. 'Have you any idea of what you've done?' she raged as she turned from the sink. 'You've made a proper fool of me and our marriage. I'm hurting badly, Adam. I wish to God I could hurt you in return.'

'Chloe, let's talk about this,' he said pleadingly. 'I'm really sorry for what happened. But can't you see that it has nothing to do with us? It's history now. We're happy, you and I, happy with our lives, happy with Mia. Everything is going fine. Why spoil all of that?'

'It was all spoiled long ago, Adam,' Chloe stormed. 'You're asking far too much of me if you think I can ignore this. And as of now, I want you out of this house.'

'You can't mean that.'

'I most certainly do. Right now. I want you to pack your bags and leave.'

'Please, Chloe,' he protested.

'I feel sick every time I look at you, you bastard, so I want you gone.'

'Chloe, you're being unreasonable—'

'No, you are,' she erupted. 'I can't possibly carry on as though nothing has happened. Don't you understand how I feel? I can't stand the sight of you any more.' In a white hot rage, she picked up Mia's sudsy dish and flung it at Adam. It missed and bounced harmlessly off the buttercup wall. She hated the look on Adam's face. Anxious, worried, regretful, his breezy confidence shattered. This new Adam made her all the more angry and distressed.

'Very well,' he said, his voice subdued. 'If that's what you want, I'll leave you in peace.'

She pretended to be busy in the kitchen as he went upstairs. She told herself she was glad when she heard him moving around, opening drawers and presses as he gathered some clothes together. She told herself she was relieved when he came downstairs hauling a suitcase. And even as he hesitated at the hall door, she willed him to be gone.

The house seemed strangely quiet after he left. Chloe went into the dining room, opened the cabinet and automatically reached for a bottle of vodka. She was just about to open it when she remembered that she was almost three months pregnant. All day long, she had forgotten about the baby. She suddenly realised that since she had met Mel on the Friday evening, she hadn't once given a thought to the new baby forming inside her.

And that was what finally reduced her to tears.

Chapter Thirty-seven

She was down on her hands and knees, scrubbing the tiled floor with an old-fashioned scrubbing brush, the kind her mother used to use on the faded linoleum floor on Saturday afternoons. But the tiles were filthy, and every time she scrubbed one clean, it crumbled into sawdust.

She was shopping in Superquinn. She was pushing a trolley around. The trolley was empty and she wondered why everyone was floating past, fingers pointing at her, laughing at her, until she looked down at herself and saw that she was wearing dirty rags that barely covered her.

Someone was crying. Chloe heard the sobs quite clearly. They laced her dreams and roused her to half wakefulness. They seemed to go on for ages.

Eventually she dragged herself out of bed and checked on Mia. But Mia was fast asleep, tucked up in her cot, the picture of innocent bliss. When Chloe got into bed again and settled herself on the lilac pillows and tried to shut her aching eyes, the hazy tail end of her dreams closed around her and she realised that the sobs had come from her.

Morning brought a renewal of the nightmare. Another night over, another day to get through. Only now it was Monday. Mia had to be dropped off at the crèche and there was a whole day in the office to cope with.

She was good at coping, wasn't she, she told her face in the mirror as she carefully blended in extra concealer to cover the circles under her eyes. She could manage fine, she assured herself as she backed her Beetle out of the driveway.

And there was no real need for anyone to know that she had sent Adam packing, or that her life was in smithereens, was there?

She was halfway down the road when she realised that she had left Mia's bag sitting on the countertop in the kitchen. Then she couldn't find her door keys. She rummaged for ages in her bag, spilling everything out onto the passenger seat of the car, before she eventually remembered that they were in the pocket of her jacket.

* * *

447

In a three star hotel in the Temple Bar district of Dublin city centre, Adam was getting ready for work. He frowned at his tired reflection in the mirror as he knotted his tie. He had been awake half the night, thanks to his thoughts chasing themselves around and around and a gang of drunken revellers who had no conception of the fact that it was a Sunday night and that Monday was a normal working day for most people.

As he picked up his briefcase and strode towards the door, he wondered how Chloe was getting on. Her distressed face had haunted his thoughts since he had stalked out of the house on Saturday evening. He lifted his mobile and punched in a number as he hurried down the staircase to the foyer.

'Hello?' Mel's voice was groggy.

'Mel, Adam here, and I'll dispense with apologies for disturbing you at this hour of the morning. Some of us are already up and about our business.'

'What do you want?' She was more alert now.

'I'm asking you to stay away from Chloe. And I'm hoping that this time you'll listen to me.'

'Stay away? Why?'

'You know exactly why, Mel.' His voice was cold. 'I've told her what happened between us and she's taken it very badly.'

'You've actually told her?'

'Yes. I was left with little choice after your well-chosen remarks last Friday night.' He had reached the foyer, exited the hotel and went out into the damp July morning.

'Yeah, well, I didn't do it on purpose. It's just that she had the nerve to tell me I needed a complete overhaul. Especially if I wanted to get a man of my own. A man like you. I felt a bit mad and I told her you didn't always find me so dull. I definitely think Abbey Manor has gone to her head.'

'Yes, it probably has,' Adam said. 'Chloe's put a lot of effort into it. She's only ever wanted the best for us. That included you as well. Now it's all been thrown back in her face.'

'C'mon, Adam,' Mel's voice taunted in his ear. 'Don't tell me you weren't able to talk your way out of it. The man with the silver tongue.'

'Aren't you the least bit concerned about Chloe?' Adam barked. 'She's supposed to be your friend, after all. She's so upset about what happened that she's thrown me out of the house. She says our marriage is over.'

There was silence at the other end of the phone.

Adam stalked towards the car park in Fleet Street. 'Happy now? You can sneer all you like at me, Mel. I don't care if you think I've finally got my just desserts. But don't go upsetting Chloe again. She doesn't deserve it.'

'She's actually thrown you out?'

'What did you expect? That she'd put out the flags?'

'I didn't think you'd tell her all the gory details, Adam.'

449

'You just wanted to shake us up, was that it?'

'I thought you'd wangle your way out of it, somehow or other.'

'Has it crossed your mind that perhaps I didn't want to?' Adam snapped. 'Maybe I didn't want to have any secrets lurking between Chloe and me.' He reached the car park and he had to put down his briefcase as he searched for his parking ticket in his suit pockets. Too late, he remembered that he had left it on the dressing table back in the hotel room.

Damn and blast.

'I can scarcely believe you're that noble,' Mel's tone was sarcastic. 'My guess is you were afraid I'd tell her anyway and it would be better if you got your word in first.'

'You can think what you like. I really don't care.'

'I'm no threat any more, is that it?'

'You were never a threat, Mel.'

'Then why didn't you tell Chloe about us ages ago? Why wait til now?'

'I didn't want to hurt her.'

'You mean you didn't want to rock the boat on your comfy middle-class life.'

'I know you don't have a good opinion of me, and that's also something Chloe was hoping to change,' Adam said as he turned around and began to stride back to the hotel. 'Chloe was hoping you'd realise she did the right thing when she married me. But for some reason or other, Mel, you decided to put the boot in.'

'Well, I got a bit pissed off when you were being held up as the perfect example of a loyal husband and I knew otherwise.'

'Hold on a minute, you're forgetting something,' Adam snapped. 'What happened between us was a once-off, unfortunate mistake. Chloe and I weren't even engaged at the time. You don't know what kind of a husband I've been to Chloe over the past three years. You haven't been around, have you? I'm far from perfect, I'll admit, but I do love Chloe. I know she tries hard to get everything right and she sometimes goes overboard, but she means the world to me. And so does Mia.'

'What are you going to do now?' Mel asked in a subdued voice.

'I'm keeping out of her hair for a few days. Giving her time to cool down. Right now she doesn't want to look at me and I hope you're satisfied. You know, Mel, I could almost think that you just couldn't bear to see Chloe happy.'

* * *

'Henry, it's Mel.'

'So you've decided to talk to me, have you?'

'I need to ask you something.'

'Your curiosity has got the better of you and you're wondering what I was doing waiting patiently outside your bed-sit.'

'Henry, this isn't the time for a joke.'

'What's wrong?'

Mel gripped her mobile. She had rehearsed exactly what to say but somehow, now that she was talking to Henry, the words wouldn't come.

'Mel, what is it?' Henry asked and he sounded so patient that she wanted to cry.

'Look, I need you to do something for me.'

'Of course,' he agreed.

'I need you to go around and see Chloe, see if she's all right.' She tried to keep her voice even. Who cared if Henry knew what had happened? It wouldn't make one whit of a difference. Not now.

'Oh. You're not asking me over for dinner then.'

''Fraid not. Anyway, you wouldn't want to come.'

'At least let me make that decision. What's wrong with Chloe?'

'She's thrown Adam out.'

'She's what?'

'She's thrown him out and I just wondered if you could check and see if she's all right.'

'Henry to the rescue, you mean. How come I'm always picking up waifs and strays?'

'You're the only one I could think of. Just knock on the door and see if she's okay.'

'Pardon me for being a bit thick here, Mel, but you're her friend. Surely she should be crying on your shoulder?'

'No way.' Mel's voice was muted.

'Why ever not?' Henry asked.

'Because I'm the reason she threw Adam out.' And with that parting shot, Mel ended the call.

* * *

The sun was finally breaking through in a sudden blaze of sunshine after a dull July evening when Chloe answered the door. For a minute she couldn't see with the glare of the sun in her eyes, then realised that Henry was standing in the porch in front of her. She had half hoped it was Adam, returning to beg forgiveness, and her heart did a double flip before it sank to her toes.

'Henry! What do you want?'

'Can I come in?'

'It doesn't suit right now.'

'Not even for a few minutes?'

'No.'

'Is Adam around?' he asked cagily.

'You know, don't you?' Chloe accused him.

'Know what?'

'Don't look so innocent, Henry, it's written all over your face.'

'Well, I've heard that things aren't right between you two and I was concerned.'

'You can go straight back to Adam and tell him he needn't send you to do his dirty work.'

'It's nothing to do with Adam. I haven't talked to him since last week,' Henry said. 'Mel sent me. She phoned me and asked me to check on you.'

Chloe began to laugh. 'She must have one hell of a guilty conscience.'

Henry looked at her blankly.

'Don't you know?' Chloe demanded. 'Or did Mel kindly leave that out of her version of events?'

'Sorry, Chloe, I'm lost.'

'Didn't she tell you she slept with Adam and that's why I've thrown him out?'

Henry frowned and shook his head. He turned from the doorway and stared up the avenue so that Chloe couldn't see the expression on his face.

'Ha! Surprise, surprise, my husband and my friend, in bed together. Is it any wonder I've shown him the door? And you can tell my friend,' Chloe sneered, 'that I don't want to hear of her or see her again.'

'Somehow or other, Chloe, I doubt I'll be talking to her,' Henry said as he abruptly turned on his heel and marched down the driveway.

Chloe went back to the kitchen. In the few minutes she had been at the door, Mia had managed to open a press. She was sitting in the middle of the tiles, covered in a thick dusting of flour, along with the cake tins and baking trays she had also managed to pull out.

'Mia! You bold girl!' Chloe picked up her daughter and shook her, and only when Mia began to scream did she realise what she was about. Chloe stopped, appalled at herself. She began to cry, sinking to the floor, and sitting on the powdery tiles, she cried and cried and rocked the warm little body of her daughter back and forth in her arms.

Where had she gone wrong? She had done everything she possibly could to make their dream lives complete. How could everything go so horribly wrong? How the hell had it all been thrown back in her face?

* * *

Adam began to phone. He phoned every evening that week. He asked after her and Mia. Each time Chloe told him to get lost. Each time she told him she didn't want to talk. She shouted and screamed and yelled at him and ordered him to keep away from the house and she slammed the phone down on him time and time again.

And every night she slept alone in the wide, king-sized bed. Or more to the point, she tried to sleep, but the bed seemed huge and empty and cold.

Adam called to the house the following Saturday and demanded to see Mia.

'I told you to stay away,' she said as she confronted him in the hall, all at once glad and horrified to see him.

'I want to see Mia. That's all.'

'Mia's fine,' she glowered at him.

'I just want to have a look,' he insisted as he moved past her into the kitchen. She caught the whiff of his aftershave and it made her feel sick.

'Then you're out of here.'

'Okay, okay.'

When she went shopping that afternoon in Superquinn she put a bottle of his favourite Merlot into her trolley without thinking. When she reached home and unpacked the shopping and realised her mistake, she promptly opened the wine and poured every drop down the sink, watching the red wine swirling around the stainless steel sink with a fascinated horror.

When her mother phoned she pretended everything was fine. She and Adam were up to their tonsils, she said cheerfully. Especially Adam. He had a rush job on at the moment and was in the office day and night.

And when she bumped into Kaz in the local newsagents on Sunday morning, with Mia screaming blue murder in her buggy, and Kaz asked her if everything was all right, she stuck to the same story.

'Are you in work today?' Kaz frowned.

'No, why?'

'Isn't that your uniform you're wearing?'

'Oh, this.' Chloe forced a laugh. 'I'm in such a rush this morning that I just grabbed the nearest thing. I'm so busy that I completely forgot to buy milk. That's why Mia is screaming. She hasn't had her breakfast yet.'

'You're slipping up, Chloe,' Kaz teased. 'Running out of milk and not glammed up in your Sunday best? I'll have to talk to Adam about this. Where is he this morning?'

'Up to his tonsils, rush job, you know,' Chloe laughingly shrugged as she wished the floor would open up and swallow her.

She went home and feverishly tore off her uniform suit. She pulled on her best Ralph Lauren trousers, but she couldn't do up the zip. Her tummy was expanding already. In the end she grabbed her tracksuit. After all, did it matter what she wore around the house when no one was going to see her?

She burst out crying when she realised she had put on a wash at the wrong temperature and Mia's Winnie the Pooh cardigan had shrunk to a doll-like size. She automatically took three pieces of chicken out of the freezer for dinner, and when she realised her mistake, she flung one across the room so hard that she knocked over a mug on the drainer. It gave her a certain grim satisfaction.

The following morning, her hand was shaking so hard when she put her key into the ignition of the car that she had to take a gurgling Mia out of the car seat, go back into the house and phone in sick to work.

And then that evening, when Mia was in bed, Mel phoned.

'I've nothing to say to you,' Chloe said coldly.

'Chloe, please, hold on, just let me talk to you for a minute.' Mel's words came out in a rush, as though she was afraid Chloe would hang up.

'Go to hell, you bitch.'

'I deserve all that and much more, I know, but just listen to me, please? Just give me five minutes.'

'Do you know what you are?'

'Believe me, I'm not proud of myself, Chloe, or of what happened. I'm really, really sorry. You've no idea how badly I feel about it all. If there was anything I could do…if only I could only turn back the clock…'

Her friend's voice was full of remorse, but Chloe ignored it. 'You interfering bitch. Don't expect me to *ever* forgive you.'

'I'm not expecting you to forgive me, I know I don't deserve it, but please forgive Adam?'

'What? Are you out of your mind? Did he put you up to this?'

'No way, he told me not to contact you, not to upset you further, but I had to ring you, Chloe. The whole thing was a ghastly mistake. It meant nothing.'

'You made love to my husband and it meant *nothing*?'

'It meant nothing in the sense that it was just…it was a mad moment, Chloe, please believe me. It was all a horrible accident.'

'Some accident.'

'Adam called to the flat looking for you that night,' Mel was babbling. 'It was *you* he wanted. He was disappointed when I opened the door. I asked him in because I was feeling lonely.'

458

'Lonely? Thought you were thrilled to be getting the hell out of Ireland.'

'I drank too much that night and started feeling depressed about my family. We were both hammered. We didn't make *love*, Chloe, far from it. It was just – God – a reaction, a silly, stupid blunder. Hate me for the rest of your life, okay, but can't you at least forgive Adam?'

'How dare you lecture me!'

'I'm sorry,' Mel said hastily. 'I'm really, really sorry. Say what you like to me, I'm a rotten bitch, I know. Blame me for everything if you like, I deserve it. But Adam loves you. And I know you love him. Don't throw away everything you have.'

'I can't believe I'm hearing this. You, of all people, urging forgiveness. What a joke. It's even funnier than saying that Adam loves me. And that was a great stunt you pulled, sending Henry around. No doubt he's reported back to you.'

'No,' Mel said slowly. 'I haven't seen him. And I don't really expect to.'

'Funny, that's more or less what he said,' Chloe snapped.

Mel was silent for a minute. 'It wasn't a stunt, Chloe,' she continued. 'I felt really terrible when I heard what happened and I just wanted to make sure you were okay.'

'Get lost. It's a bit late for your guilty conscience to activate itself.'

Chloe's attention was caught by the vase of tiger

459

lilies on the hall table. She looked at the curved shaped of the lilies, the soft peachy petals, the sunlight through the leaded panel in the hall door shooting rainbow hues through the cut glass vase. How dare they look so beautiful, she simmered, when right now her life resembled nothing short of a black, bottomless pit? How dare they look so perfect when her life was a total shambles?

'It's not too late for you and Adam,' Mel's voice rang in her ear. 'Listen to me, Chloe, he loves you. Don't let this spoil things for you. Please don't become like me, all dried up and cynical.'

'I dunno, Mel. I'm beginning to think you were right all along,' Chloe said smartly. 'Marriage isn't worth the paper it's written on.'

'Maybe that's what I thought once upon a time, but I was wrong.'

'You were wrong?' Chloe echoed.

'Yeah, wrong about you and Adam. You were right to marry him, Chloe. You're made for each other. And what Adam feels for you is a helluva lot stronger and far more important than any silly, stupid thing we did. You mean the world to him, you and Mia. Would it make any difference if I told you I was jealous?' Mel spoke haltingly.

'Jealous? Don't tell me you decided to break us up because you were jealous?'

'I had no intentions of wrecking your life, but I felt kinda mad the other night over…a few things, and I wasn't thinking straight. And I'm jealous of what you and Adam have now – the closeness, the sense of belonging to each other, his love for you, and your wonderful little daughter. Because somehow or other, I just can't seem to find it for myself.'

Chloe thought for a moment that Mel sounded as though she was crying. But she was obviously mistaken. In those first frantic days after leaving Galway, when she had finally dried her tears, she had said she'd never, ever cry again.

And then Mel quietly hung up.

The phone call made things worse. She had blocked things from her mind after Adam had walked out of the house. Now she couldn't get the pictures out of her head, pictures of Mel and Adam together, limbs entwined, Adam thrusting into Mel with that look of desire in his blue eyes, Mel responding and urging him on.

She took the phone off the hook and switched off her mobile. She fled up the stairs and tore off her clothes. She ran a bath, filling the tub with water as hot as she could bear, and immersed herself in it and scrubbed her body as hard as she could. She splashed her face over and over so that she wouldn't feel the rivers of tears pouring down her cheeks.

She stayed off work another day. Another day of drifting around the house, watching the hours go by, wandering from room to room, looking after Mia as she suddenly and gleefully discovered how to run.

'Wait til I tell your dad,' she caught herself saying as she chased her small daughter up the hall, her chubby little legs going like pistons. Then she remembered he wouldn't be coming home that evening, and she felt empty and hollow and so lonely that he wasn't around to share this small triumph.

The next day, as though Mia had suddenly decided to go all out, she began to feed herself, dipping her spoon into her strawberry yoghurt with a flourish and getting quite a lot of it into her mouth. Once again, there was no daddy around to beam with admiration and tell her she was brilliant.

Was this it? Was this what it would be like? An emptiness, a house that meant nothing without his presence in the evening, a daughter missing out on her beloved daddy's attention? Only he wasn't her beloved daddy, Chloe corrected herself. How could he be, when he had cheated on her mother?

And how dare Mel, of all people, suggest that she forgive him?

Chapter Thirty-eight

There was a slight drizzle falling as Mel, her arms laden, walked down the path to her red Ford Fiesta. It was another damp Friday afternoon, and a great start to the August bank holiday weekend.

She made two trips from her bed-sit to her car before all her belongings were packed away. Everything she had in this world fit into the boot, including whatever Henry had been minding for her and anything she had brought back from her travels. Once again, as she had packed up, she had come across her fluffy little dolphin with the white underbelly.

The only thing that has saved your life, she told it as she wagged a cross finger, is the fact that you came halfway around the world with me. And somehow it didn't seem right that the innocent furry dolphin should end up in a grotty Dublin City Council rubbish tip amongst mounds of household waste. So instead of throwing it in the bin, she sat it on the shelf in the rear window of her car.

She threw a final look around her bed-sit, and leaving her key on the table, she pulled the door closed behind her. She wasn't sorry to be getting out of the cramped, shabby room. She was only too glad to make an escape.

She got into her car, moved out into the traffic and turned on the wipers to rid the windscreen of the light misting drizzle. She drove outbound along the Naas Road towards the busy Red Cow round-about and the M50, joining the stream of traffic moving along the northbound M50. At the next exit she swung left for the N4, the west, and Galway.

She couldn't make sense of things any more, such as why she had bothered to come home from Australia, why she had driven a wedge between Chloe and Adam, or why someone called Samantha filled her full of irrational rage. The empty space inside her seemed worse than ever now, so it seemed only right to go back to the beginning, back to where she had started. Maybe if she made sense of the beginning, everything else would fall into place.

Alice Saunders had been ecstatic when Mel phoned. 'I can't believe I'm going to see you again! Your room is ready for you, of course, and I hope you have plenty of photos and stories of your travels.'

'I have indeed, Gran.'

'Good. You know your parents are home for good?'

'I know. Mum e-mailed last week.'

The further west Mel drove, the brighter the sky became. She barely noticed when the drizzle stopped, or when the grey skies began an imperceptible lift. By the time she reached Athlone, there was a hint of sunshine breaking through the clouds. It was usually the other way around, she recalled, raining in the west and brighter over the eastern part of the country.

And the landscape had changed. Mel couldn't get over the amount of new housing estates spreading out from the towns and villages, the new bypasses, the general air of prosperity compared to even four years ago. New hotels and luxury apartment blocks were springing up at the edges of towns, and of course the traffic. She slowed down coming into Ballinasloe and joined the tailback of traffic edging through the town. She had barely got used to Dublin city traffic, but by the looks of things, it was equally bad throughout the countryside.

Change was everywhere. Nothing stayed the same. She didn't know whether to feel glad or sad; all she knew was that as her trusty little Fiesta ate up the miles to Galway, she had a sense of feeling somewhat lighter in herself.

There was another huge tailback in Loughrea, where it took almost half an hour getting through the town. She should have stopped for a break, but she had been too anxious to keep going. In the town of Craughwell, the sun had finally broken through, and again she saw more spanking new housing estates and a jumble of colourful window boxes. The landscape now was more familiar, dry stone walls and roadside hedgerows and verges tumbling with summer colour.

She hit another queue of traffic for the Oranmore roundabout, but it was only when she saw the row of high flags drifting across the sunny evening air, the police hovering on snarling motorcycles as they directed the lines of traffic and the roar of helicopters lifting into the skies that it dawned on her – Ballybrit. The Galway races. Her heart lifted with memories of long-ago excitements.

She had picked a great time to come home.

Come home? Mel almost stalled her Fiesta as she frantically looked for the Spiddal road. The outskirts of Galway had changed beyond all recognition. She found the turn and indicated appropriately. Yes, she supposed as she double checked the signpost, she had the feeling that she was finally coming home. She wasn't running away, not this time, not any more.

* * *

'I'm sorry I didn't get a chance to talk to Mel,' Samantha sighed as she picked up a striped T-shirt and folded it neatly into her suitcase.

466

Henry frowned. 'What did you want to talk to her for?' It was Friday evening and he sat on the couch with a bottle of Budweiser as he watched the news on RTÉ1. Samantha was going through a pile of her tops, ironing some and packing others directly into her case. She was finally moving out, into a house-share with two of her pals from Athlone who had just arrived to live in Dublin.

'I'm thinking of going to Australia next year, and she'd be able to fill me in on everything.'

'I don't know that I'd recommend going to Mel for advice.'

'Why not? She seemed to know what she was about. Anyway, I thought you and she were friends.'

'Yes, we were.' Henry emphasised the verb.

'Oh. Like that, is it?' Samantha looked at him curiously. 'What happened?'

'The same old story, as old as time,' Henry sighed. 'She did the dirt on Chloe, something I never expected of her.'

'She *what?*' Samantha was incredulous.

'Adam and Chloe have split up, because Mel and Adam have been at it together.'

'No.' Samantha was round-eyed. 'You mean Chloe's Adam. And Mel?' Her voice rose. 'I don't believe you.'

'Neither would I have, only I heard it from Chloe herself. She's kicked Adam out.'

Samantha shook her head. 'That doesn't make sense. Mel and Adam? No way. Mel's not the type to deliberately betray a friend. He'd never attract her anyway, he's too, I dunno, too sophisticated for Mel. It's almost as bad as thinking you and me, Henry…' Samantha began to laugh.

'Chloe thought you and I were an item,' Henry told her.

'Did she now?'

'She even thought you were pregnant.'

'What gave her that idea?' Samantha had moved over to another pile of clothes, but now she stopped and looked at Henry curiously.

'I suppose it was your reaction to Mia,' Henry shrugged. 'She even thought I was the father.'

'That's mad! Didn't you explain?'

'I made the mistake of assuming that Adam recognised you, which obviously he didn't, but no, I didn't get a chance to explain to Chloe. Anyway, I didn't think you wanted all and sundry knowing your business.'

'It's all the same to me now,' Samantha shrugged. 'But look, Henry, if Chloe was so far off the mark with me, God knows how wrong she is about Mel and Adam. There's no way Mel and Adam… it's ludicrous. And she didn't take to their posh house any more than I did. She more or less told me that she preferred your apartment.'

'She did? When?'

'The day she called to collect her things, you were out buying wine, remember? She wouldn't stay, but I'm not surprised. I was in bits. I was still going around in my dressing gown with my underwear draped all over the rads. God knows what she thought.'

'Remind me about that day,' Henry asked her.

* * *

'Hello, Chloe.'

'Oh hi, Mum.' Chloe took a deep breath and tried to relax. She had been half tempted not to answer the phone. Just keep things light and friendly, she reminded herself. She'd had plenty of practice, after all, when she had returned to work last Wednesday, pretending that she was just over a sore throat. Yes thanks, that was why she looked so pale, but yes, she was definitely on the mend.

'Any news?' Irene asked.

'No, everything's fine.'

'Is Adam still working those mad hours?'

'Yes, he's very busy.'

'Any plans for the weekend?'

'I've nothing organised at the moment.'

'Good. How about coming over here for dinner over the weekend? Sunday or Monday, whichever suits? It would give you a break and we could take Mia to the park. And if you want me to babysit… I'm sure you and Adam could do with a night out, especially the way he's been working lately.'

'I'll have to think about it, Mum.'

'Think about it?' Irene sounded puzzled. 'It

469

shouldn't be a major decision, Chloe. I'm only suggesting coming to me for dinner and I'll throw in a spot of babysitting. Ordinary things that happen between mothers and daughters.'

'Yes, but I'm not sure what my plans are.'

'I thought you didn't have any plans.'

'I said I've nothing organised just yet.'

'I dunno, Chloe. The neighbours around here are almost plagued with their grandchildren. They're always in and out of their houses. But I never have that complaint. I sometimes feel like I'm not really wanted.' Irene laughed ruefully.

'Don't be silly, Mum, you know I'm busy at the weekends, catching up after the week.'

'And here I am, trying to save you a bit of cooking, and you won't take me up on it? Unless, of course, you and Adam are going out to some posh restaurant. Naturally, I don't want to interfere.'

'I told you, Mum, I don't know what we're doing. It depends on Adam and how his project is coming along.'

'Don't tell me he's working over the bank holiday weekend?'

'He probably will be.'

'That's crazy, Chloe. He'll run himself into the ground. And for what? So you can buy two more brand new cars next year?'

Chloe remained silent and tried to count to ten.

Chapter Thirty-nine

Alice Saunders was thrilled to see her granddaughter. She threw welcoming arms around her and her face was wreathed in smiles as she drew her into the bungalow. Mel unpacked in her flower-sprigged bedroom. She looked around at the clean lavender sheets, the candlewick bedspread and the heavy blue curtains, the jug of bluebells on the dressing table. She checked in the wardrobe for her walking jacket and knew by the fresh scent that her gran had recently washed it in readiness. She looked out at the view of the fields and the hill behind the house, the springy grass and the straggling dry-stone walls, and she immediately felt at home.

She spent the weekend chilling out, going for walks on the beach and relaxing in her gran's back garden. The weather stayed warm and dry, the skies clear and infinitely blue, and Spiddal was busy with visitors. Nothing much had changed in the time she'd been away. There were some newly renovated bed and breakfast homes and fresh paint on most of the village premises, but the beach was the same as ever, the coast of north Clare floating in a haze on the horizon, the blue-grey seas lapping along the shore, the skyline stretching away. She thought of Sydney Harbour and the Marina Mirage, the sense of excitement and activity, but this was a different excitement, a fresh, unspoiled landscape that was quietly familiar, to which she belonged heart and soul.

Her gran's house was the same as ever, too, even down to the row of family portraits on the front room windowsill. Mel looked at the schoolgirl, prim and proper in her uniform, but now she felt no sense of outrage or injustice, just a feeling of warm recognition for the schoolgirl she had once been. She looked at her parents and remembered the two people who had been in love. Were still in love. She felt different, softer somehow around the edges as she moved around the comforting famil-iarity of her gran's bungalow, very far removed from the spiky, stubborn Mel who had fled to Dublin all those years ago.

Her gran seemed to have become smaller and her hair even whiter, but the spark in her green eyes was the same as she pored over Mel's collection of photographs and asked her all about Australia. On the Sunday evening, as they finished watching the news on the television and sat companionably in the sitting room, she asked Mel about her love life.

'I was beginning to think I'd never see you again,' she admitted. 'I was full sure some Australian would snatch you up and you might never come home. Just as well for me that they're all wearing blinkers over there.'

Mel laughed. 'No fear of me being snatched up, so you needn't have worried.'

'Was there any romance?' her gran enquired with a mischievous glint.

'No, Gran,' Mel smiled. 'None whatsoever.'

'That's hard to believe. The lads out there must be as bad as the Irish, pure blind when it comes to a lovely young girl like yourself.'

'I'm fine as I am,' Mel shrugged.

'You're more than fine, Alannah.' Alice reached out and patted her on the arm. 'You're only gorgeous. And to think I really didn't know if I'd see you again.'

'Well, I'm here now, and it doesn't look like anyone is about to cart me off.'

'It would be nice if some day you had someone to love,' her gran said wistfully.

'Things are different nowadays, Gran.'

'Don't I know? I read the papers and I watch the telly. You young people are all having a great time, and rightly so. But there comes a time when it's nice to have a man of your own, someone to love, and maybe a wee baby. Unless, maybe you don't want…?' Her gran left the question hanging in the air.

Up to now Mel would have scoffed at her gran and told her there was far more to life than a man and a couple of babies, but now, in the restful atmosphere of her gran's sitting room, she found herself suddenly confiding in her.

'There was someone, and I thought…' she began.

'Oh?'

'It's not going to be, because his girlfriend is pregnant. And besides that…'

'Yes?' Alice encouraged, her eyes soft and concerned.

'I did something stupid before I went to Australia, I made a silly mistake, and now, years later, it's come back to hurt people. It was something I never intended to happen, I had too much to drink…'

To her absolute horror, Mel began to cry, and once she had started, she couldn't stop. Sitting on her gran's comfortable sofa, she dropped her head into her hands and cried as though her heart was about to break.

'Alannah! What on earth's the matter? Don't upset yourself so!' Alice was suddenly alarmed.

'God, Gran, everything is so mixed up inside me,' Mel said in a muffled voice as she struggled for breath.

'Sure, isn't it a crazy mixed up world we're living

in,' Alice said, fluttering helplessly around her granddaughter. 'Please don't take on so, don't upset yourself. Whatever it is, it can be sorted.'

'I don't think so.' Mel slowly shook her head. 'One night when I had too much to drink I did something very foolish,' she continued, mopping her streaming eyes. 'It was just before I went to Australia, and now Chloe's found out and I've wrecked her marriage and her life…'

Alice sighed. 'Will you whist, Alannah. I won't even ask what happened. All I can say is you're not the first person and you won't be the last to do something silly. We *all* make mistakes, that's how we grow and learn.'

'I'm no better than my father. And when I think of what a self-righteous prig I was…how all these years I wouldn't even talk to him…' Mel sobbed.

Alice took her granddaughter in her arms. 'Hush, child. It's part of the human condition, we get hurt, and unfortunately we hurt others.' She waited until Mel's sobs had subsided a little and then she smiled gently at her. 'You were never a prig. Young, impetuous and idealistic, yes, just as I was at your age, just as most young people are.'

'I was really mad with him, Gran.'

'Of course you were.'

'He must have been really furious when he heard I jacked in college.'

'Oh, he was,' Alice smiled. 'You gave us all a fright when you gave up your studies and stormed

475

off to Dublin. But then you redeemed yourself a little by going to college at night, didn't you?'

'That was partly thanks to Chloe.' Mel blew her nose in her hanky. 'She had more than enough ambition for the two of us. And she managed to persuade me that there had to be more to life. She was determined that we were going on to bigger and better things. And she definitely did, only now I've gone and wrecked it all on her.' Mel started to cry again. She didn't care that her gran must have by now put two and two together and figured out what had happened. She didn't care if her gran was shocked or horrified by her behaviour. It was all she deserved. 'Oh, Gran, what am I going to do?'

'Hush, child.' Her gran hugged her. 'You have to learn to live with yourself, first of all. You have to accept yourself as you are, a beautiful, intelligent, kindhearted – no, let me finish,' she insisted as Mel shook her head. 'You're a beautiful person, Alannah, but you're also human, so naturally you make mistakes.'

'This was a major boo boo.' Mel gave her a watery grin.

'I think we're all entitled to one of those,' Alice said stoutly. 'The important thing is to forgive yourself. And don't turn your back on everything and everybody on account of a mistake, major or otherwise.'

'I had to go halfway around the world and come back again before I found that out.'

'And some poor creatures go through their whole lives and never manage to forgive themselves, let alone others.'

'But I've hurt Chloe badly and she can't see beyond her hurt at the moment.'

'Give her time. And give her some space. But make sure you talk to her again. Whatever you do, don't isolate her or allow her to isolate herself.'

'I've tried to talk to her, but she wouldn't listen.'

'Does her husband love her?'

'Oh yes, he does,' Mel nodded.

'Then how could you possibly have wrecked her life?' Alice smiled.

'But she's thrown him out.'

'I'm sure he'll find his way back. He will if he loves her enough.'

'She means everything to him and I've already told her that. But right now she doesn't believe me.'

'Well, try again and keep trying until you convince her to look beyond your mistake.'

'Yes, maybe you're right,' Mel sighed. Her tears were gone now, replaced by a sense of utter exhaustion, and she knew that as soon as her head hit the lavender-scented pillow, she would sleep soundly for the night.

'I *am* right,' her gran's eyes twinkled. 'I haven't lived to this ripe old age without learning from my own mistakes! And don't be too hard on yourself, Alannah. Tell me about this lad you mentioned. Did he love you?' Alice asked softly.

477

'I think he would have, if I had let him. But I pushed him away and now he has a new girlfriend, and she's expecting his baby.' Mel shrugged and tried to put on a brave face in spite of the sore ache in her heart.

'I see. What's his name?' Alice asked.

'Henry.'

* * *

'Where the hell are you holed up?' Henry demanded.

'Henry?' Adam answered his mobile.

'What's going on? I've been trying to get you all weekend, but you weren't answering my calls.'

'I've other things on my mind.'

'So I gathered.'

'As you seem to already know, I'm living apart from Chloe right now.'

'Can we have a chat?'

'I'd like that, thanks. Say, the Westin at eight thirty tomorrow night?'

He was on a fool's errand, Henry told himself as he battled his way along Dame Street through the hordes of people out for the night. It was Monday night of the bank holiday weekend, and town was buzzing. The fine weather in the west of the country had finally spread eastwards and it was a mild, sunny evening. He should be doing something more exciting, he told himself, instead of raking over the ashes of Adam and Chloe's marriage. But he had to know for sure.

478

They were halfway through their pints of Guinness before Adam broached the subject. 'How did you know about Chloe and me?'

'How long did you think you could keep it a secret?' Henry demanded.

'I didn't think it would last this long. I thought Chloe would have taken me back by now.'

'So she did throw you out.'

'Yes, didn't you know?'

'I'm just trying to get the facts straight. Things can be easily misinterpreted, you know, like thinking that Samantha's my latest lover. At least that gave us a laugh. Did you really not recognise her, Adam? She only lived a mile away from us in Athlone and she was in and out of the house many a time.'

'Yeah, like about ten years ago.' Adam stared into his pint. 'There's a hell of difference between an eight-year-old school kid and the sexy siren Samantha's turned into.'

'That's only for show. She's just trying to find her feet again.'

'All the same, you can't expect me to have recognised her after all these years.'

'Tell me about Chloe. And Mel.'

Adam shot him a glance. 'Sounds like you know already.'

'It *was* Mel, then?' All of a sudden, Henry's pint tasted bitter and he resisted the urge to throw it in Adam's face. He shouldn't have bothered to meet Adam. He should be out on the town somewhere.

But he had scarcely been out on the town since he had come back from Australia. It didn't hold any interest for him whatsoever. He had a constant picture in his head of Mel and the way he'd left her standing on the beach in Port Douglas. Their fleeting goodbye hug was forever stamped on his heart. When he looked back, he could have kicked himself for meekly getting on the plane to Sydney. He had felt a rush of hope when he heard Mel was leaving Australia. But since her arrival home, things seemed to have gone from bad to worse. Now it looked like he would have to pull himself together somehow, and get back into the swing of things again, take Samantha's lead and pick up his life again.

'Go on,' he almost snarled. 'It *was* you and Mel, wasn't it?'

Adam sighed. 'Yes and no.'

'Either it was or it wasn't,' Henry snapped.

'It meant nothing, one of those drunken encounters – don't tell me you didn't have any of those in your time – it was over in seconds, and I was so pissed I don't really know how I even managed it. Trouble is, Chloe thinks it's the end of our marriage.'

'Well it would be, wouldn't it, if you had sex with her best friend?'

Adam looked into space. He gulped a considerable amount of his pint before he answered. 'Don't remind me. Thing is, Chloe and I weren't even engaged. It was all off. I was totally hammered when I called to the flat. Mel answered the door and I kind of remember she seemed to be upset about something. She had downed most of a bottle of Southern Comfort, not that it gave her any comfort,' Adam laughed harshly.

'Hold on a minute, when exactly was this?' Henry asked, trying to follow the thread of Adam's rambling explanation.

'It was just before Mel went to Australia. Chloe and I had spilt up, remember?'

'Before…? But I got the impression from Chloe that it had just happened recently,' Henry said slowly.

'No way. It happened years ago, when we had split up. Believe me, I've never stopped regretting it. And neither has Mel. That's why she stayed away for so long. I've tried to make up for it to Chloe, and I was full sure our marriage would be a success. I've tried to tell her it's past history, but she isn't having any of it.'

'I suppose it shouldn't really matter,' Henry said slowly.

'I'm glad you agree with me. So you think that Chloe will come around in time?'

'Oh, I wasn't thinking of Chloe,' Henry told him.

'What, then?'

'I was thinking of Mel.'

Chapter Forty

When Chloe walked into the Premier Elect office at ten past nine on Tuesday morning, Emer looked at her in surprise.

'Chloe! What are you doing here this morning?' she asked as she wheeled around from the photo-copying machine.

'Coming to work, of course. Why?' Chloe demanded. She stopped in her tracks and felt cold all over. She must know. Somehow word had got out that she had shown Adam the door, and Emer thought she'd be too upset to come to work. And if Emer knew, then who else? God. This was all she needed. Wait til the grapevine got hold of this. The whole office would be a no-go area.

'I thought you were going to the meeting,' Emer explained.

'What meeting?' Chloe's voice was suddenly hoarse.

'Debbie Driscoll's meeting with the customer service managers…' Emer's voice faltered. 'Don't tell me you've forgotten about it.'

'Of course I didn't,' Chloe snapped, recovering her composure. 'I had to come by the office to pick up some figures, that's all.'

Pick up some figures? What figures? What meeting? She was horrified to realise that her mind was completely blank. Her legs were trembling as she walked over to her desk and dropped her bag. Her vision was blurred as she leafed through files on her desk and her hands were shaking so much that a bundle of papers slipped out of her grasp and slewed across the carpeted floor.

'Hold on, Chloe, I'll give you a hand,' Emer offered. She bent down to retrieve the papers.

'No, I'm fine, thanks,' Chloe said abruptly, gathering everything together into a messy pile. Fine? Anything but. She switched on her computer and logged into her account and checked her calendar of events. And right enough, there it was, full details of the meeting, including the agenda.

Debbie had sent the memo around last week, requesting the Dublin-based customer service managers to meet in head office that morning to discuss interim results of the latest customer satisfaction survey, and everyone was to bring whatever information they had collated so far. Chloe had been working on a preliminary report, but now, of course, she couldn't find it. She couldn't remember where she had put it any more than she had remembered the meeting that morning. How on earth had she forgotten about it in the space of a bank holiday weekend?

A bank holiday weekend when she had spent the three days holed up in the house with Mia, afraid that Emma or Kaz would notice something amiss, petrified that her mother might take it upon herself to visit her out of the blue. A weekend when she had switched off her mobile and unplugged the phone, and the only person she had talked to was Adam when he had turned up on Sunday morning and asked to see Mia.

Not that she'd had much of a conversation with him. He had taken Mia out in his car and brought her home three hours later. Chloe didn't even ask him where he'd been as he dropped his little daughter back. Mia had promptly dissolved into floods of tears as he waved her goodbye.

Chloe had felt like crying too, but she had no tears left by now, only a hollow ache somewhere deep inside of her. After another sleepless night, she had been so relieved to drop Mia at the crèche as normal and get to work in one piece that she had totally forgotten she was supposed to be at the head office just about now.

This was a disaster. Never in her professional career had she been so careless. She closed her eyes briefly and tried to take a deep breath, but she couldn't even breathe properly because her heart felt as though it was lodged in her throat.

She tried to prioritise. Phone Debbie and tell her she had been held up. Find her draft report. It had to be somewhere on her desk. Then she would have to get a taxi up to head office. Getting her car and driving up wasn't an option, she rapidly calculated, it would take too long to find parking. She eventually found her interim report, ready and waiting in a large manila envelope in her out tray. She grabbed it with relief and picked up the phone to order a taxi.

The taxi took an age. In city centre traffic, it weaved dangerously between bus lanes, trucks and cars. Chloe sat in the back seat, feeling almost weak as she clutched her briefcase. How could she have been so stupid as to forget a meeting, a meeting with Debbie of all people? Her skin prickled with acute embarrassment at the thoughts of arriving so late.

'Good morning, Chloe,' Debbie said pointedly as she slunk into the meeting room in head office almost forty minutes late. She took her place at the table, with the half a dozen other customer service managers. Tara Conroy, as perfectly groomed as ever, smiled cattily across at her and Chloe felt like scratching her eyes out.

'Sorry I'm late, Debbie, you see—'

Debbie put up her hand. 'Spare us the excuses, Chloe,' she said crisply. 'We've work to get on with and we're behind as it is. Now Tara, would you mind presenting your interim findings?'

A couple of Chloe's colleagues smiled sympathetically as Chloe opened her briefcase and took out her papers, but it didn't make her feel any better. The last place she wanted to be was at the receiving end of their sympathy.

Tara rose to her feet. 'I have copies for everyone,' she began, distributing some handouts around the table.

'Good thinking,' Debbie smiled approvingly.

Chloe's stomach clenched as she glanced through Tara's report. Not only was it was glaringly clear that Tara had put a huge amount of effort into her interim report – far more effort than Chloe had put into hers – but in her rush to get to the meeting, Chloe hadn't even thought about the basic necessity of making copies for everyone else.

Bloody brilliant. She was really going to be shown up now.

She was a failure, a total failure. She couldn't handle her marriage and neither could she handle her career. All her efforts, all her ambitions, had crumbled into dust. She scarcely heard Tara's little speech. There was a peculiar buzzing sound in her ears and she was suddenly nauseous. She was painfully aware that Tara sounded more confident than ever, more self-assured and a hundred times more efficient than Chloe felt at that moment. The group discussed the salient points of Tara's report, most of the discussion flowing over Chloe's head, and Debbie thanked Tara for her excellent work.

And then it was Chloe's turn.

She took a deep breath and nailed a bright smile to her face and slowly rose to her feet. 'What I have here is very much a draft report,' she began. She swallowed hard and tried to clear her muzzy head. 'Customers were very slow to return their survey forms and so I don't even have a minimum number of replies.'

Debbie frowned. 'That doesn't sound very promising, Chloe. Surely you initiated some follow up?'

'Yes, but—'

Debbie cut across her. 'Out of the replies you did receive, can we have your initial findings? I presume you have copies…?'

'Well, er, the photocopier was on the blink this morning,' Chloe fibbed. Her voice was thin and seemed to come from very far away.

'This morning?' Debbie looked disbelieving.

'Yes, em, that is…'

She never got to explain or elaborate any further. The noise in her ears increased to a tidal roar and there was a funny taste in her mouth. Everything swam in front of her, she saw two Debbie Driscolls looking at her impatiently, two Tara Conroys calmly smirking, before she slumped quietly to the floor.

* * *

Debbie immediately called off the meeting. She took charge, helping Chloe up into a sitting position on her chair, ordering her to drink some water, then putting her head between her legs. With her nose humiliatingly pressed against the green of her uniform skirt, Chloe heard Debbie sending Tara off to the canteen to fetch some weak tea and toast. She asked everyone else to return to their respective offices. When Tara returned from the canteen and Chloe finally raised her head, Debbie rattled a hundred and one questions at her.

Was she ill? Was she on any medication? What was her doctor's name? Did she want to call the doctor? Did she want to go to the bathroom? Was there any particular reason why she had passed out?

Chloe shook her head in reply. She felt a cold sweat beading her face and her hands trembled as she forced down a piece of toast and drank some hot, weak tea. After a while her breathing calmed a little and she began to feel better. Tara and Debbie were talking in low murmurs and watching her anxiously, and everyone else had gone.

'I'll be fine in a minute, sorry about that Debbie,' she croaked. 'Sorry I disrupted the meeting.'

'Nonsense, Chloe. Don't be concerned about the meeting, that'll keep for another day,' Debbie said briskly. 'I'm far more concerned with you, and you won't be fine in a minute. You're going straight home to bed, and what's more, I'm driving you.'

'There's no need—'

'There's every need. You're in no fit state. Tara's parked outside, she's going to bring us over to your office to pick up your car. It's all arranged. I'm driving you home, and then I'll get a taxi back into town.'

'Really, Debbie, there's no need. I'm sure I can manage to get home myself.'

'That's beside the point. I'm not allowing you to drive home, full stop.'

'I can't put you to this trouble,' Chloe protested.

'Chloe, I'm not doing this for the fun of it,' Debbie said firmly. 'I'd be in a lot more trouble if I didn't look after you properly and ensure your safety. And as far as I'm concerned, the only safe place for you right now is your own bed.'

Chloe felt hot and cold all over, but now it was for a different reason. Would life ever be normal again, she agonised as she handed over her car keys. And what was normal? She had completely forgotten what normal was like. Right now, it resembled some kind of hazy utopia that was far beyond her reach.

Late morning traffic was light. Driving Chloe's Volkswagen, Debbie made steady progress out through Harold's Cross en route for Abbey Manor. The sun was high in the sky and it hurt Chloe's eyes as it bounced off the rear window of the car in front.

'You'll have to give me directions in plenty of time, Chloe,' Debbie said crisply as she slowed to a halt at traffic lights. 'I'm hopeless at navigating around the outskirts of Dublin, especially with all the new roads.'

'Okay.' Chloe's voice was practically a whisper.

Debbie, hopeless? Debbie couldn't possibly be hopeless at anything. The word 'hopeless' shouldn't even be in her vocabulary, unless, of course, Chloe grimly qualified, she was talking about a certain member of her staff. She felt as though she was moving in some kind of surreal dream as Debbie turned in at the entrance to Abbey Manor and followed the directions to her house.

'This is very nice,' Debbie said approvingly as she turned into the driveway and brought the car to a stop.

Chloe glared mockingly at her four-bed detached house, with the cobble-locked driveway and landscaped front garden. She couldn't believe she was returning home like a troublesome child sent home from school. She would far rather be at her desk, competently going about her day's work, collecting Mia from the crèche as usual, watching the news on the kitchen portable as she cooked dinner for herself and Adam… But normal things she had taken for granted a few short weeks ago now seemed so impossible.

'I can't thank you enough, Debbie,' she said chastely as they got out of the car and Debbie handed her back her keys.

'Aren't you going to ask me in?' Debbie queried.

'Yes, of course, come in,' Chloe said hastily. She opened the hall door and ushered Debbie into the sitting room, darting furious eyes around in case

490

anything was out of place. But there was nothing amiss in the perfectly ordered room. All was calm and tidy and overlaid with a sweet floral scent from the bowl of yellow roses on the mantelpiece.

'You shouldn't have too long to wait for a taxi,' Chloe said. 'Will you have a cup of tea while you're waiting?'

'No thanks, Chloe, I'm fine. You're to sit back and relax. But first tell me who I should phone.'

'I can get you the local taxi numbers if you hang on a minute.'

'Sit down, Chloe, and that's an order,' Debbie insisted. 'I didn't mean taxi numbers, I can use the company service. Who can I phone for you? Who's going to come and keep an eye on you?'

'I'll be fine, Debbie,' Chloe blustered. Just get Debbie out of here fast, she fretted, as fast as possible. Then she could crawl up to bed and howl like a baby, because she sure as hell couldn't keep up a front for very much longer.

'I've no intentions of leaving you in an empty house after what happened this morning,' Debbie said sharply. She took out her mobile. 'Who will I phone, Chloe? Your husband?'

'Oh no, not Adam.'

Debbie's eyebrows rose enquiringly.

'He's away…away on business,' Chloe spluttered. 'He'll be gone for the whole week.'

'And you're trying to carry on as normal, no doubt,' Debbie commented.

'I've no problems coping by myself.'

Debbie put down her phone and eyed Chloe squarely. 'It's no reflection on yourself or your husband, Chloe, but I really don't know how you young mothers juggle with full-time jobs and babies, not to mention the hassle of commuting time. And from what I hear, nowadays crèches are usually inflexible as regards closing hours. It must be a nightmare sometimes.'

'It can be difficult,' Chloe admitted, relieved to get off the subject of Adam.

'I'd say it is.'

'But nothing you couldn't manage, Debbie,' Chloe ventured.

Debbie frowned. 'Me? You scarcely think I worked full time when my two little scoundrels were small.'

'Didn't you? I always thought…'

'Not at all. I would have cracked up long ago. I jobshared, and I had a great neighbour nearby who also jobshared. We looked after each other's children on alternate weeks and it was a terrific arrangement. I only returned to full-time duties when my youngest started secondary school. Mind you,' she added dryly, 'I sometimes wonder if I made the right decision. If you ask me, the older they get, the more worry it is.'

Chloe couldn't believe what she was hearing. It was strange enough to see Debbie Driscoll, Premier Elect's high flyer, perched on her leather sofa in her

492

Abbey Manor sitting room with her smart linen suit and expertly styled red hair. But to hear her chatting about her family and admitting that she had job-shared because she couldn't have managed a full-time job when her children were small was news to Chloe.

'You're looking a little better,' Debbie said. 'You've a bit more colour in your face. You certainly gave us all a fright this morning.'

Chloe smiled.

'Any reason why you slumped to the floor in such a spectacular fashion? I know you were dying to disrupt the meeting, but maybe you took it a bit too far?'

'I don't know how it happened,' Chloe fibbed.

'Maybe you're overdoing it a little,' Debbie said. 'It's tough nowadays trying to cope with young families and careers. Far be it from me to offer advice, and this is strictly off the record, but there's always the option of cutting down your hours a little. It was something I never regretted and I can guarantee you, it won't affect your career.'

'I'm able to manage.'

'Yes, but at what cost to yourself? I bet you just about get through the week and spend the weekend catching up. You're losing out on time with your little daughter.'

'What's this?' Chloe felt uncomfortable. 'Do you think my work is suffering?'

'Not at all. I just think you're stretching yourself as far as possible,' Debbie spoke clearly. 'And sometimes that means going into overdrive. If that happens too often…' Debbie shook her head. 'I remember the day you came back to work after your daughter was born and you insisted that nothing would change. That's not possible, Chloe. Of course things change when you have a baby who's completely dependent on you, a baby who you love to bits. There is a balance to be struck, you know, between your home life and your career. You remind me of me, in a way.'

'Do I?' Chloe croaked.

'Yes. You're conscientious. And ambitious. You don't want to let any of your standards slip because you now have a baby. That's very admirable, but very punishing for yourself if you think you can maintain the same level of output on all fronts, all of the time. Something will give eventually.' Debbie gave a short laugh. 'I'm not giving you a lecture, Chloe. I'm just speaking from the point of view of the well-being of my staff, and nothing else. It's up to you and your husband, of course, and no one else to decide your priorities. Hmm?'

'Yes, Debbie.'

'Just give yourself permission not to be a superwoman now and again, okay? And now,' she held out her phone. 'Who shall I contact?'

Chapter Forty-one

Irene's face was creased with worry when Chloe answered the door to her.

'What's wrong, Chloe? Has anything happened to Mia? Or Adam?'

'Come in, Mum. No, there's nothing wrong, nothing major.'

'I got a bit of a fright when your boss phoned and asked me to drop over. Is she still here?' Irene glanced into the sitting room.

'No, she's just left.'

'What's going on?' Irene asked as she followed Chloe through to the kitchen.

'Nothing, really, Mum,' Chloe said lightly as she put on the kettle. 'I wasn't feeling too well in work today so Debbie brought me home. She wouldn't leave until she was satisfied that I had someone to keep an eye on me, so she insisted on calling you, even though I'm fine.'

'Fine? Your boss takes the time to bring you home from work, insists on ringing me, and you think you're fine? What exactly happened this morning?'

'I just felt a little weak, but I'm okay now,' Chloe said stoutly. And all of a sudden, she began to feel exhausted.

'You can't have recovered that quickly. I hope she told you to take the rest of the week off.'

'She did, actually.'

'I bet it was more than just feeling a little weak. I'm delighted you asked her to call me. Anything I can do for you, just say the word,' Irene said briskly as she took off her jacket. 'You sit down and relax. I'll make the tea. And let's see if I can make a sandwich for us. It's almost lunchtime. Which door is the fridge hidden behind?'

'The last one on the left. Just poke around, you'll find whatever you need.' Chloe sat down at the table, feeling utterly drained. Too tired to even talk, she watched her mother prepare a plate of ham sandwiches and a pot of tea and set it all out on the table. As though she sensed Chloe's exhaustion, her mum didn't even ask which crockery she should use, just grabbed whatever was in sight.

'This is a novelty, Chloe,' Irene said as she sat down at the table. 'A lunchtime treat, just the two of us.'

'What shift are you on today?'

'I'm due in at three, but I've already phoned the supermarket and it's no problem to arrange cover for me. I told you before, don't hesitate to call on me if you need to.'

'I can't have you staying off work on my account!'

'Don't be ridiculous. You're far more important to me than a few hours stacking shelves. I'm staying put until Adam gets home, and that's that.' Irene calmly refilled her mug of tea.

Chloe took a deep breath. 'In that case, you'll have a long wait.'

'Why? Where's Adam?'

'He's away on business. In Cork.' More lies. God.

'Cork? When will he be home?'

Chloe shrugged. 'Probably the weekend.'

'Then you're coming home with me.'

'I can't do that,' Chloe objected.

'Why ever not? Your old room is still there and my car is outside. All you have to do is change out of that uniform into something more relaxing and pack a bag with a few things for Mia and yourself. We can pick her up at the crèche and off we go. Just for a couple of days. It'll give me a chance to mind my little granddaughter and you'll have a complete rest.'

'No, I can't do that…' Chloe hesitated.

'I'm not giving you any choice. You're coming with me and for once you're listening to your mum. Now that you're expecting another baby,

Chloe, you'll just have to look after yourself.' She eyed her daughter with solicitude.

'How – how did you know?'

Irene smiled. 'Call it a mother's instinct. When are you due?'

'January. Mia'll only be a year and a half.'

'All the better. You can rear them together and they'll be great company for each other.'

'Do you think so? I thought it was a bit soon…' Chloe said despondently. 'I thought it was much too soon,' she continued as her mother looked at her with concern. 'And this wasn't part of my plan,' she finished in a sudden rush of confidence.

'Oh, Chloe, don't be worrying. Life seldom turns out to plan. You'll manage fine.' Irene put down her mug and looked at her calmly. She reached across the table and patted Chloe's hand. 'Think of how much Mia means to you and just imagine that on the double. A new little baby. How wonderful. You might have to make some adjustments, but you'll cope, of course you will.'

She didn't know whether it was her mother's utmost confidence in her, her calm acceptance of the fact that another baby was on the way, and that it was wonderful, or merely the fact that she had at last shared the news that had been haunting her for over a month, but Chloe felt some of the cloud lifting. She sensed a bright chink in a corner of the huge grey pall that had overshadowed her life. To her embarrassment, she felt tears pricking her eyes, so she got up from the table in the pretence of looking for some biscuits. While she had her head stuck in a press searching for biscuits that didn't exist, she told her mum that yes, she would come back home with her, just for a couple of days.

* * *

Mia's eyes lit up when they arrived at the crèche. She abandoned the toys she had been playing with and ran over to them on little chubby legs, her arms outstretched. She was starting to talk now, mostly gibberish, but one or two words were quite clear, and Irene swore that she heard her call her 'Ganny'.

She insisted that Chloe went to bed for the afternoon. She put fresh sheets on her old bed and said she was taking Mia to the park, so she wouldn't be disturbed. It was strange to be back in her old room. Chloe could hardly remember the last time she had slept there. The room was all at once different and familiar. Her brothers had commandeered a corner for their computer and the bookshelf was filled with disks and games, but some of her old teddies were still sitting on the shelf over the bed. Whatever Chloe hadn't taken with her had been put up into the attic and was probably still there, she mused as she lay calmly in bed and let the quietness of the house settle around her.

She slept for several hours, and when she awoke, she felt refreshed. She went downstairs, feeling a little embarrassed at being back in the family fold again, but she needn't have worried. Her dad was reading the paper in front of the telly and beyond asking Chloe how she felt, he didn't make undue fuss. He didn't dare. He was under strict orders from Irene.

'Hello love, sleep well?' her mum asked.

'Yes, thanks. Where's Mia?'

'She's in the front room with the boys. It's a wonder they didn't wake you up, the racket they're making.'

And only she saw it with her eyes, Chloe would never have believed it. Her two brothers, whom she had often dismissed as no brainers, were doing their level best to show their little niece how to play the guitar, and Mia was enjoying every minute.

Chloe stayed on in bed the following morning at her mum's insistence. She heard Mrs Cullen coming in, asking her mum if she needed anything from the shops. She heard her making a big fuss of Mia, telling her she was the cutest little girl in the whole wide world. She listened to her daughter's peals of laughter and heard her mum say that she didn't really need any shopping but she was dying to go out with Mia in her buggy and show her off to everyone, whereupon Mrs Cullen suggested they go together, in case Irene needed a hand with the buggy. First of all, though, they would have a cup of tea and some of the lovely fruit scones that Irene had baked.

Chloe lay back in bed and felt somehow comforted.

She wasn't expecting Henry to phone. When Mrs Cullen and her mum and Mia left for the shops, she switched on her phone just in case Adam tried to contact her. Thank God for mobiles. He didn't have to know she was in her mum's. She could just as easily be in work. She had barely entered her pin number when Henry got through.

'Chloe! Thank God you answered!'

Chloe's heart lurched, and the previous twenty-four hours of relaxation was almost shattered as she automatically wondered what had happened to Adam.

'Why, what's happened to Adam?'

'Sorry if I alarmed you, there's nothing wrong with him, apart from a battered heart, of course. I just feel that I've spent the last few days trying to reach unreachable people on their mobiles. Believe me, it's extremely frustrating. I'm trying to find Mel. Have you any idea where she is? I spent all yesterday evening waiting outside her bed-sit, but there was no sign of her. Eventually someone took pity on me and told me that she had moved out last weekend.'

'I've no idea where Mel is,' Chloe said crossly. 'Why don't you phone her? I'm sure you have her number, half the world has her number as far as I can see.'

'Don't be like that, Chloe,' he said. 'What happened between Mel and Adam was most unfortunate

501

and both of them still regret it. He's tried to make up for it the past few years, hasn't he? He's worked hard to give you everything you've ever wanted and make you happy. '

'Easy for you to talk, Henry, it doesn't affect you.'

'It could indeed, only I've chosen not to let it come between Mel and I.'

'What do you mean, Mel and you?'

'That's why I have to find her, Chloe, and her mobile is powered off. Anyway, even if I did get through, chances are she'd disconnect me. I have to see her face to face.'

'I don't know where she is,' Chloe said sharply. 'More than likely she's run off again. She could run all the way to Galway for all I care.'

'Galway. She has a gran in Galway, hasn't she?'

'Not quite, her gran lives in Spiddal, just outside—'

'Yes, yes, I know where it is. Thanks, Chloe, you're a star,' Henry said cheerfully. 'And give Adam hell when you take him back. Although you probably won't want to. Give him hell, I mean. He looks like he's going through that already. Poor bloke.'

'Men. You always stick together, don't you?' Chloe fumed.

Take him back, said Henry.

Forgive him, said Mel.

God knows what her mother would have to say.

Chapter Forty-two

Chloe told her mother about Adam later that evening. They were out having a meal together, something they seldom had the opportunity to do. That night, with her two brothers babysitting Mia, and as Chloe intended going home the next day, it seemed the ideal chance.

'Are you sure you feel up to going home tomorrow?' her mum asked as they sat by the window in the Chinese restaurant and waited for their meal. The restaurant was quiet; it was early yet and the young couple at the next table were totally absorbed in each other.

Chloe tore her eyes away from the couple. Once upon a time… She mentally pulled herself together.

'Definitely. I've had a great rest, thanks. But I'll have to get back to normal.'

Normal? What a joke.

'There's no rush, you know.'

'I'll wait until tomorrow evening,' Chloe said. 'That will give me practically another day to relax.'

'I'd prefer if you waited until Adam was home.'

Silence fell and stretched between them and Chloe was relieved that their order arrived. Waiters were busy arranging dishes in front of them, bringing more water, a small carafe of house wine – one glass of red would do Chloe all the good in the world, her mum insisted. Chloe tried to eat her beef chow mein, but the food seemed to stick in her throat.

She waited until her mum had finished most of her chicken curry and then she told her about Adam. After all, her mum would find out sooner or later, and she could scarcely continue with the pretence of Adam being away on business. So quietly, and with a minimum of fuss, she told her that she and Adam had had a serious disagreement and she had asked him to move out of the house.

'Oh, Chloe! No!' Irene's face was so shocked that Chloe was momentarily taken aback.

'Yes, Mum. Adam and I are now separated.' It was the first time she had actually spoken the words and her wobbly voice seemed to echo over and over. She moved her dinner around on her plate to avoid looking at her mother's distressed face.

'You can't mean this, Chloe.'

'I'm afraid I do.'

'Lots of couples have rows. I'm sure it will sort itself out?' Irene gave her daughter a hopeful look.

'No, it won't just sort itself out,' Chloe said with determination.

'Look, Chloe.' Irene hesitated and took a gulp of her wine before continuing. 'I certainly don't want to interfere, but you don't throw your husband out of the home at the first sign of trouble. There'd be no marriages left in Ireland if we all did that. I came close to throwing your dad out a few times, and where would I be now if I'd been stubborn and obstinate?'

'I'm not being stubborn,' Chloe simmered. 'What Adam did was unforgivable.'

Her mum gave her a worried smile. 'Yes, it usually seems unforgivable in the heat of the moment. But after a couple of days, when you calm down and you're able to look at things from every perspective...'

'Adam's gone almost three weeks, mum. It wasn't just a silly row. It was a major problem.'

'What? Three weeks? And all this time...' Irene's voice trailed away. 'So he's not really in Cork on business?'

Chloe shook her head.

'You can't mean this. Three weeks? Tell me it was just a silly row and you'll sort yourselves out in time. You're both working far too hard, and if you ask me, that's the main problem. You're both stretched so much that even a little disagreement can seem like the last straw.'

'No, Mum, this wasn't just a little disagreement.'

'Come here til I give you a cuddle,' her mum said as she reached towards her. 'I'm just…oh God, Chloe, I never expected this.'

To Chloe's horror, Irene began to cry, dabbing hopelessly at her eyes with her napkin. She gulped the rest of her wine and pushed her plate of chicken curry to one side. At the table next to them, the young couple threw curious glances in their direction.

'Mum!' Chloe hissed. 'I'm supposed to be the one who cries. You're supposed to be on my side.'

'Of course I'm on your side,' her mum sniffed. 'That's why I'm crying. You've just told me that you've had a huge row with your husband and that your marriage is on the rocks. This is terrible, Chloe. And you and Adam…' Irene shook her head. 'Never in a million years did I expect this. Not Adam. Oh God, tell me this isn't happening.'

'It very much is. Now stop crying or you'll have me starting off. We'll look a right pair of eejits.'

The waiter arrived at their table and hovered attentively, and Chloe nodded mutely as he asked if he could clear away the plates. She refused the dessert menu and Irene ordered two coffees.

'It's a brandy I need,' she said ruefully as she dabbed at her eyes one more time and finally made an effort to pull herself together. 'I never expected this. Not you and Adam. I know by the way he looks at you that you and Mia are everything to him. I just can't believe he'd do something to throw all that away.'

'Believe me, he did,' Chloe said grimly.

But they weren't actually married at the time, were they? They weren't even engaged.

But her friend, of all people.

'I always thought Adam was so, well, reliable and trustworthy,' her mother continued. 'And he was so proud of you and Mia. You should have heard him on the phone to me when he was organising your birthday weekend away. He was determined to make it as good as possible. I was full sure he loved you to bits. I can't believe he'd suddenly turn around and put your marriage at risk. It doesn't make sense.' She sounded totally mystified.

Chloe shrugged.

'I mean, when I think of how he spoke of you, how happy he sounded just two short months ago,' Irene continued. 'I can't understand what went wrong between then and now.'

'It's something that happened a while ago,' Chloe admitted, secretly wondering if she were mad to be confiding in her mum like this. 'I only found out recently.'

'Oh, Chloe,' Irene looked devastated. 'What on earth could Adam have done that was so dreadful? No, on second thought, I don't want to know. All

I can guess is that it must be something absolutely terrible if you're turning your back on him, and that doesn't add up for me.'

Their coffees arrived and Chloe stirred her spoon around and around in the frothy liquid.

'If it happened a while ago,' Irene continued, 'does it really matter now? Does he not deserve a second chance?'

'Mum, please,' Chloe glared.

'Okay, okay, I'm just trying to help. Have you and Adam talked this through? I mean really talked?' her mum asked.

'No, we've mostly rowed,' Chloe answered despondently.

'How does he feel about things?'

Chloe shrugged. 'He's not a bit happy, but I don't see how I can just forgive and forget.'

'And you're sure you really want to separate and say goodbye to your marriage?'

'I told you, Mum, it's over. I don't even want to talk to him.'

Irene sighed. 'You'll have to discuss it properly with him. There are certain procedures you have to follow. There's Mia to be considered, maintenance and custody and visiting rights. Then you'll have to sort out what will happen with the house, and all your possessions. All your financial arrangements will have to be agreed.'

'I suppose you're right.'

'It's not a question of being right, Chloe. It's a

question of the practical realities. You'll have to see a solicitor.'

'A solicitor?'

'Yes, you'll need a solicitor to process a legal separation. You can always go to Family Mediation to iron out some basic agreements.'

'You seem to know a lot about it.'

Irene laughed mirthlessly. 'You get to pick up bits of information in my job. The local supermarket is a great nerve centre for gossip. Between wife beaters and alcoholics and fifty-somethings running off with girls young enough to be their daughters, there's always plenty of colourful news. For your own sake, Chloe, you'll need a formal agreement on everything.'

Chloe began to feel sick, as though she was moving in a scenario that was totally unreal. Was this how the end of a marriage looked? A formal separation, signed and sealed. A banker's draft on the same day each month. Adam bringing Mia to the zoo, to McDonald's, trying to while away the hours, trying to be the best dad possible in strained circumstances. The man who only recently had shared her life and her love and her bed, becoming nothing better than a formal visitor. Tearing apart a home, dividing all their favourite possessions...

She didn't care about Abbey Manor. It was only a collection of pristine rooms. It meant nothing to her without Adam. She had spent the last three weeks climbing the stylish, pristine walls.

But Mia? And talking to Adam about custody and visiting rights and maintenance? It all seemed so totally crazy. And the new baby, of course. A fresh wave of panic washed over her. The new baby would never have a proper daddy around. But this was what she wanted. This was why she had thrown Adam out of the house. She wanted to end their marriage, and she wanted to end it because she couldn't trust him any more.

'When are you seeing Adam again?' Irene asked her.

'He'll be calling over on Saturday afternoon to see Mia,' Chloe answered.

'I still can't believe that Adam would be irresponsible enough to cause his marriage to break up. And I find it very hard to believe that he'll let his marriage fall apart, and you with a new baby on the way.'

There was something in Chloe's face that made Irene gasp. 'Chloe! Does he know?'

'Know what?' Chloe mustered an innocent expression onto her face.

'Does Adam know about the baby?' Irene demanded.

Chloe remained silent.

'This is ridiculous. You'll have to tell him,' Irene insisted.

'I'm going to,' Chloe said. 'But it shouldn't make any difference. I'd never take him back on account of having another baby.'

'I agree with you there,' her mum said. 'You don't use an innocent baby to paper over the cracks of a broken marriage. But knowing the kind of father that Adam is, if he's not happy now, he'll be even more horrified to think you're breaking up with another baby on the way. Does he know that you're staying with me for a couple of days?'

Chloe shook her head mutely.

'Or that you almost collapsed in work?' Irene continued remorselessly.

'Let's go home, Mum,' Chloe sighed, 'while we're still talking to each other.'

Chapter Forty-three

She was up late the following morning. She lingered comfortably in bed for a few moments, listening to the sounds of the house around her, the radio on in the kitchen, her mum pottering around and chatting to Mia and Mia making an effort to answer back. Normal household sounds that were very relaxing and soothing.

She was surprised to realise that lying back on the pillows in her old bed was so restful. She had been anxious to put her past life behind her when she had moved into the flat with Mel. But it wasn't so bad after all, was it?

She thought of the way her mum had dropped everything to look after her for a few days, how her dad had tread carefully around her so as not to put his big size tens in it, how her brothers had taken a beaming Mia under their respective wings. And the succession of neighbours calling to see if they could help, and fussing over her happy little daughter. Her mum enjoying the attention, and absolutely thrilled to have Chloe and Mia to look after for a little while.

'These lie-ins are getting to be a bad habit,' she joked as she went downstairs.

'That's the whole point of having you over,' her mum said. 'As soon as you've had breakfast I'm bringing you grocery shopping. It'll give you a chance to pick up anything you might need at home.'

'Good idea. Thanks, Mum.'

Chloe began to wilt again after the shopping and went back to bed early in the afternoon for another nap.

'Go while you have the chance,' her mum urged. 'Look, are you sure about going home? You can always stay another night.'

'No, I'll get going after dinner,' Chloe said as she went back upstairs one last time. If she stayed another day she would never want to go back to the cold isolation of Abbey Manor. She wondered if Kaz and Emma had noticed her absence. Probably not. Then again, she had never really encouraged them to be all that close, had she?

When she awoke, she knew it was late afternoon by the way the sun was slanting across the wall of her bedroom. And again she lay still, absorbing the quiet of the house, hearing the sounds from outside, traffic, children playing, but she let them wash over her. This time, when she went downstairs, Mia was nowhere to be seen and her mum was busy in the kitchen chopping a pile of vegetables.

'Where's Mia?' Chloe asked.

'Sit down and have a cup of tea.' Irene gave her a hesitant smile.

'Mum. Where's Mia?'

'She's out.'

'Out?'

'Yes, out with her daddy.' Irene was brisk. She scooped up the vegetables and put them into a pot.

'Adam? What's he doing here? God, Mum, you haven't gone and told him, have you?'

'Will you relax? No, of course not. I haven't told him anything.'

'Then how come he called here?'

'He phoned your office, apparently, and heard you were out sick. And your mobile was switched off this morning. So he tore home to Abbey Manor, and when there was no sign of you, he phoned me in a state of panic. He's out now with Mia. He brought her to the park.'

'How come I've a funny feeling you're not as innocent as you sound?'

'Search me. That's the truth, Chloe,' her mum shrugged.

Chloe sat down at the table, as her legs were suddenly threatening to give way.

'Adam Kavanagh in the local park with Mia, and on a Thursday afternoon,' she shook her head.

'There's nothing wrong with the local park,' her mum said defensively as she put on the kettle.

Chloe raised her eyes to heaven.

'If you're that worried, why don't you follow them over? You can rescue them if necessary and tell them that the dinner is almost ready.'

'Dinner?'

'Oh, didn't I say? Adam's joining us, and it'll give you a chance to behave like two mature adults instead of rowing all the time.'

'Bloody brilliant.'

'I meant what I said, Chloe. It'll give you the opportunity to open proper lines of communication, so that you can start taking formal steps towards getting your official separation worked out. You can't go on in a sort of limbo.'

* * *

It was years since Chloe had been to the local park. Her childhood recollection was one of scuffed, untidy grass, hundreds of young boys chasing a football around and around and getting in everyone's way, and a constant supply of dogs running and sniffing in the undergrowth.

All that had changed.

The park, on a sunny August evening, was an oasis of calm and tranquillity. Outside, the rush hour traffic began to increase, but inside the railings, the park was quiet and peaceful. It had obviously been landscaped in recent years. At the far end of the park, Chloe could see where a football pitch had been marked out, with proper goalposts and changing rooms. Up at the near end of the park, the grass was neatly trimmed and the tangled undergrowth was no more. Banks of summer flowers were grouped between lengths of old railway sleepers. Swathes of young saplings had been planted and they glowed a bright, feathery green in the August sunshine. Wooden benches were dotted here and there overlooking the small lake in the centre.

Adam and Mia were feeding the ducks.

They didn't see her, so Chloe watched for a while, unobserved. She watched her little daughter in her small denim pinafore and bright pink blouse as she lobbed pieces of bread into the lake. Adam was sitting on his hunkers, breaking off small pieces of bread and passing them to her slowly and patiently. She heard Mia's shrieks of delight as the ducks cut a trail through the water and pounced on the bread and sent spiralling ripples out across the calm surface. She heard Adam laugh out loud as Mia suddenly made a run for it, testing out her little chubby legs.

Then lightly and easily, Adam hoisted Mia up onto his tall shoulders so that she could aim further out onto the lake, to the smaller ducks that were being edged out of the way by their bigger and stronger counterparts. After a while, when the bread was all gone, Adam lifted Mia down again, and with infinite care, he strapped her into her buggy and began to stroll around the perimeter of the lake, stopping occasionally to allow her to look at the ducks, now satisfied and replete.

This is what it would be like in the future, Chloe thought. Just Adam and Mia, out together. Without her.

They had almost come full circle around the lake. Soon they would spot her, so she forced a smile on her face and moved forward to meet them.

'Look Mia, here comes Mummy,' she heard Adam say.

Mia chuckled and waggled her legs.

'This is a nice surprise,' Adam said, his blue eyes looking genuinely pleased.

Chloe was just about to give him a sharp reply when she decided to hold her tongue. It was a lovely evening, Mia was flushed and happy and they were going back to have dinner in her mum's. There was no real point in getting off on the wrong foot, or starting a row. Not at the moment. So instead she shrugged and said that she had felt like a bit of fresh air.

'Nice here, isn't it?' Adam said.

'Yes, it's improved a lot since my childhood,' she answered, falling into step beside him.

'Your mother was telling me that you were off work for a few days.'

'That's right. I just took some time out.'

'You look more rested. You work far too hard, you know. You should take time out more often.'

'I might. I might even cut back on my hours a little.'

'I think that's a great idea.'

She felt a lot more rested, more relaxed, Chloe realised. But she couldn't say the same for Adam. He looked tired and haggard, almost as though he hadn't had a proper night's sleep since she had thrown him out. And in spite of his smile, there was something in his eyes that she had never seen before, some kind of pain that caught at her heart.

They left the park, Adam pushing the buggy, Chloe walking alongside as they turned right and headed for her mum's house. They didn't look like a couple on the verge of a legal separation. They looked like a normal family, out for an evening's walk. They were even having a normal enough conversation.

Two grown adults, behaving maturely and opening the lines of communication, Chloe reminded herself. Nothing more.

Dinner at her mum's was pleasant and relaxing, even though they all scarcely fit around the table. Irene had insisted on waiting until Chloe's dad and Brian and Rory were home so that they could all sit down together. Chloe privately wondered if her mum thought that in the circumstances, the more the merrier.

Irene had prepared shepherd's pie with fresh

vegetables and Brian and Rory were impressed with Mia's skilful efforts at feeding herself. And if Adam was surprised at his little girl's newfound dexterity, he wisely kept silent. Instead he exchanged a surprised glance with Chloe as Mia competently wielded her spoon. Chloe proudly smiled back, forgetting for the moment that she was at loggerheads with her husband.

Their main course was followed by freshly baked apple tart and custard and Adam raved about Irene's cookery talents.

'That's just years of practice,' Irene scoffed. 'Chloe'll be as good, even better, in due course, won't you Chloe?'

'Of course.' Once again, Chloe had no option but to smile across the table at Adam, and the smile he gave her in return was full of mischievous intent. She turned to her dad then, in an effort to ignore Adam, but she sensed him watching her with roguish blue eyes as though he was fully aware of her purpose.

After the meal, Chloe helped her mother tidy up. The boys proudly showed Adam the tricks they had taught Mia on the guitar and her dad fell asleep in front of the telly.

'Thanks for everything, Mum,' Chloe said as they finally switched on the dishwasher in the small kitchen.

'Chloe, any time. It was a pleasure to have you and Mia. I've told you before, I'm just a phone call away. You do feel up to going home, don't you?'

'Yes. I'll have to get back into some sort of routine.'

'Don't forget, I'm here any time you need me. Don't you dare wait until you collapse in work before you look for help again.'

'I won't, I promise.'

'I was wondering…' Irene hesitated.

'Yes?'

'It might be an idea if Adam were to drop you home, you and Mia?'

'What?'

'Just a thought. It would save me dragging myself out again. And now that you're on speaking terms, you could maybe begin to sort out where you're going from here.'

'Well…'

'If you didn't all leave together,' her mum pointed out, 'your dad and the boys would start asking questions. Remember, they still think Adam has been away on business. Do you feel like filling them in?'

'No,' Chloe answered hastily. 'Not tonight.'

'Then that's settled.'

* * *

The sunny evening had slowly melted into a dusky twilight by the time Adam put Chloe's shopping and overnight bag into the boot.

'Is this it?' Adam asked in surprise.

'Yes,' Chloe said curtly.

'Where's all Mia's stuff?'

'I didn't need it.'

Chloe insisted on sitting in the back of the car with Mia, even though she was secure in her travel seat. This way, she could keep some space between herself and Adam. She waved goodbye to her parents and brothers, promising to see them soon.

They drove through the twilight in silence. Chloe was conscious of Adam's alert eyes; she could see them every time she glanced over at the rearview mirror, as he continually checked the traffic and threw an eye to her and Mia.

'She's gone asleep,' he smiled fleetingly at Chloe as he approached the M50 roundabout.

Chloe automatically smiled back. She looked up at the tall circles of motorway lights over the interchange as they twinkled brightly against a violet-streaked sky, and for a moment she wished that they could go on like this forever, the three of them wrapped in a cosy world of their own, as the car purred through the purple evening against a slipstream of passing traffic and under a necklace of starry lights. Adam turned the car radio on low, so as not to disturb Mia, to an easy listening station and Chloe relaxed back in her seat. She felt warm and cocooned against the realities of life.

The DJ's voice was low and intimate as he announced the next song, and Lou Reed's husky version of 'A Perfect Day' filtered around as the car purred along.

Chloe listened to the crystal clear piano notes as though for the first time. She thought of the evening they had just shared and realised that it had been every bit as perfect as any day you could wish for. She pictured Mia in the park with Adam, feeding the ducks on the glinting lake, her clear and childish laughter, Adam swinging her onto his shoulders, Adam settling Mia into her buggy afterwards and throwing her a warm smile in greeting as she joined her husband and daughter.

She thought of the dinner table and their shared sense of pride as Mia gloried in feeding herself, and Adam's mischievous, heart-melting smile as her mother assured him of Chloe's cookery potential. And now, the journey through the velvety evening, and the feeling of security with Adam's steady hands on the wheel, his attentive eyes as he drove his precious cargo home.

You mean the world to him, you and Mia. Mel's words floated into her mind. All of a sudden, she couldn't bear to meet his eyes in the mirror, so she pretended to be asleep, because she felt as though she was going into some sort of free fall once more.

Only this was different.

They could go on like this, having more perfect days. Something else Mel had said came back to her, something to the effect that what Adam felt for her was far bigger and more important than any silly, stupid mistake. She thought of her friend's remorse, and the way Adam always put her happiness first. Why should something stupid that had happened years ago spoil what they had now? It would only spoil it all if she allowed it to. If she chose, she could decide to leave those few mad moments where they belonged.

In the past.

They swept in through the entrance to Abbey Manor. The estate was quiet. It was dark now and lights glowed from houses as they drove around towards the cul de sac and home.

'Chloe, wake up,' Adam murmured.

Chloe feigned wakefulness.

'I'll bring everything in and then I'll come back for Mia,' he said. 'I suppose she's to go straight to bed?'

'Yes, it would be best.'

Chloe clambered out of the car on suddenly shaky legs as Adam took her bags and shopping out of the boot. The night was mild and calm as she followed Adam up the driveway and waited in the hall. She watched as Adam went back down the driveway, released the buckle of Mia's seat, lifted her carefully and carried her into the hallway.

'Here we are, one sleeping daughter. Will I bring her upstairs for you?' he asked.

'Yes, please.'

'Right so, and then I'll leave you in peace.'

His face was unusually subdued, and their perfect evening might never have been. In a matter of moments he would be gone. He would come back down the stairs and walk out into the night, leaving her alone with her thoughts in the cold, empty bed.

But it didn't have to be this way. It would only take a few words to begin to put things right again, wouldn't it? Just a few words…

'Adam…I…'

'Yes?'

Don't go. I think we should talk.' Now that she had voiced the words she felt suddenly breathless.

Adam looked alarmed and he seemed to tighten his grip on Mia. 'Talk about what?'

Chloe swallowed. 'Maybe we could talk about … giving it another go.'

Relief flashed in his blue eyes. 'Another go? Us?'

Her heart felt lighter as she nodded.

'Does that mean I'm forgiven?' he asked tentatively.

'Not quite.' She gave him a half smile. 'It means you have a lot of making up to do.'

'Chloe, that sounds marvellous!' Without letting go of Mia, Adam quietly shut the hall door and curved his free arm around her. 'You know I love you,' he murmured, hugging her close to him.

'Yes, I do,' she whispered, as she hugged him back.

Chapter Forty-four

'You're looking better already,' Alice said. It was Friday evening and they had just finished their meal. Alice handed her granddaughter a slice of freshly baked apple crumble.

'Better? Why? What was wrong with me?' Mel asked with a mischievous gleam in her eye. 'Most people thought I looked great when I came home from Australia.'

'You had a nice bit of a colour, but you were far too thin. Even after a week of fresh Connemara air and sunshine and plenty of nourishing food, I can see the difference already. You look like a new woman.'

'Good. I feel exactly like a new woman, and guess where I'm off to this evening?'

'Where?'

'I'm going into Galway. I'm going to see Mum and Dad.'

'Alannah! Jesus, Mary and Joseph!' Her gran hurriedly crossed herself. 'Are you sure?'

'Absolutely,' Mel said with determination.

'Will you be coming back, or…' Alice's face was a mask of agitation.

'Of course I'll be back. I'll be back in time to have a nightcap with you. Don't worry, Gran, I'm not running away this time. Promise,' Mel smiled, then on a softer note she added, 'You told me to forgive myself. Well, there's something I have to do first.'

The sun was a red ball in the western sky as she backed her Fiesta out of her gran's front garden and took the road to Galway and her parents' home. Alice waved from the doorway and Mel waved back cheerfully as though a visit to her parents was the most natural thing in the world.

She had dressed much as usual, beige jeans and a white sweatshirt. She'd had her hair lightly trimmed and it fell in soft layers around her face. At the very last minute she had sprayed herself lightly with perfume, a present to herself as she came through duty free in Singapore.

The journey was all too swift, the traffic light at that hour on a Friday evening, and she barely had time to gather her thoughts or practise what she wanted to say before she was parking her car. The house was situated on a hilly incline just outside Galway town, and in the near distance, across the rooftops of neighbouring houses, she could see the shimmering expanse of Galway Bay, now blushed a silky pink by the setting sun.

She sat quietly for a moment and took several deep breaths. She had come a long way since she had fled this house to go to Dublin. She had gone halfway around the world and then come back again. The years fell away as she got out of the car and crunched up the gravel driveway. There were two cars parked in front of the double garage, a navy Mercedes that she guessed belonged to her father, and a silver Alfa Romeo that was probably her mother's.

She walked up the granite steps to the porch, reached the hall door and hesitated, and for one final moment she searched her mind for an appropriate greeting, but there was no need to collect her thoughts or think of something to say, because her father opened the door and as she reached out to him, he wordlessly took her into his arms.

* * *

In broad daylight on a Saturday afternoon, Henry McBride was well and truly lost.

His journey from Dublin had been uneventful, and apart from traffic delays in Ballinasloe and Loughrea, he had eaten up the miles. He hadn't anticipated any problems in Galway, but it had been a while since he had visited the city, and between new roundabouts and shopping centres and business parks, he had become hopelessly lost.

He tried to curb his growing impatience as he asked two teenage girls for directions to Spiddal. They took one look at him and fled down the road. He supposed he couldn't blame them. God knows what he looked like, with his auburn hair sticking up all over his head and the irritable frown on his face. He was holding up the traffic, so he pulled out again and drove further up the road, and with a surge of relief he spotted a garage a few hundred yards ahead.

He had to repeat the instructions the garage hand gave him three times before he was satisfied.

* * *

'I'm going for a walk,' Mel told her gran.

'Do that, Alannah,' Alice smiled. 'It's a lovely evening again. I don't know what we've done to deserve this glorious weather. Take advantage of it while you can. I'm going to lie down for a while, I'm a bit tired.'

'That's my fault. I kept you up late last night, didn't I?' Mel grinned.

'You did indeed. But it was worthwhile, wasn't it?'

'It was,' Mel smiled back. 'Have your rest, for we're all going out to dinner tomorrow, remember?

Dad's booked a table for the four of us in a new restaurant in Galway. And you'd better be there.'

'I wouldn't miss it for the world. Never thought I'd see the day.'

'Tell you the truth, neither did I,' Mel admitted.

Neither did I, she repeated to herself as she pulled on a soft pink hooded top over her white T-shirt and cut-off jeans and headed out the door into the tranquil sunny evening.

* * *

Henry hadn't quite decided what he would do when he reached Spiddal. He had managed to find Mel in Port Douglas, hadn't he? And that was over on the other side of the world. He would surely find her in Spiddal. If she was there, of course.

He drove along the country road from Galway city, every mile bringing him closer and closer to Spiddal and, he hoped, to Mel. The hedgerows and grassy banks lining the road spilled flashes of colour into the golden August sunshine as the car swept along, and now and again to his left, he caught glimpses of the blue of the sea.

When he reached the village of Spiddal, he parked his car and went into a bright, welcoming pub. The outside was bedecked with hanging baskets stirring in the sunshine, the inside filled with the aroma of freshly cooked food and packed to the rafters with noisy holiday makers.

He ordered a bottle of Ballygowan and raising his voice, he asked the barman if he had any idea where Mel Saunders lived.

'Mel Saunders? Never heard of the name.'

'Tall girl with dark hair, been away for a while?'

'Nope. Name means nothing to me,' the barman shrugged.

Okay, maybe they didn't know Mel. But how about her gran? Only he wasn't sure what her gran's name was. Could be Mrs Saunders, sure, could also be any name under the sun, depending on which side of the family she was on.

'Do you know any Saunders at all?'

'Afraid not. Hey, Mick, do you know any Saunders around here?' he called over to another barman, an older man who looked as though he had worked in the pub all his life. The chap sitting at the table near Henry chose that moment to deliver the punch line of a joke and the crowd he was with erupted. In the middle of the commotion, Henry barely made out the older barman's words. Had he been able to lip read, he would have been fine; as it was, he had to turn to the noisy table and request a bit of quiet before he gathered that he had to go up the road for about a mile or so and turn right.

He was trying to figure out what exactly constituted a country mile when he almost overran a laneway to his right-hand side. He reversed slightly and parked on the verge and decided to go it on foot.

530

There were no replies at the first two houses and he was just about to head back down to the main road when he noticed the gable end of a third house a little further up the lane. High fuchsia hedges, drenched in evening sunshine, bounded the front wall and trapped scented heat in the front garden. He was knocking at the hall door before he spotted the red car tucked into a corner of the garden.

Mel had a red car, hadn't she? Isn't that what Samantha had said? She collected her belongings and drove off in a little red car?

He knocked again, his impatience almost spilling over, and eventually an elderly lady with soft white hair opened the door. She peered at him through sleepy eyes and regarded him suspiciously.

'Sorry for disturbing you, but I'm looking for Mel? Mel Saunders?' Henry asked expectantly. He was disgusted to realise that he had his fingers crossed behind his back.

'I'm afraid there's nobody here of that name, young man,' the elderly lady told him. 'I'm Mrs Saunders, but there's nobody living here by the name of Mel.'

He felt a crushing sense of disappointment. He was so sure he had been on the right track. He had no option now but to leave this old lady in peace. It looked like he had interrupted her nap and once more he apologised for disturbing her as he turned and walked down the driveway. He glanced over at the car again and felt like kicking it.

And then he spotted something that made his heart somersault. Something small and fluffy and grey that was sitting in the back window of the car. He wheeled around and marched back up the driveway.

'She calls herself Mel, but I don't think it's her proper name. She's tall and dark haired, and absolutely beautiful,' Henry said, grinning widely. 'And she has the most amazing pair of green eyes. Come to think of it, they're not unlike your own,' he finished.

Alice's face was one huge smile as she held open the door and said, 'You must be Henry. What on earth kept you?'

* * *

The tide was coming in. It sucked at the shingle beach and ran foamy rivulets in amongst drifts of seaweed and clusters of rocks, forming small swirling pools that emptied and refilled with each incoming surge of the tide. Seagulls drifted lazily in the salt-scented air. The sun had momentarily disappeared, swathed behind a light layer of cloud, and although it was early in the evening, the sky was drained of colour. It hung suspended like a pearly grey bowl over the darker grey of the murmuring sea. The north Clare coast was a smudge on the horizon between sea and sky.

This end of the beach was quiet. Most visitors flocked to the main crescent of sand right in the heart of Spiddal village, but Mel preferred to walk here, slightly up the coast, where it was more secluded and where there were only a few solitary walkers like herself. Soon she would have to head back, as the incoming tide swallowed up the shore.

She picked up a smooth shiny stone and hurled it into the water, heard the plopping sound it made as it sank, picked up another and had taken careful aim when someone behind her threw a stone that skimmed the water expertly half a dozen times before it sank to the sandy floor.

Determinedly, she aimed her stone and threw, but once again it sank without trace, swallowed up by the waves. And again, another stone traced an arc slightly to the right of her and skimmed the surface of the grey seas several times before it disappeared.

She turned to see who this expert might be, and came face to face with Henry. She wasn't too surprised to see him, for she had been thinking about him quite a lot, and in the hazy light of the cool evening, it felt almost as though she was dreaming. Then she realised that it wasn't a dream, that he was standing in front of her, wearing a pair of denim jeans and a big smile.

God, she wasn't able for this.

'Go away,' she said.

'That's a lovely welcome,' he said calmly.

'I said, go away.'

'I've no intentions of going anywhere,' he stated. 'Do you realise you've led me in quite a merry dance…Miranda Eleanor?'

Her name rolled off his tongue like poetry and it caused her heart to quiver. Her face was a mask of puzzlement as she faced him. 'Where were… how come…were you up at my gran's?'

'I was,' Henry told her. 'We had a very interesting chat. She's lovely, your gran, just like you said.'

'You had no right to come barging down here,' Mel said heatedly.

'On the contrary, I had every right.'

'I've nothing to say to you, so I suggest you leave.'

'I'm not leaving until you listen to what I have to say,' Henry said, and his easy manner vanished. All of a sudden he looked like he meant business. 'Have you any idea how long it took me to find you? We could begin with Tuesday night, when I set up a vigil outside your flat, continue on to Wednesday evening when I finally realised you had absconded. Then a phone call to Chloe, put two and two together, drive down here on the off chance, frighten the wits out of two teenagers on the outskirts of Galway, almost cause a riot in the pub down the road when I asked a party to quiet down so I could hear the barman's instructions…' He moved closer and closer to Mel as he spoke until he was standing right beside her.

'Okay, okay, but don't come any closer,' Mel said, backing away.

'Your gran was right. She told me you could be as prickly as barbed wire.'

'She *what*?'

Henry smiled. 'And I told her I knew that already. She also said that despite your suit of armour, you could be very easily hurt.'

'Did she now.' Mel folded her arms defensively across her front.

'And I told her I also knew that already.' Henry paused. 'And then she said you had a heart of gold…Miranda Eleanor.'

She forced herself to ignore the poetic tone of voice again. 'Is that so?'

'And I said I knew that already too. But she also gave me a warning.'

'She did?'

'Yes. She told me that if I did any damage to your heart of gold, that I'd have her to answer to.'

'Well, naturally she's on my side.'

'And she's quite a feisty lady, so I've no intentions of bringing the full wrath of your gran down on my head. I promise I'll never damage your heart.'

'Henry!'

'She also had one final word of advice for me.'

'Yes?' Mel's heart was beating so fast she thought it was going to suffocate her.

'She said – now let me remember this correctly – oh yes, she said that on no account was I to let you get away this time. Or I would have to answer to her. For the rest of my life.'

He was standing so close that she could see the fine dusting of auburn hairs around his upper lip

535

and the look in his tawny eyes seemed to melt even her toes.

'There's one major problem,' Mel said stubbornly.

'Only one?' His eyes twinkled.

'Yes. Samantha.'

Henry smiled. 'Don't you know? Samantha's my cousin. Her boyfriend ditched her and then she had a miscarriage, all in the space of a week. So she came to Dublin to get away from Athlone and she ended up temporarily borrowing my swanky new sofa bed. She's now fully recovered, she's a little older and wiser and has just moved into a house with her pals.'

'Oh.'

'I really have reformed, Miranda Eleanor.'

'I bet you got tired keeping count of your conquests.'

'Believe it or not, I fell in love. For the past few months my heart has been on the other side of the world.'

Mel's breath caught in her throat.

'Why did you really come home from Australia?' he asked, his eyes searching hers.

She shook her head.

'Don't be afraid, just tell me.'

She sighed quietly. 'I kept seeing something…in my dreams. Wherever I was, anywhere, it began to drive me mad.'

'What did you keep seeing?'

'Your face.'

He smiled. 'That'll do for starters.'

'But there's another problem,' she added hurriedly.

'If it's anything to do with nine-to-five boring bank managers or millstones of mortgages that last forever, I don't want to know.'

She shook her head. 'That doesn't matter.'

'Doesn't matter? That's a relief. I didn't fancy giving up my permanent and pensionable job, never mind my apartment.'

'You weren't seriously going to? You're joking.'

'I'm not joking. But we will need food on the table and somewhere to put our heads at night. Of course, we can always take a sleeping bag and camp out on the Aran Islands.'

Mel smiled as if she couldn't believe what she was hearing.

'Talking of sleeping bags, did you ever, after I left…?'

Mel shook her head. Speech was impossible.

'Good. I want that pleasure to be all mine…and yours, of course.' He reached out and touched a tendril of her dark hair. It was the first time he had touched her so, and she shivered.

She had to tell him. 'There's something…a problem…maybe you know already…'

'My love, anything that happened in the past is over and done with, okay?'

My love? Oh, God. 'But Chloe…and Adam… I've really hurt her.'

'They'll sort themselves out, wait and see. Chloe will bounce back. You can't put your life on hold on account of that ridiculous carry on. And your gran would kill me if I allowed you to. You scarcely want to be responsible for that, do you?'

She smiled.

He said, 'Miranda Eleanor. What a beautiful name.'

'Not so beautiful when you're fifteen and you're getting slagged for always being top of the class.'

'How does it compare with Henry Alphonsus?'

'No!'

'Yep,' he grinned. 'Our grans will have a field day when they get together.'

'My gran never calls me anything but Alannah.'

'That's even more lovely, but not quite as lovely as you.' He looked at her steadily and Mel felt as though the empty space inside her was slowly filling up with so much joy and happiness that it was about to overflow.

They were still standing in the same spot on the beach and there was a kind of hushed expectancy in the evening air as Henry finally reached for Mel and she went into his arms. He held her close for several moments, his arms wrapped around her as though he was never going to let her go. She was almost as tall as he, so her head fit neatly into the crook of his neck. She stood quietly, absorbing the scent of him, getting used to the hard feel of his body against hers, the rise and fall of his chest, the beat of his heart and the answering leap in hers. Then he released his hold a little and held her slightly away from him and she felt his hands on her hair as he let it ripple through his fingers, and pushed it back gently from her face.

'You know, I've never really kissed you. Not properly,' he murmured as he looked at her mouth.

'Have you not?' Her voice was hoarse.

He gave her a startled glance. 'I hope you're joking. I'd hate to think I had kissed you and you had forgotten all about it.'

Mel grinned at him. 'Maybe if I see what it's like, then I'll remember.'

Finally, he closed his eyes, held her tight, and began to kiss her.

Oh, God.

He never had.

No one ever had.

Not like this. Never, ever like this.

A corner of the sun peeped out from behind a shredded cloud and turned his auburn hair a fiery red. It shone in Mel's green eyes as they stopped kissing for a moment and smiled at each other. Henry impulsively lifted her up. He whirled around and around with Mel in his arms before setting her down again. And this time when they kissed, it seemed as though they were never going to stop.

They didn't notice the indulgent glances of other couples strolling by.

They didn't notice the sun finally breaking free of the wispy clouds and flooding the sky with golden light.

And they never noticed the tide coming in.

The lacy foam eddied around their feet, swirling back and forth, back and forth, all the time gaining ground. It became bolder and bolder, surging quickly around Henry's Nikes and Mel's white sandals. A cheeky wave, more audacious than the rest, gathered strength, crested and fragmented into a thousand glittering drops as it hit against their ankles.

'I can't stop,' Henry murmured as he lifted his mouth off hers for a millisecond.

'I don't want you to,' Mel whispered, her green eyes shining.

Eventually, of course, they had to. Henry said he didn't mind if they were swept out to the Aran Islands, but Mel pointed out that they didn't have a sleeping bag and it could get very chilly at night. Then Henry remembered that he had been invited to join the family for dinner the next day, so he took her by the hand, and laughing breathlessly they raced up past the shoreline, over the rock pools and slippery seaweed, with the lacy waves laughing at their heels.

Epilogue

Ryan Adam Kavanagh comes into their lives on a sunny January morning, quietly and calmly. Adam holds Chloe's hand tightly. He leans over to kiss her damp forehead, smooth back her hair and murmurs that she's brilliant. She smiles back and feels a quiet, inner contentment spreading out from her heart.

Together they cuddle their new son. He is a perfect little miracle, with tender, satiny skin, a crumpled face, feathery blond hair and tiny crescent fingernails on perfect, dimpled fingers. He gives a huge yawn with his miniature mouth, flexes his tiny feet and fixes them with a curious, un-focused stare. They bring him home to Abbey Manor and Adam feels humble and full of gratitude as he carries his son in through the hall door.

Mia is delighted with her new 'boy baby' and Adam asks her to mind his teddies until he's big enough to look after them himself. He buys his son a tiny Man U top to match the one he has already bought for Mia. Chloe laughs and says she hopes he doesn't think they're going to produce an entire football team. She needs time out to spend with both her daughter and son, after all. Adam kisses the top of her head and says she can have all the time out in the world.

The baby is christened on a mild Sunday at the end of April. Just a quiet celebration, Chloe has decided. The most important people are the baby himself, his little sister, his parents, grandparents and, of course, the godparents.

She dresses her son in miniature white garments and blue ribboned bootees and blows kisses on his velvety tummy as he smiles and gurgles and kicks his legs. Adam's parents arrive and relax in the sitting room. Chloe's parents arrive, and Irene brings apple tarts and cream and goes down to the kitchen to put the finishing touches to the buffet. Chloe dresses in a soft grey suit and twirls at her reflection in the bedroom mirror. When she thinks of the last few months, she'd never have guessed she could come this far.

The godparents are last to arrive. It's almost time to leave for the church. Then there's the sound of car doors banging outside and footsteps on the path. In a flurry of hugs and kisses, Mel and Henry arrive. Mia is picked up and whirled around, her childish laughter flowing like a crystal clear stream around the hall. Then Mel leans into the Moses basket and gently lifts out her new godson. Her face is tender as she cuddles the warm bundle in her arms and turns around to smile at Henry.

From across the room, Chloe sees the look Henry gives Mel. It's as if she's the only person in the room and his eyes are warm with the knowledge of something wonderful waiting in the wings. And Chloe suddenly spots the glint of diamonds on Mel's left hand. She feels laughter bubbling up inside her and some kind of happiness lifting her soul as she flies across the room to hug her friend.

Also by
Mary Bond

Sexy, dark-haired Eve Andrews likes nothing better than to flit around Dublin enticing admirers, then ruthlessly dumping them as soon as she gets bored. Her main ambition in life is to have a blast - that is, until she meets Alex Gallagher...

Daisy O'Neill is Eve's cousin, as shy and retiring as Eve is upfront. So, when handsome Sam Heffernan suggests they get together, she can't for the life of her work out why.

What neither cousin knows is that her destiny has been shaped by events in the past, and when love beckons at last, each will have to overcome the legacy of her childhood: Daisy finds that, no matter how far she runs, she can't escape the sense of loss which shadows her. And Eve will learn the hard way that manipulating others isn't necessarily the key to finding everlasting happiness. One thing is for sure, both women are set on a shattering collision course, with altogether unexpected consequences.

Available wherever books are sold, or order online at
www.gillmacmillan.ie to save **20%**